WANTED BY
THE MARSHAL

RYSHIA KENNIE

HER DETECTIVE'S
SECRET INTENT

TARA TAYLOR QUINN

MILLS & BOON

First Published in Great Britain 2019
by Mills & Boon, an imprint of HarperCollins*Publishers*
1 London Bridge Street, London, SE1 9GF

Wanted by the Marshal © 2019 Patricia Detta
Her Detective's Secret Intent © 2019 TTQ Books LLC

ISBN: 978-0-263-27438-7

0919

MIX
Paper from
responsible sources
FSC™ C007454

This book is produced from independently certified FSC™ paper to ensure responsible forest management.

For more information visit: www.harpercollins.co.uk/green

Printed and bound in Spain
by CPI, Barcelona

WANTED BY
THE MARSHAL

RYSHIA KENNIE

This book is dedicated to you, the reader. Enjoy!

Chapter One

Cheyenne, Wyoming
Late spring

Kiera Connell grabbed her bag and headed with a smile to the exit of the Prairie Seniors' Care Home. Few things made her happier than her work here. In fact, she often came in for extra hours beyond those they paid. She supposed it was because of her own lack of family that made being here so special, made her feel so included. She'd lost her mother when she was a toddler and the aunt who had raised her had died seven years ago. The seniors and the other caregivers were, to her, like family. Today, she'd filled in on an earlier shift before working her scheduled evening shift. It was late, and her car was in for repairs. It was a nice night and only a twenty-minute walk home. She planned not to waste any time getting out the door.

Her hand was on the knob when a quavering voice stopped her.

"Kiera? Do you have a minute?"

She turned around without hesitation. "Sure, Ann," she said. She guessed that the elderly woman had hurried down the hall after her as fast as her walker would take her. Kiera must have been caught up in her own thoughts, for she hadn't heard the shuffle of Ann's feet as she had struggled to follow.

"What's up?"

"I wondered if you could pick up a magazine for me tomorrow."

"I will," Kiera said as she put a reassuring hand on her arm. She'd promised she'd run the errand for her only an hour ago. She'd also promised an hour before that. But Ann, like many of the other residents, had dementia. "I'll get one with racy pictures."

Ann smiled. "You're a tease," she replied. "But thank you."

"I'll see you tomorrow," Kiera promised. "Now get some sleep."

After watching Ann turn slowly around and make her way painfully down the hallway, she headed for the exit. But she glanced back and saw Ann take a wrong turn to get to her room. It was a simple setup, a small facility, but for someone with memory loss, nothing was simple.

Kiera dropped her bag and hurried down the hall. She could leave Ann to find her way to her room on her own. She knew that she would eventually get there. For one corridor only met another and circled back to the starting point. She could wait and let the plan of the hallways take Ann the long route back to where she wanted to go. But she couldn't do that. It wasn't in her nature. She slowed her step as she walked beside the woman. She chatted to Ann about her day, her plans for tomorrow and the promised magazine. It was a conversation she'd had three other times since supper. Once, when she'd brought Ann's medication. Once, when she made sure that she was ready for bed and again when she checked on her later in the evening. She'd completed the same ritual for half a dozen other people as well, but Ann was one of her favorites. While some of the work was repetitive, it was the people that made this job one of the best she'd ever had. As a nurse-practitioner, it was her that the staff turned to when health issues cropped up. She loved the challenge of keeping this community of seniors healthy. She loved it every bit as much as she loved being part of their support structure.

"Kiera," her supervisor, Beth, called as she left Ann in her room and headed back down the corridor. "What are you still doing here?"

"I was delayed."

"Ann again?" Beth shook her head and smiled. There was no danger of Ann overhearing their almost maternal hovering; she'd disappeared into her room. And, like many of the residents, she was hearing impaired. "I could have given her a hand."

"I know," Kiera replied. "But I was here so…" The words trailed off as she shrugged. She looked at her watch. It was almost midnight.

"Are you sure you don't want to take a cab home?" Beth asked. "It's late."

"I'll be fine. It's a warm night and a short walk."

"Be careful," Beth warned with a wave.

She gave a wave back and headed out the door. It was a beautiful late spring night. She was walking down well-lit streets in an area of the city where she'd always felt safe. The air seemed to caress her skin. She walked by one of the city's eight-foot-tall, artist-painted, decorative cowboy boots. A streetlight splashed light on the gold-and-brass spur and revealed a cloud-studded, bright blue Wyoming sky above a mountain range. The beautiful scene was painted on the body of the boot. The boots were all unique and were displayed randomly throughout the city. They were one of the many things that made

Cheyenne special to her. Tonight, this one marked the halfway point, ten minutes from home.

She began to hum a little tune. And, as she walked by a local coffee shop, she noticed a man sitting slouched on an outside bench. It wasn't unusual to see the occasional homeless person in the area, especially during the warmer weather. She thought nothing of it and instead considered jogging the rest of the way home.

"Miss."

The soft male voice came out of nowhere and startled her. But there was no threat in the voice, only a kind of lost hopelessness. She'd heard that tone before. The streetlight pushed the shadows away as another man in a ragged T-shirt and baggy jeans rose from the sidewalk where he'd been sitting cross-legged with cup and a sign asking for help.

He approached her slowly, with a slight limp.

"I'm sorry," he said in a soft voice. "Could you spare some change?"

"Of course," she said and reached into her pocket and pulled out some coins. She dropped them into the cup. He looked thin and grubby. She guessed he might be in his late twenties but not much older. It wasn't a sight that she was unfamiliar with. Occasionally, she volunteered at a nearby soup kitchen. There, she often saw people like him who were homeless or just down on their luck. She sometimes wondered what had brought them to such a desperate state. Whatever the reasons, she couldn't turn down someone in need.

"Have a coffee on me."

He nodded. But it was as if his interest was elsewhere. She turned in the direction that seemed to have caught his attention. And as she turned, she saw the hooded figure approaching. They were alone; the man on the bench had disappeared as if sensing trouble. There was no time to run. There was no time to scream. It was over before she knew that it had happened.

When she opened her eyes again, her arms and shoulders ached. The breeze that had lifted her hair earlier, and which she'd taken joy in walking in, was gone. She was no longer on the street but in what seemed to be a house. Everything was dimly lit, and she could see the shadowy shape of the room: large, empty and rather rank smelling. Her wrists and ankles were tied with rope that was so tight it cut into her skin.

Escape.

And yet, as much as she knew that she needed to get away, she couldn't. Even without the ropes that restrained her, her body was weak and didn't seem to want to respond. Her head spun. She guessed that she might have a concussion. The smell of must and disuse closed around her. Her heart pounded so hard that her chest hurt.

Stay calm, she told herself as she took deep breaths. *That's the only way you're going to figure a way out of this.* But her head reeled, and she passed out. When she came to, everything was dark. She lay still, trying to figure out where she was, who had done this to her and what they wanted. She had to clear her mind. She had to still her fear so that she could think straight. She was focusing like she'd never done before. Hours of yoga, of meditation, were being used in a way she had never thought possible. As soon as she cleared her mind, she realized that, again, she wasn't alone. She could smell rank body odor. She cringed and waited for what might come next.

"I'm going to enjoy every minute with you."

The voice came out of nowhere, sliding through the darkness like a stream of venom.

Kiera thought she might throw up. She held back a shudder.

She knew that voice. It was the homeless man who had asked her for money. That seemed both forever and only minutes ago. Time was lost to her. Her head spun as he whispered a long litany of sexual pleasures he would demand from her. She could smell something rancid on his breath that made her stomach twist and bile rise in her throat. His finger ran along her arm and she held back a shudder. Instinct told her that fear would entice him. Show no fear was second only to escape.

"And then," he said, drawing his words out as if he were about to offer her a unique treasure. "When I am through with you, you will die."

She'd never been more terrified. He didn't need ropes or restraints of any sort—she couldn't have moved if she'd wanted to. It was as if she were part of a TV program. It was as if everything that happened was part of that program, part of that fantasy. She'd wake up soon and it would all be over. A silent shiver crawled through her. This was real life. A nightmare.

"Not until I have my turn."

Kiera didn't know who or what they were, or if the voice was male or female. She only knew that the second voice made her skin crawl.

They moved away from her. Now their voices were low, too low to hear. She passed out again after that. When she awoke, she sensed that she was alone. Time passed. It was broken only by changes in her consciousness. There were moments that she fought with her restraints. There were moments where she drifted back into unconsciousness. In the moments she was conscious, she lived in a state of panic where she feared she would die.

The next time consciousness returned she was aware

of a painful ache in her hands. The pain came from lack of circulation, for not only were her wrists tied, but she'd been partially lying on her hands. She shifted, taking the weight of her body off her hands. Something smelled different, a scent that was heavier, like pine and mold strung together. And there was the sense that she'd been moved. She pushed her hands against what felt like a wooden wall and moved them up as high as she could reach. Then, she rolled away from the wall and pain shot through her legs as her fingers touched another wall. Wherever she was, she was in a place much different from the cavernous room she'd first been in. She guessed the size by feel, determining that she had about a foot of space in either direction. As she rolled over again, she could feel wood against her lower back and against her legs. It felt like it was touching her skin, but she'd been wearing pants and a tunic. The only bare skin was her arms, at least that was the way it had been. Kiera felt with her fingers along her leg and felt skin rather than cloth. Further exploration told her that there were large tears in her pants and in her tunic.

Her clothes were torn but still there. She felt in the darkness as surprise ran through her. Considering what had happened, what she'd heard, this wasn't what she'd anticipated. Something had changed, and she didn't know what. She remembered the threats. She knew where this was going. They were frightening her, dragging things out. It was clear in the things they'd said. They wanted her terrified and they'd accomplished that. That they wanted to rape her wasn't in doubt. Their words only confirmed that, but for some reason that hadn't happened. Not yet. She didn't know why but for now she'd been lucky. But she sensed that time was running out.

There was only one option: she had to get out of

here, get away from them before the worst happened. She didn't want to contemplate, again, what that might be. But the possibilities of worst were engraved in her tortured mind. Rape, as they'd promised, or worse—she took a deep, almost panicked breath—death.

The taste of dust and disuse was in her mouth as she began to chew at the rope that bound her wrists. Minutes passed. It could have been hours. Time blended into itself and had no meaning. All she had was hope and she needed to cling to that. Desperate, she tried to pull her wrists apart. Something seemed to give but the rope didn't break.

Kiera rolled over and something sharp bit into her skin. She felt for it awkwardly, twisting her body to get more reach. Something pierced her finger and she bit back a cry of pain but continued her exploration and discovered a nail jutting about a half inch out of the wood. Excitement raced through her. Finally, a tool to free herself. She shimmied closer and began to rub the rope that was binding her wrists against it. Minutes passed and then, the rope snapped. The force of it had her falling backward, missing the nail that had freed her and hitting her head against the wall. She lay like that for seconds as she caught her breath. Then she began to shake her wrists, trying to return circulation to her numb hands. But as blood began to flow, the pain overwhelmed her. She cradled her hands and had to bite her lip to stop from crying out.

Silence and darkness crowded around her. As she lay waiting for the pain to dissipate, a thin stream of light flicked across the room and then disappeared as quickly as it appeared. Her heart leaped. Was it possible that the light came from outside? Where else would it come from? Was it the headlights of a car? Was she near a street or was it just her captors turning a light on and off in another room? The light had appeared to move before it disappeared. Its very presence suggested a possibility. Her heart pounded at the first sign of hope before she struggled to her feet. She felt in the darkness a little over four feet above the floor where the light had seemed to come from. The wall felt different. The wood wasn't as solid and seemed out of line with the rest of the wall. It was a subtle difference, but enough to hint that it might cover something. Her heart raced at what this might mean. She began to pick at the wood. She scratched and clawed with her fingernails and was surprised when a piece broke off easily as if it was not only thin but rotted. Determined, she dug harder. In places the wood was almost like butter while in others it was hard and resistant. Splinters dug into her skin, embedding under her nails. The pain made her eyes water. She didn't stop. Her gut screamed one thing. This was her chance to live.

The wood chipped away piece by piece, sliver by sliver. Now she didn't think of the pain or of the warm trickle that ran down her fingers, and then down her wrists. Vaguely, she knew it was blood. She knew that she was bleeding. It didn't matter. For she knew now, what she'd only guessed before, there was a window behind the wood covering.

The possibility of freedom began to appear as she could see vague shapes, enough to figure that she was looking at an alley. Now half of the window was uncovered. It was enough. She ripped her already torn pants off at the knee and wrapped the material around her hand. Her body shook with stress, with anticipation. She took a deep breath and hauled her arm back. She drove her fist through the window with all the strength she had. The glass shattered. She could feel the slick warmth of blood as it ran down her arm. She forced her mind to think of only one thing—escape. With that thought, she yanked out two more pieces of glass, clearing the bottom half of the window enough so that she could get out.

Freedom.

Kiera sank to the floor and began untying the rope that bound her ankles. She looked up often, her heart pounding. She feared that her captors would burst in at any moment. They'd punish her for what she'd done— kill her even. It wasn't a thought she could entertain. She couldn't think of that. There was no time to speculate.

Finally, she pulled the last knot free and stood up.

There was a sense that time was slipping away. There were furtive noises on the other side of the wall, the one to the right of the window she'd just uncovered. She had to go now. And even though she wasn't a big woman, she knew it would be a tight squeeze. Seconds later, one leg was outside; a breeze ran across her skin and she barely acknowledged that. The jagged edges of glass that she hadn't been able to clear away ripped the places where her skin was bare. The pain only reminded her to keep going, that she wanted to live.

The night air was heaven as it sent goose bumps across her exposed flesh. Her heart raced. Her captors could be anywhere. They could be behind her now.

Kiera flipped over so that she was on her back and didn't land on her head into the unknown darkness. But, with the majority of her body out, she lost her grip. She landed on a pile of plastic garbage bags that broke her fall. For seconds, she lay there, shocked, terrified and exhilarated all at once.

Freedom at last.

Something sharp bit into her side as she struggled to her feet and pain shot through her. Finally, she stood in the darkness shaken and disorientated. She took a breath and then another. And she told herself that if she ever got out of this, if she were truly free, she'd be setting up a safe-ride program for all the workers at the care home.

A streetlight glimmered in the distance. She limped as fast as she could toward the light, and the possibility of freedom.

Cheyenne, Wyoming
One week later

US MARSHAL TRAVIS JOHNSON knew that he should be looking forward to the low-key case he'd just been presented with, especially after his last assignment. It had been high-octane from beginning to end as they'd cornered a drug lord who had made it through two international borders and numerous state lines. But, the truth was, he loved action and he loved a challenge.

"I've received notice that Kiera Connell was discharged from the hospital yesterday." The look James Perez, the FBI lead on this case, gave him was grave.

Travis nodded. He knew the case. He knew that the woman was the only survivor of a serial killer who had terrorized women from coast to coast for well over a year.

"She's safe but we're afraid she might run if she feels otherwise. At this point, no need of twenty-four-seven protection, just a presence that gives her a sense of security. I want you to head the team that will protect her." James shrugged with a half smile. "I wouldn't dump this on you, but considering the high-profile status of this case, we need the best protecting her."

"No worries," he said. He wasn't surprised that James had considered the pressure this might put on him. James was one of the most considerate men he knew. They'd known each other for years, worked together many times, and had eventually become friends who shared many interests including a mutual love of baseball.

"You read the file?"

Travis nodded. He'd followed the case over the past year. The file had only sharpened the details.

"Yeah, I did," he said with a grimace. It didn't matter how long he was in law enforcement, or how many cases he saw, the depths of mankind's depravity could still surprise him. "There appears to be no connection between the witness and killer."

"There isn't, at least that we know. I doubt that will change. From everything the witness said, she's never seen him before."

"That seems to be the usual for this killer. Picks random women," Travis said grimly. Eleven women had died at this man's hands and other than the fact that they were female and attractive, there were no other commonalities. They ranged in age from twenty to forty, their ethnic roots as varied as their ages.

"As you know, she was found here." James turned his computer around. He pointed it out on the detailed map of one of the most neglected areas of the city. "Five o'clock in the morning, a transit driver on her way to work found her. She called it in immediately and stayed with the victim until police and an ambulance arrived."

"A Good Samaritan."

"I salute them almost every day on this job," James said with sincerity.

Travis couldn't agree more. The unsung heroes. The civilians who went above and beyond were an invaluable resource that often went unpraised and unnoticed.

"She was damn lucky," Travis said. Having her alive and able to ID the killer was a huge break in a case that, as horrific as it was, unfortunately, was titillating. The media had had a field day following the trail of the killer and that news had gained a growing body of followers over the months of the spree. Now those killings were being tied to others hinting that the killer might have been active much longer than authorities had known. That was the dark side of humanity. They loved tragedies and horrors, as long as they had no personal connection to them, of course. He pushed the chair back and stood up. Despite what he'd said, he was anxious to get back into action even if it was as non-challenging as babysitting a potential witness who was no longer in danger. The perp had been put behind bars.

"She was lucky. She escaped before she could be assaulted or worse. According to what she told authorities, she wasn't sexually assaulted. She was backhanded a number of times. She has some fairly serious bruising on her left cheek."

Travis swore at the thought of it even though he knew that in the scope of things, that assault was minor.

"Unfortunately, that wasn't the worst this piece of sludge did to other women. Besides the concussion, she has dozens of wood splinters in her hands—and yet none of that stopped her from getting away."

He pushed the file at Travis. "She's spent more time in the hospital for psychiatric evaluation than anything else."

A phone rang.

Travis looked at the picture on the file as James took the call. The dark-haired beauty who had smiled with lighthearted innocence for the photo was frozen in a moment in time when she couldn't imagine the nightmare that was to follow. Since the picture was taken, she'd come close to death. The thought made him feel slightly sick.

"Just a heads-up," James said as he put the phone aside. "She's insistent that she return to work as soon as possible."

"What?"

He looked up, shocked that that would even be a consideration after everything she'd been through.

"I've suggested at least a two-to-three-weeks' wait on that."

Travis said nothing. There was nothing to say, for in reality, he had no say. It was up to the FBI. For him it was an assignment, nothing more. The only thing he knew was that everything about this case was troubling.

Her attacker, Eric Solomon, the man now known as a serial killer who had silently hunted, killed and raped women across the country, was behind bars. Something about the emergency call had triggered an instinctive reaction by the detective in charge that night. He'd felt something off and deployed unmarked vehicles without sirens or flashing lights. The victim had been taken to the hospital while officers had converged quietly on the deserted house where the victim claimed she'd been held. The perpetrator had been caught when he'd returned minutes later and had been unprepared for what awaited him. There, the baby-faced man had been surprised by the police presence. He'd turned to run and been caught and arrested on the spot. The evidence had almost been too easy. The victim's DNA was lodged under his fingernails and strands of her long hair were twisted around his ring finger like a trophy. Once the victim had identified him in a lineup of photos, it was clear that they had their man. He was now awaiting trial.

"In all my years, I've never dealt with this kind of

situation," James said. "The perp is behind bars and the victim is still terrified for her life. She thinks there's another killer out there."

"Could it be a delusion brought on by post-traumatic stress?"

"We're definitely considering that possibility. In fact, that is why she was held in the hospital a day or two longer than necessary," James said. "Right now, as you know, our biggest concern is that she might be saying one thing and planning another. I think her talk of going back to work is only a ploy to let us believe she's alright. Truth is, I think she's far from it."

James glanced at his phone as it dinged a message and pushed it away. "I've never seen a victim escape something as dire as she did in quite the way she did. She has a mind of her own and where that might lead her…" He leaned forward. His blue eyes stood out more than usual against his tan complexion. "I can't take any chances with this. We need her on the stand. But…" He paused. "This witness appears to have more guts than any I've seen before."

Travis had to agree with that. For the woman had literally clawed her way out of a closet and broken out through a boarded-up window by crawling through an impossibly small opening. Then, she'd run barefoot down a dark, neglected alley to safety. And when she'd been brought in, James had told him how deadly calm she'd been. There had been no tears or hysterics, only a shaky voice as she'd reported what happened. The tears had come later according to hospital staff but even then, there'd been few. According to the file, and James had confirmed it, she'd been solid in her testimony that would incriminate the perpetrator of one of the worst serial killer rampages the country had seen in recent years. She was a five-star witness and had identified Eric Solomon from a picture lineup presented to her while she was still in the hospital. But there was only one glaring glitch, and it was the fact that she claimed to have heard two voices—both she believed to be men and both with the intent to hurt her. That belief was a glitch that cast a shadow on both her stability and her believability. It was her insistence, with a complete lack of supporting physical evidence, that the killer hadn't worked alone.

Chapter Two

The covers were twisted, some on the bed, some off. The room was still in darkness as Kiera fought with a sheet and finally reached over and flipped on the bedside light. She'd thought she'd heard a sound, something out of the ordinary. Seconds passed. She clutched the sheet as the fridge fan clicked on. The soft whirring seemed loud in the night silence.

"It's the fridge," she muttered as if saying those words would reassure her, as if they would change everything.

It was her second night back in her own home, in her own bed. It had been over a week since the attack. When she'd been discharged from the hospital, she'd been more than ready to pick up her life where it had left off. Except, that wasn't the way it was. The condo she called home no longer felt like one. The funky, crafty style she'd created by shopping flea markets and craft sales, the style that had felt so completely her and so homey, felt foreign. She'd been on edge since she'd come home. And a police officer had been assigned to patrol her area. He made a regular pass of her property, checking in often and would continue, the officer had assured her, until a US marshal took over. While she wasn't under twenty-four-hour surveillance, she was promised a patrol car in her neighborhood and a regular check-in.

She grabbed the book she was reading and her blanket. After heading to the kitchen to start the coffee maker, she curled up on the couch while it brewed. But the cozy mystery lay unopened on her lap despite the fact that it was one that she'd anxiously been waiting to read. She sat quietly, trying to think of anything but the trauma she'd endured.

She looked over at the half-grown cat she'd so recently taken in. Her name was Lucy. Both the name and her reason for being here were fate more than choice. She'd taken the cat so one of the residents at the home where she worked wouldn't lose contact with her pet and would still be able to see her. Now the adolescent cat was curled up on her raspberry-and-blue flowered armchair. Lucy had claimed that chair from the minute she'd been brought home. Kiera stood up and went to sit on the edge of the chair and ran her fingers through Lucy's soft fur. The cat batted at her hand and curled up tighter, presenting her with her back.

"You win," she said with a smile and went back to the couch. But, despite the cat's rejection, it felt good to have her here, to have another living being sharing her space. In fact, she'd picked the cat up from her friend's house the minute she'd been discharged from the hospital. But she knew that she needed more than Lucy to move past the trauma. She needed to dive back into the work she loved. Returning to her routine would get rid of the fear and uncertainty that had rooted in the midst of her life like a field of thistles. Even now, she missed her colleagues' banter and the everyday comings and goings of the care home. The thought of that brought a touch of normalcy to the sense of unreality she'd had since she'd been kidnapped.

She stood up, paced and then sat down again. She

knew that the experts disagreed with that theory. They thought that counseling sessions and rest were the answer. She didn't need counselors or psychiatrists or any other health professional to talk her into wellness. What she needed, besides her life back, was to know that both her kidnappers were behind bars. That would make her feel so much better than any therapist ever could. But the authorities thought they had her attacker. No one believed that there were two involved in the attack for there was no physical evidence. Instead, the FBI had assigned a team of marshals to protect her. They weren't here yet, and secretly she felt that they were putting them in place more to ensure that she didn't skip town than to protect her. It was a feeling based on the way they'd phrased things as they laid their protection plan out to her. Whatever they thought about that—they were wrong.

It was five minutes to five o'clock.

The phone rang.

"It's a prank," she muttered. "Someone with a sick sense of humor." That's what the police officer had said when she'd told him that she'd gotten two calls early yesterday morning. One a hang up and the second heavy breathing. He hadn't taken the calls seriously at all. In fact, he'd called the incidents unfortunate and bad timing, following so closely on the heels of all she'd been through.

Yet, in her heart she didn't believe any of that. Her gut knew it would happen again and her hand shook as she answered.

"Hello," she said and fought to keep the tremor from her voice. "What do you want?"

She was talking to dead air. They'd hung up just as they'd done yesterday at exactly this time.

If they followed yesterday morning's pattern, they'd call again. In exactly ten minutes.

She hit End and wished that she could hurl the phone across the room.

She got up, dropping the blanket and the book on the couch as she went into her bedroom and over to the night-stand. She hesitated a second before opening the drawer. She looked at the gun lying there as if that would some-how make her feel better. The gun had rested in the bot-tom of her aunt's purse for forty years, or so the woman who had raised her had claimed. She'd kept the gun after she had died, as a memento, nothing more. She didn't like guns. And, for the longest time, aside from getting a per-mit to carry a concealed weapon, she'd kept it in a locked storage box. Despite the promise of police surveillance, being checked in on didn't feel like it was enough. In her fear, she'd taken the gun out of the locked storage box the day after she left the hospital. Her life had turned on its head. Her aunt had been right, one should always be prepared. If she'd had the gun with her that fateful night, maybe she would never have been taken.

"Auntie Nan, you may have known what you were talking about," she said. Her voice was soft, reflective. She looked upward as if somehow, somewhere, her aunt would be listening.

"Damn it." She hated this, hated the fact that her life was in shreds and now she was the victim of some idiot. A prank caller on top of everything else was too much. For she knew her freedom would soon be curtailed by personal protection. A man prowling her property night and day was not something she wanted, and not, accord-ing to the FBI, anything she could avoid.

A US marshal was security she didn't need. They'd soon be here anyway. What she wanted hadn't seemed to matter in over a week. First the kidnapping and now in its aftermath, the surveillance, protection they liked to call it. Despite their insistence of vigilance, the irony was their reasons for it. They didn't believe her claims that there was another killer. Instead, they feared that she would run. There was no danger in either option. She wouldn't run and there was another killer. But Cheyenne wasn't a place where a serial killer could continue his sick activities and not get caught. It wasn't a place where he could blend in. It was a small city and that made it difficult to hide. Whoever the second killer was, he'd follow a pattern already established over the last year and head to a larger center where there was more opportunity. She was as sure of that as she was that the second killer existed. She tried to tell herself she was safe, that the fact that only one killer was behind bars, didn't matter. She tried to tell herself that the killer that authorities insisted didn't exist, was no threat to her but they would be a threat to another woman in some other town or city in this country. But despite thinking that, she wasn't so sure that she was safe or, that it was over. She wasn't a forensic expert or a psychiatrist, but she knew a little about serial killers. She'd met one face-to-face and she'd been in the presence of the other.

The other. She shuddered for it was the thought of that—of the one on the loose that terrified her most.

The one they hadn't caught, the one they didn't believe in, that one had been the leader. At least, that's what she sensed. She also sensed that nothing would stop them. They'd go on, find a new partner, maybe work alone. But the end result would be that someone else would die. She shuddered. Someone had to stop the killing and to do that someone had to believe her.

At five minutes after five o'clock in the morning, the

phone rang again. There was no point hesitating. That wouldn't make any of this go away. She answered.

The deep breathing started. As it had before, it went on for a minute. This time she said nothing after the first hello, not for thirty seconds. Then she demanded that this end. She demanded an identity. She got neither of her demands. The phone call ended exactly thirty seconds after that.

She tossed the phone to the other end of the couch as if distance would make a statement, end the harassment. Prank calls were what she had thought yesterday. But now she sensed something else was at play, as a sense of déjà vu almost choked her.

THE SUN HAD only begun to rise when Travis turned the corner onto the quiet residential street. The assignment was low-key. That's what he'd thought going in. He'd also learned a long time ago that situations like this could turn on a dime. And a second read of the file gave him a feeling that something was off. It was because of that, because he trusted his instincts, that he was here this early. His shift didn't start for another three hours. Something told him that he needed to be more proactive than normal.

He wanted to get a clear handle on things. He wanted an uninterrupted look at what he was dealing with. That included not only the witness but her environment as it was now—undisturbed. Less than a minute later, he pulled up to the three-story off-white condo building in the middle of the block. The ground-floor unit was the one that the witness, Kiera Connell, resided in. She'd purchased it a year ago. He knew that because he'd already run a check on the property. It was built five years ago, and she was the second owner. They were trivial facts but even in a low-threat case like this, it was his habit to research such things. Even though there was a driveway, he parked the SUV in the parking lot a group of similar buildings shared. It was too early in the morning to knock on her door and introduce himself. The entire building, including her condo, was still in darkness. He could see the darker shadows of flowers in the flower bed. Everything seemed to be in place—neat and organized.

He wondered what the inside of her place was like and he wondered what the occupant was like. He didn't know what she'd been like before the incident. But he could only guess that now she would be in need of support and counseling for many months, or even years, to come. She'd survived a vicious attack by a serial killer who had left a trail of women dead. The women had all been raped and then murdered, all except the first two. They'd been murdered without any evidence of sexual assault. That wasn't odd but rather an indicator that the perpetrator had evolved. An attack like that could leave the victim broken and unable to return to their former life. He hoped that wasn't the case. But the law of averages wasn't in her favor. It was too bad. According to the file, she'd been a determined young woman. She had carved a career for herself despite adversity. But a file never told the whole story, nor did the authorities who led the investigation. To keep her safe, he needed to know who she was as a person. That was for later; for now he'd scout out the area. The advantage of this early hour was that he could do so without any distractions. He was lead on the team of marshals who would protect Kiera Connell. The danger to the witness was minimal. Despite the low risk of danger, he was working the case like he did any other.

On this assignment, he'd had shorter notice than most. It was up to him and his team to keep her safe and make sure she kept it together until the trial was over. The feds had pinned their case not only on the evidence they'd collected but on the testimony of the only witness.

He'd learned as much as he could about the woman who was his latest assignment. It fascinated him that she was the only victim who had escaped. That a twenty-five-year-old nurse, with little life experience, had been the one to do it—that, to him, was mind-blowing. Although, he couldn't imagine how messed up she must be from the experience at the madman's hands. He felt for her. But he still would rather bow out of this assignment. For, he saw little challenge. The perp was behind bars and he and his team were effectively babysitters to a witness who was too important for authorities to take any chances on. She was the key to ending a killing spree that had lasted far too long. For they suspected it had gone on long before they'd become aware of it. All that aside, bowing out was, unfortunately, not an option.

He looked at his watch. It was twenty to six. He'd been up since four after only five hours of sleep. It wasn't a big sleep loss, only an hour less than he usually got. He shrugged the thought away. It wasn't a factor. The amount of time that had passed since he'd arrived was. He'd learned a long time ago that time could slip away if not tracked and organized. Time was critical for it could mean life or death. That was why he always kept a tight schedule and a close eye on the time.

A window at the front of her property was open a crack. It was the swing-out kind that, if one was into such things, could open from the outside. He frowned at that. No matter that the killer was behind bars—open windows low to the ground were begging for a crime to happen. He stood at the corner of the condo. The sun was rising. Streaks of sunlight were making it easy to see without the aid of a flashlight. He took a step forward meaning to scout the entire perimeter of the unit.

"Freeze! Take one more step and I'll shoot."

The woman's voice came out of nowhere. He'd been broadsided. *Damn it*, he thought. He'd been caught with his pants figuratively down. He turned and saw out of the corner of his eye the barrel of a handgun. He didn't dare turn right around, even though he wanted to. But he didn't plan to die today, or any day in the immediate future.

"Drop your weapon!"

There was no way in hell that was happening. His mind ticked through the options. He could take her down, but he had to get closer. He hoped her attention was on his weapon as he dropped it to his side, still holding it in his left hand. At the same time, he took a step backward, toward her.

"Do it!" she snapped. "And don't take another step."

"I'm a US—"

"I don't care who you are," she interrupted. "Put your hands where I can see them and drop your gun."

He slid his gun into his holster and lifted both hands in the air. He had his badge in one hand, having pulled it out from the side of his holster as he'd holstered the gun. "I'm going to toss my badge—"

"No!" she interrupted. "You'll throw nothing."

Damn it, he thought again. He was furious with himself. She'd snuck up on him. But she hadn't come out of nowhere. He should have sensed that he wasn't alone. He should have known. *Hell*, he thought. He should have expected it, been prepared for it. It was the basic tenet of any scout pack—Be Prepared—never mind a US marshal. He'd missed the signs that she was near. And because of that, he was at the wrong end of a gun. Was he getting old? His friends had teased him about that only a week earlier over a couple of beers. They'd been celebrating his thirtieth birthday. He discounted that thought. He worked hard to be at the top of his game. Still, that didn't change the fact that he'd screwed up—big time.

"Who are you?" he asked. If nothing else, he deserved to know who was threatening him. More important, he needed to put himself back where he belonged, in charge of this situation.

She fired a shot that kicked up dirt two feet to his right.

"What the hell!" he roared and almost spun around, stopping himself with sheer willpower.

"Another word and you're a dead man," she retorted.

A thought came to him that was as outrageous as it was possible. After all, it was her condo that he was standing outside. The more he thought it, the more the idea gained plausibility. Was it possible that this was the witness he'd come to protect?

"I'm here to—"

"Do you not understand English? Shut up," she said.

The words were angry and spoken with no hesitation, no hysteria and no tears. That wasn't what he expected if she was the witness. But if it wasn't her, who was she?

"Turn around," she ordered. "And do it slowly."

There was something about her voice. A silken edge that in another time and another place might have been erotic. He couldn't help the thought. It was a voice that could do things to a man in the darkness of the night.

He found it interesting that her voice vibrated a bit as if she was nervous or traumatized. Had she never held a gun before? It was a possibility. And a possibility where he'd been lucky that she hadn't hit him.

He pivoted on a heel. He wanted to give her the impression of how little he cared about her demands, or the fact that she had the advantage. She needed to know that he didn't fear her.

But when he faced her, he could only stare. For the woman holding a gun on him with a grim but determined expression was the face on the witness's file. He was facing the very woman he was to protect, and the file picture had done her no justice. In the picture she'd been pretty; in real life she was so much more than that. The rising sun highlighted her dark hair, giving it a glossy sheen that framed her beautiful face. She was petite, no more than a few inches over five feet. She was slim and yet voluptuous in a way that made him fight to keep his eyes up and on her face. It was an attraction that he hadn't felt in a very long time, if ever. She mesmerized him with a look.

He was pinned by green eyes. They were eyes that would have held him forever if it weren't for the gun that she had yet to lower. The moment shifted everything he knew about this case. A simple, uncomplicated assignment had just become difficult. Difficult in ways he'd never imagined.

Chapter Three

"Kiera Connell?"

"How do you know me?" Kiera's voice cracked as it had off and on since her ordeal. She hoped that it wasn't on the edge of breaking or of her losing it like she had for an hour only yesterday. She couldn't afford to lose her voice when a strange man was roaming her property. After everything she'd been through this was beyond disconcerting. She wanted to ask who he was, why he was here but she feared that her voice wouldn't hold out. That he knew her name was interesting but not startling. There was a list of owners in the common area. The question that was more troubling was—had he been casing the place?

"I don't."

The easy way he spoke combined with his soulful brown eyes seemed to say that none of this bothered him. That this was just an everyday occurrence. Who was he?

He took a step forward.

"Take another step and you die."

It was a stupid thing to say and she knew it. She'd already threatened him with death once and despite her threats, she doubted if she could kill him. Pull the trigger, yes, she'd already done that. But that had all been for show. If she was going to threaten to kill, she should be able to make good on that threat. She'd only shot the gun at the shooting range and then here, when she'd dusted the top of a dandelion to prove her point. She didn't like the feeling of aiming a killing weapon at another human being, at any being.

"Who are you and what are you doing slinking around my place in the dark?"

Except it wasn't dark anymore. The sun had cleared the night shadows and the neighborhood was coming to life. Soon one of her neighbors would be wondering what was going on. On the upside, she was sure that if someone were to see their little tableau, they would be quick to call the police. This wasn't the kind of neighborhood where guns and violence were common. In fact, she'd never seen or heard of an incident in the time she'd been here.

"Travis Johnson…" He broke off as if reconsidering saying anything else but instead took a step forward.

"Stop!" Her throat hurt at the effort, but it didn't break. She clenched the gun so tight that her palm was beginning to sweat.

She frowned. He hadn't ditched his gun as she'd demanded, only holstered it. She wasn't sure how she'd let that get past her. She guessed that she would have had to shoot him for him to relinquish the weapon as she'd demanded. Except for the weapon which he was careful to keep his hand away from, he was complying. Not once had he tried to overpower her, to take the gun from her. Considering how fit he looked, she guessed he could have easily been able to overpower her. Instead, he'd let her remain in control, let the situation play out. Except for the gun, none of his mannerisms indicated that he was the trespasser or thief that she'd first thought. His voice was low and calm as if having a gun held to him was a normal way to begin his day. His stance was relaxed, as if she were no threat. That annoyed her.

Despite the discomfort, she held the gun tighter. It was as if by doing that she was safe—protected even more than before. Her eyes met his. His brown eyes were steady and in an odd way honest. Yet something ran under his calm surface. She speculated that he hid a harder, darker side. The thought of that made her hold back a shiver. She needed no more darker sides. She'd faced more darkness than she ever wanted to see in this lifetime. And yet it wasn't over. There was still the trial. And there was still… She pulled her thoughts back from another terrifying reality. One that was hers alone, for no one else believed her.

"Okay, Travis Johnson. Why are you on my property?"

"I'm a US marshal," he said quickly, as if afraid that she was going to cut him off again.

She couldn't hide the look of disbelief on her face. Despite her earlier analysis, there was something about him that made her think of the bad boy in high school and not of someone in law enforcement. Except, this was no boy. He was tall and broad shouldered, with a rough but good-looking face and a tough-as-nails attitude. With the early morning shadows lifted, it was clear that he likely wasn't a common thief. Besides, she doubted if one would be this confident after being caught red-handed trespassing.

"Identification?"

He held out something that glinted in the early morning sun. "My badge."

It looked official enough. And she had been told there would be protection.

"You can call—"

"I don't need you to tell me who I can call," she said and couldn't keep the bite from her words. She didn't like the way he was looking at her. She had too many men look at her like that and the last thing she needed was another. Except if she were honest, there was no lust in his eyes, only an intense determination. She didn't like that either.

Despite that, she lowered the gun. She held it stiff and inches away from her hip. "So, you're the protection I was promised."

"Yes," he said. "Along with two other US marshals. We are your security team from now through the trial." He shifted as if contemplating moving a step closer.

"Don't move," she demanded.

"I have to say I've never had a witness react like this before," he said looking down at the lowered gun.

"I'm betting that you've never met someone who escaped a serial killer either," she said. She couldn't help herself. Even in this situation she wasn't about to take guff from anyone. She told it like it was; she always had.

"No." He shook his head. "You're right. You're the first." He took a step forward, his hand out. She held out her hand and noticed that he had to reach and take a step forward to accept it. She hated her small size in a situation like this for it made her feel at a disadvantage. He took her hand and it seemed to be swallowed in his as he gave it a firm shake and let go.

"Marshal Travis Johnson. Here to protect you and make sure that your testimony is given, and that piece of trash is put away for good."

There was something in the tone of his voice that held a doubt she couldn't identify, as if he questioned his assignment.

"You think there might be a problem?" she asked.

"No problem," he said. "Look, let's go inside and talk there before you have your neighbors wondering what's going on." He eyed the gun. "You might want to put that away."

"This way," she said and ignored his suggestion as she brushed past him. Their eyes met as she passed. His seemed to see beyond what she'd left unsaid, as if he knew her very thoughts. She looked away. He might be here to protect her, but he had no idea what he was up against. For there was another threat. The fact that it was faceless didn't make it any less deadly.

"Would you like a drink? Water, coffee?" Kiera asked as she closed the back door to her condo.

"Coffee, please."

"Follow me," she said with a no-nonsense tone of voice, as she led the way to the kitchen.

The unit was compact with only one bedroom, a living area and the kitchen. Despite the small space, everything seemed neat and organized. There was a homey feel to the way she'd decorated, and the smell of coffee seemed to permeate everything.

"Have a seat," she said. "I'll just be a minute. I obviously need to put this away." She raised her gun hand mere inches, enough to make it clear that it was the gun she was putting away.

And with that she turned and disappeared into the bedroom. He heard a drawer open and close, and then she returned empty handed and went to the cupboard, pulling out two cups and lifting the coffee carafe and pouring them each a cup.

He felt out of place, too big for the space and very much as though he were intruding. He accepted the coffee cup from her and noticed that her hand shook. He wished there was something he could do to take the fear away from her but knew he had nothing to offer but his presence. Her fears existed in the past and in the unknown of her future.

They sat across from each other and for a minute neither of them said anything. She'd been through hell and he didn't know what he should address first. He ran through a list of things that he knew he needed to ask, to tell her. Where to begin eluded him. When he looked at her he saw the way she rubbed her thumb against the tablecloth and when she looked up, he noticed the whiteness of her lips, and that's when he knew just how much stress she was under.

Another minute went by and the silence was heavier, more awkward.

"I'm glad I have my aunt's gun," she said in a soft voice that broke the silence.

"If you find yourself in a situation in the future where you need to pull a weapon to defend yourself, just remember—you have to be ready to use it." He paused. "You weren't today, were you? I don't count a wild shot, completely off mark, as prepared."

"I don't know, maybe."

"Maybe is as good as no, and in another situation, hesitation would have been fatal—for you."

"Then I can't hesitate."

"Exactly," he said. "On the upside, I'm here to make sure that you never need that gun. If it's not me, it will be another marshal making sure you're safe. Although, we'll need some help from you."

"What do you need?"

"The truth and—" he paused "—your trust. That means that if there's anything you haven't said, anything you're holding off saying, you need to tell me."

"I've already told the FBI everything I know," she said. "And they don't believe all of it."

"Everything?" he asked. He hoped that she'd give him something that could be used in the case. She'd seen one face only and she'd identified him, for now that was what they had to work with.

"He wasn't working alone," she said. "I heard…"

Her voice dropped as his heart sank.

She couldn't repeat this, not in court. It would make her testimony questionable if she spouted those beliefs like facts with no physical evidence to back them up. They needed an ID on a killer, nothing else. Certainly not a belief that had no support, no evidence, no backing of any kind and seemed more fantasy than reality.

"Kiera, we can't assume…"

"Not without evidence," she said with a nod of her head. "I realize that. But there's something else. I don't think it's connected, but it's frightening."

"What's going on, Kiera?" he asked hoping that maybe going along with her might be a better way to eventually get her off this particular track.

"I'm getting anonymous calls," she said. "In the early hours. Yesterday was the first morning I was home since the attack and that's when they started. There was another this morning. They were both the same. The phone rings at five minutes to five o'clock in the morning and then again at five minutes after five."

That much he hadn't heard. Had it been reported? He doubted it, for it was a fairly glaring oversight and James was nothing but thorough. Another thought hit him. He pulled out his phone as he stood up. His knee caught on the table. Coffee slopped from his cup. It just missed the embroidered tablecloth.

"I'm sorry," he said. But he could only think of what she'd said. Five minutes after five o'clock in the morning was the time the 911 call had come in. The facts from the time she was found and how it had rolled out as the authorities took charge were engraved in his mind. The time of her rescue wasn't public knowledge. He couldn't imagine the time being anything more than a coincidence though. He wasn't sure if even she knew the exact time of her escape. He wasn't sure if anyone had told her. She might only know it was early in the morning, unless she had asked. Either way, he didn't like the sound of any of this. The bus driver who had first found her knew the time, as did the police and the first responders. Would one of them have leaked the information? Except for the bus driver, that would be a breach of confidentiality and mean immediate firing. He made a mental note to mention the possibility that there was a leak to James. The thought, even the possibility, that someone had taken that information and used it to harass her was, to say the least, disconcerting.

She was back with a dishrag in her hand.

"Let me," he said. He took the cloth from her and wiped up the coffee just as it had come close to creeping onto the edges of the tablecloth.

"Got it," he said handing the cloth back. The tablecloth was unique, and he guessed that it was handmade. He'd seen his mother and his aunts embroider many such pieces. This one was a beautiful, vibrant garden scene.

"You embroider?"

"No," she said with a smile. "I found it at a craft sale." She leaned over to take the dishrag and wiped a drop he'd missed.

A minute later she sat down. It seemed that she moved slowly every time she was forced to sit anywhere near him.

"Have you reported the calls?" he asked despite the obvious tension.

"Yes," she said. "Sort of. I spoke to the police officer who was here yesterday but no, unless he put a report forward, which I doubt, they weren't officially reported. I left that to him." She got up as if she was unable to sit, as if his proximity made her nervous.

"Kiera? Are you alright?"

"Would you like more coffee?" she asked with her back to him.

"No thanks. Look, I'm sorry that this is happening. I'm sorry—"

She turned around and there was a pallor to her face. "It's alright. It's me. This is just all so difficult."

He'd taken the wrong approach. He'd been in her face since the beginning, but he wasn't used to dealing with a woman traumatized in quite the way she had been.

"Look, I'll have another cup of coffee, if you'll have one too."

A look of relief crossed her face. And a few minutes later they were talking easily about the craft sales in the area and he was silently thanking the women in his life, in his family, for his knowledge of such things. Ten minutes later she was looking, if not relaxed, at least not so tense that she'd leap at the slightest sound.

"Kiera, I hate to ask this, but you said the anonymous calls you received the last two nights or more specifically, early morning, weren't reported. Why not?"

She shrugged and was quiet for a minute. He gave her time to get her thoughts together and wondered what she was afraid of revealing and why.

"Like I said, I told the police officer the other night, after the first occurrence. He told me there was nothing to be frightened of, that a prank call was just the luck of the draw."

"He brushed them off?" Travis asked as he fought

outrage and tried not to let that emotion show in his voice. "You didn't tell him the time and that there were two of them?"

"I told him all of it," she said. "He didn't believe any of it was part of what happened. I don't believe that. Someone needs to know."

Damn it, Travis thought. There'd been no mention of this, no report. Heads would roll. He pushed the anger back and instead focused his attention on her.

"Tell me about the phone calls," he encouraged in a gentler tone.

She looked at him with relief.

"And don't hesitate to tell me anything from here on out."

She nodded and something in the set of her chin seemed less tense.

"The call occurred again this morning. Two calls, two early morning calls in a row. It begins with a ring and a hang up. Then, ten minutes later, five minutes after five o'clock, they call again. The second call is always heavy breathing for about a minute before they disconnect."

He was quiet, considering what she had said.

"Here." She tossed her phone to him. "The calls are there. They're listed as unknown but the time, duration…"

He looked at the phone's history that confirmed what she'd already said, although he'd never doubted her—at least on that fact.

"We may get along yet," she said with a cough. She covered her mouth and turned away. "Excuse me," she said. "How long did you say I was stuck with you and—" she coughed again and then turned, gave a slight smile, as politeness disappeared "—and, as my aunt would have said, your ilk."

"Right until the bitter end, sweetheart," he said, glad to, again, see the hint of attitude. It gave him hope that she'd be able to overcome the trauma she'd endured. She was a strong woman. That was what the therapist had put in his report, and he'd been right. Not many could endure what she had.

"You have no idea what that might mean."

"You'll be safe, I promise," he said although he knew that wasn't what she'd been alluding to but rather the unknown that lay between now and the trial.

"Will I?" she asked.

He looked into her eyes and saw heartbreak and fear. Both were emotions that tore at his heart in a way no woman had affected him in a long time. But she'd been through more than he could imagine. And other than preventing further threats, he couldn't change what had happened. He couldn't stop the fear, for that arose from a horrifying experience that he could not change. He could only hope that his protection made her feel safe despite prank calls in the middle of the night. He could only try his best to help her face the nightmare she'd endured.

"The calls, they're just opportunistic pranks, aren't they?" She asked the question with hope in her voice. She turned away, her shoulders slouched.

"Kiera," he began. "I'm sorry you weren't taken seriously." He thought of the police officer who'd blown the first calls off. He'd be having a few words with him. "They might be pranks." He wanted to say that they also might not. But all of this was guesswork and needed investigation, monitoring. "I'll handle this."

She turned around to face him. "I can't stop thinking about the phone calls and why they chose me, now of all times. My name wasn't made public. It's a stretch to think that there'd be a connection at all. But the time the last one comes in is about the same time in the morning when I was rescued—give or take. I don't know the exact time—I never asked."

He knew the exact time. He also knew that she was right.

It seemed too coincidental. It seemed too everything. Had someone leaked information and this was their idea of a prank? He hoped not. He hoped it was an unfortunate coincidence. If they continued, he'd have her phone rerouted and the calls handled. She needed time to heal and get on with her life. The calls were obviously frightening her, threatening her peace of mind. And, because of that, they had to end.

He stood up. His gut told him that something else was going on, that this case wasn't as straightforward as everyone thought. There might not be a second serial killer, but something was off, something had been missed.

"I'll be doing some back and forth from the office to here. But I'll be available by phone and I'll be in and out throughout the day. There'll never be a moment when you can't reach me or one of my team." Seeing how frightened she looked, he made a snap decision. He would be here for her until daylight tomorrow. "Tonight, if you get any more of these calls, I'll be in my vehicle, in your driveway. Get me."

"I will," she said softly. "That's guaranteed."

But it wasn't her next words so much as the finality with which she said them that, despite what he believed, made his blood chill.

"Whoever wanted me dead. Whoever I escaped from. One of them is still out there."

Chapter Four

Kiera struggled to catch her breath. Her heart pounded so wildly that her chest ached. Her life depended on escape and yet she couldn't move. She was tied, gagged and stuffed into a space so small that when she rolled over she touched a wall on either side. Her legs were numb from lack of circulation. She was trapped and there was nothing but darkness. She didn't know how long she'd been here or how long before it was over. Over— Her heart raced, for that could mean she lived but it could also mean she died. She took a breath. She fought to still her pounding heart. Fought to keep her mind off all the horrible possibilities. She had to keep sane.

KIERA WOKE WITH a gasp. She was sitting up. The sheets were tangled around her. The pillow was on the floor and the quilt had slid off the bed. She gulped air as if she were drowning. Despite her pounding heart she reached for the phone. She knew what happened next, for it had happened before.

But the phone sat cold and silent in her palm. The phone calls had, in such a short time, become an unwanted ritual. She looked at her phone. It wasn't time. It was too early for the calls that she had begun to both expect and dread.

She shivered not from cold but from dread. She prayed for this to go away, for the nightmare to end. But no amount of wishing made it go away.

Chills ran down her spine. She grabbed the edge of the quilt and pulled it up and around herself. Despite being well into spring, it was chilly tonight. It was like the weather was a harbinger of more bad luck, as if shadows had poked dark fingers into a life that had once been full of hope and love. It was a life she'd built from the broken fragments of the family she'd lost. It was a life that was hard-won and one she loved. She fingered the edge of the quilt as if that would calm her. But the anticipation of what was to come and what had happened in the too-recent past lay heavily on her.

The bedside lamp sent a warm glow over the quilt. She took deep breaths as she'd learned to do in beginner's level meditation. She'd begun the course weeks ago, when her life had been normal.

Normal.

She tried to concentrate on the quilt and on the vibrant colors that she'd admired when she'd first seen it at a local craft sale. She ran her thumb back and forth across the finely stitched embroidery. She'd spent hours furnishing and decorating her condo. She'd made it hers with bright pictures and homey touches, like the quilt and the handmade tablecloth that covered her kitchen table. She'd loved her place—it was the first home she'd ever owned, and it was totally hers. But now, she felt as if she sat in the middle of a stranger's things. Nothing gave her solace. Instead, she felt edgy and out of sorts. Almost five minutes to five o'clock in the morning. The phone would ring very soon and as much as she feared that, she feared who it might be more.

Everything she knew about this caller was unprovable. Yesterday she'd taken a chance by telling Travis. Despite saying he would be there for her, she knew that he doubted her claim that the phone calls were tied to the killer she'd escaped. She didn't blame him for doubting. The authorities believed that the killer was behind bars. She'd have been surprised if his reaction had been any different. In a similar situation, she knew she'd do the same. For there was no evidence, no proof of anything, never mind that he had an accomplice.

The phone rang. She didn't dare breathe. Instead, she looked at it as if it were an evil stepsister. She wanted to toss it across the room but that would end none of this. It rang again. And, she knew with a sick feeling, that this was far from over.

She gritted her teeth. Whoever this was, whatever it was, it wasn't going to bring her down. She shivered and hit Answer.

"Hello?"

Silence.

"Answer me, damn it."

The call ended.

She wanted to pitch the phone across the room. Instead, she set it down. But she knew that in ten minutes, if it followed the pattern of the last few nights, the phone would ring again. She tried to calm herself by remembering what Travis had said and remembering the fact that he was still here, just feet away. She'd invited him inside but he'd refused.

She stood looking out her living room window. Her front yard was shrouded in darkness. She wondered if there was someone out there, waiting in the dark. An entity more terrifying even than what she had escaped—out there and still looking for her. She pushed the thought away and looked to her left. There, she could see the shadow of Travis's SUV. Somehow, knowing he was there made her feel safe but didn't remove her dread as she waited for what would come next.

She wished that she could believe the authorities, believe that she was safe. She wished that she could believe that no more women would die. But she wasn't so sure. What she was sure of was that not that long ago she'd had a job she loved, people she cared about and a life. Then everything had changed. She knew it didn't mean that was over. Although she wanted so badly to go back to that, to a normal life, to a place where the nightmare hadn't happened. But she knew that nothing would change what had happened, time would only blunt the brutal memory. Eventually she'd go back to work, to her regular life and to the people she considered friends and family. When she did, she knew it would be different, and eventually she knew that would be okay.

She shuddered and crossed her arms tightly as if that would provide some comfort. She desperately wanted her old life back. She wished that she could hit Restart and go back to the way things used to be. But there was no going back, she'd been through a trauma that had been life changing.

Her testimony, as the only known survivor of a serial killer, would hopefully seal one killer's fate. For now, that had to be enough. It was time to concentrate on her own health, at least that's what the therapist would have her believe. But he was in the same camp as the other authorities. No one believed that there was more than one killer. But she knew that she hadn't imagined the second voice. She knew in her heart that the man who had tried to kill her and, if she hadn't escaped that closet, would have succeeded and left her like almost a dozen other women in a shallow unmarked grave—hadn't been killing alone. But, with no evidence of any of that, her claim was dismissed. Even the therapist had blown it off. He'd stated that she may have suffered an auditory hallucination. He'd come to that conclusion when she had described the second voice as one that she couldn't peg as either male or female but as something distant and sexless. He had then offered a label for the experience. Apparently, what she'd heard was a normal symptom after a trauma like one which she had experienced.

Her mind went back to the call, the one that always followed the first. Her hands shook at the thought. She had made Travis a promise. She'd promised she'd get him if she had trouble or if she received a phone call where no one answered, as it had in the last two early mornings. Although he didn't believe there was a connection between the phone call and her earlier trauma, she knew that he was here to protect her, to help her even and right now, he was all she had.

She didn't think to grab her robe from the closet. Instead, she padded to the front door in the light shorts and T-shirt she'd slept in, her bare feet quiet against the cool laminate flooring.

She hesitated at the door. Doubts rose and made her rethink her decision. Should she get him—should she leave it? In the scope of what she'd endured, the phone call was nothing. More than likely a prank call as he'd suggested. Before she could decide one way or another, an abrupt knock sounded. She jumped back with an involuntary shriek.

She looked through the peephole.

Travis.

She barely knew him and yet it was like seeing a long-lost friend. She fixated on one important fact; he was on her side. She unlocked the door and stood aside to let him pass. But he didn't. Instead his hands dropped to her shoulders and his eyes were filled with concern.

"What happened?" he asked with a frown. It was as if he already knew. "What's wrong?" He added that question on top of the other when she didn't answer. Without waiting another second, he pulled her into his arms.

It was a friend's hug, one meant to comfort. He was warm and solid against her. And while it lasted only seconds, he was exactly what she needed. It was a promise of protection that no words could offer.

He let her go as he closed the door behind him and stepped farther into the room. She followed. In the space of seconds, everything had changed. And, for the second time in twenty-four hours, she felt protected—safe.

Chapter Five

"Someone called and hung up. I'll be alright," she said before he could say anything.

He wasn't so sure. She'd been pushed to her limits and beyond. No one should have to endure what she had. He wanted to comfort her but there was nothing that he could say that would change what had happened. He could only offer his protection, his words that didn't change anything and his promise to protect.

She shivered in her light T-shirt and shorts.

He glanced to where the afghan hung over the edge of her sofa. She was meticulous about her things. He'd learned that yesterday. The arrangement of her house, the position of her belongings was as familiar as his apartment. Yesterday, he'd made it a point to get to know her environment. Now he knew what might help and what might hinder her, what he needed to know to keep her safe. He went over to the sofa and got the afghan. He brought it back and placed it over her shoulders.

"Thank you," she said as she looked at him with a gentle smile.

"You're welcome," he replied. Even though he wasn't quite sure if she was thanking him for the afghan, for noticing that she was cold—or for being here. Maybe for all three.

"For noticing." She finished on a rather lame note, as if she'd been privy to his thoughts.

He considered asking her to give him her phone, let him take charge. He wasn't sure if she was ready for that.

One thought rolled into the other. He was overthinking it all. Still, he hesitated, unsure for one of the few times in his career. He didn't want to misstep. She was fragile. In a situation like this he knew that, for the victim, control was something that was important, even if it was an illusion. That meant not taking her power away from her. In this case, he decided, she would lead.

"Was it the same as last time?"

"Yes. There was just dead air after I said hello and they hung up within seconds. I didn't say anything more. I don't know why..."

"I'm glad you didn't," he said. He couldn't help himself. He put a hand on her shoulder as his other hand lifted the edge of the afghan that trailed on the floor and wrapped it more securely around her. "That's why I came to your door. I wanted to be here, in case it happened again."

"Thank you."

He tensed. There was a quiver in her voice and it was hoarse. But when he looked at her, he knew that it wasn't tears that had changed her voice. She was tougher than that. She'd proved that by surviving her ordeal, and by confronting him yesterday. He wanted to lash out at the perpetrator. He wanted to roar with anger but there was nowhere and no one to vent his ire at.

He looked at his watch.

"The next call should be in five minutes," she said as she watched him.

A frown marred her beautiful creamy skin. The lines in her forehead only drew his attention further, to the bruise on her cheek. The bruise was only beginning to yellow. He wanted to reach out and run a thumb along it, to somehow emphasize that it would never happen again, not on his watch. Her kidnapper had backhanded her more than once according to what was reported. Reading that in the file enraged him. Hearing James mention it and now seeing the evidence again only made him want retribution, vigilante justice. None of that would happen.

"You think it will follow the same pattern as the previous nights?" He asked the unnecessary question in an attempt to divert his thoughts.

"Yes," she said, "I don't have any doubt. It's already begun."

He wished there was something he could do to stop the idiot who was doing this. This was a coward at work. A coward who was further scaring a woman who had been terrorized beyond what any human should have to endure. He wanted to get his hands on the piece of crap who was doing this.

The fact that there was nothing he could do only made him feel awkward, and too big for the small living space. The driveway surveillance had been long and monotonous and despite his orders to the other two marshals who would take turns relieving him, that there was no need to remain every minute on location, he'd remained for every hour of his shift and beyond.

His thoughts went back to the possibility of another call, minutes away. Was the caller just picking a random number? Had the caller heard a woman's voice and that had prompted him to continue his rather sick game? Or was this something deadlier, as Kiera had alluded to?

"Have a seat," she said and pointed to the couch that sat angled in a way that offered a view of both the front and back yards.

The condo was small and yet its size was inviting and reflected her personality. They'd talked yesterday beyond the parameters of the case and she'd told him that she loved to sit on the couch and read. The butter-yellow couch was completely her. In a way it seemed to reflect her warm personality. He remembered times through the day when they'd talked about something other than the case. He could see her sitting there in the lazy hours of the evening reading on that same couch. He sat on the left side. She'd already told him that the right-hand side was where she sat. She'd said that with a laugh. They both knew that with her living alone, the whole darn couch was hers, she could sit anywhere, not just on the side she said she claimed. A side she also said she preferred for it allowed her to watch the birds and squirrels come in for the seeds and peanuts that she left out for them.

"It will be okay. I promise, Kiera. The killer is locked up. He can't get to you. The calls are nothing but some jerk with nothing better to do."

"Maybe," she said. But the word held neither sureness nor fear. "But how did they get my number?"

Random chance, the explanation he'd offered when he'd first heard of the calls, hadn't sounded plausible even to his own ears. It hadn't yesterday either. He wasn't sure what the connection could possibly be. The serial killer was behind bars unable to perpetrate such calls. Possibly, someone with an evil bent. He was at a loss.

Two minutes to go.

"When you answer, put your phone on Speaker," he said as he handed the phone to her.

"I will," she agreed.

Another minute ticked by. She looked at him but didn't say anything. He'd protected other witnesses, especially in his early days as a US marshal, but none who had gone through what she had. It enraged him to think about what had been done, what she'd escaped.

She looked at him with fear in her eyes and a tense, determined look to her lips.

It was four minutes after five o'clock.

"I'm here, Kiera. It will be alright. We'll put an end to this, I promise." He squeezed her hand and she held on tight as if she never wanted to let go.

Chapter Six

At exactly five minutes after five o'clock in the morning, the phone rang just as Kiera had said that it would, just as she said it had every early morning since she'd left the hospital.

She held the phone and looked at him. "Answer?" she asked and the hand holding the phone trembled.

"Answer," Travis said without hesitation and only assurance in his voice.

But she seemed frozen, her face pale. The phone rang again.

"I'm right here," he reminded her. "Answer."

She hit Answer with a trembling finger. Despite her earlier reaction, her hello was impressive in its control. He reached over and hit Speaker.

Heavy breathing, steady, rhythmic. There was a hoarse edge to the breathing like someone with a respiratory problem.

Her face was stiff, masklike. She held the phone away from her and touched it only with her fingertips, as though it was poisonous.

He reached over and took it from her. The heavy breathing was slow and drawn out and carried on for another few seconds. Then silence.

One second, two.

Travis let it play out, let the caller lead. Finally, the silence ended with a raspy inhale and exhale. And then the words that he knew neither of them would ever forget.

"You die."

The voice was oddly sexless.

Kiera gasped and put a hand over her mouth. But it was too late.

Travis had no doubt that the caller had heard. He imagined their satisfaction at the fact that their victim was frightened. He was glad that for good measure his own phone was recording the call.

"You'll die before you'll ever testify. Die," the voice repeated.

The connection broke and the phone went dead.

"Damn it," Travis said and looked at Kiera.

She wasn't looking at him.

"Someone else is out there," she said in a whisper. "Someone else knows who I am, where I am. They never spoke before—the other calls, I mean. And that voice, it gave me chills."

He took her hands. They were limp, her palms damp. He looked into her eyes.

"They're words, Kiera. Nothing more. You're safe and I'll make sure you remain safe." Meanwhile, his mind was going through the options. Who this might be, what the level of threat might be. He needed to speak to James. They needed to discuss this development and analyze what he'd recorded.

"How do they have my number? How do they know I was a witness? Who squealed?"

She was hitting valid points. Points that had him concerned. There'd been leaks in the emergency system before—rare, but it had happened. While most were dedicated to their jobs and usually closemouthed, there had been a few over the years who had revealed information that was never meant to go public. Had it happened again? And then, of course, there was the wild card. The bus driver who had initially rescued her had sworn no oath of secrecy. The chances that the time of her rescue had been leaked were high. That would explain these calls and justify the possibility that this was just a prankster who had also discovered her identity.

"There was someone else—the man in jail wasn't acting alone."

"Kiera," he began.

She stood up.

"It doesn't matter what I say, does it?" she said angrily. "You're not going to believe me. Despite the fact that I was there." The last words sounded defeated.

"I'm not saying that." He quelled the frustration from showing in his voice. She didn't need that. These phone calls on top of everything else were too much. He took a calming breath. "I'm not discounting what you're saying, Kiera. I can't deny that there's someone out there threatening your life. I heard them. It definitely needs to be looked into. But I don't want you worrying about your safety. No matter what the intent of these calls, no matter who it is, you're safe here. I'm going to ensure that."

She moved away from him and turned her back. She was looking out to the front lawn where the rising sun was dispersing the shadows. "I heard that voice before. The night when I was taken." Her voice dropped off.

He turned to stare at her. She was determined that she'd been the victim of two kidnappers. Maybe it was time to give the theory more consideration than anyone had up to this point. He knew that it didn't fit the profile that had been built in the year-long investigation and that was why the idea was getting pushback. But profiles were not written in stone.

There was a pensive and rather frightened look on her face. "One of my kidnappers had a very unusual voice. It sounded exactly like that," she said. "But I've already told you that. I don't know why I'm bothering to do it again."

She was speaking so softly that he had to strain to hear her.

"Don't stop, Kiera," he encouraged.

"That was the voice of the second killer. I know it."

He looked at her with more than a little interest. He nodded, urging her to continue.

"It was dark," she said in a low voice that was close to a whisper. "But it was clear that there were two voices. One voice was different from the other, as different as their touch. It wasn't the one who was arrested. There were two people there—two kidnappers."

"You're sure?" he asked.

"Yes, damn it!" she said, anger flaring in her voice. "But no one believes me. They might believe me—maybe," she said with drawled-out sarcasm. "When it's too late."

"It will never be too late," he said. "That's why I'm here and I've never failed in a case. I won't fail you now."

"You promise?" she asked with a touch of hope replacing the anger.

"I promise," he said.

"These calls will end tonight," he assured her. It was easier to take the emotion out of the equation by defaulting to work and business. It was the only way to dodge what was stirring in the room, or more aptly, within him. It was an attraction he couldn't seem to stop.

"Can I keep this?" he asked as he held her phone up. "I'll get you another, a prepaid," he said as he saw the look of doubt in her face. He wanted her cooperation but with or without it she wouldn't be handling these kinds of calls. From now on, he or someone else on the team would be accepting any further prank calls. She had enough to deal with.

Slowly she nodded. And he felt humble at the fact that in that one gesture she'd offered the last of her doubt, that she'd given him her trust.

She was pale and quiet. He worried for her, for her well-being. She'd survived a lot, more than most people ever survived in a lifetime. Had the call been too much, compounded with all the trauma she'd so recently escaped?

"I need to make a call. Will you be alright for a few minutes?"

"I'll be fine," she said.

He paused.

"Really," she assured him. "I'm fine."

Outside, he pulled his phone out of his pocket and hit one of the numbers in memory, the FBI's security team. Two minutes later he'd spoken with Serene Deveraux, their security expert. She was the head of that unit and had been for as long as he had been a marshal. He quickly had her assurance that she'd do everything possible to trace the call. Around him, the surrounding homes were beginning to come to life as they prepared to begin a day that, for them, was no different from any other.

His phone buzzed. It was Serene returning his call with news that only confirmed what he already knew.

"My guess is that whoever is making the call is using a burner," she said in her usual matter-of-fact, get-the-job-done voice.

The fact that they were using a prepaid phone didn't surprise him. It was what he'd suspected.

He shoved the phone in his pocket and went inside where he could smell coffee brewing and could see Kiera in the kitchen. She moved easily around the small area. And, as much as he'd tried to be objective and treat her like any other case, he had to admit that she wasn't any other case. Her in-your-face attitude on the lawn yesterday morning was an act of defiance that defined their first meeting, an act that had both surprised and intrigued him. She'd been kick-ass from the beginning and despite the reasons for his being here, he couldn't help the fact that he was attracted to her. He kept telling himself that it was nothing more than superficial. After all, she was rounded in all the right places. A full bottom that he'd love to…

Stop it, Johnson. He pushed the thought from his mind and immediately regretted it, for that thought was replaced by that of the creep who had almost had his way with her. The anger he felt at that thought was like nothing he'd felt before. For the first time in his life he wanted a man to die. For the first time—he wanted revenge.

Chapter Seven

Travis put the bowl down. It was one of a set that were cream colored and scalloped in blue, each with a different farm scene. He guessed that they were another of Kiera's craft-sale finds. He'd just whipped eggs, and the cheese, tomato, onion and assorted spices were ready to go. He'd been in the midst of making her an omelet for breakfast. It was six o'clock, an early start to the day. It had been a day with a rough start. Getting the third set of anonymous calls had been upsetting for Kiera and something he needed to follow up on with Serene and beef up security.

He glanced over his shoulder. Kiera was nursing her coffee with a hand on either side of the cup. She was looking gaunt, as if it had all been too much. And he wondered how it could not be. It took a special kind of person to bounce back from what she'd endured. He was going to make sure that she started the day out right. With something that stuck to her ribs, as his grandmother was fond of saying. It was from her and his mother that he'd learned the art of cooking.

"It seems like a never-ending nightmare," she said.

"It will end," he assured her.

"I hope so," she said. But her voice seemed dull, almost absent of emotion.

Damn, he thought. Despite how well she'd been doing, right now she didn't look fine at all. She was sitting like a pale statue at the table. Her mind was obviously somewhere else. He could only imagine that that place was the recent and very ugly past. Was she thinking about her ordeal or about the phone call and her belief that the killer wasn't acting alone? While he had yet to admit anything to her, his gut told him that there might be some validity to her theory. But instinct and gut feelings wouldn't convince the FBI on the matter. He flipped his thoughts.

"Can I get you some more coffee?" he asked.

She didn't answer.

"Kiera?"

He sat down beside her, pulling his chair close to hers. Had he overestimated her resiliency? If needed, he'd be willing to change the shift schedule more than he already had and stay with her through all of today, as well. She needed familiarity; she needed him. He didn't allow himself to consider that last thought.

There was something that spoke of desperation in the look she gave him. He squeezed her hands, too tightly.

"Ouch. It's okay, Travis."

"Sorry," he said but even as he let her hands go, he remained beside her. He'd be her support for as long as she needed him. But her eyes were dark, brooding, filled with memories that were deep and soul disturbing. He couldn't stop looking at her. He felt for her on a level that he couldn't quite quantify. It was as if everything about her mattered—to him.

The connection caught his breath and left him speechless. It was as if there were something special that bonded them in a way neither of them could fathom. He pushed the thoughts from his mind. Seconds slipped into a minute and then two.

"I'm lucky to be alive," she murmured. "And I want to live. But someone out there wants me dead."

He didn't dispute what she was saying. There was no disputing the reality of the threat.

His mind went back to the report. A transit driver, Sophia Antonia, had found her minutes before dawn. The driver's report stated that she'd seen a woman's silhouette under the glow of the streetlight. At the time, she'd thought she'd been seeing things. But as she got closer, she'd seen Kiera weaving at the entrance of the alley. She'd seemed fragile, broken even, but she'd waved her hands over her head in a plea for help. At first, Sophia thought she was drunk or high. She said the torn medical scrubs and tunic made her realize that something was very wrong.

He marveled at how luck had both saved Kiera's life and almost taken it. She had been lucky that Sophia had been there that morning. It was a rough area of town and not the bus driver's usual route to work. But she was much earlier than usual. As a result, she'd taken the unusual route to grab a cup of coffee at a place that catered to truckers and was open at that hour of the morning.

Sophia had been blocks from her destination when she'd seen the woman stagger from the alley into the light of a nearby streetlight. At first, she hadn't intended to stop. The fact that she'd backtracked was amazing in itself. It wasn't a place or time where most would have stopped to help an unknown woman. But Sophia had claimed some instinct told her that Kiera was different, that she desperately needed help. Then, as she'd turned her car around and the headlights had shone on Kiera, she'd seen the state she was in and known then that there was something very wrong. She knew despite the time and place, she had to stop. It wasn't total bravery; Sophia admitted that she wasn't unarmed. She went nowhere without her inherited Colt Special. And with that in her hand and her phone in her back pocket, she'd gotten out of her vehicle to investigate. As she'd approached, she claimed that Kiera had stood there unmoving with her torn tunic and pants flapping in the breeze.

Then Kiera had spoken the only words she was to speak until she arrived in the hospital.

Help me.

And the transit driver had.

She'd taken Kiera to her vehicle, put her in the backseat, then called 911 and waited for help to arrive. The state Kiera was in had the woman nervous as to who might have done this to her. And she'd admitted to locking the doors and sitting poised at the wheel, with the engine running, ready to take off if necessary.

"I'm fine, Travis. It's just…" She brought his attention back to where it needed to be, on her.

"You're sure?" he asked, taking her hands in his and squeezing them.

"Positive," she said with a smile and pulled her hands free. "Hungry," she said with a tentative smile. "What's the time on that omelet?"

TEN MINUTES LATER she took the last bite and pushed the plate to the side.

"This is the best omelet I've ever tasted," she said. "You're a fantastic cook. Thank you." She stood up, picking up her plate and reaching over to pick up his. "Where'd you learn to cook like that?"

"My grandmother insisted I learn," he said with a smile as he put his hand over hers. "And my mother," he finished. "Let me clean up."

"No," she replied. "I need something to do and you said you had to go into the office."

"You're sure?" He didn't feel concern at leaving her alone. She wasn't a runner. That he was sure of and that was what the FBI had been concerned about. He knew that for the most part, James trusted his assessment. He'd make sure she was safe and he wouldn't be gone long. But, in that time, he'd arranged for the area to be patrolled by a police officer and later this afternoon Devon would take over. In the meantime, he had no qualms about her safety. He'd covered all the angles.

"Positive," she said. "I need to get back to a routine. Nothing better than dishes to take one's mind off things."

"Alright," he said, appreciating the way she was able to return to normal despite the trauma she'd been through. He guessed much of it was pretend on her part. And, while it wasn't healthy in the long run, in the short term it helped her cope. "I won't be gone long. An hour tops. You know my number—call me if there's any trouble, anything at all," he said. "I'll get a patrol car in the area while I'm gone." For she might not be a runner but he wasn't one hundred percent confident, considering her belief and the calls, about her safety.

"I'll be alright."

"Keep the doors locked," he said a few minutes later with his hand on the doorknob. "Call me..." he repeated.

"No worries," she said.

And she stood on the step as he pulled away, a lone figure who looked too small, too vulnerable. The memory of her standing there, of her vulnerability, stuck in his mind. As a result, he drove a little too fast, trying to shorten the time he was gone, the time she might be alone.

Chapter Eight

"I need electronic security in place and I need it yesterday," Travis said. He was in the FBI office in Cheyenne. He and Serene had already gone through a minute's worth of niceties. He didn't have any more time than that.

"I'm sorry to rush this but…"

"No problem," Serene interrupted. "Keep the facts coming—you know I don't do well with small talk."

Despite being head of her unit, Serena was still very hands-on. He knew that other than giving her the specs of Kiera's property, she'd handle the rest without his help.

Serene made a note of all the relevant details, asking him pertinent questions as she typed. "I'll have a man out within the hour," she said and looked up from her computer screen. "Motion detectors, cameras, the works. There won't be anything that happens around her place that we won't be on top of."

"Today?"

"Today," she promised. "Give your witness the heads-up that there'll be activity around the house. Better yet, make sure you're there."

If he didn't know her as well as he did, he would think that she was implying that he needed to be told how to do his job. But he knew that Serene didn't mean to undermine. That was just her manner. He'd known her for years and had a friendship that had begun with a series of misguided dates.

"Sit and we'll finish this up," she said without looking at him.

He pulled out a chair. They both knew the drill. He provided the information she needed and offered photos of the problem areas he'd identified. He listed the specifics almost by rote as he'd memorized them yesterday when he'd first seen the place.

"The system will be in place by early afternoon," she said as she looked up from her computer screen. Her eyes were molten and dark and, right now, razor-sharp.

"I'll set up a system that will be monitored from here. But you'll also be able to access it. I've made it inaccessible inside the unit based on what you've said of your witness."

"I can work with that," Travis said.

She looked at him. "There's something else. The phone. What are you going to do about that?"

"I bought a prepaid for her to use and I took hers. That way if there're any more of those calls she won't be receiving them." He put the phone on the desk. He'd been clear with Kiera that her family and friends wouldn't be able to contact her, but that she could still reach them. She'd promised him that she'd limit her calls and not reveal any vital information like her current situation with law enforcement or anything regarding the case, including the threatening calls. She'd agreed and said that she'd warn her friends that she'd be out of communication for a time.

He'd been surprised that it wasn't an issue for her and more surprised when he learned that she had no close family. In fact, he'd not only been surprised but floored. He knew that she had been orphaned. He knew that she'd been raised by an aunt and he knew what the file had said, but he hadn't taken that information literally. In the back of his mind he'd always thought that there was someone.

He couldn't imagine being alone like that. He couldn't imagine not having to make sure there was some way to communicate with people who had always been there for you. In his vibrant and close-knit family, that wouldn't happen. His family had deep roots in Cheyenne although some of them had since scattered farther afield. But none of them would be okay with being out of touch with him. In fact, they'd proven their need to stay in touch over the years—and when he could be, he was there for them, always leaving a way for them to be in contact. Only last week, he'd stopped by his aunt's apartment to help her move a dresser, and minutes ago he'd made a quick call to check on his mother, as his father was on a business trip. The fact that Kiera had no biological family was something he couldn't comprehend. But she claimed her family were her friends, even her coworkers. And she'd been concerned about them and relieved when he'd told her that she could call them using her prepaid. The phone's number would be blocked. She'd already been instructed not to give the phone number out. He wasn't ready to trust anyone, not even her inner circle.

"Excellent," Serene said bringing him out of his thoughts of Kiera. "We'll monitor the calls. I'll try to run a trace on anything suspicious. Give me the number of the prepaid and I'll forward anything personal directly to her."

"That's it," he said a minute later as he stood up. "Anything else and I'll be in touch."

With the surveillance issue in motion, he headed down the hall.

You'll die before you'll ever testify.

The words were dire. They were not words that could or should be ignored. Crank call or not, he couldn't assume that it was benign. His gut was telling him that there was weight behind the threat, that it might not be chance that had her receiving those calls. That was why he was here.

His steps echoed as he strode down the hallway. A minute later he was outside James's office.

He gave one hard knock on the door. The sound echoed down the corridor. He didn't knock twice. James was expecting him. His hand was on the doorknob when he heard the greeting and was told to come inside.

"What's going on, Trav?" James asked after Travis had taken a seat. "I heard you're lining up electronic security on the witness's home."

"I did. Kiera's been receiving anonymous phone calls since she returned home." He went into the details of the calls.

"Have you witnessed any of these calls?" James interrupted.

Travis was not fazed by the interruption. He would have been more disturbed if James hadn't interrupted. For that was his habit. He was an interactive, if slightly abrasive, listener. The only time that fact changed was if the topic had no interest or relevance for him.

"Not until early this morning. The last call was five after five. For the first time there was a voice." He paused. "She's adamant that there were two perps that night."

James was looking at him with interest.

"Serene has determined that the calls were made on burners."

"So, there's no way of linking them to a person, an account," James said thoughtfully.

"No. And they appear to have been made from various points throughout the city."

He looked over James's shoulder where he could see a partial view of Cheyenne's skyline. Cheyenne was a small city. It wasn't a place where one expected a woman to be afraid for her life. But crime occurred everywhere, even where it was least expected. If nothing else, his career had taught him that.

James sat back with a look of concern on his face. He laced his fingers and batted his thumbs. "Initially, our biggest threat was the chance of the witness disappearing. Running if she felt threatened. This will only exacerbate the potential for that problem."

Travis didn't say anything to that. The possibility that the witness would run had been a concern for the feds since the beginning. They based that fear on the fact that their witness was insistent on her belief that there was more than one perpetrator. Another threat could cause her risk of flight to increase. He wasn't so sure that they were right. After meeting Kiera, after seeing how much she cared for her condo, how much she cared for the cat she'd adopted and how much she loved her life and job—he saw no risk of flight.

"I don't think running is a problem. I think we have a different situation to be concerned about," he said. "The last call threatened her with death."

"Did the others?" James asked without skipping a beat at the switch in direction the conversation was taking.

"She says no. According to her, no one spoke during the other calls. The first of the set was only a hang-up and the second was heavy breathing. Like I said, according to Kiera, always at the same time, same duration. Until this morning when the last call changed everything."

"This has been going on for three mornings, if we include today. And she didn't feel that it might have been important to notify us immediately?"

"She mentioned the calls to the police officer on duty, the first morning they happened. But she said that, despite how distraught she was over them, he'd basically blown her off. Told her she was imagining things as a result of the trauma she'd been through."

"So not only did he push aside a key piece of evidence, he decided to play amateur psychologist." James swore, as he turned his attention to his computer. "I'll be looking into this. In a case like this something like that should not have been ignored." He frowned. "I'll be pulling him off this case, that's for sure."

His fingers flew on the keys as if making notes as he talked. Seconds passed and he stopped, pushed the computer to the side.

"So, tell me more about these phone calls."

"According to her, nothing was said, just some heavy breathing, that was it. This morning, I was at her door at five and missed the first phone call. She said they hung up after she answered. Except, they're at exactly the same time. Five minutes to five and five minutes after."

"I wish I felt comfortable saying that it was just another loon out there," James said. "Or, even that it was someone jumping on local news to get their jollies. But that seems unlikely. We've kept the information on this case pretty bare-bones, at least what the public is hearing. And the most disturbing aspect is the time that last call is coming in. The same time as her rescue." He shook his head. "That time was never released."

Travis looked at James and neither of them said anything for a minute. Then James leaned back. "Five after five was the time the emergency call came in."

Travis nodded.

"A leak? Possible. Unfortunately, it's happened before." He pushed back in his chair and looked at Travis. "So, these calls have been going on since she got home?"

"That's pretty much it," Travis said. "The last three mornings. This morning she claimed the first call came in as it always did. No one was there when she answered. I heard the second at five minutes after five exactly the time she claims that the last of each of the previous sets occurred."

James leaned forward, a frown on his face and a look of expectation in his eyes.

"I put it on speaker phone and the voice I heard was androgynous. It had no inflection, can't even verify if it was human or machine-made. What I can tell you was that the caller threatened her life. Here," he pulled out his phone. "I'll play it."

When it was over, James again pushed back his chair, this time with enough force to go back a few feet. His arms were behind his head and a frown was on his face.

"Damn," James said. "I know you've stated that she isn't giving signs of running but this could just tip things. What she experienced was unimaginable and now this."

"It's not good," Travis agreed.

"That was all there was?"

Travis nodded. "Too short to trace. But she claims that the voice she heard sounds like the voice of a second person involved in the kidnapping."

"Yet we only made one arrest. Only one killer was in our sights until this." James ran a hand through the pouf of curly black hair that centered just above the classic buzz cut on the sides of his head. "I don't like the sound of this. We can't afford to ignore it. Of course, if you have no trace, we have nothing to go on."

"I've given Kiera's phone to Serene to monitor and given Kiera a prepaid. She's setting up surveillance."

James didn't acknowledge the phone transfer but instead said, "Good call on the surveillance."

Travis said nothing. What he'd done was only another detail like all the others—part of his job. He changed the subject.

"She's different than I expected even from your initial report," he said, determined to address some of the key components of this assignment.

"What do you mean different?" James asked.

"She's more grounded than you think. I don't see a flight risk at all. In fact, I'd say just the opposite. She's determined that justice is served. But these phone calls…" He shook his head. "A death threat isn't something to discount. Could there be a leak? Did someone talk about what happened, mention the time that she was found?"

"I hope to hell not," James said. "I trust my team."

"There's the hospital, the emergency crew, a string of people involved. It only takes one of them to open their mouth."

"I'll put someone on it. Heads will be rolling if that's the case."

"And she might be right. Maybe this is a perp that's flown under the wire."

"A second kidnapper." James shook his head. "One thing I've learned in this job is never say never."

He stood up. "Whatever the motivation for the calls, we can't ignore this. Keep our witness safe and keep me up to date. In the meantime." He looked at his watch. "I've got another case breathing up my tail. I'll have to trust you on this one as I always do." He said the last with a laugh.

Travis didn't ask what else James had on his plate. He

didn't need to know. He had one mission and one mission only, and that was keeping Kiera not only alive, but safe. He wouldn't jeopardize either one of those mandates for details not related to her and her case.

Chapter Nine

Arranging surveillance, meeting with James—all of it had taken longer than Travis had expected. It was early afternoon by the time he returned to Kiera's condo. Serene had promised the security would be in place by the end of the afternoon. In the meantime, he needed to update Kiera on all that had happened.

Her front door opened before he'd reached the end of the sidewalk. Kiera stood with one hand on the door and the other on the jamb. She smiled, and he felt a welcome like he had come home. He shook the feeling off.

"How'd it go?" she asked as she ushered him inside and closed the door.

The unease and troubled demeanor that had radiated off her this morning was gone. Now there was an aura about her that he found calming. That surprised him considering all she'd been through. But there was so much about her that was a surprise. She wasn't fitting the profile her file had painted. He couldn't pigeonhole her and he found that refreshing.

"The feds have agreed to electronic surveillance. Your condo and the area around it will be monitored twenty-four-seven," Travis said. He regretted what he'd said, how he'd said it, when he saw the look on her face. He regretted that he hadn't alerted her to his intentions before he left. But, for him, this type of procedure was standard. He'd forgotten, that for her, it wasn't.

"Is that necessary?"

"Better safe than sorry," he replied. "The anonymous phone calls are likely nothing more than someone with a sick sense of humor. But we'll have an eye on your place just to make sure." She'd already said that she believed the voice sounded like the second kidnapper. Repeating that fact now wouldn't move the case forward but it would more than likely upset her. Upset was not what he wanted their star witness to be so, for now, he downplayed.

"You mean close my bedroom door when I'm changing?" she asked with a slight smile.

It took him a minute to react. He hadn't expected a joke. In fact, it hit him so sideways that he didn't react at all.

"Kidding," she said before he could answer.

She went to the fridge and opened it, bringing out two bottles of water.

"Here," she said. "I imagine you haven't had a break or a drink since you left."

"Your instincts are spot on," he said with a laugh and she offered him an answering smile as she sat down on the couch.

He took the drink she offered. Flavored water, lemon, something they admitted they both liked.

"Thank you," he said as he chugged back a couple of generous swallows before recapping it. He sat down on the couch beside her.

"As you already know, I won't be here every day," he said. "There'll be other marshals taking shifts." He looked at his watch. "Devon Gowan is due in half an hour. He'll be taking the next shift." The shifts were long but not as long as the time he'd spent. He'd stayed until he knew things were stable and Kiera felt safe. "But if you need me, call—I'll more than likely be in the vicinity."

"I could have guessed that."

This time the smile she gave him was rather quirky and her eyes had a look. It was like she knew everything about him.

"Really?"

"You're not that hard to read, Travis," she said. "You don't give up control easily and you feel responsible for me. Although you shouldn't. Despite what's happened I have been taking care of myself for a long time."

"I know," he said feeling slightly chastised. "Reece Blackburn will take the shift after Devon. Just so you know who's who."

"I'll be fine, really," she said. "I have everything I need including the update you gave me on the men who will replace you—Devon and then Reece. You're a worrier, aren't you?" she asked with a smile.

He was glad to hear the light, almost teasing tone in her voice. She'd been weighted down with enough darkness. Unfortunately, until this trial was over, it was a darkness that was a long way from ending. She'd been through hell. He imagined that a trauma like she'd been through was forever burned in one's memory, an inescapable nightmare. She'd literally escaped both rape and death. For her to tease, to see humor in anything now, so soon after was, he hoped, a promising sign.

"You worry too much, Trav."

The diminutive of his name stuck in his mind. Only those closest to him ever called him that. He wondered what that meant in the scope of their relationship. Did she feel the connection he felt? He pushed the thoughts away. There was no relationship, not like that—not ever.

"Is there something else?" she asked.

"No," he said. "There's been nothing more. But we aren't taking any chances with your safety. Last night's threat was enough. I want you to stay inside. Like I said, we'll have a marshal on the grounds most of the time and video surveillance twenty-four-seven. Any sign of a problem and someone will be at your door in minutes."

The smile was gone. Her face was pale.

It was his fault for reminding her of the drama that was currently her life. "I'm sorry..."

"No." She shook her head. "Thank you. I appreciate all of this."

"Remember, you're safe. Help is one phone call away. I or someone else will be continually cruising the area. We have surveillance in place—there's no chance of anyone getting to you. Plus, the serial killer who began all this is locked up. He can't get to you."

"He can't," she said, her green eyes shining with determination as they focused on him. "There's more than one. There's..." she said.

She could be right. As he'd admitted to James, he was beginning to believe there had to be something to it.

"I know, there's nothing to prove what the crazy woman claims," she said with a hint of resentment in her voice. "You're wrong. I can't give you details but I know there was another person. It's not just my imagination."

He'd tried not to frown, to keep his face placid. And yet, some of what she said was right. This case wasn't over because the killer went to jail; there was something else, something they'd all missed.

"I heard both of them the night they took me," she persisted.

"I know what you think, about there being two serial killers, a partnership. It's rare but I haven't discounted it. In fact, I spoke to my superior about it."

She leaned back against the wall, as if standing without support was too much.

"If there's someone else out there, we'll catch them, I promise."

She nodded, her lips tense. But a look of gratitude was in her eyes as she took a step toward him.

"Thank you," she said. "For believing."

She touched his arm and the heat of her touch seemed to sear his skin.

"I appreciate everything you've done but I've at least had a few hours' sleep. You need to rest," she said. Her eyes seemed to take in everything about him. "We've been joined at the hip for the last thirty-two hours," she continued. "And spending the night in your vehicle was no way to get a good night's rest. You can't be watching me almost twenty-four-seven. And," she interrupted when he was about to state his argument to her accurate observation. "I know you haven't been here all the time. And you don't need to be. No one does. It's enough to know that you're a phone call away and that there will soon be a monitoring system. Having someone here the majority of the time is more than enough. Being watched by someone in your office, well, I couldn't be safer." She lifted her hand from his arm, but the heat didn't dissipate; she was still too close.

His phone dinged. It was a text message from Devon.

She stood up and went to the window, looking out.

"Devon will be here in a few minutes," he said to Kiera as he joined her.

"Good," she said with a smile. "You'll be able to get some sleep."

She turned and gave him a gentle push toward the door.

"Hey," he said with a playful tone to his voice.

"Get going," she said with a smile.

"Determined, are you?" he flirted. *Damn it, man, cool it*, he chastised himself.

"Always," she replied with a serious tone.

He knew that she'd been running her own life too long to play by other's rules. It was a trait he'd picked up on immediately after reading her file. It was there that he'd read of her guardian's death. It was there that he'd learned how she'd been independent since the age of eighteen. It impressed him even now to know that she'd put herself through a master's degree in nursing while never losing sight of her goal. She'd worked toward her chosen career while holding a part-time job and living alone.

At the door, he turned to face her.

"You haven't had much sleep yourself," he said.

He was leaving her safety in the hands of another man. Despite the fact that Devon was a friend, it didn't sit well. He didn't want to think of all the reasons why that might be the case. He couldn't go there, for to go there—to where his feelings lay—would break the barriers he was attempting to build.

"I'm fine," she said as if she could read his mind. "Quit worrying. A bath and a nap are all I need."

"Keep your door locked. Devon will be around. He may check in from time to time but if that becomes bothersome, just tell him."

She gave him a smile that didn't quite reach her eyes this time.

"Thanks, Travis. All of this makes me feel better, especially after last night."

"We'll keep you safe. You have my number…"

"I have my gun too," she reminded him as she'd done earlier.

He said nothing. He didn't need to be reminded of that. She had a Colt .45 in her possession. She also had no training, no practice with firearms that he knew of. A gun in the hands of someone not used to firing it could be deadlier than someone who was unarmed. The weapon could be used against her. He could only hope that that situation didn't occur. Instead he skated over the comment. He'd instructed Devon to notify him if anything changed, even a feeling of an imminent change—anything at all. He wanted to know. In the meantime, she'd be all right. She had to be.

"By the way," she said, interrupting his thoughts. "Your security installation expert—I believe that's what he called himself—he called me from the driveway before ever getting out of his vehicle. I'm not sure what he expected to find here, a fire-breathing dragon? What the heck did you say to him?"

Travis chuckled. "I didn't say anything. At least nothing that wasn't true." He'd warned Jed that she was jumpy as a result of all that had happened and she also had a weapon. Jed had obviously taken the necessary precautions not to surprise her.

A knock on the door interrupted his rather drawn-out goodbye. His hand was on the doorknob. He wasn't ready to hand her safety over to anyone else completley, even someone as skilled as Devon. But no one was at their peak with no sleep and if he were honest he'd admit that he'd reached his limit. He was done. He was only human, and he needed sleep. He opened the door.

"Looking a little worn, pal," Devon Gowan said as he entered the condo. "Age getting to you?"

"Thanks," Travis said with a grin. Devon had been part of the group that had gone out for drinks to celebrate Travis's thirtieth birthday. At the jokes about old age and turning thirty, Devon had only laughed as he'd reached his thirty-fifth over six months ago. Thirty, he'd joked, was a nothing birthday.

Devon held out his hand to Kiera. "Devon. Good to meet you."

Kiera took it without hesitation. "I'm glad you're here." She nodded toward Travis.

"He needs a break."

Travis couldn't help but smile. There was a maternal note to her voice that he hadn't heard before. He was feeling slightly better about leaving her.

"Thought I'd at least introduce myself and after that I'll make myself scarce," Devon said. "I won't get in your way. All I ask is that you remain on your property. And if for any reason you plan to leave—I need to know. Although I'd prefer…"

"That I stay here."

"Yes, ma'am." He gave her a nod. "Here's my number if you need to call."

He and Travis exchanged some final details and a minute later the door closed behind Devon.

Kiera looked at him with doubt in her eyes.

"He's good," Travis assured her.

"He's not you," she said.

He wasn't sure what she meant by that and he wasn't going to put any meaning into it. He couldn't. She was an assignment, nothing more. Still, he hesitated. If leaving had been difficult before, it was worse now. She was more than an assignment. Although even admitting it to himself felt wrong. He needed to put a stop to his feelings.

"Go," she said and gave him a light push. "Get some sleep. I'll be fine."

He hoped she was right as he closed the door behind him.

RAGE RAN WHITE HOT through every pore.

Eric should be here and he wasn't because of that

cursed nurse. Because of their last victim. The nurse thought she'd gotten away. She was wrong. Her rotten scent could be sniffed out; she'd be found. For one, her name was on her tag and even though Eric had panicked and thrown her purse into a Dumpster, it hadn't been hard to find where she lived. For the first time since they'd begun the spree, they'd stayed near the city where their last victim was taken. In every other kill, they'd been hundreds of miles away before the body got cold. Now there was no leaving, not until the work was done, not until Kiera Connell was dead.

The pen snapped, and a drop of red ink hit one hand and landed on the edge of her freshly pressed T-shirt. The red stain looked like blood. And it was a reminder that blood was life and the ability to take life was power.

She'd planned to go back to Denver. There they could set up house together—rest, have a stay-cation before they hit the road again. That had been her plan all along. Once they'd finished with the latest victim, they'd retire for a while. Whether it was a month or two, or even a year, she didn't know. But the plan had been solid, she'd already made steps in that direction. That had all been before Eric had fallen into the hands of the law.

Anger raced through her. For now, all that was ruined. They'd left the victim restrained and cruised the city, dragging out the moment when they could enjoy their captive. It's what they always did—the best was saved for last: rape and murder. It was like holding off opening a Christmas present. At least that's how she's explained it to Eric when she'd first begun the ritual. This time, she'd agreed to grab them something to eat and dropped Eric off. She knew that he'd wait for her. For he never raped unless she was there to watch. But the bitch had somehow escaped either in the time they'd cruised around together anticipating the final moments with her or while she'd been getting takeout and Eric had gone to the nearest convenience store for the cigarettes he refused to give up. He'd been back first and had obviously missed signs that the law's trap lay in wait. She'd been just behind him, far enough back to get away. Now, all that was left was revenge.

Kiera Connell had stolen the only person who mattered. And the phone calls had done nothing to release the anger. None of them, not even the rage and threat spewed on the last call. Kiera had ruined everything. Kiera needed to die, long and slow and painfully.

In the meantime, patience was all that was left.

But nothing came easy, nothing ever had. Even Eric had taken years to find. First there'd been enduring a marriage to someone who had put food on the table and grief in their bed. Years of abuse had ended in a brutal, messy way. A hammer in mid rant had ended it all. The burial spot would never be found. *Gone and run off* was as good an excuse as any when people asked, but few did. Now that was all in the past. The new life, the new name—all of it was the start of a life that had once been only a dream.

There'd been lonely years in between but it was then that the skills of the craft were honed. First on transients found along secondary highways, at least in the days before Eric.

Eric.

They'd had years of bliss. But, now it was over, he was gone and only anger was left.

Eric.

He'd been a teenage runaway, eager to learn—to be molded into the man he had become. Despite her rough marriage, she hadn't been that old herself. She'd been twenty-eight to his sixteen when she'd found him. He'd already spent a few years on the street. It was perfect. She was old enough to know more than he but young enough to understand him. And for years their sadistic crime spree had flown under the radar. But, as their crimes became more ambitious and the missing women began to add up, their actions gained notoriety. For the last year, people had lived in fear of them. It had been a wonderful time, a glorious time. The highs they'd felt during those exhilarating months as they'd crisscrossed the country were now only memories. The highs needed to come back but alone it was impossible. There was only one thing to do. While it wouldn't fix everything, it would give some satisfaction.

Justice.

To get justice, the last victim, the traitor, needed to die.

The authorities thought they could protect their star witness. They thought she was safe with Eric behind bars. They believed that Eric had run a one-man show.

What a laugh.

He didn't have it in him to have enjoyed and killed as many women as they had. On his own he was messy and far from able to plan and maneuver into the future. Alone, he would have been caught a long time ago.

The window of the van that had been home for the last three weeks needed to be washed. The van replaced the vehicle before, and the one before that. The vehicles had been temporary homes stolen from neglected and troubled places where the odds of their loss being reported was minimal to none. It was chilly. Was Eric cold? It was hard to stop worrying about someone who had been your responsibility for so many years. It was impossible to stop thinking of him now for he'd been everything, son—partner in crime.

This must finish on their terms, for Eric. Justice for Eric. It was the one thing that needed to be done. It was the only thing that would make everything right. The kill that was the most important and the one that would be the last. And whether it was or not, the excitement at the thought was like no other.

Chapter Ten

Early the next day, Travis knew one fact—sleep was pointless. As much as he needed sleep, as much as he had promised Kiera that he'd get some, he'd only managed a few hours. He wouldn't have gotten even that much if, for the last half day, James hadn't been tied up with another case. But James would be in his office now and while he could call, in a situation like this he always found face-to-face to be better. Fifteen minutes later he found himself again in James's office.

"Grab a coffee and have a seat," James said. "I can only imagine that you've had some long nights."

"That goes without saying," he said. He poured a cup of coffee out of the carafe that was always at the ready in James's office. He put the carafe down and pulled out a chair that sat at an angle from James's desk. He was anxious to see what, if anything, was new. He hoped that there was a lead on the anonymous phone calls.

"Exactly as you thought, Travis. Serene confirmed that they're using prepaid phones. There's no way of tracking who made the calls," James said. "What we do know is that whoever made them did it from a variety of locations within the city. They were all made from the edges of downtown."

Within the city.

"Someone could have Kiera's ID in their hands. Her bag was never found," Travis said. His gut screamed that these calls were connected but...

"If we didn't have the perpetrator behind bars, that would be a troubling fact," James said. "Or, if I believed at all that there was a second perp still on the loose. I've looked at the evidence and I can't go there, Trav." He pushed away from the desk and leaned back in his chair. "Unfortunately, the wrong person picked up her ID and decided to play games with her rather than return it. And now they've made a sadistic game of it. A crime in itself but not the crime you think."

"I see where you're coming from, but I think it's more than that, James. I've got a bad feeling. And Kiera is still convinced that there's more than one killer."

"Convince me," James said as he locked his hands behind his head. "We have the killer behind bars and there've been no killings since he's been incarcerated. Never mind the fact that the evidence indicated he was acting alone. But it's becoming increasingly clear that these calls are not something we can discount. What the hell are they? What's the connection? I'm just not getting this."

"I agree. They're serious," Travis said. "I've gone through the history over and over. After her discharge from the hospital she becomes the victim of telephone harassment. And that harassment has carried on for three nights, or to be exact, three pre-dawn calls, the second call always occurring at exactly the same time that the original 911 call came in. And then the last call is a threat on her life." He smacked a hand on James's desk. "Damn it. I don't know what the connection is, if any. All of it is too coincidental. And none of it can be overlooked. A threat on her life. She needs more protection than we're giving her."

"I agree." James pushed his chair back from his desk, his hands interlocked behind his head.

"Is it possible that there is something that we're missing?"

James shook his head. "I don't know, Travis. I know that using a prepaid phone was more than likely the work of someone who didn't want to get caught. I agree with you there. It definitely involved planning. But planning for what?" He turned to the window as if the answer would lie there. "I can't imagine there could be a connection. It seems like too much of a long shot. And a second serial killer—other than the witness claiming that she heard someone else—there's no evidence at all to take us in that direction. A yearlong investigation turned up no evidence that there was anything more than the one man, Eric Solomon."

Travis stood up. He was frustrated at not having an answer, at not being able to solve this, to give it all a proper fix that would make Kiera perfectly safe. To do that, he needed answers. "I know two serial killers is a long shot. I agree with you there. But these calls, whoever and whatever they are, have to end."

"So, we've reached an agreement. The protection will be upped. Make the protection twenty-four-seven. From here on in, your team is on-site. We can't take the risk. Until we've figured out what the hell is going on, we play it safe."

Five minutes later, Travis left James's office. He was somewhat satisfied but still troubled. The evidence they had was heading in a direction that he didn't like. It was the same direction, the same theory, that Kiera believed and which, until now, he'd discounted. That had all spun on its head. Now her claim of two killers seemed even less of an impossibility. And, while James had yet to agree to such a theory, they were much closer to all being on the same page. Much closer than they had been yesterday.

He headed to the cafeteria where he grabbed a tray and a roast beef sandwich. Just before the till, he took an iced tea from the cooler, paid and found himself a seat in the far corner where he wouldn't be disturbed. He unwrapped the sandwich and started to eat, but his mind was elsewhere. He was thinking of everything that had transpired and brought them to this point. It was time to get his crew on board. The other marshals needed to know that the parameters of the assignment had changed. With Kiera's insistence that there was a second perpetrator and the reality of the phone calls, they had to tighten security. They'd thought the perpetrator was behind bars and that she was safe. If there was a second killer, she could be in danger. As a result, there would be no more being out of sight of the property for even a lunch break. He guessed they'd agree once they heard the circumstances, not that they had a choice.

He opened the app that allowed him to see the view from the cameras on Kiera's property. He panned the area at the front of the house. The grounds were quiet. He moved to the camera on the other side of her property and his finger froze before he could flip to another screen. For what he saw was the back of someone at the corner of her unit. There was no disputing that someone appeared to be casing her condo. It clearly wasn't Devon. Whoever it was, they were considerably shorter than that and Devon would have no reason to wear a hoodie or skulk around the property in such a manner. This was a stranger—someone who shouldn't be on the property, a trespasser. A moment later, the person was gone.

He swore and dropped the remains of his sandwich into the wrapper.

He was too far away. He punched Devon's number and waited. One ring, two. His fingers drummed on the table. A young man looked over at him. He recognized him as a new hire that James had mentioned. He was of no relevance. He was still training, an agent who was working with Serene at the moment. He looked through him, even as the guy watched him. He looked away. He had no time to worry about other people's curiosity. The phone continued to ring. Three rings and then four. Devon needed to get on this like yesterday except Devon wasn't answering. He hadn't ended the call before he was up and heading out the door.

He burst outside and within seconds was in the parking lot.

He bit off an expletive as he ran for his SUV and his mind checked off all the possibilities. He punched Devon's number again. Devon might have missed the call for a valid reason—a call to nature, who knew? Devon was his best hope to deal with the trespasser. But, as before, the phone rang unanswered before hitting voice mail.

Another curse flew. Where the hell was he and why wasn't he answering his phone? He'd have a word or two with him when this was over. His mind ran through the possibilities. He thought of calling Kiera, of warning her, and remembered her penchant for taking care of herself. She'd be more likely to want to face the trespasser with her gun. That could place her in worse danger than she might be in already. He had to get there before the unthinkable happened.

He was behind the wheel and had the SUV in gear almost in one motion. He was off with a screech of tires, driving as fast as he dared. Too fast, and without the warning sirens of an emergency vehicle, he'd endanger more lives than he was trying to save. He wanted to gun the engine and instead he had to slow down as he spotted kids playing. They were dangerously close to the street. He was in a residential area, no place for speeding. He had one eye on the children as he watched the speedometer and kept moving. He'd considered calling the police but even a few minutes ago, they'd have gotten there no sooner than he would, and the last thing he wanted was the chaos of multiple responders. All that aside, he had to get there. And he had to get there soon.

Kiera's life was at stake.

KIERA FELT LIKE she was trapped in her condo and had been for days. Yet it had been only five days since she'd been discharged from the hospital and a week before that since this whole horrid ordeal began and her life turned upside down. Wednesday, middle of the week, a day she often found herself scheduled at work. Work— a lifetime ago.

Since her discharge from the hospital, she hadn't gone farther than her own front yard. She was almost a prisoner in the house she loved so much. Travis popping in from time to time had made the confinement tolerable, even pleasant up until yesterday. But today staying another minute inside her condo felt unbearable. Without Travis's casual conversation, interspersed with shop talk she'd have been bored out of her mind. But having him there had livened up the day and made her feel less confined. Even his delving into more details of the horror that her life had become and the event that had changed her normal, even with that he'd kept her on edge in different ways, for she didn't know how she felt about him. He both entertained and interested her. The spark of attraction, of course, had helped and the time had flown by. But all that had changed since he'd left. Devon remained outside and, while he was a nice man, he didn't excite her the way Travis had. She guessed it worked both ways and maybe that's why Devon kept to himself. He'd check in every few hours and then only for a minute or less. That wasn't the same. She missed Travis.

Travis.

She couldn't help thinking of him. He was like no man she'd met before. She wished she'd met him under different circumstances, that might have changed everything. Maybe they could date like normal human beings. But she was normal no longer. She was a victim of crime. She was a witness. She'd been in the company of an evil that she didn't want to imagine, never mind think of. She wanted to forget that it had happened, but she couldn't. For she'd never escaped, not really. The danger had followed her. She knew it. She sensed it.

She shivered. Something felt different. She felt alone— vulnerable.

Devon had left on an errand and to grab an early lunch. He'd popped his head in to tell her that and she'd invited him to share lunch with her. If nothing else, she could use the company. But he was adamant about not imposing on her in any way. At the time, she hadn't disagreed even though she could have used the company.

While she was not privy to his thoughts, it seemed he wanted to reassure her. And he had reminded her that he'd be only a phone call away. Except, he'd left his phone behind. It was all because she'd asked for a minute of his time before he left. It was then that he'd dropped his phone. She'd found it beside the garbage after his car had pulled away. She thought it might have slipped out of his pocket when he was moving one of the boxes of recyclables.

Since then she'd heard it ring a few times but left it. Who was calling Devon and why was none of her business. She heard the phone ring again and turned away from it.

She had to get out. She felt trapped, like the walls were closing in. She needed fresh air. Despite her earlier thoughts and unease, she'd never felt anything but safe in this neighborhood. She didn't think any of that had changed. She hadn't jogged in almost two weeks and she missed it. She wouldn't venture farther than her block. She'd just do a repetitive circuit of the block until she ran off some steam. In her bedroom, she changed into a worn tank top and shorts.

She guessed that Travis wouldn't like this idea either. But there had been no physical danger since she'd returned home, and one thing she'd learned about him was that he could be overcautious. So, while she wouldn't be talked out of this, she would follow the rules. With Devon gone, she'd let the FBI know what she was doing. She put in a call at the number at FBI headquarters that was for any updates or problems with surveillance. The woman she talked to was insistent that she not do this. Kiera didn't give the argument much space. She wasn't asking permission, only giving a courtesy notification. She hung up before the woman could present further argument. The phone rang immediately after and she ignored it. She wasn't going to argue the point. The fresh air would help her feel better. Jogging was something she enjoyed and something that she hadn't done since the attack. Getting back into familiar routines was critical to recovery. The therapist had told her so and she agreed. Routine would remind her that, despite what had happened, she wasn't a victim and the incident shouldn't define her.

She jogged in place, then did some stretches. And as she did, a sense of déjà vu ran through her and she wondered if this might be a mistake. She shrugged off the feeling. The outdoors, fresh air and a bit of freedom were calling to her. After all, what could happen on a street she knew well where not a car had gone by in almost an hour. She couldn't be any safer. She pushed the doubts from her mind and went to get her sneakers.

Chapter Eleven

Travis's phone buzzed once.

"You've got trouble," Serene said without hesitation. "There's an intruder at your client's condo. I had a visual on the surveillance camera. Gangly, wearing a black hoodie. In the last few seconds they've slipped off the monitor. I didn't get much of a look. Couldn't determine sex, age, nothing."

"I saw the intruder earlier. I'm already on my way," Travis said. "Thanks for the details."

"It's worse. Just prior to that the client phoned me. She told me that she is going jogging."

"What? Tell me you stopped her. When did this happen?"

"I told her not to do it. But she disconnected before I could make a convincing argument. It was immediately after that that I got the visual on the intruder." Her voice was laced with frustration and concern. "Since then, I've called her numerous times. She's not answering."

"Where's Devon?" he growled out the question. While he hadn't given the order for twenty-four-hour surveillance yet, it was still expected that the marshals were twenty-four-seven in touch. Devon had been free to go for a break, thirty minutes or so at a time. What he hadn't been free to do was be out of contact.

As far as the twenty-four-hour surveillance, that was new and the onus was on him to let his men know. He'd been on his way to do that. In the meantime, Devon needed to be answering his phone. He'd been going back to Kiera's property anyway, he'd tell Devon then. A delay of minutes wasn't a concern, or so he'd thought at the time. It seemed only minutes ago when Kiera had contacted him to let him know everything was fine. She'd been reading a book, relaxed. Everything was okay.

"Have you contacted Devon?"

"I tried. No answer," Serene replied with frustration lacing her words. "I don't like this. One of them should be answering their phone. Something's wrong."

His heart thumped at the scene she was painting. He could only guess at why Kiera had contacted Serene instead of Devon or him. But why hadn't she contacted Devon or him instead? Why had she said she was reading a book one minute and then phoned Serene to say she was going jogging? Even as he asked the question, he knew the answer. The book was a smoke screen. He wouldn't have been as easy as Serene to skirt around. He would have demanded that she put the notion of jogging aside well before she'd had the opportunity to hang up. In fact, he would have anticipated that reaction, and he would have laid down the law before she'd ever stated her purpose. He would have used her own suspicions against her, and he knew that would have stopped her.

"Damn," Travis said. The curse was mild and didn't make him feel any better. He wanted to say so much worse and that wouldn't change anything either. He took a breath. They needed a physical presence, to stand between Kiera and danger.

"There's been nothing in the last thirty seconds or so," Serene said.

"I've got this." He disconnected and at the same time bore down on the accelerator. He was speeding in an area that was industrial, free of pedestrians, where he wouldn't endanger anyone. But, within minutes, he was back in a residential area and again had to watch his speed.

He gripped the wheel, his palms sweaty, his lips tight. Where was she? What was she doing? Was she safe or... He couldn't think of the latter, of the possibilities.

She was in danger with no one to defend her. Her bag had never been found. There'd been a death threat. Was it possible that someone knew where she lived? It was no question. Time was against him but despite that, he knew that he had to get there in time to intervene. He had the wheel in a death grip. That she'd gone against his advice was more than frustrating. At the same time, he realized why she'd done it. She was going stir crazy. He would feel the same in her situation. But he hoped all that didn't make her feel that it was worth the risk. Still, he could picture her checking the neighborhood, seeing no one and feeling safe. Odds were she was but he wasn't good with odds.

This was his fault. He should have realized that she needed to get out. That she needed to do something other than sit in her condo. He should have facilitated that, arranged safe outings in order to prevent this situation from happening.

He was as close to panic as he'd ever been. He called Kiera again. It was the third time. Like the other calls, it went straight to voice mail. He bit back his frustration. There was someone casing her condo and neither she nor Devon were answering their phones.

"Sweet hell," Travis muttered under his breath. He sped up when he could. And, within seconds, again found himself easing off the accelerator. He coasted through a red light on a street that was empty of other vehicles or pedestrians. He ordered Siri to dial Devon again. The phone rang and rang—no one answered.

Frustrated, he slammed the palm of his hand against the steering wheel. Two blocks and he turned the corner heading for a route where speed would not be an issue. Just as he thought that, a cargo truck pulled out in front of him.

He swore again as he swerved around the three-quarter-ton lumber truck. Minutes passed, and the distance closed. Five more blocks. Five blocks of not knowing if she was safe or what might be happening. A murderer could very well be about to take another victim.

He couldn't think of any other reason why the trespasser was there. He didn't believe in coincidence. He didn't believe in a lot of things. But what he believed right now scared him like nothing ever had. Kiera's life was in danger. He knew that instinctively. That was one thing he never questioned, his instincts.

He took the corner at a speed that laid rubber on the pavement. Two blocks to go. A woman walking her dog stepped out and he swerved around them. He could see her in the rearview mirror. She was pumping her fist at him with the dog yanking on its lead and barking at him. He slowed down. He gripped the wheel, his lips compressed.

Two more blocks.

Would he be too late? The thought of that repeated like a metronome in his head, the beat dull and relentless, moving toward possible doom.

He couldn't be too late. He had to make it on time.

He couldn't believe that this was happening. He'd made his last drive by Kiera's place at eleven o'clock last night. At that time, he'd run into Devon and been given a bit of a hard time about getting too attached to a client, and about stepping in when he wasn't needed. He was right. He didn't need to be there. It was Devon's shift. As a result, he'd taken the ribbing as it was meant—joking laced with truth. He and Devon went a long way back. They'd gone to the university together and been friends ever since.

He dialed Devon's phone again. No answer.

If something happened to her…or Devon… It was a possibility he hadn't considered until now. But it was Kiera he worried about most. She was the target.

He had to remain focused. He took the last corner with a screech of tires.

KIERA HADN'T LIKED the FBI contact's reaction to her phone call. She didn't like being told what to do or not do. She hadn't called to get their permission. She'd called only as a courtesy. Despite the threatening phone calls, she felt safe in her own house and in her own neighborhood. She hadn't been out alone, or at all, since she'd welcomed Travis to the neighborhood. She smiled as she remembered that greeting. Her gun in his face wasn't exactly welcoming. Fortunately, Devon had had a more civilized introduction.

But all that was behind her. Now she was sick of her restrictions. Staying indoors had been fine those first days but now she'd begun to feel slightly claustrophobic. It was either get outside or go insane. She had a bad case of cabin fever.

The neighbor's dog was quiet. She'd used him as a barometer since she'd moved in. If there was a stranger in the area, he barked. She could usually hear him even if he was inside. The silence gave her comfort. Nothing was afoot, at least nothing that the dog had sensed. And, even if it was, she had her gun. It was in the gun belt that she'd purchased when she'd first inherited the weapon. The last time she'd worn it had been to the shooting range. It could be used two different ways, concealed and unconcealed. It could hide quite nicely under a T-shirt worn near the beltline, so she wouldn't be frightening the neighbors with an in-your-face weapon. And she wouldn't be unarmed either.

She looked at her watch. Devon had told her that he'd be back in half an hour. That was forty-five minutes ago.

She bent down to make sure her shoelace was tied.

It was time to reclaim her life, one little piece at a time.

Chapter Twelve

Travis felt as if time had run out. He couldn't stop the panicked feeling of doom. It was like nothing he'd felt before. And even though he was close to Kiera's condo, he wasn't close enough.

Every minute made the possibility that Kiera was injured or worse, all the more real. He needed to floor the accelerator and yet he couldn't. Running over a pedestrian or causing an accident wasn't the answer. Two tragedies would not fix anything.

Kiera.

Was she safe? What had happened since the last time he'd spoken to her? He tried to keep his mind off the possibilities. But his mind wouldn't stop reeling through the what-ifs and might-have-beens. He was afraid that he'd be too late. He couldn't take his mind off that possibility.

He parked at the end of the avenue that met with her street. He couldn't take the SUV any farther, not without making his presence known to whoever was lurking around her unit. From here he could see down her street. There was no activity, no cars, no people. Despite everything, despite a heartbeat that was revved for action, on the street everything appeared normal. He closed the driver's door with a controlled shut meant to be soundless. For he didn't know where the intruder might be or if they were gone. He went in on foot, across the lawn along the outside of the condos. Each building was three stories with two units on every floor. Her unit was on the main floor. As he moved along, he scoured the area for movement, for anything out of the ordinary.

Nothing.

Her building was in the middle of the block and the intruder could be anywhere, if he was here at all. Not even a dog's bark broke the silence. There was no one in sight as he came closer to her unit. There was nothing to indicate trouble.

Kiera might already be injured or worse. He needed her safe. He wouldn't have it any other way and yet his mind was already going to much more dire possibilities. The intruder had broken into her place. He should have called her, warned her. Kiera injured—dead, the unwanted possibility ran through his mind.

Not possible. Anger fueled his denial. He refocused his thoughts, focusing on the situation only, factoring emotion out of it. This was business first—emotion had no place, never had—and even now, he told himself futilely, it never would.

He had his gun in both hands. There were few people home now. He'd done the research days earlier. The block included not only the condos but single-family homes across the street. Most of the residents on the block were daytime workers of various kinds. The mix of people included six middle school children and two high schoolers. They were gone for the day. The others, four seniors, one unemployed and one night worker, were in the minority and what they might think should they look out a shuttered window was not a consideration. As long as they stayed indoors, there was no problem. He cleared his mind as he moved across front lawns, keeping under

cover as much as possible until he was at her condo.
There was nothing out of the ordinary. The blinds were
down as he'd told Kiera to keep them. The condos on
either side were silent; the driveways were empty. But
none of that was unusual, it was a working-class neighborhood and it was the middle of the day. Outside, there
was no sign of Kiera. Was she out jogging as she'd said
she would be?

He moved along the perimeter. He needed to make
sure the area was safe, the threat gone before he checked
on her. There was a bank of shrubs on the west side of the
building. It was an end unit, so whoever had been casing
her place could well have moved around or even be inside. His grip tightened on the gun handle and anger was
white-hot in his gut at the thought that someone might
be threatening her. But there was no sign of forced entry
from the front. That left the back. He turned to go in that
direction and that's when he sensed something was off.
That's when the small hairs rose on the back of his neck
and he felt that he wasn't alone.

SOMETHING WASN'T RIGHT.

The feeling had been strong enough for Kiera to
give up the idea of jogging more than five minutes ago.
She'd done one circuit of the block and stopped midway
through a second. A feeling of déjà vu and a chill swept
through her at the same time. Everything felt still, too
still, and a knot had formed in her gut as she felt as if
she'd been transported to a place she'd been before—a
dark, frightening place. The quiet, the feeling of being
alone and the only person outside had overwhelmed her
and she'd ended her jog. There was something not right
and her instincts screamed for her to return home. If
there was one thing she'd learned after the nightmare

she'd survived was to follow her instinct. So instead of continuing her jog, she'd gone inside where she'd double-checked the door locks, front and back. Then, she put her sneakers away. In her socked feet, she went to the bedroom, opened the nightstand and took her aunt's gun from under her t-shirt. She hesitated before putting it away. The weapon felt foreign and cold in her hand; even the memories it invoked of her aunt were gone. A chill ran through her, for nothing seemed as it should be. Something was shifting, something dark and gray and… Something was very wrong. Her intuition was in overdrive. She opened the drawer and took the gun back out.

With her other hand, she reached for her phone. The prepaid Travis had gotten for her was so small in comparison to her smartphone that she'd forgotten twice where she'd put it. Now it was gone, again.

She frowned. She traced her steps back. Her mind had been on Devon's phone and how he'd forgotten it. She hadn't been thinking about where she'd placed her phone and now she couldn't remember where she'd set it. With her mind on the missing phone, she placed the gun on the end table.

"Irresponsible," she muttered.

She glanced around and got down on her hands and knees. Finally, she found it under the couch cushions where, if anyone had called, she'd never have heard it. She guessed that it had slipped out of her pocket after she'd called and alerted the woman in charge of her surveillance of her intent to go jogging. She'd been sitting on the couch when she'd made the call and she'd thought that she'd slipped the phone into her pocket. Obviously, it had slipped out.

She looked out the window. Nothing had changed and yet her gut was tight and strumming like a wrong note playing again and again. She looked at her watch. Devon had left to grab lunch and assured her he'd be back in thirty minutes or less. If there was trouble, as she sensed now, she'd phone Travis. He was her go-to man anyway, the one she depended on. The truth was there'd been something building between them from the very beginning.

"What the hell are you thinking, girl?" she chastised herself. She was acting like a woman in love, or more aptly in lust, rather than a woman in crisis.

The street was silent. The last vehicle she had seen seemed like forever ago. It had belonged to a neighbor at the end of the block. She turned and put the gun on the end table. There was no threat. It had been her imagination. She was overreacting again. But she couldn't help it. She'd been through things that most people never face in a lifetime. She needed time. She knew that. She went to the kitchen to grab a cup of coffee. She added a dash of sugar to the dark brew and carried the drink back to the living area. Seconds ticked slowly by and felt like minutes. She set the coffee down by the gun.

She picked up a book. Despite the fact that it was the latest cozy mystery by her favorite author, it held no interest. Somehow reading about crime of any sort wasn't comforting. But she needed something to do. She'd cleaned the house thoroughly two days ago and there wasn't a dust ball anywhere. She thought of Prairie Seniors' Care Home and realized how much she missed the work and the people.

She was itching to go back, to be useful again. She smiled as Lucy wove herself between her legs with a deep, satisfied purr. Then the cat leaped up beside her and curled up for a nap. She thought of the cat's easy nature and how she'd settled quickly into her new home.

Now, six months later, they were a team—both considered each other family, or so Kiera would like to think.

She looked at her watch. Two minutes had gone by and it had seemed like forever. She was feeling particularly anxious and she wasn't sure why. She'd opened the blinds at an angle that she could see out, but no one could see in. It was against Travis's warning. But she needed to see what was going on—so far nothing.

Something moved at the edge of her condo. She didn't have a full view from her window and her heart raced before relief rushed through her.

Travis.

She'd recognize him anywhere.

He was near the cotoneaster shrub a few feet from her main entrance.

She frowned.

His back was to her and she sensed that something was wrong. Just the way he held himself, the way he hadn't come to her door as soon as he'd arrived. That wasn't normal. Usually he came immediately to check on her. Something was up.

She thought of stepping out, asking him what was going on, why he was here. But then something else caught her attention. There was a movement in the opposite direction. She caught it from the corner of her eye. She crouched down so the window ledge was now at eye level and she was at the corner of the window frame—out of sight. She watched but the movement didn't repeat and there was nothing and no one in sight.

Her heart seemed to knock in her rib cage and her hands shook as something intuitive told her that Travis wasn't the only one on her front lawn. Someone else who he hadn't seen was there, hidden by shrubbery. Maybe it was the neighbor's cat, but instinct told her it wasn't.

Her heart thumped at the thought that Travis might be in danger.

Something shifted and nothing was the same. Now she could see who was at the other end of her unit. She could see the top of a faded black hoodie. Whoever they were, they were almost the length of her unit from Travis and they were definitely shadowing him and moving closer. It was also clear the way they kept furtively to the bushes, that they didn't want to be seen. Obviously, they were up to no good. They were hunched over. And she couldn't see their face.

The faded black garment was too big and sagged over their frame. Male or female, it was impossible to tell. She backed up from the corner of the window where she'd been peeking out. She bit back the tremor that ran through her. She had to warn Travis and yet she knew that as soon as she opened that front door she'd make his stalker aware of her presence. That might put Travis in as much danger as he was now, maybe more. As she contemplated her choices, the stalker disappeared from sight. Her heart was locked in her throat.

She had to do something. Knocking on the window would alert them both. With Travis at a disadvantage, unaware of whoever was stalking him, that wasn't the answer. It was up to her to protect him. She didn't think for a minute of the irony of that thought. Instead, she raced to the table and grabbed the gun. She fumbled with the safety as she hurried to the door. She'd never felt so nervous. Life and death weighed on her shoulders. She could almost hear the pounding of her heart. Her fingers wouldn't cooperate as they slipped on the lock, finally unlocking it with one hand while holding the gun with the other.

She opened the door and it was then that she saw that

she was already too late. Travis's stalker was to his left, screened by shrubbery. The person had a metal bar raised high over their head and was standing directly behind him but out of his line of vision. Only a few feet separated them.

Everything was happening so fast, too fast. None of it was real and it was occurring in blips of time that were less than seconds and felt so much longer. The metal bar was coming down about to hit Travis's head. The stalker turned, looking at her as Kiera froze. She knew she didn't have a clear shot, not one that didn't run the risk of shooting Travis. In the strange tableau that seemed to be moving slowly through a fog, the hoodie slipped and partially revealed braided gray-streaked black hair and the face of a middle-aged woman.

No! Her scream was silent. Her throat seemed closed, her broken voice frozen in fear. There was only one option. She had to take the woman out. But she had no time to line up the shot. She had to make do with a quick shot, a warning shot and hope it was enough. She held the gun with shaking hands and fired. At the same time, metal flashed; a crowbar or something like it was swinging at Travis's head.

Travis crumpled to the ground. She fired again but the woman bolted across the lawn and disappeared from sight. It had all happened in seconds and yet it had seemed like forever.

Kiera's heart was in her throat and tears were in her eyes as she rushed to Travis's side.

She was too late.

"Travis, no!"

Her cry did nothing. He was dead and her heart broke.

Chapter Thirteen

Kiera dropped to her knees beside Travis.

She was terrified. She feared he was dead. And even if he wasn't, the danger wasn't over. She clutched the gun in one shaking hand like it was a lifeline. But, as her aunt had promised so long ago, the gun had been a game changer. She'd scared off his attacker with it, even stopped the attack. Except it hadn't been enough.

She took a breath, stilling the first rush of fear. Her professional instincts were kicking in. This was a medical emergency and she'd dealt with these before. She couldn't think the worst. She could only deal with the present. He had to be alive.

She was frozen in place at the thought, the very idea that he might not survive. She needed to check his pulse. She had to take charge of this situation. She took a deep breath as if needing courage before reaching for his wrist. But she'd barely touched it, felt the heat of his skin against hers and she dropped it.

This wasn't like her. She didn't hesitate. She'd handled many medical crises in her short career. But this was different. This was Travis. She was scared for the worst and because of that she didn't want to know the truth. She didn't want to know that there was no hope. None of that was an excuse. She pushed back into a squat that put inches of space between them.

Your auntie raised no coward.

It was a mantra she'd lived by in the years since her aunt's funeral. That mantra had seen her through the last few teenage years alone. Without the guidance of her aunt, she'd made the journey to get a profession, become an adult and stand on her own two feet, alone. Now this was on her, on no one else. Whether he was alive or dead, she needed to take care of this. She reached for his wrist and felt for a pulse. The strong beat almost took her breath away.

He was alive.

She was overwhelmed with relief and memories. Only yesterday when she'd teased him. Only a few mornings ago, he'd been with her as they listened to the phone call that had terrified her and threatened her life. She thought of how he'd held her after the first phone call and just before the life-threatening phone call.

He'd been there for her in more ways than he needed to be.

Now he needed help. But he needed more than a nurse-practitioner who had no medical equipment on hand had to offer. As she thought that, a familiar vehicle took the corner onto the driveway too fast and skidded to a stop. Relief flooded through her as Devon leaped out, slammed the car door and bolted up the driveway. His revolver was in both hands, and there was a look of intense determination on his face as the gun moved left and right as if trolling for danger.

"He was attacked," she said. "By someone with a metal bar."

Devon had both hands on his gun, ready for anything. "Where are they?"

"Disappeared around the house."

Devon holstered the gun and was down on his knees beside her.

"Is he…?"

"He's alive and his pulse is strong," she broke in before he could ask the question that had only so recently terrified her. "He was hit on the back of the head."

"How the hell did this happen?" Devon asked. "The area was clear before I left."

She shook her head and stood up. She had no answers. She hardly knew herself what had happened. She only knew what she'd seen.

"Where did they come from?"

"From that direction," she pointed in the opposite direction. "I caught a glimpse from the window." Her voice choked but she pushed on. "There was no chance to warn him." There was more. There was one detail that could change everything. She held back, not sure how Devon or even Travis would react.

"I was too late," she said instead with honest and sincere regret.

She shivered. The air was cool and hinted at the possibility of rain.

Devon reached down and took Travis's phone from his back pocket.

Kiera's legs felt suddenly weak. She dropped to her knees beside Travis.

"Thanks, Serene, I'll keep you posted." Devon finished his conversation and squatted down beside Kiera. "I'm going to make sure the area is clear. Serene has an ambulance on the way. You're alright here?"

She nodded and barely glanced up as Devon left them.

"Travis," she whispered in his ear as she bent close to

him. She barely knew him and yet she knew that it would tear out her heart to lose him.

She felt along his skull, feeling for injury and also noticing the soft texture of his hair. It was short, cropped off not in a stylish way, but one that was practical, one that fit his profession. Her hand went as far to the back as it could, her fingers gently probing. She felt what she presumed was blood. She pulled her hand free. Head wounds tended to bleed profusely. Her hand was bloody. But that told her only what she already knew, that he'd been hit on the back of the head. He could have a concussion. The seriousness of that could only be determined by medical tests like an X-ray.

She stood up, swinging around at the sound of footsteps behind her.

"I'm sorry—I didn't mean to frighten you," Devon said. He looked down at Travis. "I don't understand what happened. Did he scare off the intruder before?"

"No," Kiera interrupted him. "He never saw his attacker."

"Never saw— Then how?"

"There was an intruder, armed with a steel bar," Kiera said breathlessly, barely looking at him before turning back to Travis.

"How long ago?"

"A minute, maybe two," she replied. "Whoever it was disappeared. I think they went around the corner of the condo. I'm not sure. I…" Her voice broke.

"I fired a couple of shots but I was too late. The stalker snuck up on him." She looked at the gun with regret. "I never got a clear shot. My shots may have scared them off. I don't know."

"Good work."

Relief flooded through Kiera at the sound of Travis's

voice. It was husky and quieter than she knew it to be. It didn't matter. He was not only alive but conscious.

"Ouch," he said as he sat up. His hand went to the back of his head and came back, as hers had, smeared with blood.

"Crap, you're bleeding, man," Devon said.

"What the hell happened?" Travis asked.

"You were hit on the back of the head," Kiera said. "They snuck up behind you."

"That explains it," he said in a dry tone that in another situation might be an attempt at humor. "My head hurts like it's about to explode."

"We'll get you to the hospital," Kiera said. She took his arm as if she might help him up.

"No!" He pulled away. "No," he repeated less forcefully.

"There's an ambulance en route," Kiera said.

"I'll be fine."

"Once you're looked at, maybe," she replied.

"Unbelievable, this shouldn't have happened," Devon said. "I should have been here."

"You couldn't have known," she said. "No one did."

"Someone could have," Travis snarled as he struggled to his feet. "Where were you?" he asked glaring at Devon.

"The area was secure. At least I thought so," Devon said. "I screwed up."

"You're not kidding," Travis took a step forward, the look on his face like he was going to punch the other man.

Kiera grabbed Travis's arm. "We misjudged. I told him to go, to take a break. He's allowed breaks. I remember you saying so."

"No, Kiera. This is on me," Devon said.

"No," Kiera said. "It isn't. It was my choice, my insistence. I felt comfortable and I'm not about to run and you knew it. That was the only reason you were here, to make sure I didn't run. At least that's what I thought until now."

"Where were you?" Travis asked Devon. "A break is one thing man, but you were gone a lot longer. You were out of contact. You…"

"Completely and totally screwed up. I dropped my phone and didn't know it was missing. And by the time I realized it I'd already ordered my lunch. The food was delayed…"

"Let me get this straight," he interrupted. "You waited for your food rather than get your ass back here for your phone."

"Travis, please. It's alright. I'm not going anywhere. You know that. It's not his fault," Kiera pleaded. "No one could have predicted an intruder…"

The scowl on Devon's face said otherwise. She wished that she could ease the guilt that she knew he was feeling. While he hadn't spent the time with her that Travis had, she liked him.

"Damn it, I hold you responsible, but I blame myself as well," Travis said. "It was my call. I told you to take breaks."

"I took a break as you'd agreed and I was gone longer than I'd said," Devon replied. "A lot longer. And dropping the phone…"

"Was a major screwup," Travis replied.

"I found it after you left," Kiera added.

"There's nothing I can say except it won't happen again," Devon said.

"It better not," Travis replied. "You reported it?"

"I did. The least I could do considering…" Devon said. "You'd be right to have me removed from the case."

"Don't tempt me," Travis said. "You called it in? I thought your phone was missing."

"I borrowed yours and notified Serene of the incident. Catch," Devon said as he tossed the phone.

Travis caught it easily in one hand.

Devon glanced at Kiera with a crooked grin. "I think our boy might be right. He'll be fine."

"I hope so," Kiera said. She agreed that his eye-hand coordination seemed unaffected.

"Is the area clear?" Travis asked.

"Yeah," Devon replied. "I checked inside and nothing around her unit, front or back. I just did a cursory of the outside, but I'm going to take another look at the perimeter," Devon said to Travis. He headed across the lawn, widening the scope of his first search.

Kiera struggled to hold back tears. He could have died. She could have died. Death had again stared her in the face. Worse, it had almost taken him from her. She didn't know if she could have survived that.

"Kiera?" His voice was softer, deeper than normal. It was as if speaking was an effort. And she imagined, considering what had happened, that it was. And yet he was still in the game, only minutes after taking a blow to the head.

She pushed a stray hair off her face as if that would focus her mind where it needed to be. And yet she didn't want to go there. She didn't know if she had the courage to go there. It was terrifying. For that place brought forth other possibilities. Like who and what his attacker might have been and why they were here at her condo. Had Travis just been in the way? Had they been trying to get to her? Was she a danger to everyone she knew and everyone she cared about?

Travis sat down. Sweat gleamed on his forehead.

"You need to stay seated and let your head clear," she said and couldn't help the chastising tone of her voice.

She was relieved to put her attention, at least temporarily, to medical matters.

He grabbed her hand and pulled her down toward him. "I'll be fine," he said with steel in his voice. He pulled her closer. His hand was hot against her wrist. There was a hint of the shaving cream he'd used that morning that seemed to curl around her. The scent of him reminded her of early morning and lemons.

The grounds were quiet. Devon was coming around the corner. He was on the opposite side of her unit. And from the look on his face, he hadn't found any more information than they already had.

Travis ran the back of his palm across his forehead. "Did you see anything else? Anything?"

The questions were a relief to Kiera. For despite the fact that he was conscious and speaking, she didn't know how badly he was injured. A head injury was always frightening. His questions showed that he was not only aware of what happened, but that the hit on the head hadn't scrambled his brains.

"It all happened so quickly. You could have died. I should have…"

"You should have done nothing more than you already did. Without you I'd be dead."

She shook her head. "I should have shot sooner. I should have…"

"You probably didn't have a clear shot and you're not a marksman, so you waited," Travis said. "Understandable. But despite all that, you saved my life. If you hadn't been there, I would have been dead. There's no question of that. Don't doubt yourself. I can only say thank you."

"Don't thank me…"

"There's no one else to thank. I'm not sure how or

what happened, how I missed it. But I'm alive because of you."

"If I'd…"

"Stop." He held up a hand. "Tell me what you saw but no more about it being your fault. It's not." He paused as if for emphasis. "You did everything you could."

Kiera took a deep breath. "She hit you in the back of the head. It looked like she used a crowbar. That's my best guess. The sun was glinting and making it hard to see."

"She?" Devon said. He'd just returned from his search of the area. "Are you suggesting that his attacker was female?"

She swallowed back all the resistance and pushback that she knew was to come. It was time to stand her ground, speak of what she knew. "Yes. A woman, middle-aged. I caught a glimpse of her face."

"Where are you going with this?" Travis asked.

"Don't you see? There's a connection between my kidnapping, the phone calls and this." Kiera said with determination and frustration lacing her voice. "There were two killers, exactly as I told you. And one of them is back to get me."

Chapter Fourteen

"Are you alright?" Travis asked a few minutes later when they were inside her condo.

"I'm fine," Kiera assured him. "It's you we're worried about." She'd waited outside on her stoop as he'd spoken privately to Devon and then put in a phone call to the local police. Since then the ambulance had arrived. They'd pulled into the driveway with lights and sirens off as requested. The paramedics had checked the head wound, cleaned it up and agreed with her assessment. Although all parties agreed they'd prefer if he followed up. And again, Travis refused. But at least there was a consensus that odds were he had no concussion and he'd had on the spot treatment from professionals with equipment she didn't have access to.

He glanced at Devon and she didn't miss the subtle nod they exchanged.

"I'll check the neighborhood," Devon said.

Silence filled the room for a few seconds after Devon left.

"How's your head?"

"Fine," Travis said.

"I'll get you some water," she said, for his voice sounded choked, hoarse even.

"Did you get a good look at who did it?" he asked after

she'd returned a minute later and seconds after he'd taken a swallow of the water she'd brought him.

She shook her head. "Kind of yes and kind of no. It was a quick look and I saw only part of her face."

"Tell me again what you saw?" he said. "The details."

She sat down beside him and he took her hands in his.

She held on to his hands tight as the image of that face flooded her memory. "Long black hair, streaked with gray, and braided. I think she was middle aged, her face was tanned and lined. At least the part of her face that I saw. I never made eye contact. She turned away in just a split second."

"I know you only remember seeing one of your kidnappers. But was there anything familiar about her? Anything that triggered a memory?"

And they both knew what he was asking. Was she the elusive second kidnapper?

She shivered. "I only heard him. At least, I thought it was a man, but the voice—" she frowned "—could have been either male or female. That's all I have and your attacker didn't speak, and I didn't completely see her face."

His hand turned hers over and his thumb stroked her palm. The action was both surprising and comforting, and completely not the Travis she knew. He tried his best to keep their relationship professional.

As if reading her thoughts, he squeezed her hand and let go. "We'll talk about this later. In the meantime, I need to report what happened today."

He stood up, pulling her to her feet. "You'll be okay for an hour or so? Devon will be here. This time he won't be leaving. And there'll be a police cruiser in the area. I won't be long, but I need to file the report on this. I'll send a sketch artist here and let Devon know to expect them."

"No worries," she said. "The question is, are you okay?"

"I'm fine," he said as she walked with him to the door. He opened it and stood in the doorway, looking at her as if contemplating something about her, or the situation or both. She wasn't sure what was going through his mind.

"Kiera…" His voice dropped off as if he were considering what he wanted to say or even how he was going to say it.

"What?" she asked.

"I just want you to know, that I'm completely behind you. We have one killer behind bars but I know that there's someone else out there. Whether this was her or not, we'll get them sooner or later, Kiera. One killer at a time."

She shivered. "She found me." It was as much a question as it was at statement.

"Maybe, but she's at a disadvantage. You've seen her and you'll never be alone."

"I have my gun. I'll keep the doors locked and…" She looked at him, remembered that he'd been wounded protecting her. "You be careful tool"

He touched her cheek. "Call me if you need me, if you're scared at all—anything. We'll make sure you're safe. Promise."

"What about you?" she asked.

"I'll be alright," he said and the look in his eyes said he appreciated her concern. "You worry too much," he said as he pushed a strand of hair that had escaped her ponytail back from her cheek. He took her by the waist, pulling her closer to him. "I like that."

"Do you?" she said in a voice that was soft, almost provocative.

For heaven's sake, she thought, *you're flirting with the man who almost died protecting you*. It was an outrageous thought. Yet, she wanted nothing but to run her hands along the firm lines of his body.

She didn't have any warning when he kissed her. It was hot and hard and wet all at the same time. It was passion and the promise of more. It was the perfect kiss as she melted into him, kissing him back, mating her tongue with his. She fit against him like they were meant to be. She ached for this kiss to never end, for it to become more.

But with it came the knowledge that in the aftermath of what had happened, nothing could come of this. She pulled away. She needed to keep her head straight, her wits about her, and so did he.

"Go. You've got work to do," she said in a voice that didn't sound like hers at all. It felt strange and distant, and far from sincere. "Go," she encouraged.

He looked at her strangely as if he didn't believe what she was saying. And then a curtain seemed to come down and there was a distance between them again. It was like a professional space that breached the growing personal connection. She breathed a sigh of relief. That was the truth of their relationship. She was a client or a case, whatever it was that marshals called their assignments—nothing more.

Travis looked at his smartwatch. "Give me an hour, no more, and I'll be back. You'll be okay?" he repeated as if repetition would assure that she would be.

"I'll be fine," she said. She pointed to the end table where her gun lay. "I have the old standby, Devon and apparently part of the police department." It was a relief to know that he trusted her and knew she wasn't going to take off. This was the safest place she could be.

"You do."

"I'm not worried," she said. "Do what you need to."

"I DON'T LIKE THIS," James said twenty minutes later. "Especially the fact that you were attacked. Damn it, you could have been killed."

"I'm fine," Travis assured him once again.

James shoved back in his chair and stood up. "That's the one good thing to come out of this conversation. The rest…" He shook his head. "The two-kidnapper theory, the fact that no evidence of their existence was ever found over an almost fourteen-month investigation, seems implausible. Except, and here's where I contradict myself, there's been too much happening for it not to all be related. I just can't get over the fact that one killer may have flown so far under the radar."

"Except now they're out and not so quiet," Travis said. "The phone calls, the attack on me—casing Kiera's place. All of it. What if Kiera's right? What if the one that got away is now after her?"

It was a question for which they didn't have the answer. But he needed to talk this out. The theory of two killers, the attack—all of it added up to a threat to their witness, a threat to Kiera.

"We can't dismiss the idea that we don't have this case locked up," Travis said.

James frowned. "I don't like anything that came down this afternoon. Especially that I can't marry any of these incidents up to solid facts. I don't want any of this affecting her testimony."

"It won't. With any luck we'll have the pair of them locked up well before then."

"Sounds like best case scenario. If there are two killers. Otherwise, if they're all separate events then we have a variety of crimes happening and only one commonality—Kiera. All the crime happens around her. All the crime happens after she escapes the serial killer," James said slowly, contemplating the suggestion as if it had become fact. "Interesting, if we factor in the possibility that someone acquired leaked information."

"Not likely," Travis said.

"Agreed," James replied. "But a remote possibility."

"Never mind that—just look at the evidence. The phone calls, the stalker. You start piling the evidence together and it's adding up to a big something."

"Like I said, I can't disagree," James said slowly. "What I can say is that this is completely out of the ordinary. It's not the pattern that the average serial killer follows. Of course, there're exceptions, there always are. Even so, the specific cases of couples working together are rare. The Wests in England for one. But, in that case, she wasn't the dominant player, he was."

The more Travis thought about the recent events, the more convinced he became. But the more evidence they could gather, the better. He intended to sit down and talk to Kiera. The memories were still coming back, so the possibility of her remembering something new, something more tangible, in the next few days was a possibility. He knew the FBI would speak to her in the days leading up to the trial but somehow, he believed that he might have more success. She trusted him. In a way, the desire she ignited in him aside, they were friends.

"In the meantime, we know there's a threat—that fact no one disputes. So we need to move our witness to a safe house."

"I agree," Travis said with a feeling of relief. That was one item off the table. There was no discussion, done deal. He knew James would get that in the works and it was only a matter of alerting Kiera. He pushed that from his mind, knowing that convincing her might not be so easy. Despite her claims that another killer was still at large, she was anxious to go back to work and return to the life she'd put on pause since the incident. He'd convince her one way or another. He had no choice. What he had now was another issue—one almost as big as the one they'd just put to bed.

James leaned forward, his elbows on his desk. "I'm sensing another request in the works." He looked Travis in the eye as if forcing the point.

"I'd like to interview Eric Solomon," he said as he moved to the next item on his agenda.

"You'd like to what?" James said in a voice that was strained. It was a voice that barely held back his outrage at Travis's request. "What do you expect that will accomplish? He's already been interviewed and said next to nothing."

"I'm not sure," Travis said, unsurprised at the reaction. "Considering everything that's happened, the playing field has shifted."

"In your opinion."

Travis shrugged off the interruption. "Different questions, different interviewer, might get a different response. Maybe a different insight."

"You think he'll let something slip?"

"Maybe he can help us connect the dots."

"The odds are that he may say nothing at all," James said.

"True. But we also might gain some insight. Plus, he's had time to think. Maybe he'll reveal something that will give us that connection."

"Doubtful. While he hasn't lawyered up yet—that doesn't mean he won't request one. And that will change everything. Right now, he's just refused."

Travis was silent for a second digesting that interesting piece of information. "That aside, it would be negligent not to let me interview."

"How so?"

"It's a shot. Something might have changed. I know it's changed for us. This assignment isn't what I expected and maybe Eric is willing to shed some light on it."

James was shaking his head.

"We have the chance of changing the odds," Travis finished as he saw the stormy look on James's face. "Especially sending someone like me in." He held up his hand, staving off James's interruption. "Why? Because, I wasn't part of the original arrest so I'm unknown to the perp. The bonus? I'm actively involved in the case. But he doesn't know that. I have an inside scoop on the possibility of a twist…"

"There is no twist," James said with gritted teeth. "At least none that has any backing."

"So, let me do it."

"I don't know, Travis."

"What will it hurt?"

James shrugged. "Fair enough. I don't think you can do any harm. Maybe this idea of there being a partner in these crimes is a theory that dies as a result of this interview. I can only hope, because that surely complicates things. In the meantime, maybe you're right, it definitely has the potential to change things—or not." He shrugged.

"Agreed. Fifteen minutes, that's all I ask."

In the hall a door slammed shut. Someone laughed. Silence settled thick and uneasy between them as they sat on either side of the old oak desk.

"Alright, fifteen minutes and not a minute more. I'll arrange it ASAP. Let's say tomorrow at ten o'clock."

Travis stood up. "Thanks," he said to his friend and, for the duration of this case, superior. It was an awkward situation but one that they so far were handling without injury to their friendship.

"Don't thank me yet. You could walk out of there looking like an idiot."

"I'll buy the round," Travis said. "But if I'm right…"

"No chance of that."

"If I'm right that changes everything."

"Agreed," James said with a frown. "We can both hope that the theory is as whacked as it sounds. Neither one of us needs this complication."

Travis didn't disagree. He hoped that James was right. And he prayed that Kiera was wrong, but he feared she was very right. If that was the case, there was another killer on the loose, exactly as she'd said. And this time, they might very well have Kiera in their sights.

Chapter Fifteen

Travis had already had two cups of coffee when he arrived the next morning in Rawlings, Wyoming. It was a little after nine thirty in the morning. The Rawlings State Penitentiary was where the notorious serial killer, Eric Solomon, was being held as he awaited trial.

It was Thursday, exactly fifteen minutes before ten, when Travis entered the facility. He immediately felt trapped, confined, as he always did within the walls of a prison. He hated this aspect of his job, for prisons always made him feel claustrophobic. There was no reason for the feeling, no past trauma or phobia that he could put his finger on. Maybe it was just a subconscious aversion at the thought of being confined.

He pushed the thoughts from his mind and went through clearance. He was then ushered to the interrogation room. He was fifteen minutes early. He'd planned that, for he'd known that by the time he cleared security and made the necessary pleasantries with the officials, he'd be right on time.

As he entered the room and the door clanged behind him, the noises of the prison fell away and he pulled out a chair and sat down. It was the position in which he began any interview with someone who was incarcerated. It was less threatening than standing. He glanced at his smartwatch to make sure he was still ahead of schedule and to mark his time. He was now five minutes early. From everything he knew from the file and what James had told him, the murderer had said little. As a result, the odds that he'd open up to Travis were slim, but he still had hope. That the possibility was there meant that he had to take it. He knew that was the reason James had agreed—the faint hope of information.

Five minutes later the metal door opened. A medium-sized man, with blond hair that curled over his ears and average looks, leaned nonchalantly against the door-frame. His face was boyish and younger looking than Travis had expected. Eric Solomon was only two months younger than he was and yet he looked a decade younger. His youthful face helped make him look trustworthy. It was what had lured too many women to their deaths.

Travis tried to maintain a friendly look while feeling nothing but loathing for this man who had brutally killed so many women. He had to clench his hands at his sides and struggle to keep a pleasant expression. This piece of crap had threatened Kiera, had touched her, torn her clothes and meant to violate and then kill her. He couldn't think of that, for the rage it built in him would become uncontrollable in seconds. He'd stand up and take this piece of trash's throat in his hands and…

Damn it, Johnson. Cool it.

He couldn't. He'd kill him for what he'd thought that he could do to the woman he cared about.

He took a mental step back. What the hell was he thinking? He didn't care about Kierra not in that way, not in a romantic way. He hated this piece of trash. That was it.

There was no getting around it. It was too soon. He didn't know her. It didn't matter. He was falling for her.

Focus, damn it.

The guard gave the man a push. Eric took another step inside. The step was reluctant, forced on him from behind. He gave Travis a bland look that showed little emotion as he was forced to take another step into the room by a second shove from the guard.

"Behave yourself," the guard ordered. "Fifteen minutes," he said as he looked at Travis.

Travis gave him a nod and the guard walked out closing the door behind him with a distinctive click.

Travis made a snap decision. He guessed that sitting for this interview wasn't going to work, or at least sitting and waiting for him to sit wasn't working. He needed to meet him halfway. Pride was standing between them and, to eliminate that problem, they needed to be on equal footing. He stood up and held out his hand.

"Eric?"

"Marshal Johnson," Eric said with a sarcastic look.

"Travis."

Just like that, Eric smiled at him, the previous antagonism gone.

Travis guessed it was an act not unlike his own.

"Have a seat," Travis said as he reached for his own chair.

Travis pulled out the chair, and he sat down.

So did Eric.

They did it almost in sync.

Travis watched the murderer with casual nonchalance. He didn't slouch in his chair. But he didn't sit up straight either. He did everything not to appear threatening. Now, facing the man who was accused of such horrendous things, he wondered what could have brought him to that while tamping down the feeling of outrage that Kiera had been so close to dying at this man's hand.

He took a breath and focused on objectivity. This was his one chance. He'd read the file. Eric Solomon had had every dysfunctional trigger necessary through his childhood to raise him into the killer he'd become. He was a classic case. He'd come from a fragmented and dysfunctional family. He had a father who had disappeared before he was six, a stepfather who had been abusive and a mother who'd been mostly absent.

Travis knew that children could overcome those odds; many did. Not Eric. He'd run away from home at thirteen and disappeared off the authorities' radar. Following that, there'd been a long period of silence, until now.

Although he'd seen the file picture, it didn't reflect what Travis saw now—an open, friendly face. It was an illusion, he knew that. The initial assessment had indicated that the suspect was a sociopath. It was clear that Eric was giving him what he thought he wanted.

Eric silently watched with obvious reluctance and then slouched as he faced Travis with his arms folded. His face was tense, resistant. He barely looked at Travis. In fact, he didn't look at anything at all except the top of the desk that separated them.

His well-toned frame made it clear that he spent a good deal of time working out. Travis wondered if he spent any time contemplating the lives he had taken. He guessed the opposite might be true, that he might think about taking more. Fortunately, he could no longer do that. The question remained, was there someone out there who could. Someone who would carry on where he'd left off? Was Kiera's theory valid at all? Was what he and James speculated a reality?

"You killed a lot of people, Eric," he said without inflection. He slouched back in his chair. He didn't make eye contact but rather looked over the man's shoulder. His words were designed to be exactly as they sounded, unimpressed.

"You been living under a rock?" Eric snarled. "That's old news."

"You're right, it is," Travis replied, deciding to go straight for the heart. "Bet you wish that traitor who rode along with you got some justice too."

Silence met that comment.

Eric's lips tightened. His eyes flicked right and then left and didn't quite meet his. Travis pulled back in his chair as if putting as much distance as possible between them.

Seconds ticked by and Eric slouched further down in his seat as if by that he were proving his disinterest.

"You've been wronged. I can see that," Travis said knowing that the sudden changes in mood were on the accused murderer's file. He was extremely unpredictable.

Silence filled the room and seconds ticked by.

Eric shifted on the rock-hard metal chair. He glanced at the clock on the wall. Then he leaned forward, an ugly look on his face as if he were about to physically attack.

"Where is she? Where is the bitch that put me here?"

Travis didn't say anything immediately. He didn't want to give Eric Kiera's name.

"If she's not dead yet, she will be soon." He shook his head and his next words put all doubts to rest. "I should have raped her when I had the chance."

At that, it took everything Travis had not to lunge across the table and choke the life from this piece of crap. He'd dealt with a lot of slime in his time but never had it been so personal.

"Got under your skin, didn't I? Tell me where she is and maybe I'll tell you a bit more of what you want?"

He wouldn't let Eric see how much the turn in conversation had gotten to him. Instead he flipped the interrogation back to where it belonged—on the killer.

"Would you have started killing without him, Eric?" He asked, taking charge of the interview. He didn't wait for an answer. He held the killer's eyes as if the truth might be hidden there. "You weren't alone, were you?"

Eric cursed.

"Your partner was the reason that you got into this mess wasn't he, Eric?"

He'd been winging it for the last few minutes, relying on the fact that there might be some hate on Eric's part over what had happened to him. That was, if any of this had any validity, if the relationship existed at all, if there was another killer.

He met the accused serial killer's insolent gaze with a "couldn't care less" look of his own. Eyes told a lot about someone. In this case, the accused's eyes were a dusty blue, innocent as a baby's except there didn't seem to be any depth to them. They reflected the overhead fluorescent light: flat, barren—emotionless. Travis sat back, stretching his legs out, keeping his arms free, his hands on the desk.

"So, now they're free and you're here. This isn't what you deserve."

"I don't know what you're talking about."

Travis ignored that. "What do you think? I think he has himself a new partner, someone else to enjoy his pursuits with."

Silence was thick in the room. The dull clang of metal echoed down the hall. Eric's mouth tightened. His arms folded across his chest as he leaned back. Whether on purpose or by accident, he was copying Travis's pose.

Precious seconds ticked by; a minute passed. And then, just as he prepared to launch his attack from another angle, Eric sat up and leaned forward. His expressionless eyes, eyes that made Travis want to take a step back, met his.

"She deserves to die alongside me," Eric muttered.

She.

That one word seemed to vibrate between them. He couldn't believe what he'd just heard. It was amazing that he'd revealed anything at all, Travis thought. He pushed that reaction back, concentrating on keeping his face emotionless.

"I can understand that feeling," Travis said.

Eric said nothing.

"We're close to making that happen, but we need your help to do it," Travis said ignoring the animosity that felt alive between them. He stated the lie without a trace of guilt. If that was what it took to flush the truth out of this murderous piece of trash, that was what he would do. "She's out having fun, living the life and you're here…" He shook his head. "For how long?"

Eric remained silent.

"You've been wronged. I can see that," Travis said.

"She started all this," Eric said unexpectedly as he shook his head. "She's the reason I'm here. It wasn't my fault."

He sat up straighter, drawing himself back, almost defensive.

"I believe you," Travis encouraged.

"Do you?" he said with the original sulky edge that had lessened slightly as if he were feeling slightly more talkative. "She always said we'd be together forever, that she'd never leave me. And now I'm here and…" His face shut down, as if he knew that he'd said too much. He shoved back from the table.

"Eric," Travis began. "I can help you." In the back of

his mind he could only thank whatever stars had aligned that Eric hadn't demanded a lawyer be present. It was a possibility that might have deep-sixed this idea before it had even begun.

"Help me what?" he snarled. "I'm going to die in this hole and you know it."

"You help me, and I can help you," he said. "If you're sentenced…"

"I don't need your help," he gritted through clenched teeth. Spittle fell on the table. "It's over. I don't need you or any of your twisted promises." He stood up in a rush and the chair clattered backward. Behind him the door swung open. Before either of them could move farther, the guard was in the room. In seconds, he'd grabbed onto him.

Eric's eyes met his.

It wasn't the first time he'd faced evil and it wouldn't be the last. Still, he was glad to walk out the gates of the prison and leave Eric Solomon far behind.

The trip hadn't been as successful as he'd hoped. He'd proven only one thing. He had confirmation from the killer himself that he hadn't acted alone. More amazingly, he'd also had confirmation that the other killer was female. But whether Eric would ever admit to that in court was another matter. They'd work on that when the time came. Most important, he knew that he needed to get Kiera into a safe house and they needed to do it faster than James had thought. They needed one now.

Travis was on the phone to James before he hit the road. He explained the situation and an hour later he was heading back to Cheyenne with orders to get Kiera packed and ready for her new life. He wasn't sure how that would go over. What he did know was that there was an APB out on a woman who might be the second serial killer. A woman who might have only one goal in mind, making sure that her last victim died.

This time the little over two-hour drive that stretched out in front of him felt endless. As he left Rawlins's city limits behind, he'd never felt more determined in his life. It was during the drive that he was able to contemplate, really think about how much Kiera had come to mean to him.

Even after this short time, he couldn't imagine his life without her. Despite that, he knew they were too different, their lives too disparate to ever pursue a relationship. He didn't know from one moment to the next where he might be or what he might be assigned to. And Kiera, she had her job, her love of her elderly patients and her passion for helping. He knew all that despite the little time he'd spent with her and he wanted so much more. He was blindly falling for her without knowing her like he should. And he didn't know if she felt the same way or not. It was too early in the game and yet his mother had always said that it had been that way with his father. It had been that way with two aunts and uncles as well—it was the way his family worked. They were romantics. He pushed his what-ifs aside and only hoped that she'd give him the chance to get to know her, a chance outside the boundaries of this case.

It was when he was on the last leg home with fifteen minutes to go that he heard the news that made fear run through him like it never had before, even when he'd faced off against the most dangerous criminals. There'd been an attempted prison break at the Rawlins state prison. No further details were released.

"Damn it!" He slapped the steering wheel. He was still too far away. He ordered Siri to give James a call. She answered back in her usual precise tones with a hint of an electronic accent and told him that Jane wasn't in his directory. He smacked his palm against the steering wheel again in frustration but gave the order again, this time slowing his voice down, and he had much better luck.

"No word yet on what happened," James said. "I believe it was stopped in time."

Believe wasn't a word that gave him any comfort. Had the break been stopped? One name ran through his mind.

Eric Solomon.

Chapter Sixteen

Travis pulled into the FBI office in Cheyenne at exactly one o'clock in the afternoon. The journey between Rawlins and Cheyenne had seemed to last forever. Only five minutes ago, he'd spoken to Reece, the marshal taking the current shift with Kiera. Reece had assured him that everything was well, there was nothing out of the ordinary. Considering all that had happened in the recent past, he'd drawn in a relieved breath at the news. Reece, not unlike Devon, was good. Travis was surrounded by good men, the best. Only last year, Reece had been instrumental in taking down a terrorist group. He could rely on any number of colleagues, but Reece Blackburn, like Devon, stood out. Assured by the call, he headed for the FBI office to report what had occurred with his visit to Eric. Thirty minutes later, inside the FBI building, he bypassed the elevator, for even a minute wait would have been intolerable, and took the stairs two at a time.

But the physical exercise didn't take the anxiety away. He didn't want to be here. He didn't want to be away from Kiera another minute. But there was no choice. There were things that needed to be done and things that he needed to speak to James about. They were specifics that needed to be put in place, and a plan that had to be put in motion to keep Kiera safe.

"James," he said as he stood in the doorway.

James nodded but his eyes remained on the laptop.

Travis took a seat as James contemplated the screen before looking up.

Travis told James the details of what had happened.

"Interesting," James said thoughtfully. He looked at the file on his laptop. "So, here's the new arrangement effective almost immediately. A safe house in Denver. Memorize the address and I'll be in touch," he said. "With the new information, well, this isn't a safe situation. Especially with the admission from Solomon. You and Kiera are officially a couple until this is over. Unfortunately, the place won't be ready until tomorrow morning. I'd suggest a hotel room in Denver. Have her use your last name, pose as a married couple. Maybe flip to her second name for good measure. I don't think you need any more than that—at least for now."

"Thanks, man," he said. "For getting this done so quickly."

James nodded. "Good luck," he said. But the look he gave him held something else that looked suspiciously like regret.

Travis didn't have time to consider what any of that might mean. He wasted no time in getting out of the office and heading to where he needed to be—with Kiera. No matter how good Reece was, he needed to be there by her side.

Fifteen minutes later and two blocks from Kiera's house and it seemed like the distance between the FBI office and her home had increased dramatically. It was taking forever to get there. His mind was awash with thoughts, with what needed to be done.

It was two o'clock in the afternoon. He promised himself that he'd have Kiera away from here and on the road by three.

But minutes after Reece had left Kiera's condo, Travis walked over to Kiera and sat down on the sofa beside her. It was time to lay out for her the drastic shift in plans. It wasn't a job he relished for he didn't know how she would take it. He wasn't sure if she would cooperate and if she didn't, he didn't know if he could convince her to change her mind.

There was no way to preface this, so he met it head-on. "Kiera, it's not safe for you here."

She frowned, her eyes narrowing. "I don't like where this is going." She looked him in the eye as she stroked Lucy and the cat purred. "This is our home. I…"

He looked down. Damn, he hadn't thought about the cat or factored in its importance to her. An error right out of the gate wasn't good.

"After what happened, Kiera, we can't take the chance that it might happen again. We have to move to a safe house."

"What do you mean?" she asked. "You and the other marshals are protecting me until the trial. I'm safe."

"You weren't safe yesterday afternoon."

"But I'm safe now," she insisted. "You make me safe."

He met the look in her eyes, saw apprehension and something else—fear. He took her hands in both of his, ignored the cat and pulled her close. The cat meowed. The damn cat could complain all she wanted, he thought. His lips brushed Kiera's and then he was pulling her against him. He kissed her deeper as her soft yet firm figure pressed against him. And he only wanted her closer, tighter.

When he let her go, she gave him a befuddled look.

"I'm starting work next Monday," she said after more

than a minute had passed, as if that somehow changed what had happened. She shifted a few inches away from him, her lips still heightened in color, prettily blushed from his kiss.

"They're expecting me. They need me." It was as if she believed he would argue and she had her defenses in place.

She wasn't wrong. It wouldn't happen, it couldn't.

"Kiera, you can't stay here. They can get a temp in— I've already spoken to your supervisor."

"You what?" her voice went up in volume. "How dare you." She stood up. "I can't— I don't need…" She shook her head as if there were no words to say how upset she was. She walked a few feet away, her back to him. What was clear was that she was dodging the idea of a move altogether.

He followed her. He put his hands on her shoulders. He turned her around to look at him. No matter what she thought—this was happening. He wasn't taking any chances, not with her life—ever.

Her eyes never left his. They sparked with passion, with denial and with all the life he loved so much about her.

"You had no right."

"I'm responsible for your life," he said. It was true, for it was what it all came down to.

"You're nothing more than a bodyguard," she said as if downplaying his work might help her win the argument. "And I don't need one. I'm fine on my own. I'm armed." She looked over her shoulder and he followed her gaze to where the vintage Colt .45 sat on the coffee table.

"You didn't think so yesterday or the day before that," he said with strained patience. There were other arguments he could draw on like where and where she could not take the gun. All he wanted to do was check the time and hit the road. He drew on every ounce of patience he had. "What's changed? I've got that you have the gun, but don't think I don't know how you feel about using it. Odds are you couldn't shoot anyone if you tried. In fact, the last time around you scared the intruder off but I'm guessing that wasn't what you meant to do."

She looked at him with denial in her eyes.

He leaned over and kissed her again. And in the seconds after that kiss, everything changed between them.

Her upper lip quirked in the suggestion of a smile. "I could hear my aunt's voice telling me to crease their ear. Except, I was afraid. Afraid that I'd miss, kill her and you. So, I shot high." She didn't look at him. "I could have creased her ear. I've been to the shooting range. Months ago..." Her voice trailed off.

He guessed that she was realizing that a little practice did not make perfect.

"And work isn't an option," he said arguing a point that was in his mind, moot. He had a bigger issue to deal with but first he had to steer her from this one. "You'd endanger the residents of the care home."

She looked at him with tears in her eyes. She unfolded her arms. "Alright," she said. "I won't go back to work, not yet."

"Agreed. Not until I catch this piece of sludge and put them behind bars." The truth was, he was ready to put her over his shoulder and take her out of here kicking and screaming. But that wouldn't work. He needed her buy-in and he needed it quickly.

"Just because our security team claims that there have been no early morning calls doesn't mean that it's over. In fact—"

"It could mean something worse," she murmured.

"It already has meant worse," he said. "You were stalked and I was attacked."

They had little time. They needed to get packed and get on the road. Even with a drive that was under two hours, barring traffic, they needed to leave as quickly as possible. As it was, they'd be hitting rush-hour traffic in Denver. There was no getting around that. The traffic rush began now and would last well through the supper hour. Still, he wanted to get on the road and put distance between her and the danger that he now knew lurked here. But he couldn't push her and risk any opposition. He waffled about which approach would be best.

She didn't say anything. Instead she fell back down onto her sofa as if every bone and muscle in her body had turned to jelly.

"You've got to leave, with me, Kiera. To a safe house. You and me."

"Why? What's changed?"

"I went to Rawlins, to the federal jail."

A hand went to her mouth. "You saw him."

"I did. And he confirmed what we'd already come to believe, that there were two people that night and only one of them is in jail."

"And I'm the only witness," she said in a whisper and sank down onto the edge of the couch.

"Exactly," he said. "I'll tell you all of it on the road." He sat down beside her.

"We're that pushed for time?"

"I want us on the road by three at the outside," he said. "You're okay?"

She nodded. And he could see in her eyes and the set of her lips that they were finally on the same page.

"The safe house won't be set up until tomorrow but the important thing is that we're out of here, out of Cheyenne."

"I hate this," she muttered. "There's no other way?"

"No other way," he confirmed in a low voice that only emphasized the situation. He was pleasantly surprised at her reaction, by the lack of pushback from her. After her reaction about her job, he'd only assumed the worst.

"Okay," she said and stood up. "I'll get packed."

"Just like that?" he asked. He couldn't predict her.

"There's no choice is there? I mean, the only thing that seems to have stopped are the phone calls."

She was right there. According to Serene there'd been no calls since the third morning she was home. There'd been a dead-end on traces. In the meantime, he'd obtained a pre-paid phone for Kiera.

"No choice," he agreed. "And it's a hotel for us tonight," he said. "I'll tell you—"

She held up her hand. "I'm not ready to hear what he said. I..." Her voice shook. "Give me time on that. I need to know. I just don't... It gives me the chills, like I was there in that closet all over again."

"I get it. You'll ask in your own good time."

"I will," she said with a smile. "And probably sooner than you think. In the meantime, what else aren't you telling me?"

"One other thing." He hesitated to say it, unsure of how she was going to react. There was a split-second hesitation "We're going to be married for a while."

"Alright," she replied.

"Then we're good to go," he said, as if the cavalier words could make up for his shock at her easy acceptance of the new situation. They were heading into the unknown. He'd expected reluctance, fear even. And he was relieved that she reacted with none of that.

His phone rang. He looked at it and at Kiera. "I have to take this," he said.

She nodded as he stood up and went to the front door. He hit Answer as he opened the door and went outside.

It was James.

"You ready to head out?"

"Twenty minutes out," he replied. He didn't mention that he had yet to convince Kiera that this was the only way to keep her safe. "I'll message you when I'm there."

"Have you rolled out the situation for her?"

"She's aware we're going to a safe house."

"So. You have told her that she's going to be your wife for a while? Possibly gotten her agreement?" James chuckled as if already anticipating her response.

"The laughs on you," he said with a smile. "She knows and it's not an issue."

Travis disconnected seconds later and went back into the condo. He didn't look forward to what he only saw as long and anxious hours ahead.

Chapter Seventeen

They'd been on the road for thirty minutes. The prairie rolled out on either side of them, as the distant mountains rose in the background. He glanced over at Kiera. Anytime he had in the past, like now, it seemed that her eyes hadn't left the road. It was as if they needed to be there, as if she were the one driving. He sensed her tension. He knew leaving her home, her job and her life in Cheyenne wasn't easy for her. He also knew that the move was the safest option.

The cat meowed for the first time since the trip began. He had to admit that despite his reservations, so far, the animal had been no trouble.

"Lucy," Kiera said as she turned to slip her fingers through the wire front of the carrier. "Not that long and we'll be there. Promise."

She spoke as if the cat understood. He'd heard that this was a trait of many pet owners. Her bond with the animal was like a foreign language to him. He'd never had a pet. Neither his lifestyle nor his personality left him open to the idea.

"You're quiet," he said as another mile passed. He glanced over at her, hoping if nothing else to start a conversation on how she was feeling, on how this impacted her. Anything would be preferable to the silence.

"I'm completely stressed by this. Leaving my home, leaving everything I treasure behind." She shook her head. "It's impossible to process. It's all been so much, too much."

She was silent for a minute.

He didn't say anything. He couldn't imagine all she'd been through and all she still needed to do to finally put this behind her. She was right, it was too much, and yet more kept being asked of her. There was no choice. But he admired the fact that with little complaint, she shouldered it all.

Minutes passed. He could feel her eyes on him. He glanced over. The late afternoon sun highlighted her high cheekbones, her natural beauty evident even without a trace of makeup.

"I hate that this is happening," she said after silence had again become heavy, uncomfortable between them.

"It's not forever," he promised. "After the trial, or maybe sooner, you'll be able to go home. One day, it will be as if none of this ever happened," he said. He wasn't sure if that would ever be the case. But she needed something to look forward to. She needed the silver lining, not the dark cloud that she'd so recently escaped.

"One day," she said in a quiet voice. She turned to watch a herd of elk in the distance, as if the sight would bring that normalcy into her life, as if it might bring it sooner.

So far, it had been an easy drive. But Wyoming was like that, miles of straight, uncongested roads. With a small population, traffic jams didn't exist. It was one of the things he loved about the state. Of course, there was more to it than that. He could also add the mountains, the wildlife and the raw, untouched prairie. All those things were reasons that he'd jumped at the chance when a position had come up here. The bonus, of course, had been the fact that this was the state where he had grown up and where the majority of his family still lived.

Minutes and miles passed. The scenery hadn't changed, only another herd of elk and a lone deer provided any change from the miles of prairie. They traveled in silence for a few miles.

"It will never be the same will it?" she asked as they neared the Colorado border. "My life, I mean."

He didn't know what to say. He guessed that what she had said wasn't really a question.

A minute passed and then two.

"You didn't believe there were two people who took me, did you? Even after calls and the threat," she said.

"That's not exactly true," he said glancing at her. "After the phone threats I still had doubts. But I was considering what you said and pushing to investigate the possibility. Then, after I was attacked…" He glanced at her. "If I'd known you better, I would have believed sooner. I'm sorry, you were right."

"Sometimes I think none of it was real, that it was just one horrifying hallucination."

"Right," he replied. "And that's the problem."

"You need evidence," she said.

"Exactly. Without it, you have us in a corner. As a marshal, it's my job not to take everything at face value. I'm obliged to question." He glanced at her. "There aren't any lawyers now. He's refused representation. But I can see that changing. Eventually he'll come to his senses. The lawyers will be worse—you realize that?"

Worse was an understatement. The defendant's attorney, should he acquire one, could literally tear her apart.

"I know," she said softly and yet with an edge in her

voice. "Don't worry. Whatever happens, I'll survive," she promised.

He knew that she'd survived a lot in her life. Her mother had died when she was three. She'd never known her father. Her mother had been a single parent. What Kiera knew was that her father had been too young and too uninterested. He'd never offered support and declared he wanted nothing to do with her. Her parents had parted ways shortly after her mother learned she was pregnant. For Kiera it had never been a big deal. Even after losing her mother, she'd never thought to find the man who had fathered her. She had no interest and claimed she never would. Her aunt had raised her after that but had died only a half dozen years ago. As much as Travis cared about his aunts and uncles, he wasn't sure what it would be like to lose your only family member, the aunt who raised you. He knew that her aunt had no children and he could only think how lonely that would be with no siblings, no raucous family gatherings. It seemed odd to him.

"Like you survived your childhood?"

"No!" There was a note of surprise in her voice. "It wasn't like that. My childhood wasn't anything that needed surviving. Not at all. Aunt Nan was wonderful. Besides, I was so young when my mother died that I only have a few memories. Good ones but nothing traumatic. It was Aunt Nan's passing that killed me. I was eighteen. And after that, it was just me.

"What about you?" she asked.

He smiled, for he realized that in the time he'd spent with her it had been more him grilling her, and, of course, he had the advantage of having a file on her.

"Three brothers, a sister, my mom and dad, grandparents and a herd of cousins, aunts and uncles… Some days the list seems endless."

"Do you stay in touch with them?"

He smiled. "All the time," he said. "But it's more like they stay in touch with me." He thought how spoiled he really was and how little effort he had to put in to keep in touch. They did, as his mother would call it, all the heavy lifting. But once a year he had his grilling extravaganza for the entire clan. There was no set date due to his job and the unpredictability of his assignments. But it was tradition. And, on the first good weather weekend that he was home, he fired up the grill for the event. It was an event that he planned at least a week in advance.

"You're lucky," she replied and there was a wistful tone to her voice. "I'm betting you had fun growing up," she said. "Lots of baseball games?"

"A sport that I don't excel at," he admitted.

"What were you good at?"

"Golf," he said. "Not the sport to win the girls over, so I migrated to football in high school."

"Golf," she repeated. "If it makes you feel any better, Aunt Nan was an older mother and her idea of sports was bowling. I actually can still bowl a fairly good game."

The conversation stayed for a few minutes on safe ground, exploring the worlds of their childhoods before lapsing again into silence.

Ten minutes passed, then fifteen. The scenery was changing. They were getting close to the state border. She shifted in her seat as if she were ready to get out, stretch her legs and end this road trip.

The mountains were drifting farther back. The road felt less closed in.

"Okay, tell me, what did the creep say when you went

to see him? Tell me what you can," she said. Her voice was soft and yet no less commanding.

"He basically said that he wasn't acting alone. And he confirmed that he had a partner and that she's female."

"What the lowly witness had already told them," she said with a hint of an edge in her voice. She looked at him. "Was it you who suggested that I be moved?"

"Pretty much. Although…" He didn't finish. He wasn't sure if he wanted to finish.

"Although?" she repeated. "That leads me to believe there's more."

There's always more, Travis thought. "It wasn't an easy decision to be made all around. But once the evidence of a second killer became a real possibility, once a stalker entered the picture, there's no way that we could do anything else but get you immediately to a safe place." His eyes were focused solely on the road for it was moving into prime time for deer and antelope to be crossing the highway. The animals were in grazing mode and not adverse to running, without warning, across the highway.

There was silence again for a few minutes as the late-afternoon sun danced across the prairie and the mountains retreated farther into the background. They crossed the Colorado border and the traffic slowly began to pick up. Time passed and soon they were no longer in laid-back, wide-open country. The uninhabited prairie slowly morphed into towns and then cities and eventually the urban and commercial sprawl that spread tentacles along the highway and led to the metropolis of Denver.

"How long?" she asked with a quiver in her voice. "How long before I can go home?"

His eyes were on the road. But the truth was he didn't want to look at her. He couldn't stand tears. He didn't know what to do. It wasn't as if he could hug her or even just make it better with words. He was driving. He had to stay focused and there was really no time limit he could give her. *Until it's over* wasn't the answer she wanted to hear.

He could feel her eyes on him. He knew that she wouldn't let go of the question. She'd wait patiently.

"It will be alright. We'll get you home, hopefully soon."

"I hope so," she whispered.

And, in the silence, he vowed that he would keep the promise of getting her home soon.

It was a promise he didn't know how he was going to keep.

Chapter Eighteen

They'd been on the road since midafternoon and the trip was close to over. It was almost five o'clock—the worst time to be hitting the outskirts of Denver. He looked over at Kiera. She was quiet as if caught in her own thoughts.

She glanced at him. "You okay?"

"Why do you ask?"

"You've been driving the whole way and it's crazy busy."

"Denver in rush hour. You've never been here?"

"No." She shook her head. "There wasn't money for trips, not after Aunt Nan died, and even before. We had to follow a fairly tight budget."

He imagined what she must make of seeing the urban sprawl that was Denver. The endless box stores as they neared the city, the vehicles that were bumper-to-bumper, the hectic pace of a large city so different from Cheyenne.

He gave her a glance and a quick smile. Not that he didn't enjoy his visits to Denver, not that it wasn't a beautiful city but the urban sprawl that led into it was only another reminder of why he loved the wide-open spaces of Wyoming.

"I'm beginning to appreciate Cheyenne," Kiera said as if she had read his thoughts. "This is too busy for me."

He kept his eyes on the road. But he couldn't agree

with her more. Denver was an attractive city, but Cheyenne was the perfect size, at least for him.

They'd passed a number of hotel and motel advertisements. He'd already pinpointed a hotel a mile from where they were. It would be a relief to get off the road.

"I found a hotel close to the house we'll be moving to tomorrow."

"Alright," she replied. "I'm assuming you're checking in."

"I am," he said. With her having no ID, he would complete the registration at the hotel. His name was on no one's radar and using his name, acting as a couple, was part of the plan. Five minutes later he was taking their bags to their room.

"Are you hungry?" he asked. It was close to suppertime and he hadn't eaten since breakfast. He wasn't sure about her.

"Starved," she replied.

Guilt ran through him that he hadn't stopped and grabbed snacks for them while they'd been on the road. "There's a restaurant beside the hotel."

"Let's go," she said as she headed to the door. He guessed when she said she was hungry, she'd meant it.

"You said you grew up in Wyoming, or did I get that wrong?" she asked fifteen minutes later. They'd been seated at a table in a restaurant that also had a large bar, where televisions were set up overhead for prime sports viewing. They placed their orders before getting back to the conversation.

"Except for a brief time in North Dakota."

"What was that like?"

He didn't want to tell her a single thing. They'd already spoken of their childhoods and while there was a lot more that could be said, he'd said enough for now.

He only wanted to look at her. He was fascinated by everything about her. From how she picked up her napkin and rearranged it so that her cutlery was neatly laid over it, to how she seemed to take everything in—enjoying it all, despite their reasons for being here, despite the trip to get here.

Their food arrived and they chatted amicably, like friends, clearly skirting all the reasons they were in Denver. It was a nice break.

An hour later they were back at their hotel room. He held the door open for her and she walked by leaving a light scent of cinnamon behind her. He followed and tried to keep his eyes off the easy swing of her body. Her arms were well-toned, and he guessed that was a result of working out. It was something else they had in common. His job dictated that he be fit but truthfully, he'd work out despite it. The gym was a place that invigorated him, and a week didn't go by without at least two visits to it.

In their room, she looked at her watch. "It's only eight o'clock. Do you want to watch a movie?"

"Sure," he replied. He'd sat down on the edge of the bed nearest the door and the cat immediately curled up in a ball on his lap. He wasn't sure how that had happened. Tentatively, he stroked the top of its head. The animal purred and cuddled closer to his belly.

"How did you end up with the cat?"

"Lucy? One of our new residents rescued her. Two months later she had a stroke and ended up in the care home. So, I took Lucy. It works out well. I can bring her to work occasionally and Margaret can see her pet."

"They don't allow animals?"

She shook her head. "Visiting is fine but not living there. Many of the residents love animals but can't take care of them. Having them visit is the next best thing.

They bring in cats and dogs usually, but…" She smiled. "I've seen the occasional rabbit come in. As far as Margaret and Lucy, I bring her in at least once a week. It's not just Margaret who loves seeing her. She brings so many smiles. You can't imagine." She took Lucy from him and plunked down on one of two queen-size beds closest to the window. The cat batted her chin and she chuckled. "Margaret and Lucy are handling the arrangement fine and I think Lucy has truly settled in."

She put the cat down. "We need snacks," she said, changing the subject. "For the movie," she finished when he didn't answer. "Should I go and get…"

"No," he said abruptly and knew from the way that the smile had left her lips, that he had been too harsh. "I'm sorry. I meant that I will get them."

Five minutes later he was back with drinks, chips and a chocolate bar to share. She'd admitted earlier that she loved chocolate but couldn't eat a whole bar. She found it too sweet.

"To share," he said when he saw her frown at the bar.

"You remembered," she said, and the frown was replaced by a smile.

He settled down on the bed closest to the door. The movie was a comedy. She'd picked it and it was perfect considering the state of her life. They laughed and shared the junk food. It was strange for he felt like they were a team as darkness collected outside.

The credits were rolling when he turned off the television.

Kiera had yawned numerous times in the last hour.

"Time for bed," he said. The words were more of a fact than a question. It had been a long day for both of them.

She nodded. "Definitely."

She'd already claimed the bed nearest the window and

that suited him perfectly. They were on the fifth floor—there was no chance of danger coming from the window. He preferred to be closest to the door. In case of intrusion or disaster, that was both the danger point and the escape route. It was easier for him to ensure her safety if he had control of the exit.

Fifteen minutes later, she was sleeping, and Travis was staring at the ceiling. Knowing she was a few feet away only awakened desires that he was struggling to keep under control. A shared room had been a bad idea. He'd be glad to be settled in the safe house and put some space between them.

He closed his eyes. But it was impossible to sleep. He wondered how long they would have to keep her hidden. He hoped that it would be a short time. He hoped that they could catch the killer soon. But he knew the odds were slim. They had no new intelligence. They had no idea who she was and only the assumption that the person who had attacked him was also a serial killer. If that was the case, they had Kiera's sketchy description to go on. James had indicated that based on his interview, the FBI would interrogate Eric again. But he had his doubts on whether the killer would give any more information.

An hour later, he was dozing off when a scream woke him. He turned on the light. Kiera was thrashing around. Sweat gleamed on her skin.

"No," she said. "No, please." The covers twisted around her and her hair streamed over the pillow.

He got up and went over to her.

"Kiera."

"No!" She clawed at the covers.

He took her hands in his. She didn't wake up, but the touch seemed to calm her. She stopped struggling.

Lucy mewed from her carrier.

"Travis," Kiera murmured but her eyes didn't open.

"I'm here, sweetheart," he said and lay down on the bed beside her. He didn't know if she heard him, for she wasn't awake. He put an arm around her and she snuggled close to him. Finally, she settled and seemed to go into a deeper sleep. He lay there as seconds ticked into minutes. The cat mewed again. He dropped one hand down and stuck a finger into the carrier, stroking the soft fur. The mewing stopped. The cat purred and then dropped into silence. Finally, he reached over and turned off the bedside lamp. Both Kiera and her cat were asleep as he lay awake listening in the darkness. With Kiera warm and trusting in his arms, he knew that his life had just drastically and irrevocably changed. For the first time in his life, he'd given his heart away.

OVER BREAKFAST, as they wasted time until the safe house would be ready at ten o'clock, they bantered like they never had with each other before. He wasn't sure how they got there, but somehow or other, one of them had taken them back to stories of childhood. It was an easier conversation compared to others they had had. The intensity of the last week, the horror that she'd escaped—all of it was put aside as memories of bucolic childhoods and crazy kid antics drew them closer to each other. The stories had him appreciating the child who had made the strongest woman he knew. He wondered what her aunt had been like to have raised a woman like Kiera.

He'd learned that she'd been a video game fanatic as a ten-year-old. In turn he'd shared that, as a boy, he'd been a baseball addict, watching as many televised games as he could. Except, as he'd said earlier, what he'd been good at was golf. He'd even admitted to her that golf wasn't something the other kids admired, not like being the star pitcher or quarterback. So, he'd become competent at the sports the girls admired—baseball and football, but he'd never been the best player.

She'd smiled at that.

They'd exchanged stories—stupid childhood acts that now only made them laugh. While her childhood had been more difficult than his, it seemed her aunt had been dedicated to making it the best it could be.

"She was amazing," Kiera said softly. "Aunt Nan loved nothing better than having fun. I couldn't have asked for a better childhood." She laughed. "Did you ever make homemade ice pops?"

He smiled, enjoying this side of her. She could easily hop from one story to another. She wove laughter through her stories and asked him questions when he didn't immediately provide a story of his own.

"As a matter of fact, yes. With fruit juice."

She made a face. "Ours too. But at the time—they were good. I think my aunt thought they were healthy." She smiled. "Despite losing my mom, I can't complain about my childhood."

Silence followed after that.

When he thought of it later, he knew that it had been a strange conversation to have. Two adults drifting back into childhood memories not once but twice—he remembered the conversation on the road, passing the time as they got here—to this place, this time. Both conversations had served the sole purpose of taking them away for a few minutes from a situation that was too dire to contemplate. But the conversation also made him far too aware that there was little he didn't like about her. He just wished that it all boiled down to like. But he feared that it was building to more than that and he had nowhere to go, nowhere to run from an emotion that threatened to bring him to his knees.

He mentally pulled his emotions from the abyss. She depended on him to protect her. Seducing her, thinking of seducing her, none of that was part of the protection he was expected to offer. He needed to play this one by the book. And the book said no romance on an assignment. His intentions were good, but he made the mistake of looking at her, meeting her eyes. And he knew that whatever the rules were, she was in charge of the game. If she chose to break the rules, there was nothing he could do to stop her.

Chapter Nineteen

Later that morning, Travis pulled up to the low-rise beige apartment building where the safe house was located. It was one of eight apartment units in a lower-middle-class area that was built decades ago. It was the kind of area that was in need of a loving touch. It was a part of town that was occupied by people too busy making a living to give much consideration to looks. Or to notice strangers, thankfully.

"This is it?" Kiera asked but it was more statement than question.

He glanced over. She seemed tense, worried even.

He put a hand over both of hers.

"It will be alright," he said.

She looked at him. "It had better be, hadn't it?" She took in an audible breath before finishing her thought. "There isn't any other choice."

He squeezed her hand and let it go. There was nothing he could say that would change any of this. James had said that the apartment would be set up for them first thing in the morning and he'd confirmed that that was completed over an hour ago. Everything was ready to go. There was no room for doubt. This was the only choice they had to keep her safe.

Although, he thought that the FBI couldn't have picked

a better area of the city. He realized that the choice was intentional. But, in his mind, he wanted the best for Kiera. Even in a situation like this. But this wasn't the best, not in comfort or status. What it was, was the best place to hide. It was in areas like this where nothing and no one seemed to stand out. It was the type of area that seemed to exist in every city. The housing was a jumble of beige and brown cheaply built mass housing units. It was a place in the city that had no real appeal. It was a place where it was easy to get lost, to disappear amidst neighbors only concerned with keeping their heads above water.

He unlocked the door to the second-floor apartment and ushered Kiera inside. She had a large bag and he carried another bag for the cat, along with the cat itself, in its carrier. He had a knapsack that he'd slung over his shoulder. He'd learned over the years to travel light. It didn't matter how long he'd be here, he could wash or buy more things if necessary.

He set Kiera's bags and the cat carrier down. He would let Kiera arrange the cat's things. He thought that putting her and her pet's things in place would help her feel more at home or at least settle in more quickly.

"I hope we won't be here for too long," she worried. "The shelter at home needs volunteers. We provide meals for disadvantaged and homeless. Come summer, many of the volunteers go on vacation. I usually give extra hours then." She looked up at him. "We won't be here that long, will we?"

"I hope not," he replied.

"Ann must be wondering where I am," she said, and he knew that she was referring to one of the seniors in the care home where she worked. "And Margaret, I hope she's not missing Lucy too much."

He didn't reply. She didn't seem to expect one as she walked away. He watched as she opened the fridge. He knew it would be well-stocked. That was standard in any situation like this.

"Lasagna sound good for supper?" she asked.

"Supper? How about lunch?"

She laughed. "Thinking ahead. There's lasagna in the fridge and a whole lot more—milk, cheese, some cold cuts and a stack of microwavable dinners." She opened a cupboard door and shut it. "And cereal and coffee too. We won't starve."

"I'll get some coffee started."

"Sounds good to me." She closed the fridge.

"This isn't a bad setup," she said a few minutes later. She'd scoured the place checking out each room. It didn't take her long. The place was small—five hundred square feet at most.

He glanced at his watch. It was eleven o'clock and his stomach rumbled.

"I'll make sandwiches later, for lunch. That is if they've left us any bread," he offered.

She didn't answer. He watched her, unable to drag his eyes away from hips that were more generous than one would expect with her small frame. Despite that, in his mind, they were perfect. Everything about her was perfect.

SUSAN BERKER COULDN'T get the last victim out of her mind. Kiera Connell was the one who had changed everything. It was because of her that Eric was in jail. It was because of her that her best friend and lover had been taken from her. She needed to not only finish what they'd started, but to get revenge. She could have none of that unless she found their last victim. But she'd disappeared. There was no sign of her. She'd guessed that she was in witness protection and the odds of finding her were remote. But she wasn't ready to give up. Even though Kiera Connell was in the hands of a US marshal and he'd taken her underground, it wasn't over. A crumb, that was all she needed. She cruised the only thing that might give her that crumb, social media. For days there was nothing on Kiera's social media, but she hadn't given up and her patience had paid off. Only an hour ago she'd hacked her account to see a brief conversation Kiera had had with her supervisor. She'd included a picture of a cat, to be given to one of the residents. And in that picture was the answer to where the feds had her hidden.

"One of the stupidest moves you've ever made. Your heart won over your brain," Susan said and felt happiness bubble up within her for the first time since she'd lost Eric. This was finally going to end well. Not exactly as she planned. But she'd adapt, write her own ending rather than one imposed by the authorities.

She could hardly wait. She looked at her watch. Denver, Colorado, that was less than two hours away. She clutched the wheel of the old white camper van with both hands. They were hands that were suntanned from too much time on the road, too much time behind the wheel. But for the last few years, she'd driven coast-to-coast, stopping only for the excitement of the hunt and of the sex that followed. It was what she lived for, that and Eric.

Past tense and all because…

She'd kill her. She put her foot on the gas. The thought turned her on almost as much as sex. Almost.

She had all the time in the world and she wouldn't let this one go. Kiera reminded her too much of the first young woman she'd ever kidnapped. The irony of it was that her runaway victim had returned to Denver, the place where Susan had grown up. It was also the place she'd escaped from all those years ago. She still knew the city's secrets and she knew where to find the victim. No one could hide from her there. For Denver was where it had all begun and where, if things worked out like she hoped, it would all end.

Chapter Twenty

Travis heard water running in the bathroom.

She was in the shower—naked. Washing her thick dark hair—caressing her skin with soapy fingers...

The thought broke off with a huge effort on his part. He had to divorce himself from them, for they only created an imagined image. It was an image that took him to a place there was no recovery, no going back from. If he went to that place, he'd be turned on every time he looked at her. He wondered how much of this he could stand. He needed to keep his distance and yet there was no distance to be had. The safe house wasn't meant for two people. While it was the best that could be done on short notice, it wasn't the best for them. But it was all they had and if it was to keep her safe then he'd fight the attraction that had no place between them. For, he'd rather be here, fighting his own desires than fearing for her life in Cheyenne.

But thin walls did little to mute the steady beat of the water and the sound did nothing for his hyped imagination. He needed to get out of here, get away. But there was nowhere to go. He was here to keep her safe. He needed to be with her and he wanted to be with her. In the shower—naked.

He couldn't stand another minute. He went to the door

and opened it, and then he remembered the damn cat. He closed the door. It didn't matter, the hallway was stuffy, and outside the night air was too warm anyway to cool him down at all.

There was no television in the apartment. They were definitely living bare bones, at least for the moment. With nothing to divert his thoughts he grabbed a travel magazine he'd shoved in his pack. When he had time, he loved to travel, especially places where he could hike or ski. Last year he'd been to the Swiss Alps and the year before that, the Canadian Rockies. He didn't have a trip planned yet but...

He pitched the magazine aside. It skidded across the worn wooden coffee table before stopping in a precarious hang at the edge. The magazine had done nothing to ease his mind. This assignment, this safe house, was going to be much more challenging than he'd ever imagined. Here, there was no avoiding each other. That hadn't mattered before. But it mattered now. His attraction to her had escalated to the point that, for him, there was no turning back. He wanted her in every way a man wants a woman. He couldn't go there. But the space was so incredibly small that there was little opportunity to avoid the attraction that was threatening to overwhelm him.

IF SHE'D BEEN a braver woman, Kiera would have turned the tap from hot to cold. But, despite growing up in Wyoming, she hated the feeling of being cold. All that aside, she wasn't sure if cold water would have done anything for her unwanted feelings other than make her damned uncomfortable. She wasn't sure if it was because the last two years had been a dry spell as far as romance was concerned, or he was just that hot. But something about Travis had had her falling for him the minute she'd laid eyes on him. She wanted him like she hadn't wanted a man in a long time, if ever. Her mind kept turning to inappropriate thoughts. She wanted nothing more than to run her hands along his skin, to feel the muscle that defined a body that was as much eye candy as it was alluring. But it wasn't that. It was him, his strength, the way he looked at her, even the awkward way he'd picked up Lucy. Uncomfortable, yet willing to put himself out there. There was nothing about him that she didn't like. The problem was that she feared that it was more than like.

"Get it together," she muttered reaching for the soap. She had to get rid of these thoughts, her feelings—her need for him, her desire for him. But the feelings were growing with every minute they spent together.

She tried to think of the practical, the place she was in life. She tried to think of this apartment and where she would be kept safe until the trial. It was exactly like Travis had said. Here, she needed for nothing. Everything had been provided. Everything except a safe place where she could retreat from the unrelenting attraction she felt for the man assigned to protect her. She couldn't escape him. Somehow, she had to learn to deal with that attraction. She didn't know how she'd survive days trapped with him in this small apartment. For it was different than when they'd been at her place. There she'd been distracted by the nightmare that she'd so recently escaped and the phone calls that had followed. There, she'd had a bit more space. But even then, she'd been aware of him.

Without danger distracting her at every turn there was nothing to stop her awareness of the man assigned to protect her. He was no longer safely in her driveway, making cameo appearances. Now he was front and center, and she wanted him.

"Damn it," she muttered as she rinsed conditioner

from her hair and turned off the shower. Ordinarily, she loved time in the shower. She'd often spend extra minutes just letting the water wash over her. The water and the quiet time settled her mind on many occasions.

Not today.

Everything was too different. Her life was upside down and the only constant right now was Lucy.

Lucy. She hadn't taken care of her, hadn't thought of her except to release her from her carrier.

"Darn it," she muttered. What had she been thinking? But she knew what she'd been thinking, outrageous irresponsible thoughts that had no relevance here.

It was a relief to have the concern for her pet push away her inappropriate feelings for the man who was her protector. She hadn't put food out for her, nor had she unpacked the litter box. She'd been too caught up in her own needs, or more important, her need to escape her desire.

When she stepped out of the bathroom with her hair still damp and dressed in jogging pants and a sweatshirt she stopped and smiled. Lucy was standing over her bowl and eating; her water bowl was on her other side and to the right and in the far corner, she saw the litter box.

"I was going to put that in the bathroom, kind of out of sight," he said.

She looked at him with a smile. "Perfect."

Everything about him was perfect.

"Are you going to shower?" she asked.

"Not now," he replied. "I've only got part of the family fed." He laughed.

"Thank you, Travis," she said softly, taking in his sexier-than-hell physique and totally falling for his softer side. He was everything a man could be, everything she'd dreamed of and what every man, until now, had failed to be. His only downside was his damn job. Despite that, she looked at him with new appreciation and if it were possible, heightened attraction.

She wasn't sure when he'd closed the space between them. She only knew the moment when his hands were on her shoulders. The moment when heat streaked through her, seeming to curl in her belly and ignite her desire all over again as anticipation amped it all. She was pressed against him like he would never let her go. Her arms were around his neck and she didn't remember putting them there. She was caught in the moment, in the feel of his lips on hers, on the need for more and deeper. Her body easily folded into his. But her lips didn't immediately react to his kiss, it was like her brain wouldn't turn off, wouldn't allow her body to do what it knew to do instinctively. For a second and then two, she didn't react. Her lips were stiff against his. This was what she'd wanted since the first day she'd met him and none of what was happening felt real. She'd frozen in place.

"I'm sorry," he said pulling away. "That should never have happened."

"Never be sorry." Her voice sounded strange even to her own ears. There was a husky edge to it. All she knew was that she wanted more and that, if necessary, she would make it happen. That had only been a teaser. She reached up, taking his face between her two outstretched hands. His eyes met hers in an erotic, almost hypnotic way, as if the dance she now led was hers alone.

"Never," she repeated against his lips and turned the kiss from tentative to one that couldn't be stopped.

"I've never met anyone like you," he whispered against her lips.

She didn't say anything. She wanted him now. She didn't want delays and talking meant delaying.

She knew in her heart that she wanted him with everything she had as she ran her hands down his back, feeling the defined lines of a body that was sculpted through hard work and many hours at the gym. Like the man, his body was defined by will and character. It took determination to maintain such a sculpted body and she appreciated every hour he'd worked and every inch of skin that he'd toned.

"Beautiful," she murmured.

He pulled back but didn't let her go. Instead he gave her a rather quirky, possibly self-deprecating smile. "That's a first."

"No one's ever told you that before?"

"It's you who's beautiful, sweetheart."

His hand skimmed her cheek as if reluctant to take it to the level to which she'd already led him. She felt the edge of disappointment when he turned the tables, taking their passionate game back a notch.

But the disappointment lasted only seconds before he made his intentions clear.

"Come," he said softly, taking her hand and leading her to the bedroom.

In the small bedroom, she again took the lead as she sank down onto the bed and pulled him with her. She was on her side, as she slipped her hand under his T-shirt, skimming the hard-toned flesh. He let her for a minute, maybe two—the time melted away.

"Kiera." He spoke her name in a way that was as provocative as his naked skin against her hand.

She pulled his shirt off and caught her breath. She'd known he had a beautiful body and that wasn't even one of the reasons she was here with him now. She'd also fallen for the spirit that shone so beautifully from him. He was perfection—toned and hard, golden tanned skin that reflected his active job with hours spent outdoors.

Her breath caught as she ran her hand along his flesh, feeling the tingle of her palm and the tingles of anticipation that ran through her body. She wanted more.

He wasn't going to give her more. He stilled her hands in their erotic exploration.

Disappointment ran through her at the rejection and was soon masked by expectation as his hands began to run over her, making her hotter than she could stand.

"Travis..." She wanted to feel him, touch him. She wanted her skin against his.

"Let me," he said in a gravelly murmur.

He pulled her blouse over her head. The cool air gently wafting through the room seemed to kiss her skin and she shivered. But that was immediately followed by the warm, erotic touch of his lips on her neck. She shivered as the caress dipped to her shoulder.

His hand rode over her bra before he had it unfastened, as her attention was on discovering the definition of his chest, of the slim taper of his hips.

"Stop," she said and grabbed his fingers that had been caressing her breasts, kissing his fingertips. Then she sat up, turning around, her knees taking her weight as she straddled him and slipped his jeans down over his legs and off. His underwear followed.

But he hadn't stopped. He'd been making putty of her body while she was doing that. His caresses had her so hot that she could barely think.

She barely noticed as her bra fell away, she could hardly say when the rest of her clothes followed, for his fingers danced across her skin and sent sensations rising in a mercurial flood that was quickly reaching the point of unstoppable. She wanted him, and she wanted him now.

He kissed her, hot and passionately, his hand running

over her body, gently squeezing her breast. Her arms were around his neck, her lips on his as her tongue danced against his.

Even the second when he slipped on the condom was a second too long. And when he entered her it felt as if she'd been waiting for this moment, this man, all of her life. It was where she wanted to be again, and again and again.

Later, in his arms it was as if she'd never been anywhere else, as if it had always only been the two of them. As if nothing had come before. And the nightmare, for now, had slipped away, masked by the warmth of his arms and the beating of his heart against hers. For now, it was just the two of them, made safe in a world of their own.

Chapter Twenty-One

Kiera looked at her watch. The watch felt foreign for she was used to her smartphone but she'd left that behind. She grimaced. It was only ten o'clock and felt like three. They'd been in Denver for four days and this morning began their fifth full day. The days were long but the nights… She smiled wistfully. The nights were like nothing she'd ever imagined. She felt hot just thinking of the positions they'd tried and the games they'd played. The nights made the days worthwhile.

An hour had passed since Travis had left. He'd gone for milk and bread—standard supplies for their small kitchen. She wondered if there was another reason for his supposed grocery run. For, despite how intimately she knew him, there were things about him that she didn't know at all, things he kept close to the vest. The tall, strong, silent type could be utterly frustrating.

He'd been gone too long. She felt edgy, out of sorts and she didn't know why. In his absence, she was realizing that his presence was part of the reason she felt safe. She paced the room, holding Lucy for as long as the cat would tolerate it. Minutes later, she set her down and the cat paced, obviously wanting to go out. She didn't blame her. Neither of them had been outside since they'd moved to Denver. She would have loved to put a harness and lead on the cat and take her for a walk. She smiled at the thought. Her neighbors in Cheyenne had laughed when they'd first seen her walk the cat. But she was a firm believer in the fact that a cat should be no more left to roam free than a dog. She was in the minority in that thinking.

"I'm sorry, Luce, not today."

The phone that Travis had picked up for her rang. New phone, different number and still her heart jumped at the sound. She answered on the first ring.

"Where've you been?"

"You're sounding jealous, sweetheart," he said with a laugh. "Did you think I was with someone else?"

"Oh, give it a rest," she said but the disdain was missing from her voice. Instead there was a smile and a small laugh. It felt like she'd known him forever.

"Meet me in the parking lot and I'll take you for lunch," Travis said. "I think you need a break from that shoebox we've been cooped up in. Maybe a burger."

"Sounds fantastic," she replied.

She hung up with a rush of happiness. Leaving the apartment, going outside, made her feel like they'd successfully left the danger behind. Soon, everything would be alright.

TRAVIS HAD TO SMILE as he disconnected. Kiera had sounded like a long-term girlfriend or a wife. She was playing her part well. Too well. It was hard for him to pretend, for it made the growing feelings he had for her feel justified. Except they were in a fake marriage, a made-up relationship. She was going by her middle name Jenna and using his last name, Johnson. Fake or not, somewhere along the way, the relationship had become, to a certain point, real. Never would he have thought that the victim of a brutal crime would be the woman he fell for. It was neither the time nor the place for a romantic relationship. Except he didn't know if he could turn it around or if he even wanted to. She was the woman in his bed, the woman he wanted in his life, and he couldn't see himself walking away from that. The passion he felt for her had been played out every night since they'd reached the safe house. There was no going back for him and he hoped for Kiera too.

He pushed the thoughts from his mind. He was two minutes away from the place that they now called home. It was the home that they would be living in for the next few months. He couldn't imagine where their relationship would go in that amount of time. It frightened him as nothing in his life ever had.

The parking lot was just behind their apartment building and shared with two other buildings in the area. He was just about to turn in when movement caught his eye. Someone was in the lot. That wasn't unusual. Even as he hoped it was Kiera, his gut screamed that something was wrong. His foot was on the brake, as he put the vehicle in Park. Then he saw her. She had her dark hair braided as she liked to do. She'd said it kept her long hair out of her face.

Kiera.

He smiled. He was looking forward to seeing her, even though it had only been a little over an hour since he'd left. The truth was that he never tired of her optimistic chatter.

Then something else caught his eye and dread locked in his gut. She wasn't alone. He opened the door and got out, closing it as softly as he could, his eyes never leaving the scene in front of him.

Something shifted. Now he had a clear view. He

couldn't believe what he was seeing. She was struggling. Being held—against her will.

What the hell?

Kiera's hooded captor was half a foot taller than her. She was held with an arm around her neck. As the pair struggled, he could see a glint—the possibility that her attacker held a gun.

Anger boiled within him. He'd made a colossal error, thinking that she was safe. Now she was in danger because of that mistake, his mistake.

Dread raced through him.

He was moving closer, cautiously to keep his presence undetected. He was at the edge of the parking lot, hidden by shrubs. Her captor was holding her in a choke hold. She was in a position that ensured that at this distance, he couldn't get a clean shot without risking hitting Kiera. And, as he considered his options, she was being forced backward, farther away across the parking lot. He couldn't reach her in time. And he feared that if her attacker became aware of his presence and of his intent, they would as likely kill her as not. But, if she left the parking lot with her abductor, the outcome would more than likely be the same. There was no choice. He had to take her kidnapper out. But from here, he didn't have a clear shot.

He swore through clenched teeth. Despite the angry words, it was fear that raced through his veins. He wouldn't let this happen. He couldn't, not now when he'd found the woman he wanted to spend his life with, the woman he loved. Not now, when the life of the woman he loved was at stake. There was no way he could lose her now. It wasn't going to happen. Someone would die. His attention focused on her attacker. It wouldn't be Kiera.

But, despite the weapon in his hand, his assessment

of the situation wasn't optimistic. He might have a shot if he could get closer. The weight of the Glock was unforgiving in his hand, reminding him of its success rate. Except here, he had no chance of an open shot. Unless of course he could get a head shot. The only way to free her was first to get closer and second, to get Kiera out of the way. He wasn't sure how he was going to accomplish either of those things without making his presence known.

And, as he was faced with a no-win situation and no other options, the unthinkable happened. Kiera was free. He'd seen her push back as if she might have driven an elbow into her captor. It didn't matter how it had happened. It was his opportunity. With no seconds to lose, he fired, giving his position away. But her captor twisted in time and bolted away, unscathed. A shot was fired at him, as they stopped for a second to turn and shoot. The shot was wild. Then the hooded assailant was running toward a vintage van, thirty feet behind her.

Kiera was nowhere in sight.

Panic flooded him as he ran toward the scene. Where the hell was Kiera? Had she been caught in the crossfire? He couldn't lose her, not now. He was running as if his life depended on it, except he was running toward danger. For Kiera's life depended on him. And, as the soles of his sneakers hit the pavement, life and death flashed before him as he ran faster than he ever had before.

Kiera.

She lay in a heap on the pavement, like a sack of potatoes that had been dropped and left. Whether she was injured or not, he didn't know. He only bent down long enough to put his fingers on her wrist and feel her pulse. It was steady. There was no more time. She was alive and he had a window of opportunity to end this—to stop the kidnapper.

But the scene had changed in mere seconds. It was like a kaleidoscope shifting without warning. The attacker was behind the wheel of an old van, which was very like one he remembered as a kid, a camping van. It was at least twenty years old. He was too late to get a clear shot. But he could cripple the van. Maybe slow them down by taking out a tire. And then, that option was taken off the table as the van spun around and took off in a squeal of tires as the sun glinted off the worn paint, the plate smeared with dirt and unreadable, as it sped out of the parking lot.

He fell to his knees beside Kiera. She was struggling to stand with a hand on the pavement steadying herself.

"Are you hurt?"

"No." Her voice broke. "Just scraped."

He saw the quiver of her body, realized how traumatized she was and took her in his arms. She was alive and that was all he had prayed for. Still, he had a sinking feeling that he was at war and the battle he'd lost was crucial to the victor's success. He shoved the thought aside.

"Damn it," he muttered, frustrated that her kidnapper had gotten away. They'd been so close. The van was out of sight; he could only call the attack in. Still, he was angry that he couldn't do more. The anger was muted only by the knowledge that Kiera was safe. He'd succeeded in saving the one thing that was important, the one person who mattered. Her arms were around his neck, her heart was beating against his chest. He held her as if he would hold her forever. And he would, except in this situation they needed to move. Whoever had attacked her had gotten too close. The safe house was compromised.

"You're sure?" he asked.

"Shaken," she said.

"Was the van in the parking lot when you arrived?"

"I'm not sure. I didn't see it. It was so sudden. I was grabbed from behind."

Her body shook even as he held her.

"I managed to get away from her. I didn't think I could. She's unbelievably strong," Kiera said in a trembling voice against his shoulder.

Admiration ran deep in him. She had more guts than almost anyone he knew. She was emotionally steady despite escaping possible death for the second time.

"Did you see them?"

"Her," she corrected. "And no. I didn't. She was behind me." She shuddered. "I knew that voice." Her own voice shook. "I remember it the night I was kidnapped."

Travis bit off the curse that didn't come close to tamping his frustration. If Kiera was right and if the theory of a second serial killer held, that meant that the killer had again proved herself far more resourceful and as a result, deadlier, than the one they had in custody. For, she'd not only found Kiera, but she'd flown completely under the authority's radar. Again.

"Are you alright?"

Kiera's voice was soft and full of concern, yet there was determination, a thread of steel running through it.

He looked at her with disbelieving admiration. Even now, she was thinking of someone else.

"I'm fine, Kiera," he said.

But, despite the unimaginable trauma she'd been through, it wasn't over. Whoever had attacked her had gotten too close. He didn't doubt that they wanted to finish what they'd started so many days ago. It was a more tangled web than they'd thought. And the key to that web had disappeared—again.

Chapter Twenty-Two

Travis held Kiera's hand as he began to scour the area where the attack had happened, and then where the van had been. In the meantime, he didn't plan to let her out of his sight. Yet, he needed to make a thorough examination of the area.

"Travis."

He looked at her quizzically.

"I'm not two," she said but there was no censure in her tone, only a resigned edge and a half smile.

"I know," he squeezed her hand. "Call me overcautious."

"I don't need to," she said with a shaky laugh. "That quality is pretty clear."

There was nothing to say to that. He had other thoughts, bigger thoughts on his mind, like finding out who the woman was who was terrorizing Kiera. How had she tracked them to the safe house?

He was on the phone to put in a brief report, notifying James and getting a search going on the van.

"What are you thinking?" she asked as he disconnected. "How she found me?"

"Yes. I have no answers. But I know one thing. The safe house is compromised. We'll have to move."

"I'm sorry."

He stopped. He'd expected her to be frightened, angry but not sorry.

"What do you mean you're sorry?" The words were quick. He had little time. He thought of cordoning off the area, but he had no time for that. He had a matter of minutes to examine the crime scene before someone arrived to get their car, park their car—who knew what—and contaminated the area. In the process, he also had to make sure that Kiera was safe. He was afraid. Afraid that he might lose her again. He'd never felt this way. In fact, it was like he was far more traumatized than she was—far more concerned. He needed physical contact, the heat of her skin against his to reassure him that she hadn't been kidnapped or worse. He needed to imprint her skin on his to remind him that she was alive and safe and where she needed to be, at his side. Or, more appropriately, make sure that she was where he needed her to be.

"Travis, I'm alright," she assured him. "You can let go of my hand."

"Okay," he agreed for all it took was her voice to make him realize that he was overdoing it. "Stay beside me."

"Alright but, Travis. I can identify her."

Sweet mother, he thought.

"This time I saw her face more clearly. The last time wasn't enough to recognize her in a crowd, except maybe by her hair but that's easily changed. This time was different."

Elation ran through him. They'd get a sketch artist and see what they could come up with. He'd reported the attempted kidnapping only seconds ago and the FBI's forensic response team would be sent out to gather any evidence. He didn't want to leave anything to the chance of it disappearing between now and when evidence could be gathered properly. He could see nothing but a dark oil stain where the van had parked. Then, he turned and saw a small white object standing out against the dark pavement.

He went over, bent down and picked up what appeared to be a keychain tag. He turned it over. And on second glance he knew that he was looking at another kind of tag, similar to his own, a gym fob. He looked at the lettering and saw the name—All Seasons Fitness.

Kiera was right behind him. He knew that instinctively. And then the warmth of her arm brushed against his.

"What do you have?" she asked in a voice that was calm despite what she'd just been through.

"I'm not sure," he replied as he looked at her and didn't bother to mask the admiration he felt. Attacked in a parking lot, almost kidnapped and she wasn't falling apart. Of course, he thought with regret, she'd been through so much worse. Yet it worried him that she seemed so okay now. That wasn't normal.

"It could be nothing or it could be everything. What I know for sure it that it's a gym fob and it was dropped very near where the van she escaped in was parked."

"You mean it might have belonged to the woman who tried to kidnap me." Her voice shook as she said the words. "It might be a way to track her?"

"It's a long shot but it could be a clue," he replied, relieved to hear the shake in her voice. Shaking nerves was a normal reaction for what she'd gone through. He put his arm over her shoulder drawing her close, trying to offer her some comfort, some assurance that she was safe. But he'd promised that once before and failed in his promise. He doubted he'd ever forgive himself for that.

"Are you alright?" Travis asked. He couldn't believe it had happened again, and on his watch. He'd thought she was safe, that she was secure. And instead, now their cover was blown.

"Do you really think that it was hers?" Kiera asked as she looked at the key fob. "Somehow, I can't imagine someone with such a sick bent doing something as normal as going to a gym."

"I agree," he said. "But I can't discount the possibility. And you'd be surprised. Many violent offenders keep relatively normal lives."

"A front," she said.

"Exactly."

"That could put an interesting aspect to her personality."

"How so?"

"Well, if it's the case, she's concerned about her physical health and strength." She frowned and looked at him. "Am I right?"

"The hazards of her line of work," he said.

"And this might be a clue," she said looking at the fob.

There was a determined look in her eyes and he realized that she was never going to roll over and play the victim. She hadn't from the very beginning. No matter what happened she was willing to fight. He also knew that she wasn't going to do it alone. He was going to be by her side every step of the way.

He had to focus on what might be a crucial bit of evidence or nothing at all. The gym fob. It was the standard type used by most gyms to keep a record of their clients. It was used to gain entry, the bar code tracking the number of times a client appeared at the gym.

Five minutes later they were back at the apartment. She was sitting on the couch with a worried look on her face and he was punching in Serene's number.

She answered on the first ring.

"What's up?"

"Can you check a gym called All Seasons Fitness?"

"Sure. Can I ask why?" she asked.

At another time he would have found her question amusing. Now he only found it a time-consuming irritant. That aside, the question wasn't unexpected. Serene had always said that she'd love to do field work. Despite her abrupt, get-it-done manner, questions weren't unexpected. Her curiosity was boundless and sometimes he thought her talent might be wasted, confined as it was in the office.

"It's complicated," he said. "I found a key fob that may be connected to the case."

"Enough said," she responded in a voice that was still filled with curiosity.

"If you can, I need the closest gym. Also, can you give me their locations throughout Denver, if any, and if they have a presence in Wyoming. I need the exact location of the gym where this fob belongs and to who. I need that right away."

"On it," she replied. A minute later she had the specification of the gym for that key fob along with a string of other locations for the gym across the country. "One problem, I had a hard time getting any information on the account. The tag is scraped up and that's all the information I can glean from it. Nothing on the individual it might belong to."

With that resource exhausted, he disconnected from Serene and turned to Kiera. She was looking at him with interest. She'd been listening to his end of the conversation and had drawn her own conclusions. "You think there's a connection between this and the killer, to Cheyenne?"

"It's a long shot, Kiera. This might be nothing or…"

"It might be everything," she said in a soft voice that he had to strain to hear.

"I wouldn't say everything," he replied putting his arm around her shoulders. "In the meantime, are you up for a little detective work?" It was no question. For if she said no, he wasn't sure what he was going to do. What he did know was that he couldn't leave her alone. Whoever was after her, they'd found her here. They knew she was in Denver. They'd been compromised. James was already getting them another safe house. In the meantime, he needed to keep her with him.

"You think it's not safe for me to remain alone?"

"Not here," he replied. "I'm going to the gym and you're coming along. I'm not taking any chances."

"Then I'm not taking any chances either," she said.

He frowned, puzzled at what that might mean until he saw her scoop up Lucy and put her in her carrier.

"You're kidding me?"

But he knew as soon as the words were out of his mouth, that she wasn't kidding, she was deadly serious. He could see that in the frown and the sparkle in her eye that told him she was determined. That nothing was stopping her.

"Until it's safe, she's coming with us."

The way she'd looked at him, the tone of her voice, it was enough for him to know that there was no point arguing, at least for now. He was only going to the gym, whose address Serene had given him, to ask a few questions. There was no way that the cat was a problem, an annoyance but nothing more than that. He could deal with the inconvenience, as long as he knew that Kiera was safe.

"Alright," he said as if there'd ever been a choice. And in that moment, he knew. He saw the love that she had to give—the empathy she had; he knew that when this assignme

nt was over, he couldn't leave her. He was hers, if she'd have him.

SUSAN WAS CURSING under her breath. She'd failed. That was a fact she couldn't accept. She could accept it no more than she could accept the fact that Eric was in jail waiting to die. She knew that would be the outcome. There was solid evidence against him—she knew, she'd followed the case religiously.

She missed him. And she was angry that it had to be this way. But she knew that someone had to be held responsible and she'd given the authorities a fall guy for when her luck ran out. It had worked exactly as she'd planned. He'd been set up and there was not a stick of evidence that anyone else existed.

Until… She fisted one hand. Until they'd taken the last victim. If the victim hadn't escaped, all of this wouldn't have happened. Kiera had destroyed her family, destroyed her life. And for that, she deserved to die. Except, once she was dead their evidence wasn't so solid against Eric.

That didn't really matter. She was resigned to the fact that their partnership was over. It was getting stale anyway. She was ready for new blood. She passed a teenager on a bicycle. Someone like him, she thought. Not today. But one day she would go out trolling and find herself another teenager. One who she could raise, turn into a man who would make her not so much proud as satisfied.

That was all one could ask for in life.

She turned a corner. It was another mile to the rental house she'd found so recently. Another alias, another strange house. It didn't matter. What mattered was tying up the loose ends and making sure that Kiera Connell died. But first she needed to take out her bodyguard so she could get to her. She thought of working out—she was always able to think at the gym. She belonged to a franchise where she could exercise pretty much in any city she was in. She scrounged through her bag. Her key fob was gone!

"Damn," she muttered. Mentally, she retraced her steps. The key had been in her pocket. Where had she dropped it? She needed to think.

She pulled into the driveway and stepped out. A ball rolled beside her.

"Hey, throw it back," a boy shouted.

She smiled. Her attention wasn't on him but on his companion. He'd be a looker when he grew up and soon she would need another project, another partner. The thought was fleeting as were the earlier ones. She picked up the ball and hurled it, hard and true. The move was unexpected, and it knocked the second boy off balance.

"Hey, you stupid…"

The expletive was lost on her. It didn't matter what he said. One day he would be nobody but somebody's tramp. It was what this neighborhood raised up. Sadly, he would not be hers. She had more important things to consider—closure first. She couldn't move forward without that and closure had just become much more difficult.

Chapter Twenty-Three

It was an hour before Travis and Kiera left what was no longer a safe house and headed to the location of the closest All Seasons Fitness. The route took them even farther from the city center than they already were. Here, there wasn't much as far as suburban development. And as they neared the gym, it became even more barren. They passed a tract of land that looked like it might be in the process of being developed. And farther on there were patches of neglected industrial lots. It wasn't a vibrant area and he wondered why the gym had picked this location. It was definitely on the fringes of Denver. The building that housed the gym was on the edges of a lot full of scrap metal and a run-down warehouse. On the other side he could see the start of a neighborhood of box stores. To the south there were low-cost apartments and assorted housing. It was an area ripe for developers to move in to claim land that was becoming more and more valuable.

The parking lot held a handful of cars. It looked like a location that might go belly-up soon, Travis thought.

"I'll wait here," Kiera said. "There's no point in me going in."

He wasn't so sure. Not that there was any danger and not that she wouldn't wait for him. He wasn't concerned for her safety, at least not here in this moment. Despite their speculation, the fob and this gym was a long shot. It could have been sitting in the parking lot for days and likely had been, considering its state. And, as far as this parking lot, despite the neglect of the surrounding area, it wasn't one known for a high crime rate. He still hated to leave her. But he knew that she was shaken by what had happened earlier and was more comfortable sitting in the vehicle than tagging after him. She'd said so. And here, there was nothing to cause concern. Her attacker was long gone. She was safe here and he wouldn't be gone longer than a few minutes.

She gave his hand a squeeze. "I'm fine."

"Alright," he agreed. "Keep your doors locked. You've got your phone?"

"Of course," she said with a smile.

"I won't be long."

"I'll keep Lucy company," she replied.

He nodded and wondered again how she could be so darn attached to the cat. In her situation a dog would have been better. And as far as he was concerned, no pet at all would be ideal. But it wasn't his life or his choice. He pushed the thoughts from his mind. He had other things to focus on.

He looked at the key fob. There was a good chance it had no connection with her kidnapper. He guessed that it had lain in the parking lot long before the attempted abduction. There was only an off chance that it could be the clue that turned everything on its head. Of course, he hoped for that, but he knew what the odds were. He dialed down his expectations every time he'd faced a situation like this. The hope that it was the clue that cracked the case was a long shot.

As he walked toward the entrance to the gym, a couple

of young women left with bags slung over their shoulders. He stopped at the entrance and turned, watching as they got into a VW sedan and drove away. He glanced back at the SUV where Kiera sat; she caught his eye and gave him a wave.

She was fine. He was worrying unnecessarily. The attacker was long gone, that was a given. That aside, he just didn't like her out of his sight. Especially considering everything that had happened. He needed to learn to step away in the times that he could. This was one of those times. She was away from the compromised safe house; she was with him. She couldn't be any safer.

He went into the building. There, he made his way through a large area with benches and shoe racks and wound his way to the entrance on the main floor. He decided to give the fob the acid test and used it to swipe in. The buzzer sounded, freeing the gate. The young woman at the desk looked at him with a smile.

"Here for a workout?"

"No. Actually, I found this." He held out the fob.

"I see," she said. "And it let you in. Definitely belongs here, then."

She took the fob from him and ran it under the scanner. She looked at the screen and then back at him.

She frowned.

"What's wrong?"

"I'm not getting an account coming up," she said. "It's pretty banged up. I'll see if I can find something in the records."

A minute passed.

She typed some more, frowned and then pulled out a notebook from beneath the counter. She muttered as she scanned the entries and flipped a page. Finally, she looked up. "I'll make sure she gets it."

She.

That one word was like a glaring siren between them.

"Can you tell me the name, please? I'm Travis Johnson, United States Marshal." He pulled out his ID and showed it to her.

"Yes, of course. Susan Berker."

"Is there an address, phone number? Anything else—age?"

"An age—forty-two—but no address. Only a phone number." She gave him the number.

"Anything else?" he asked.

"No." She shook her head. A curl of black hair escaped one of the dozen or so braids that were held back with a purple-and-white headband.

"We don't collect data on our clients. That's all the information we have on any of them. Sorry."

"Did she have a locker here?"

"No. She didn't. And…" She looked at the computer. "She hasn't been here in a few days. I'm sorry I couldn't be of more help."

"Excuse me," a soft voice said behind him.

He turned around to face a young woman with soft, soulful eyes and a worried expression. "I heard you asking about Susan Berker. I may be able to help you."

"Do you know where she lives?" he asked hoping for the impossible.

"Yes," she said, much to his surprise.

"I was at her place on Friday." She blushed. "She took a liking to me. I've only seen her here twice. Anyway, Friday I watched her lift weights. She was amazingly fit." She paused. "When I was in the change room, she came over and asked me if I'd like to come to her place for…" She blushed. "You know."

Travis nodded. He did know. A sexual encounter, the

details of which had no relevance to what he needed to find out.

"I said yes. But when I went to the address she gave me, she wasn't the same."

"What do you mean?"

"At first everything was okay. She gave me a hug and invited me in. Then she gave me a cup of tea. There was something off about the tea. I took a sip and couldn't drink any more. She kept pushing me to drink it."

That had Travis's attention. He guessed the tea was drugged. That put a whole new spin on what type of encounter this might have been turning into.

"Was she violent at all?"

"No." She frowned. "She wasn't happy with me when I didn't drink the tea. Then, she suggested that we play a game and brought out handcuffs. I saw the handle of a gun in her pocket and that kind of freaked me out. Everything was getting beyond weird. I told her I needed to use the washroom and slipped out her side door instead."

Minutes later, with the address entered on his smartwatch, Travis thanked her and watched as she headed to the change room. He stood to the left of the desk and mulled over what it all might mean. With answers only came new possibilities as old questions ran through his mind. How had the killer found Kiera? Was it possible they'd been tracked here and if so, how?

He contacted Serene. "Can you check if Kiera has been online since she was discharged from the hospital?" He knew that she'd been warned but he also knew of her soft heart.

Minutes later he had his answer. One interaction, one message to her boss and a picture. Her soft heart had left her vulnerable, again. Although she'd been warned to stay off social media, he guessed that she hadn't thought that one private message would be a problem. A picture of a beloved pet to remind an old woman that her cat was well cared for and safe was all that was needed. Her account had been hacked and her location traced. All it had taken was a little patience and a little tech savvy to pinpoint exactly where Kiera had gone.

KIERA LOOKED AT her watch. She was tired of waiting. It was a cool day; Lucy would be fine in the SUV for a few minutes. She unlocked the door and then she reached for the door handle. She was dying of curiosity to see if Travis had found something.

Her hand was still on the handle when the door was almost ripped open, and the handle flew out of her hands. The beginning of a scream died in her throat as she faced a wild-eyed middle-aged woman with wide gray streaks running through her long black hair. She knew her, was familiar with that face. But that was of little concern. What was, was the gun in one hand and the hate in her eyes. Or at least that's what she felt as her first instinctive reaction, that and a huge knot of fear.

"Get out!" the woman demanded in a throaty, hoarse voice that could be as much male as female. Except she was definitely female. Kiera recognized her from only three hours ago. She'd tried to abduct her once in a parking lot and somehow, despite Travis's precautions, she'd found them here. Now she had her arm and was yanking her out.

There was no time to consider any of that. Kiera fought desperately. She couldn't be taken again. For she knew the face and the voice. Her second kidnapper. Fear threatened to paralyze her, but she couldn't let it. Instead, she managed to pull away and tried to shimmy across the seat, toward the driver's seat.

"Get out!" the woman repeated. The grip on her arm was painfully tight. It was unbreakable. She was being yanked toward the door despite her efforts. She could let it continue and land on her head on the pavement or do what the woman said. There was no choice; she held a gun and she held the advantage in strength and in spades.

Out of the corner of her eye she saw the entrance to the gym and hope breathed in her heart. But it was empty. Travis was nowhere in sight.

"Now!"

The woman pulled so hard that this time only a twist of her body kept her from falling headfirst onto the pavement. She scraped her knee and managed to right herself. The gun was hard in her back, reminding her of the fact that she had no choice.

"Move!" And as she took the first step toward the beat-up white van, she knew that it was over. The chance that she could escape twice, minimal, three times defied the law of—well, everything. She swallowed back the bitter taste of dread and prayed that Travis was as good as he claimed to be.

Chapter Twenty-Four

It was an ugly word and it exploded from Travis in a burst of horror and anger as he raced across the parking lot. He'd seen the struggle as he'd reached to open the door. Kiera was pushed into the driver's side of an old white van and a woman jumped in behind her. The van was taking off with a squeal of tires as he raced out of the building. He ran like he'd never run before. But it was futile. The van was out of the parking lot and speeding down a side road. His heart pounded. He couldn't believe that this had happened, again. Anger and disbelief raged through him. He'd failed. He flung open the door of his vehicle and faced the fact that she was gone. Only Kiera's cat peered at him from her carrier.

He started the SUV and had it in gear almost in one motion. He wouldn't let this happen to her, not twice in one day, not three times in a lifetime. He was peeling out of the parking lot after the van. The state of his tires and the amount of rubber he was leaving behind on the pavement was not a consideration. He couldn't believe that this could have happened again, that it was happening at all. The van was already out of sight as he left the parking lot in hot pursuit. They'd taken an intersecting road and disappeared. All he had now was the address the woman in the gym had given him. He had to hope that was where she was headed. It was all he had. He couldn't consider that he might have erroneous information.

The woman at the gym had indicated that it wasn't that far away. He put in a call to James and soon the FBI agent's voice filled the SUV.

"Wait for backup," James said. "I'm serious, Travis. The last thing you need to do is endanger yourself, as well."

"I'm sorry, James. I can't promise you that," he said as he disconnected the call. He let it ring after that. He had no further need to talk to James. James knew nothing that would help him; he had only demands that would hold him back from chasing the pair down. He knew James would get backup out. But he couldn't wait for anyone, not with Kiera again in the hands of a mad woman. Instead, he punched in the address on his GPS. Normally, he would have pulled over. Normally, he would have cared about distracted driving. The only thing that mattered was getting to Kiera in time to save her.

"Hang in there, Kiera," he muttered. He was speeding along a road that bordered an industrial section. That was the only bit of luck he'd had so far. He could speed without qualms in this area.

He couldn't lose her now. Not when he'd finally realized how much she'd come to mean to him. He took a corner so hard that the carrier slid across the seat and the cat let out a startled meow.

"Sorry," he muttered and didn't give a thought to the fact that he'd apologized to a cat. There was only one thing, one woman on his mind. He had to get to her in time. He had to stop this atrocity before it went any further.

The GPS had him at two miles away from his target. Two miles was nothing and yet it was everything. Within a minute he was in a residential area that seemed filled with worn, broken-down houses. He noticed a child's tricycle that looked like it was abandoned in the front yard, left to rust in the elements. Again, they were fleeting thoughts. He had to slow down—tricycles meant kids, families. His hands ached from a too-hard grip on the wheel. He was taking a chance. He didn't know if this was where they were headed. He only hoped he was right. If he was wrong, Kiera could be lost to him. He tried to push the thought from his mind. But the doubt kept returning and the dread of it made his stomach ache and his head pound with fear. The killer could be taking her anywhere. The address the woman had given him may or may not have been her home. It could be anything— belong to anyone.

The sprawl of Denver was unending. Even here, on the edges of industrial commerce, where the majority of the houses were neglected, a crane loomed in the distance. He was a few blocks away. He took another corner too fast, and this time he offered no apology when the cat's carrier slid again across the seat of the SUV.

Another block, the housing seemed even worse, more dilapidated, more neglected. Another kid's bicycle lay across the sidewalk like it was dropped and forgotten. A block ahead and three houses in, he stopped one house back from a worn brick bungalow. It was the kind built thirty years ago in a boom that had poor construction married to high demand and an influx of lower-middle-class workers. The house had seen better days. He turned off the engine. And, despite the urgency that was knotting his gut, he sat and took account of the situation. The white van was in the driveway. There was no one on the street. All was quiet which was good and also disconcerting. A door slammed, followed by a dog's bark.

His gun was out, kept to his side where it wasn't the first thing anyone might see of him. He closed the door in a controlled move, so the door clicked shut. Everything was silent. But they hadn't been there that long. They couldn't be. He was only minutes behind them.

He moved cautiously, bent over as he went up the drive on the side of the van farthest from the house. He peered in a window of the vehicle. Nothing. As he already guessed, the van was empty. A crumpled sweater lay on the backseat and a potato chip wrapper was on the floor. Otherwise there was no dirt or dust. It looked like it had been recently cleaned.

He wondered at that. Despite the van's age and environment, it had been kept meticulously clean. His answer was only speculation and something he pushed to the back of his thoughts. But, if she was continuing their murderous spree, even without her partner, then this was probably the vehicle she was doing it in. And cleaning up any evidence as she went. He didn't take his mind to the darker place of what that evidence might be.

He rounded the van, keeping low. He couldn't go to the back or front without alerting Kiera's kidnapper. He assessed as he went. He looked for weak points—places that he could use to his advantage and get in unnoticed, unheard. The basement windows were the old pullout-with-a-lever kind. Easy to break into. He could squeeze into the basement in a pinch. It was a relief to focus on moving forward and not on what Kiera might be enduring now, at this moment.

Within seconds he was in. He dropped onto an empty concrete floor. He pressed his back against the concrete wall as he listened for noises. His heart pounded like it never had before as he feared that despite his reaction time, he might still be too late. The fear came from the fact that he could sense the emptiness. There was no life down here. He was alone. It was what he expected, and what he hoped not to find, not to be too late. He pulled out his pocket flashlight, shining it in a close range around him before spreading the beam out. There was nothing but one big concrete space. There was no development, no collection of stuff except for a trio of cardboard boxes. It was as if it was only temporary housing and not someone's home. There was shuffling upstairs, followed by a woman's cry.

He moved to the foot of the stairs. He wanted to run up and crash the party, but he couldn't. Waiting was going to kill him. He'd recognize that voice anywhere.

Kiera.

He held himself back. He couldn't burst onto the main floor. He had his gun at the ready, his breathing steady as he listened. He was trying to pinpoint the location of the sound. He heard a bang. Then, there was a sound like something or someone being dragged. He guessed they were not near the basement stairs, the sound seeming deeper, near the back of the house. He had nothing but guesses but he couldn't take the chance of wasting more time. He couldn't wait another second for every bit of time was working against Kiera. With his gun ready to fire on a second's notice he cautiously moved up the stairs. He felt with his feet in the dark, to avoid creaks that might warn of his presence. The basement door was closed. He put an ear to the door. There was silence on the other side. He couldn't pinpoint where Kiera's kidnapper was, where Kiera was—he had no visual. He had to take the chance.

He pushed the door quietly open. Nothing. He eased himself through the doorway, moving stealthily but quickly. He was at the junction of the kitchen and a hallway that led in two different directions. Left to a living area and right to what he guessed would be the bedrooms. He had his gun in both hands and the weapon led the way. He hung at the edge of the doorway. Time seemed to stand still and then he saw her. Just like that his eyes met Kiera's and his heart sank to see her bound and gagged, sitting on an old-style metal-legged kitchen chair. Before he could make a move in her direction, another movement had him turning to see a gun leveled at him. A middle-aged woman with an overtanned and wrinkled face glared at him but it was the gun in her hands that had his attention. He ducked and rolled away from Kiera, taking the trajectory of any bullet meant for him, away from her.

He came up on one knee in midroll. He was ready to shoot, to kill, to get Kiera the hell out of there. Her captor had retreated through the doorway that led to the living room. It wasn't a clean shot, but he took it anyway. She ducked behind the sofa. He moved forward and stopped.

A shot to his left took out a chunk of the doorframe. He ducked down as she jumped up and ran for the front door. He had a glimpse of her long black hair as she hunkered down. He didn't have a clear shot and took out his own chunk of drywall. Hunched and still moving, she turned and fired at him again. Plaster rained down on him; his vision blurred from the bits that got in his eye. He shot anyway, trying to take her out before she escaped or at best cause an injury. But she was out the door and gone.

He moved to the doorway; she was already in her van and taking off. He backtracked and checked the other two rooms of the house—empty.

"Kiera," he said, torn between chasing her kidnapper or making sure she was safe. There wasn't a choice.

He needed to get Kiera out of here. Hopefully, his reinforcements had arrived. And they could take care of the woman who'd abducted her. She was the woman who might well be an accomplice to multiple murders. She'd meet her own judge and jury once the feds had her. In the meantime, the feds had his location both from his phone call to James and even without, they could easily track his phone. The latter he knew they would do despite his call, in case something changed. He put in a quick call to James to let him that Kiera's kidnapper had taken off in the white van he'd reported earlier. He didn't wait for much of a response before disconnecting.

He knelt down in front of Kiera. She looked at him with her heart in her eyes and fright in the trembling of her hands.

"It'll be okay—I'll get you out of here."

She nodded and there wasn't a trace of doubt in her demeanor.

Within seconds he had the rope untied, the cloth out of her mouth.

"Let's go," he said taking her arm. There was no time for explanation, no time for comfort. He needed her out of here and safe.

"My legs won't stop shaking," she said with a quiver in her voice.

His arm was around her waist as he helped her down a small flight of stairs and out the back door. He got her into the SUV. As he was walking around the vehicle he was on the phone, giving James more detail on what had occurred. He hung up after getting a promise that reinforcements were on the way. Seconds later, he shoved the phone in his pocket and was in the driver's seat backing the SUV out and away.

"Where are we going?" she asked.

"FBI headquarters here in Denver," he replied. "The man I report to, James, will meet us there."

She didn't say anything. He took her silence as acceptance or shock. He might need to get her medical attention. Although she didn't look like she'd been physically hurt.

"Are you okay?"

"Are you asking do I need a doctor?" she said in a soft voice that was unlike her. "If you are, I'm physically fine," she said with a hint of steel in her voice. "I don't need a doctor. I need this creep caught."

Silence fell between them, but he expected that. She'd been through hell and survived imminent death. He didn't expect her to say much, not now when she was still in shock.

He was only two blocks away from the house where she'd been held when he saw the white van. It was coming at them from the opposite direction. It was driving erratically, weaving and on the wrong side of the road.

"Hell," he muttered as he swung the vehicle around with a screech of tires. "Hang on," he said as he took a corner too sharp and headed away from the van and toward where he knew there was an unpopulated area. A crash from behind and the impact sent the SUV flying. He had to manhandle the steering wheel to keep the vehicle on course.

He cursed under his breath. And regretted it immediately as he glanced at Kiera. She didn't seem to notice. It was almost like she had checked out. Considering everything she had gone through, that made sense. The van hit them again. There was no way he needed this nut job trying to drive her van up his rear in an area like this. He swung left heading for a more industrialized area. There, where litter and empty lots quickly began to replace housing, there was no danger to others. It was a few blocks north. He'd seen it coming in and soon he was there, in a run-down and seemingly abandoned industrial area. Rusted machinery replaced houses. He put his foot on the gas. With the residential housing behind him, he turned the steering wheel as hard as he could, swinging the SUV completely around before bringing it to a sudden halt.

"Get down," he said to Kiera. "And no matter what happens, stay down."

She nodded. Her face was pale, her lips were set. But she looked more determined than frightened.

He was out of the SUV, his gun in hand as the white van screeched to a halt in front of them and the woman jumped out. This was the first time he'd gotten a close look at her. In the parking lot, it had been more distant. And her eyes had never met his. Now she met him head-on. There was evil in those eyes or maybe that was just fantasy. He was too far away to tell. He needed to focus on reality, on her and what he might need to do. After all, this was the woman who had threatened Kiera's life not once but twice—and if Kiera's story checked out, three times.

"I'm a US marshal. Drop your weapon," he ordered.

She kept walking toward him.

He had seconds to make the assessment. Seconds to take in the face of evil framed by long black hair streaked with gray. She looked like she'd been through hell and that had defined her face. He blew the thoughts off—this wasn't the time.

"Stop and drop your weapon or I'll shoot."

She hesitated and kept coming. The thought ran through his mind that she wanted him to kill her. Was it possible? Was she deliberately defying his order so that he could take her out? Whatever her reasons, she was giving him no choice with her weapon still aimed at him.

"Drop it!"

In the seconds that followed everything seemed eerily silent. She was still walking toward him. The distance between them quickly diminished from a hundred feet to fifty. He could give no more chances considering the fact that she hadn't even lowered her gun. He fired. And she fell. It seemed too simple, too easy. Just like that, it was over.

He heard a car door slam and next thing he knew Kiera was in his arms. He held her as if he would never let her go. And in his mind, he knew that if she agreed that's exactly what would happen.

Chapter Twenty-Five

Three days later

"If I could imagine hell, that would be it," James said as they left the state prison.

Travis couldn't agree more. He knew that James wasn't referring to the prison but to the life Eric had been subjected to during his teenage years. Except it was hard to feel any sympathy. For one, they both agreed that what Eric had admitted was more of an attempt to shift blame and gain sympathy. If they didn't know who Eric was and what he'd become, it might have worked. As it was, the charming smile that he offered them only added a creepy feel to the end of a sordid tale. Eric was smart enough to end his tale of woe at the point in the story where he was still the victim. For they all knew that there was a point beyond that when the victim became the perpetrator. At first, charming Eric would admit to none of that. He stuck to his younger years, his own nightmare years. There was no better word to describe the environment that had shaped Eric Solomon. What he'd done to dozens of women was a different matter. When he spoke of the murders, it was always Susan's fault. He claimed that Susan had led the way. He wouldn't have done it, if Susan hadn't made him.

"That relationship was so twisted I don't think anyone could have made it up," James said. "It'll be one for the history books. A murderous woman prepping a teenage boy to be her partner for her future killing spree." He shook his head. "Unbelievable. Thank goodness these cases are rare. Hope we never have another."

"I'm with you on that," Travis said. "They both gave me the creeps."

In the end, despite a rough start, they'd gotten a full confession from Eric Solomon. On hearing that his partner, Susan Berker, was dead, his entire demeanor had changed. The tough-as-nails killer turned soft and frightened in seconds. In a way, he'd almost retreated to a juvenile phase. More important, he'd been willing to talk.

"He was her boy toy," Travis said referring to the killer behind bars and the now-dead woman. "And then he was so much more than that. I think given time, Eric could have become like her, maybe recruited his own team of killers."

"If she'd let him, that would mean stealing some of her power," James said practically. "In the end, he was every bit as guilty as she. They were in it together. What matters is he gave a full confession and neither of them will harm another woman again."

Travis nodded. It was a tragic, haunting story and it was also an ugly story. It began with the tragedy and the teenage runaway, and it ended ugly when a woman took him in and taught him her own dark cravings. Susan had raised him from a teenager to a man and escalated their crimes as he matured. But she'd always led the show. She'd been who they should have been after from the beginning. But she'd fooled them all by putting Eric out in front, and literally brainwashing him to believe that he was leading the show. It had all been a lie. He'd been positioned, just in case she needed someone to take the fall.

THEY'D BEEN BACK in Cheyenne for a week. In that time Kiera hadn't been alone. Neither of them had wanted that. Travis wanted her with him, at his side. He wanted to wake up in the morning and know that she was there, safe. Most of all he wanted her, just flat out wanted her. So, he stayed at her condo.

It was late. But they'd been up watching a movie. He had a break between assignments and she hadn't returned to work yet. Without work the next morning, they'd lost track of time. He'd treated her with kid gloves since the rescue, holding her until she fell asleep, being by her side—watching out for her. It was all he could do to help her get over the nightmare.

"I'm going back to work next week. Don't try and convince me otherwise," she said abruptly.

"Actually, I was wondering what took you so long," he said with a serious edge to his voice.

"Really?"

"Let's say that I'm not surprised," he said with a laugh. "And I'm not about to dissuade you. Just one ground rule, I'll drive you or you take a cab if I'm not available."

"Alright," she said.

He looked at her, surprised. That wasn't like Kiera. "What's up?"

"You'll see," she said with a laugh and rolled over and gave him a kiss that became a hot exploration before he pulled away.

"No," she said as she brought him back, her hand sliding down his belly and farther. He could feel himself get hard. He couldn't help it. Even a light touch, even a hint of what was to come had him hard and ready. Their clothes were gone in seconds. That's the way it always was—kid gloves didn't seem to make it to the bedroom. He put a hand over hers and with his other hand he began to run erotic patterns around her nipple, first one and then the other.

"Travis."

He silenced her with a kiss. They had all the time in the world and he was going to use that to his advantage. He ran his hand down, over her flat stomach, to the juncture of her thighs.

She inhaled sharply.

But her hands were soon working some magic of their own.

"Kiera," he began.

"I'm with you," she said hoarsely. "Let's do this."

He smiled. In another situation, he would have outright laughed. But that was Kiera's language of love. Or at least that was the way he thought of it. She had an odd way of expressing herself in the bedroom. He'd discovered that the first time he'd made love to her. And she'd repeated the odd phrase *let's do this* every time since. Now, he just considered it part of the norm. Life with Kiera would be challenging and passionate. Those thoughts disappeared as he focused on one thing and one woman.

"Travis," she said hoarsely. There was a pleading tone to her voice. He knew what she wanted. He knew what he wanted. They both wanted the same thing.

His other hand was still on her nipple as soon he had her body convulsing toward him. When he reached for a condom and entered her long minutes later it was only to the murmur of her voice and her promises of never-ending love. A man couldn't ask for more.

Epilogue

Cheyenne, Wyoming
Four months later

"I can't believe it's over," Kiera said.

Travis nodded. It had only been a week since Kiera had given her testimony and considering the atrocity of the crimes and their extent, the trial had gone quickly. While Eric Solomon had never repeated the admissions of guilt he'd revealed while awaiting trial, what they had was enough. He was now awaiting sentencing.

"Do you think it would have been different for Eric if he hadn't met Susan?" Kiera looked at him with a frown. "Was he flawed from the beginning, always meant to become a twisted killer?"

"I don't know. What I do know is that in the end, he was a grown man who had allowed himself to be molded into a sadistic killer. The boy was long gone," Travis said. The man would pay for what he had done, he thought.

In the last month, he'd insisted that Kiera take a self-defense class. His work made him well aware that anything could happen. When she'd completed that she'd informed him that she was setting up a safe-ride program so that the workers in care homes throughout the city would be safe going home late at night or early in the morning. And she was thinking ahead, thinking that something might be set up through the city for other women who worked late or early hours and might not be able to afford a cab, but needed a worry-free ride home.

Some things had changed but some had stayed the same. Despite all her plans, Kiera still insisted that she had time to volunteer at the shelter. He'd been hesitant about that and as a result he found himself volunteering right beside her. He'd soon discovered that it wasn't dangerous, that the people there were disadvantaged, exactly as she'd told him. The saying she'd tossed at him had held true—you couldn't paint everyone with the same brush.

"What are you thinking about?" Travis asked. "About the trial?"

She looked up at him. "No," she said. "I'm done with that."

This time, he believed her. For they'd already talked about everything. They didn't need to talk about it again. It was over and eventually she'd be able to put the experience on a shelf labeled Nightmare. That's what it was, a nightmare that was over. A nightmare that would never happen again, not to her—and if he could help it, not to any other woman.

Travis's arm was over her shoulders and her skin was soft against his lips as he kissed her neck and whispered in her ear. "What do you have planned for tonight?"

She looked up at him with the hint of the smile. "I heard a certain sexy marshal was going to cook me supper and woo me over dessert."

"Woo?" he said with a laugh. "Where did you dig that word up?"

A meow from the carrier had her smiling up at him. "Lucy was a hit," she said.

He smiled. This week she'd not just taken Lucy to the

care home but she'd stopped at the local animal shelter and taken two other cats from there for their first visit. It was impossible to keep up with her. He'd never met a woman more motivated to help others, or a woman more able to do it.

"How'd it go?"

"There were half a dozen residents who love cats and each had had more than one in their lifetime. Lucy had more than her share of attention. And the other two cats turned out to be perfectly behaved. They'll definitely be back." She looked at him. "There's something else…"

His smile dropped. Something else he'd learned in the weeks that they'd dated, in the weeks since he'd asked her to marry him and since she'd said yes and made him happier than he'd ever been in his life—that when she said there was something else, he should run for cover.

The most recent time she'd said that phrase meant that she thought that Lucy needed company. Fortunately, she'd solved that by taking the cat to work more frequently. The time before that she'd thought that she should meet his family.

That had meant him spending an afternoon grilling and entertaining his folks and assorted relatives. Not that he didn't love seeing them, it was just that Kiera didn't believe in waiting on anything. He had forty-eight hours' notice. And it had been a pile of work—worth it in the end. Still, he cringed when she began with something that meant she had an idea, usually something she was passionate about. He'd learned that there was a lot she was passionate about. Some of it he appreciated, like how she kept their bed and their sex life imaginatively hot. Although, he admitted, it wasn't as if he didn't do his share. Their bedroom was on fire most nights.

He waited wondering what it was this time.

"I'd like to add to the guest list."

He nodded. That seemed fairly straightforward. He'd asked her to marry him in a traditional way—he'd gotten down on one knee, ring in hand. Now they'd agreed on a small wedding in the backyard of the condo they'd bought only a month ago. The wedding was in three weeks and invitations to the fifty invited guests had just gone out; another would be no problem at all.

"Ann, one of the seniors at the home, would like to come. We could get a disabled bus for them."

"Them?" he asked wondering when Ann had become plural.

"Well, if Ann wants to go, I know there'll be others. I thought it would only be fair to invite them all."

"Twenty," he said.

"And the workers."

He did the mental math. Forty people, as the numbers of staff when you factored shifts equaled the residents.

She smiled, as if sensing where his thoughts were going. "They won't all come."

"But most will," he said with a resigned smile. "And some are already invited," he said thinking of a couple of workers who were Kiera's friends.

"Possibly," she agreed. "But there are a few volunteers, as well."

"Whatever you want, sweetheart."

He wondered if the guest list was yet solid or if there'd be more. And he imagined there would be more surprises after the wedding. Her generous spirit was only part of what he loved about her. He leaned over and kissed her again, and this time the kiss was hot and passionate as he held nothing back.

"Forever and always," she said against his lips. "I love you, Travis Johnson."

"Back at you," he said. In his life he'd never thought he'd meet her. The woman who would love him passionately and unconditionally. He'd thanked the heavens on more than one occasion that her horrific experience hadn't changed her. She was the love of his life and now that he had found her, he knew that he'd never let her go.

He couldn't wait for the wedding. It was going to be one hell of a day: family, friends, a busload of seniors and one very pampered cat. And, with three weeks to go, he never knew who or what might be added to the list. It wasn't going to be the beautiful, everything-is-coordinated kind of wedding. He imagined the wedding might well reflect the life to come. He couldn't see himself ever getting bored from that day forward.

"Always and forever," he whispered against her lips as he kissed her long and hard, sealing a pact that he knew could be nothing less than forever.

* * * * *

HER DETECTIVE'S
SECRET INTENT

TARA TAYLOR QUINN

For Drake Winchester, the brand-new little guy for whom I'd give my life.

I am so thankful you're in the world.

Chapter One

Detective Tad Newberry—currently on leave from the police force in Charlotte, North Carolina—walked into the pediatric examining room in Santa Raquel, California, forcing a big smile. In addition to the exam table, some plastic chairs, a counter with drawers and glass containers of various cotton supplies, the room boasted zoo animal prints in shades of blue and green. The floor was gray tile, eight-inch squares, and the lights were ceiling-mounted fluorescent bulbs.

After giving his surroundings a quick glance, cataloging every aspect out of habit, he focused on the seven-year-old boy dressed in jeans and a yellow T-shirt sitting on the edge of the table, swinging one of his legs back and forth—a nervous gesture, Tad surmised, not a happy or excited one.

The boy's mother, in jeans and a navy hoodie with a light green shirt underneath, stood beside him, hand about an inch behind her son on the paper-covered cushioned mat. As though she was ready to grab him at any moment. Tad glanced at her, having been prepared ahead of time, and still felt bile rise in his throat when he saw the red-and-purple puffiness taking up one entire side of her face.

Marie Williams wanted to be kept safe from her

abusive husband, but she didn't want to press charges against him. She truly believed that once they got through their divorce, she'd be fine; he'd no longer be a risk to her. At the same time, she didn't want to ruin his life.

Tad had heard the entire report. He didn't get it. But it wasn't his place to judge.

"Danny, this is Tad, the man I told you about," said the third woman in the room that sunny April morning, the one Tad knew and by whose invitation he was there. Pediatric physician's assistant Miranda Blake could easily steal Tad's entire focus if he allowed himself to relax. Something he could never do around the lovely brunette.

"Hi, Danny," he said, his gaze on the boy as he approached. "I hear you've had a bit of a tough time." Pulling up a chair, not the doctor's stool Miranda had pushed his way, he settled half a foot below the boy's eye level.

Chin almost to his chest, Danny nodded.

The boy, a beefy little guy, though not overweight, wouldn't meet his eyes.

Tad had never been married, had no kids, but he knew human nature. Leaning down, he tried to catch the boy's look. Danny turned to his mother, burying his face in her chest.

"Tad's not going to hurt you, Danny." Miranda's tone not only held authority, but that incredible sense of nurturing that had captivated him from the first time he'd heard her speak. The woman radiated caring. Not that he required it for himself.

He had other matters on his mind. Giving all his attention to the boy, he made a guess. "I'm not mad at you, son. You aren't in any kind of trouble. And I'm not a doctor or anyone in the doctor business. I'm not here to look at your injuries. I'm just here to talk."

He was there as part of an individualized plan designed by the High Risk Team in Santa Raquel—a team comprised of various working professionals who shared domestic violence information with the single goal of preventing domestic violence deaths. The current plan had been devised to protect Danny and his mother. His role, strictly volunteer, was to keep an eye on Danny anytime the boy wasn't with his mother or teachers. Specifically he was to do multiple drive-bys a day to see that all was well. Miranda, a frequent visiting member of the High Risk Team, had come up with the idea for the two of them, Danny and him, to actually meet. Her reasoning—if Danny knew him and knew he was close by, he'd be more apt to reach out if he was in trouble—was sound.

But it was only going to work if he could get Danny to trust him.

Not an easy feat for a man who'd had few dealings with kids until recently, and a little boy who'd had his trust in men destroyed by the one man he should've been able to count on—his father.

The boy didn't turn to him as Tad spoke. Danny's tennis-shoe-clad heel on his good leg was no longer lightly bumping the table. It hung completely still beside the leg he could hardly move.

That caught Tad's attention.

Danny didn't have to know or like Tad for Tad to keep an eye on him. But maybe he could do more here than help prevent further physical harm. Maybe he could help the little guy heal in other ways.

As someone who was attempting to heal himself, he found that the idea appealed to him.

"Ladies, if you'll please forgive any impropriety and feel free to turn your heads, I'd like to show Danny something on my leg." He tore the paper from the top half of the exam table, wrapped it around his waist. Then, looking at Miranda and Danny's mother for an okay and receiving nods, he awkwardly—using one hand, as though performing some kind of comic routine—managed to get his loose-fitting jeans undone and dropped them to the floor. He was a boxers kind of guy, dark blue that day, and even without the paper all pertinent parts were fully covered. It wasn't the pertinent parts that were relevant right now.

Pulling the paper up on his waist, high enough to expose his upper thigh or, more accurately, the jagged, puffy and discolored seven-inch scar slashing across the front and around the side of his leg, he said, "It doesn't look as gross now as it did. And yours won't look nearly as bad because it was a straight line, and that makes a big difference."

Standing there with his pants around his ankles, Tad might have felt embarrassed. Or inappropriate. All he felt was that he had to reach this little guy on his own level. Dealing with what was foremost on the boy's mind.

And it appeared to be working. Danny, having sat upright, was staring at the scar. Boys must still be somewhat the way he remembered himself being—fascinated by gross things.

"I fell, too," he said, leaving out the part about the explosion that had sent him flying. Just like he didn't mention that he knew Danny had been running from his enraged father when he'd tripped and impaled his leg on a plant stake in the backyard.

"It hurt like heck to move my leg for a while," he

added, because he knew Danny had months of rehab ahead of him as the muscle that had been cut in his upper thigh healed. "I go to the gym at least twice a day, three days a week, to make it stronger, and now I can walk without any limp at all." Unless he was overtired. Then a tilted gait came back to remind him of what he'd done.

He moved his leg enough to flex the muscle, which made the scar jump. "See, it works just fine now."

Glancing briefly at the two women on either side of the exam table, he asked if they'd mind turning around so he could get himself put back together. He did so in record time, except for tucking in the blue cotton polo shirt. Going strictly on instincts, as he watched the boy watching him, he lifted his shirt a few inches, showing Danny his back. "I got burned, too," he told the boy. "So, you see, I'm just here as a guy who got hurt, wanting to help another guy who got hurt."

Danny didn't speak. But he didn't turn away, either. He watched Tad. And maybe that was enough.

"What happened?" Danny's mother asked. Tad looked up and saw the compassion on her face. He chose to think of it as that, as opposed to pity, which he could not abide. He'd made a stupid choice.

But it had brought the best result possible—saving a little girl's life. Something that might have been done with less damage—to himself and others—if he'd followed protocol by waiting for the hostage negotiators and SWAT to arrive.

Or little Lola could have been hurt far worse than the minimal bruising she'd suffered from Tad's falling too heavily on her when he dived to protect her body from the blast.

"A guy was angry with me," he said, vetting his

words carefully with Danny in mind. "He had something that didn't belong to him and when I went to get it back, he…hurt me."

Lola's's father had rigged a homemade bomb to go off if anyone pushed open the antiques store's back office door, behind which he held the child hostage. Unaware that the girl was there, Tad had gone to the business, not yet open for the day, to question him about some things he'd been selling in his shop. Stolen things.

"Did they get the bad guy?" Danny's voice was surprisingly strong as he looked Tad in the eye.

"Yes, they did," he said. The man had been prepared to kill himself and his daughter, too, apparently, rather than face arrest. The child wasn't supposed to have been there. Her mother, who'd had shared custody of her and no idea that her soon to be ex-husband was in any kind of trouble, had dropped her off with him because she'd been called into work.

He'd dragged her into the back office, telling Tad and his partner to get out or he'd hurt her…

"So, anyway, if you want to come to the gym with me sometime, have your mom call me," Tad said. Marie Williams already had his cell number. "You might see me hanging out, too," he added. "You can talk to me or not, your choice. I just wanted you to know who I am and that I'll be around."

Danny said nothing more. Tad took the boy's choice at face value and left the room.

Miranda didn't hurry through the rest of her appointment with Danny and Marie Williams, but as soon as they were out of the exam room, she finished the last of her administrative responsibilities for the day. Then she was out the back door of the clinic where she worked for pediatric specialist Dr. Max Bennet, and heading to her car.

The white Chevy Equinox blended in with a million other similar-sized and -shaped white mini SUVs, which was why it fit her perfectly. She had an hour before she had to pick Ethan up, and Tad Newberry was waiting for her at a coffee shop halfway between her office and the school.

The balmy sixty-five-degree weather was perfect for her white cardigan and cartoon-spattered scrubs.

Heart pounding in an entirely new way, she drove five miles over the speed limit, switching lanes when necessary to weave past slower cars. All the while, she thought about those minutes in the exam room with the off-duty, out-of-state detective who'd shown up at a High Risk Team meeting six weeks before.

He'd dropped his pants. The move had been calculated, out of the ordinary, a somewhat shocking attempt to get Danny's attention—and build trust, too. She understood that. Admired the hell out of it, actually. He'd known that Danny felt particularly vulnerable, so he'd made himself seem—and perhaps feel—just as vulnerable.

All of that aside…she'd peeked. She shouldn't have. It had been completely unprofessional. Completely, 100 percent out of character. And she'd done it. Seen…a lot.

Blue boxers. Dark hair on legs that were tight and firm. Even now, driving to discuss the afternoon's event and how it played into the care plan the High Risk Team had developed to prevent Devon Williams from ever hurting Marie or their son again, she shied away from thinking about the ugly facts of life, and found herself picturing those jeans pooled around Tad's ankles instead.

Watching him with a very definite feminine reaction.

Wrong. It was just plain wrong of her. On so many levels.

Parking in the coffeehouse lot, seeing Tad already inside sitting at a table for two with a couple of steaming cups in front of him, she pulled herself together. Having very private fantasies was bad enough; allowing them to invade the space she shared with others was prohibited.

Period.

"That went well."

Miranda heard the sarcasm in Tad's greeting as she sat down. She felt herself immediately tuning into him.

"It did go well," she assured him. "I can't tell you what was said after you left—" he knew about her legal restrictions with regard to medical confidentiality "—but it went well. Marie asked me to tell you thanks. She feels much better knowing that you'll be adding extra drive-bys to the ones the police are already going to be doing."

Tad's next comment was angry. "Devon Williams should be in jail."

"Agreed. But since he hasn't actually physically hurt anyone—that we can prove—since Marie dropped those charges against him last year, and still insists that her current bruising comes from a fall, there's not a lot the prosecutor can do."

He knew that, too. Santa Raquel's assistant prosecutor was a new member of the High Risk Team.

"At least the judge granted her restraining order," Miranda added, wishing she was only thinking about the woman who'd just left her office. Truth was, she saw more abused children and their mothers than she'd like.

She suspected that at least five of the fifty families she saw on a regular basis dealt with that insidious disease.

"And you know as well as I do that those orders are ignored more than forty percent of the time in these kinds of cases," Tad countered.

And often victims invited the abuser back into their lives. Yeah, Miranda knew that, too. Which was part of what made the situation that much more frustrating.

Unknown to Tad, though, she wasn't just aware that it happened, she understood *how* it happened. In the most personal way possible.

"I don't get it," he said. "How can a woman marry a man after he's already abused her? It makes no sense to me."

He was talking about Marie, whose boyfriend had hit her a couple of times back in high school. Once, he'd also shoved her up to a wall with his hands around her neck.

He'd also loved and adored her when no one else had, making her vulnerable to him, and he'd scared her into thinking that marrying him was the only way to keep herself safe. And happy.

The incidents had been isolated. She'd understood that he hadn't been himself for various reasons—usually involving alcohol. But she'd believed him when he promised never to lift a hand to her again when she'd dropped charges against him the previous year.

She'd hoped.

Right up until he'd been thundering behind their son, trying to catch up to him to give him a spanking for not packing a suitcase as he'd instructed. He'd panicked Danny, who tore out of their house so fast he'd tripped and fallen on a stake she'd just put up in her garden.

"Our job is to follow the safety plan and do what

we can to see that Devon doesn't have a chance to hurt either of them again," she reminded him. "You heard Chantel. As soon as he violates that protection order, his ass is in jail."

Chantel Harris Fairbanks, a Santa Raquel detective on the High Risk Team, might be married to a millionaire banker and live in one of the town's most impressive mansions, but she was all cop when it came to her job. Even to the point of keeping her previous small apartment in town so she didn't ever lose sight of who she was and what she knew. So she wouldn't ever forget where she came from.

Miranda envied her—being able to keep her old self alive. Nothing about Miranda's former self lived on with her. Not even her name.

"And then the prosecutor can call for a dangerousness hearing," she said. It wasn't technically called that in California, but it meant that if Devon was arrested and was considered a danger, he could be held without bail.

The man had threatened to kill his wife. Twice in the past eight weeks since she'd told him she wanted a divorce. He'd actually told her how he'd dispose of her body. He'd been drinking again. And quit his job. When he'd gone to their house the week before to insist that Danny come to his apartment and stay with him for the weekend, the boy suffered his fall. And then he'd blamed his wife for that, too, taking his anger out on her face. On a list of nineteen risk factors pointing to the danger of death, Devon Williams ranked at thirteen. It only took eight for the case to be referred to the High Risk Team.

Marie was changing her routine, her working hours. Her newly married sister and brother-in-law were mov-

ing in with her for a while. She and Danny were going
to stay around crowds when they went out. She wouldn't
be going to her usual church, grocery store or hair-
dresser. Not until Devon was under control.

It wasn't just to keep her and Danny safe, but because she truly wanted Devon to succeed. She wanted
him to come through this. To find a good life for himself. To be happy.

She loved him.

And that was the part Miranda got that many others,
most others, couldn't. How a heart could still feel love
for someone who beat them.

The secrets she held close inside kept her emotions
in check during that afternoon coffee with Tad Newberry though she desperately wanted to talk to him
about them.

She couldn't. She wouldn't.

No matter how badly she hurt.

Ethan's life depended on her keeping her secrets to
herself.

And the second she'd given birth to him, his life had
become more important to her than her own.

Chapter Two

Miranda was fine right up until Tad walked her out to her car. His, an older-model black SUV, was parked down the street. He'd bought it used, he'd told her during one of their coffee sessions with a couple of others after a High Risk Team meeting. He was only in town for a year while he was on leave from his detective job back east. Michigan, she figured. That was where he'd said he'd grown up. A suburb of Detroit.

He was using his time off, he'd said, to learn more about the High Risk Team with the thought that he could help implement a version of it in his hometown.

Other than that, she knew so little about him.

And wanted to know much more.

Almost as soon as they drew up to her car, that vision of his pants around his ankles hit her again—like there was some kind of mental video player attached to her vehicle. Maybe she should buy a new car; maybe that would fulfill her wants, if not her needs. The inane thought came and went.

To be replaced by a sense of panic. Tad was different from any man she'd ever known. The way she responded to him was different.

But she couldn't be an honest half of a partnership. Any partnership.

When she'd run, the idea of having a lover, or a boyfriend, or anything along the lines of a male companion, hadn't even entered her mind. She spent two years in a women's shelter outside of Santa Raquel before moving to the city four years ago, and it hadn't been a problem since.

But now it was.

She didn't want to live the rest of her life alone.

Did she have a choice?

"Ethan's, what, six?" Tad asked, startling her out of her reverie.

"Yeah," she said. She must be tired. Working too hard. Spending too much time identifying with Marie.

The woman's case spoke to her on a personal level more than most. Probably because of Danny.

"He's in the first grade," she said, forcing herself back into the moment. Tad had met Ethan twice. Brief introductions both times.

After the second time, her son had teased her, saying she should go out on a date with Tad. They'd run into Tad at the grocery store one evening and she'd stopped to chat. Ethan's reaction had surprised her. She'd never thought of her son as thinking about her personal situation. She was Mom. That was all.

But maybe it had been her son's grinning little push that was her problem here. Was he missing a male figure in his life? Had that prompted his teasing remarks?

And was her current fascination with Tad merely reaction to that?

Just thoughts that Ethan's comment had put in her head?

Yeah, if life were that simple.

"Could I take the two of you out to dinner?" Tad asked, while her mind continued to fly off course.

Her stomach flip-flopped. She almost dropped her keys. Struggling to find a way to say no when what she wanted to do was ask how soon, she said nothing as he continued. "I'd like to spend some time with Ethan, since he's so close to Danny's age. Just to observe. It would help me get a better feel for things. In case I ever need to speak with Danny again. Dropping my drawers was a little extreme and I don't think it would work a second time."

She nodded, trying to school her features—feeling she managed, at best, a cross between a frown and the grin that was trying to break through.

Dinner was all he'd asked. To observe her son. No big deal.

And complicated as hell.

"I'm sorry about that, by the way," he said when her feelings continued to flay around inside. "The dropping of the pants thing. And thank you for not mentioning it."

"It was unconventional, not to mention unexpected, but I thought the idea was brilliant," Miranda spoke the complete truth. Probably because she could. Her tongue needed to fly along with her brain waves, but most of them weren't traveling in the same atmosphere.

"And... I like you in blue."

What? Had she lost her mind? *I like you in blue?*

Oh my God. She was flirting with him?

Dinner was definitely out.

"I'll keep that in mind." Tad's tone was so easygoing, her raging blood settled a little. A lot, actually. She felt completely put in her place.

Which meant that... "Dinner would be fine," she said, sane again. He needed her help with Danny. And Ethan would be with her. She was clearheaded every second of every day that she was with her son. She was all he had in the world, and she was conscious of that fact first and foremost. "When?"

"Tonight? Unless you have other plans? I'm already on Danny duty and am eager to get what help I can so I don't blow it with him."

His "duty" entailed a few minutes a few times a day, driving by wherever the boy was, according to the schedule Marie would text him each week, with nightly changes if there were any. Marie could call or text him if she got in a bind. Miranda knew, because she'd been sitting at the table when the plan was devised. She knew what every participant in the plan was doing—including their medical office. They were all on alert. And careful to make sure that only handpicked personnel were alone with Danny any time he was in for treatment.

That brought her back to this morning. Tad in the examining room.

She was dying to know what had happened to him in the past. The details.

But she didn't ask. Instead, she agreed to meet him at Uncle Bob's, a hamburger diner on the beach with a sandbox for kids to play in, at six.

She didn't have time to stand around and chat right now. Ethan would be out of school in ten minutes, and unlike Marie, she didn't have a team of experts watching out for her son.

Because, unlike Marie, she'd escaped her past. She was safe.

As long as she kept her mouth shut.

IN HIS RENTED apartment with a view of the ocean, Tad took a long, hot shower, turning the water to cold when the heat failed to relax him.

He was supposed to be recovering, and in the interim, doing a man he respected a favor as a private way of repenting for the wrong turn his career had taken. He was supposed to be getting his shit together, not losing it over the woman he'd been sent to find.

Pulling on a pair of black jeans one size larger than he normally wore, to accommodate the thigh that was still painful sometimes and had a tendency to swell, he took a T-shirt from the top dresser drawer. He followed that with a button-down white shirt from the closet, careful to line up the empty hanger in its proper place, and yanked open the little side drawer on the dresser for a pair of socks.

The arrangements in his apartment weren't all as he would've preferred them, but the place had come furnished and that was what he cared about. His clothes back home in North Carolina were in the house he'd purchased the previous year in an upper-middle-class neighborhood.

Reaching inside one of the socks he'd retrieved, he pulled out the burner phone that had traveled across the country with him six weeks before. Fridays were call days. North Carolina was three hours ahead of California and he didn't know how late he'd be out.

"Chief O'Connor." North Carolina's newly appointed state chief fire marshal always picked up on the first ring.

"Just checking in, sir. I told you she's working as a physician's assistant in a pediatric office and I had a chance to see her in action today. Like you, she's not afraid to think outside the box. I think you'd be proud of her." Maybe it made him a bit of a wuss that he always tried to find a way to comfort the older man during these conversations, to make him feel less alone.

But if it wasn't for Chief O'Connor's quick thinking

at a scene that hadn't even required his presence, Tad and a couple of his fellow officers could well be dead.

"And the boy?"

"Other than those two brief meetings I told you about, I haven't seen him." He'd meant to tell the chief about his dinner engagement. Didn't.

Wondered why the hell not.

He didn't like the predicament he was putting himself in.

"Yeah, best to go slowly." The older man's voice came firmly over the wire. "The last thing I want to do is tip her off…"

"I was going to ask you about that. With her ex gone, is there really a need for this secrecy?"

The question had been bothering him for a while, particularly since the Marie Williams case had sprung up that week. Miranda Blake, real name Dana O'Connor, had no way of knowing that she was out of danger. Surely she'd welcome the knowledge—and the chance to go home to the friends and family she'd been forced to leave behind when she'd changed her identity to escape a madman.

"I know my daughter, young man. This is *my* operation. My call. Dana doesn't like change. She doesn't like having her world upended. If she's happy there, in that life, I want to know about it. I'll need to figure that into how I approach her. And I'll need to figure out how I might fit into that life so I can make the transition easier for her."

Okay. Sure. But…

"Her ex…he might have family," the chief went on. "Someone who'd want contact with the boy. I've got a guy looking into that. Good investigator. I need to be absolutely certain, before I have any contact with her, even through you, that I'm not putting her in any danger or in any way making her life more difficult than it's already been. I'm not going to put my selfish need to have her back in my life ahead of her needs."

Nodding, respecting the man all over again, Tad wandered into the living room, to the window looking out toward the Pacific Ocean two streets in the distance.

"I'd be more than happy to check into any in-law family that might exist." His detective skills had earned him the right to make his own calls on the job—until he'd made a call based as much on emotion as skill, one that was so far from protocol that he'd almost gotten himself and others killed.

He'd saved the girl, though.

There was that. Always that. Every single time he relived the horror of that morning three months before.

"Forgive me for being set in my ways, but I learned a long time ago not to put all my eggs in one basket," Chief O'Connor said. "I have someone else following that lead. Someone who has no idea that you, or your job for me, even exist. I'm paying you to use your highly touted skills to find my daughter and grandson, which you've done, and to be fully focused there, to keep me informed. It's been years since I've had any word of my daughter and these weekly calls of ours…well, let's just say they're the best moments I've had in all those years. And I won't risk having any searches for her coming from the town in which she lives. There can't be anything connecting our investigation too close to her."

Tad nodded, understanding. He'd succeeded in tracking her down, via the access he continued to have to law enforcement databases of various kinds. He'd learned a great deal about her.

But he still wasn't satisfied. He didn't even know

Dana's ex's name. The cop in him needed to be certain, especially after witnessing from the sidelines the Devon Williams nightmare that week, that he was working with complete and accurate information.

In his entire career, he'd always double-checked facts himself. He wasn't a "rely on others" kind of guy.

"You're one hundred percent certain her ex is dead." His voice could be intimidating, too, when necessary.

"Yes. I have definitive proof. I give you my word on that."

Then there was nothing more to be said. He'd accepted the job. He respected the man. Hell, all of North Carolina respected him if such a thing was possible. Heroes didn't come around every day, and when they did, they didn't shine as often or as brightly as Brian O'Connor had. Again and again, over the course of a lifetime, he'd risked his life, and volunteered his time, too, to save and enrich the lives of those in his community. And his state.

If he'd grown a little eccentric over the years, Tad figured that was his right.

He owed him the news that Tad would be having dinner with his grandson in a few minutes. That he could call back later with a report the chief had been waiting for.

He owed him. And he reneged.

He'd figure that one out later.

First, he had a date to keep.

In a manner of speaking…

Chapter Three

"So…are we like…on a thing?" Ethan glanced between Miranda and Tad, his eyes rimmed by the dark-framed glasses he'd chosen because he thought they resembled the ones worn by Clark Kent, Superman's alter ego—the Superman of earlier days that Miranda had shared with him. If her son had been grinning, teasing, she might have been able to brush the moment aside.

"No." She reined in the rest of the blurted response that almost came out, changing it to a mildly firm denial. "I told you, Tad and I work together."

They'd just ordered their burgers, and all three had glasses of soda with straws sitting in front of them. The minutes they'd be waiting until their food was delivered suddenly seemed interminable.

"On a committee." Ethan nodded. "You said you work together on a committee." He looked at Tad. "Do you like my mom?"

"Of course I like your mom. Why would I eat dinner with someone I didn't like?"

"Exactly," Ethan said, pushing his glasses back up his nose. "Do you know the game *Zoo Attack*?"

Breathing a sigh of relief, Miranda took a sip of soda and let her son have at Tad. After all, the off-duty detective had asked for the meeting to get to know Ethan better.

"No. I don't know that game," Tad said, elbows resting on the arms of his chair.

"It's really cool," Ethan said. "You get to be in the zoo, taking care of animals, and then danger comes and you have to solve puzzles to save the animals…"

As she listened to her son's in-depth and enthusiastic description of his favorite video game, Miranda wanted to relax. To enjoy the moment.

There was much to enjoy. In spite of everything, she'd raised a boy who was confident enough, trusting and outgoing enough, to take charge of a conversation with a virtual stranger. A male stranger.

And she was sitting with a man who, in another lifetime, might have been someone she'd feel passionate about. Watching Tad as he seemed to give Ethan his full focus, engaging in conversation as though the conversation mattered to him, she felt again that peculiar bounce of joy inside, as though she was with someone special.

"I'd like that," Tad said, and she tuned back in, realizing, too late, that Ethan had just invited him to their house over the weekend to learn how to play *Zoo Attack* in two-player mode, which meant that they'd be racing against each other to get puzzles solved to save animals.

Tad *couldn't* come to their home. Ethan would ask, "Why not?" She could hear his voice inside her head, asking. No simple or credible-sounding reply presented itself. But the answer was unequivocal. He could not come into their home.

Home was her safe place. The only space she could be herself without fear…

"Jimmy from school is over there, Mom. Can I go play in the sandbox?"

She had to nod. To let him go. She wanted him to be independent. But she did not want, at that moment, to be left alone with a man who was getting way too far into her.

"This isn't a thing," she said as soon as her son was out of hearing range.

He nodded. "I know."

"It can't be a thing." She was sounding like an idiot. Had to get herself together.

"You seeing someone, then?" Tad asked easily. She didn't like how his total attention was suddenly on her. Eyeing her with some kind of understanding or something. She didn't like how warm that made her feel.

She was hot enough already.

Tempted to lie to him, she hesitated. Santa Raquel wasn't all that big. And her son's conversational filters were sadly untrustworthy.

"No, I'm not seeing anyone."

"Coming off a bad breakup?"

That might work. Except that Ethan seemed unusually focused on her dating situation. Could it be that now that he'd started school, he was noticing they were missing a part of their family? Was he needing that male figure in his life? Granted, there'd be plenty of kids without dads at his school and some without mothers. But many had other family, siblings, aunts and uncles, grandparents, cousins…

She'd known this time of reckoning would come. Had worried about it to no avail—figuring she'd have to let the future take care of itself on that one.

"No, I'm not coming off a breakup." She prayed he'd leave it there. Or that their food would arrive and Ethan, who always seemed to know when there were goods to shove in his mouth, would descend upon them once again.

When Tad glanced in the direction of the boys playing outside the sandbox with little cars Jimmy must have brought, Miranda guessed he was seeking a way out of their awkward moment, as well.

He looked so good, his dark hair, thickening shadow of whisker growth and brown eyes giving him a rakish aura in an oh-so-masculine form. She knew his legs were lean and strong. She'd seen them firsthand…and was he still wearing his blue boxers? Or had he showered since she'd seen him at work that morning?

"So you don't date at all, or is it just me?"

So much for the idea that he was looking for an out. He'd just slammed them right smack-dab in the middle of *too complicated*.

"You're only here for your leave." She blurted what immediately came to mind, as though that explained everything.

He didn't argue, and again she hoped she was off the hook. At least with him.

She still had to deal with herself and her deepening feelings for this man. And she would. She'd only known him six weeks. It wasn't like it would take a lifetime to get him out of her system.

Unless… What if, for the first time in her life, she was really and truly falling for someone? As in…the real thing?

Of course, that didn't matter in the long run. Her life wasn't open to *real*. Her goal was to give Ethan a chance at a good life, a life of his own. He wouldn't have to lie to anyone he met in his future. The life he lived now was his only known reality.

"You don't ever talk about Ethan's dad."

"It's not like we've had a lot of time for private conversation."

Not entirely true. They'd fallen into the habit of having coffee after every High Risk Team meeting. At the moment, as the team became a stronger force in Santa Raquel and the surrounding communities, they were meeting weekly. And she'd volunteered to go in place of her employer, Max, every single week.

Partially because of Tad, she was ashamed to admit to herself.

"Ethan's father is dead." She dropped it out of the blue. There were some truths she could tell, at least in part. Clearly everyone would realize Ethan had had a father. "He died before Ethan was born."

With no name, there'd be no chance to find a death record. To trace her to any young man who'd died during their last year of college. Or even to trace her to a particular college. Or to identify a girl who'd been friends with a boy who died. No way to discover who she really was.

"Wow. I'm so sorry."

So was she. Jeff had been one of the greatest guys she'd ever known, and he hadn't deserved the blows life had dealt him. "I miss him every day," she said, allowing one more piece of her real self through. Jeff had been the only one who ever knew the whole truth about her. The only one in her past life she'd told.

"That had to be hell, to lose him and be pregnant at the same time."

She shrugged. "You'd think so, but being pregnant, knowing that Ethan was part of him, and a new part of me, a whole new life... I'm sure that's what saved me." In more ways than Tad could ever imagine. If it hadn't been for Ethan she might never have had the strength, the clarity of mind, to get away.

Jeff, who'd been a foster kid, had believed in her, trusted her to raise his child—even knowing the truth about her life.

Tad's brows had been drawing closer together as she talked, giving Miranda the impression that she was coming on too heavy. She was suddenly aware that she wasn't in their own little cocoon, with her son playing safely in the distance. Instead, she—and Tad—were in a noisy diner with Friday-night happiness going on all around them.

She tried to think of a way to change the subject.

But she didn't manage before he asked, "How long did you know him? Ethan's father?"

"Four years."

"You were obviously close..."

Obviously. She'd had his son. Though not close in the way Tad would assume. "We were best friends." And that was all they'd been. Friends. Not a "thing." *Best friends.* With Ethan, she'd given her best friend his dying wish—a child who would always be part of him, carrying on a life that had been cut far too short.

"How long were you married?"

Her mind went blank. What did she say? Would the truth give her away somehow? She tried to think of everything she'd been told. By the lawyers who helped her legally change her identity. By Lila and Sara at The Lemonade Stand, the unique women's shelter in town that had founded the High Risk Team. Everything she'd heard during her time with the team about the ways information could travel to the wrong people.

Marriage meant records.

The haze of panic receded. "We weren't married."

She told him the truth. No one could find what didn't exist. She was safe.

And no one knew that Jeff was Ethan's father. She hadn't named him on the original North Carolina birth certificate, and their new identities certainly didn't name him. To begin with, she'd kept the secret to protect Jeff from her father's wrath; Jeff had so little time to live and she couldn't bear the thought of bringing more tension into his life. And when he'd died before Ethan was born…she'd just kept the secret.

Tad sat back, adjusted his knife on the table. Took a sip from his straw. What was he thinking?

Surely, in today's world, he didn't respect her less for having a baby outside of marriage?

She wanted to tell him that they knew Jeff was dying. That they'd decided not to marry so there couldn't be any legal chance she'd be held responsible for any of his medical bills.

It seemed to be taking an inordinately long time for their dinner to arrive. But then, it was Friday night and the place was packed. Ethan had glanced their way a few times, but was still happily engaged with Jimmy. The two were in the sandbox now, trying to plow roads for their cars around the other children playing there.

All in all, less than ten minutes had passed. It just seemed like forever.

"I haven't dated anyone since Ethan was born." She had to tell Tad something that would get them out of this awkward mess. "A conscious choice I've made." For reasons she'd never tell him, no matter how badly she wished she could.

Tad wasn't asking her out, but she was guaranteeing that he wouldn't, although her heart was clamoring for a chance to see what life with him would be like.

Even if just for the months he was there.

Because it was only for however many months he'd be there. There'd be no risk of having to live a whole life of lying to him... It would be a question of living in the moment for the few months he was around.

Which her heart was telling her would be better than nothing.

It would be great, actually, to have such a memory to take with her into the future. To hold close. A good secret to combat all the bad ones...

"In honor of his father?"

"No. But..." She searched for an explanation that would shut him down. And yet she didn't allow anything remotely credible to surface. Would it be so wrong to get to know him better? He wouldn't be staying, had an entire life, an important job, to return to.

"I haven't had the time," she finally said, wondering if leaving a door open to him was emotional suicide. Or maybe it was the only personal bliss she'd know in her life. "I'm a single mother, and not all men want to take that on. Added to that, until last year I was in school full-time and working, too." While becoming a PA had only taken two years of additional schooling, she'd been unable to take her college degree with her and had to earn that all over again, too. Thankfully she'd been able to test out of more than two years of that, having to pay just for the class equivalent, not actually retake the classes.

"So now that you're fully accredited and have more time..."

Oh, God. Was he going to ask her out? Flooded with heat, she felt she was possessed by something stronger than herself—this desire to get closer and closer to him.

She shrugged when he didn't complete his sentence.

He nodded, as though her lack of a definitive "no" was interesting.

She smiled.

He nodded again.

And dinner was served.

WHAT IN THE *hell was he doing?*

Walking the dark streets of Santa Raquel sometime after midnight, hunched in his department-issued coat with the collar turned up, Tad warded off the thirty-something-degree chill of California ocean air. He'd intended to head over two blocks to the beach, but had only gone one and then turned, choosing sidewalk instead of sand.

If it hadn't been for dinner arriving, he was pretty sure he would've asked out his client's daughter. The subject of his current job.

If he ever hoped to work in law enforcement in North Carolina again, he couldn't be pissing off the state's chief fire marshal—a man with more connections, both law enforcement and political, than Tad could ever hope to have.

Did he hope to go back to some form of law enforcement work?

He'd quit his job.

The department had refused to accept his resignation, so officially, he was on administrative leave for the year they'd agreed upon.

Time for the department to fully investigate, review and further discuss his last case or, more accurately, the one really bad decision he'd made in a career of relatively great ones. His solved-cases record was better than that of anyone in the department.

They wanted to keep him on.

They also wanted him to take some time to get his head on straight. To show them that he'd be able to regain any trust he'd lost with his peers.

But…did he hope to go back?

Noting that he'd crossed the fourth block with at least two largely cracked cement pieces, he thought about Santa Raquel's finances. Figured fixing cracks in the sidewalk of a seasonal tourist town should be on the radar. Someone could trip. Fall. Sue the municipal government.

The town, which was more resort-like than not, didn't seem to be hurting for money. Based on the number of large, well-maintained homes in the area, he supposed the town was doing just fine. Sidewalks didn't last forever. They cracked.

And a detective was bound to make one bad decision in his lifetime.

But what if he made two?

What if he asked out the daughter of his client? A woman he'd been hired to find? And keep watch over?

In his line of work, there'd been more than one occasion when the means justified the end.

Would that be the case here? Could he convince the chief that dating his daughter, casually, of course, was the best way to stick close to her? To spend time with her son?

And what about Miranda? What right did he have to mess with her life? As if she hadn't already been through enough?

She knew he was only in town for a matter of months. Their conversation that evening had gone in an unexpected—and much more personal—direction. Thanks to Ethan, who'd put the simmering tension between him and Miranda right out there.

So…if she was potentially interested in spending more time with him, say, one-on-one, knowing that it couldn't last long, would he be wrong to give it to her?

The thin line he walked was going to trip him up. He knew it.

Just as he'd known, when he made the choice to barge into that back office without waiting for SWAT and the hostage negotiators to arrive, assess the situation and do their jobs, that he was crossing a line.

He'd practically gotten himself killed. Had put every other officer on the scene at risk.

But he'd saved the girl.

It always came back to that for him.

He'd saved the girl.

Could he help save Miranda and Ethan, too?

Chapter Four

The thing about having a kid was that you couldn't just make up your mind about something and count on having it happen. When Ethan was a baby, Miranda was in charge. Or at least she'd felt she was. From the twos on, though, he'd been pretty adamant about having his own say in anything and everything, and she'd had to rethink her approach. A process that seemed to happen every day since. She had to foster his independence. And above all, keep him safe. So her mantra had become that if it didn't involve his safety or health, he could decide—which, in their world, meant he could have his way.

If it did have any kind of impact on his well-being, they did it her way. The line used to be clearly delineated. At least in her mind. And her boy had been good about accepting her decisions once she explained them to him.

That Saturday after dinner with Tad, Ethan woke up talking about *Zoo Attack*, about a new animal kingdom he was going to create and then show Tad. He'd said he'd come to their house and so, to Ethan, that meant he was coming.

Her moment to object to that idea had already gone. Tad's, too, apparently, at least according to her son.

And Miranda was left with the task of explaining to her son that sometimes adults said things they didn't really mean.

A concept he wasn't willing to accept.

"Call him, Mom, he'll come, you'll see," Ethan said for the umpteenth time that morning. Standing in a pile of dark clothes on the kitchen floor by the laundry room, he kicked up a sock to emphasize his point.

She threw the last pair of white underwear in the dryer and bent to pick up their darks before he kicked them any farther.

"He's a grown man, Ethan," she told her son. "I'm sure he's got more important things to do than play video games this weekend."

As soon as she heard the words, she wanted to retract them. Implying that her son's engagements weren't important wasn't what she'd intended to say.

"He said he *wanted* to," Ethan insisted.

But *she* didn't want him in her home. Hadn't let any man visit since she'd made the first home for her and Ethan.

Their little rented cottage was her haven. She didn't have to be as careful there to hide her secrets. Or to worry that someone might be watching her. Looking for her. Or him. Keeping their home private was paramount to her peace of mind, to her belief that she could keep them safe.

None of which she could explain to her son.

"Call him, Mom, please? You'll see, he'll come."

She took her time loading the washing machine. Pouring the soap. Filling the little ball dispenser with fabric softener and dropping that in. What should she tell Ethan?

She'd promised herself that Ethan wasn't going to grow up in fear. Jeff had trusted her with his son.

Turning, she saw him still standing there, his big blue eyes imploring her.

"Okay," she heard herself say. "You go put the clean sheets on your bed like I showed you, and I'll call him."

"Yes!" Ethan jumped up in the air and he was off.

Miranda had a knot in her gut as she pulled her cell out of her pocket. Tad was in her contacts, as were all the High Risk Team members.

She'd told Ethan she'd call.

"Miranda?" He picked up on the first ring. "Everything okay?"

"Of course," she lied, listening to the washer fill with water, the clinking of a metal button on a pair of white pants in the dryer. "Why wouldn't it be?"

"Just making sure." He didn't really sound worried and she figured he was merely being polite—not reading her mind.

"I'm sorry to bother you, but I told Ethan I'd call. He hasn't let up on me all morning about that *Attack* game."

"He's going to give me my key to the animals."

"You were being nice to him, and I appreciate that, but I'll get you out of it. The thing is, he wasn't going to take no for an answer until I called." So she did. Because she didn't have a logical reason to give Ethan that he'd understand.

"I don't want out of it." His response sent her heart thudding. "I meant to solidify something before we split up last night and forgot."

"You don't have to come here and play video games with my kid," she told him, hoping her chuckle sounded genuinely unconcerned. Although it wasn't.

"I want to…unless you have some reason for *not* wanting me to?"

What was it with these two guys? It was like they were plotting together against her. One she loved with all her being, and the other…she really liked Tad.

She was intrigued. Curious. She wanted to explore further.

Her life didn't support that choice.

At least not long-term.

"I mean, I know you're busy and—"

"I'm on leave," he reminded her with a laconic drawl. "In a town where I know very few people. Other than my daily exercises, High Risk Team meetings and checking on Danny, my day is free."

Looking around at the fairly large but still cozy living and kitchen area—all open so she didn't have to worry about anyone lurking in a corner—she tried to figure out what to do. This was why she didn't let people get too close, why the only "friends" she had were at work or The Lemonade Stand.

Not only did it keep life manageable, safe, but she'd also realized that if she ever had to run again, having no one close, in any sense, would make it easier. Less complicated.

"Or we can do it another time," Tad said, his tone as relaxed as always. Hard to believe this laid-back guy was a decorated detective. In her experience with law enforcement personnel—and she had a lot of it growing up with her fire chief father—first responders were an intense bunch. Work hard, play hard.

Get mad just as hard, at least in her father's case.

"I'm cleaning house this morning," she said. What

was she going to say? What reason could she give for not having him over that didn't make her sound crazy?

She'd been told, during her identity-change counseling, to stick to the truth as much as possible to avoid mistakes. But the truth was, there was no real reason she couldn't have people over. Her counselors had also told her to live life as normally as possible.

She was...scared.

"But it's not a big place," she continued. Hallway, bath and the two bedrooms left to sweep and mop. "If... How does one sound?"

He offered to bring lunch.

She tried to demur, but failed. He offered Mexican. She and Ethan loved Mexican.

Clicking off her phone after giving him their order, she didn't feel hungry at all. In fact, she felt nauseous.

She pushed through the sensation. Picked up her broom. Took nice, even strokes down the hall.

She'd invited Tad Newberry further into their lives.

She was doing this for Ethan.

Who better than a man who was already protecting another little boy from domestic abuse to have around her son? To help fill the male void she'd been noticing. He'd been talking about Jimmy's father a lot.

The decision to have Tad around, just for a short time, was a good one for Ethan, she told herself as she finished with their small bathroom and moved into her bedroom, listening to her son sing a goofy rendition of a kid's song blaring from the player she'd given him for Christmas.

But she could only have Tad around if she made absolutely sure that Ethan understood that the detective was only in town for a while. And kept herself constantly apprised of that fact, as well.

TAD BARELY HAD a few seconds inside the quaint little cottage not far from the beach. The front door opened to him and he was whisked through a living area and out to a back patio before he'd even had a chance to say hello.

The place smelled like disinfectant mixed with lavender. The brown leather sectional had a patched spot on one arm; the recliner and coffee and end tables were dust-free but mismatched. Wall art, generic. Floors, ceramic tile with throw rugs. Nothing out of place. Kitchen off to the left, complete with a top-of-the-cupboard microwave and built-in dishwasher. All spotless.

"Hey, Mr. Newberry! Mom says we can play on my Windows tablet, which is so cool 'cause we can pass it back and forth, instead of the computer where I usually have to play." From a too-big chair at an outdoor table for four, the blue-eyed boy stared up at him, his brown hair shaggy and cute, not quite long enough to hang in his eyes. As before, he was in blue jeans and a T-shirt.

"That's *Detective* Newberry," Miranda said from right behind Tad. "What would you like to drink?"

Ethan had a glass half filled with red liquid in front of him, and a hint of pink mustache to go with it.

"I've got tea, bottled water or punch."

He chose the tea and, taking a seat on the eight-by-eight tiled patio, dug into the bag of food he'd brought, dispensing items according to the orders placed—burrito minus the sauce for Ethan, taco salad with sour cream for his mother. From the family-run taco joint down by the beach.

Tad went with the house specialty. Tacos.

"That's Mom's seat." Ethan's voice was softer than normal as he unwrapped his burrito.

Tad's fingers slowed on his own paper-covered food. "What?"

"You're in Mom's seat. She always sits there, and if I do, she makes me move."

He'd taken the seat with his back to the wall of the house. He could see the door to the living area, and the small, nicely manicured, walled-in yard, too.

That was probably why she'd chosen it as her own. A woman who'd been scared enough to take on a new identity could experience a need to keep her back to the wall.

As quickly as possible, he moved, managing to re-settle himself before Miranda returned.

Maybe what he was doing—ingratiating himself into their worlds—was duplicitous. Making him untrust-worthy. He liked Miranda. Really liked her. More than he could remember ever liking a woman in such a short time. He couldn't tell her the truth about his mission, not yet, anyway. Not until he knew that his news wouldn't ruin her life again, upend her and cause her to start all over. From scratch. With a six-year-old child.

On the contrary, his goal was to make her life better. To take away her fear. To let her know she could live safely, free of the past.

He just wasn't at liberty to do that yet.

And didn't even want to think about it until he knew for certain that her ex-husband was dead. If he believed her, the man had been dead for years, but it wasn't like she was going to tell the truth. She'd told him the re-hearsed story attached to her assumed identity. But as much as he trusted her father—his current employer—

he wasn't a man who relied on the word of others. You never knew if someone had been given falsified proof.

He'd seen enough twists and turns in his career to make him wary. As recently as his last case—a man putting his own daughter's life at stake, preparing to kill the child while she stood there in his arms, crying...

"You need to watch me do this, Mr. Newberry," Ethan's young voice brought Tad fully back to the moment just as Miranda came outside with their drinks. "That way you'll learn for when you do your own and our animals can fight sometimes, too."

"Sorry, I had to brew more tea," Miranda said on the tail end of Ethan's words. "I added extra ice."

Which was quickly melting.

"And it's Detective Newberry, Ethan," she said again, sitting in her chair, unfolding a napkin and dropping it in her son's lap.

"I'd prefer Tad, if that's okay with you," he told her. Who knew if he was going to stay on as a detective when his leave was through?

Although he couldn't see himself being happy doing anything else.

"Is it okay, Mom? Can I call him Tad?"

Looking over the boy's head, Tad smiled at her.

She smiled back.

And lunch was good.

Chapter Five

It clearly wasn't Tad Newberry's first video game.

Nor had it seemed in any way a hardship for him to have his time engaged with Ethan's *Zoo Attack*. Miranda had lunch cleared away, the laundry finished, the dishwasher emptied, and brownies made before either of them seemed to notice that she'd left the table on the patio.

She only had one Saturday off a month and had to make it count—couldn't just sit and watch the "boys" play—but she caught herself smiling a few times as she heard the deep male voice coinciding with her son's little-boy enthusiasm. And heard the friendly dissension as they disagreed and ended up in battle. She was grinning from ear to ear as her son, with compassion in his voice, claimed victory.

She wasn't smiling so much that evening, though, when Ethan hit her up with a request to take his training wheels off his bike the next day.

"I'm done being a baby, Mom," he told her, his brow furrowed as he gazed at her with those big blue eyes. Jeff's eyes. She'd never been able to resist Jeff's pleading. And the man definitely lived on in his son. "I'm the only kid in first grade with training wheels."

The fact that she'd known it was time didn't make her

acquiescence any easier. Training wheels were a safety net. Miranda was already living more boldly than was comfortable for her. More risks weren't on her agenda.

You didn't get to choose when life handed you challenges. Jeff had certainly been proof of that. He'd been her best friend. The only person on earth who knew about the beatings. He'd been her rock. And when life had turned on him, she'd been his rock, too.

Which was why, at nine o'clock Sunday morning, after breakfast and dishes and making beds and washing up—and anything else she could come up with to stall—she was outside on the driveway of her rented haven, a screwdriver in hand, granting Jeff's son's request.

Jeff couldn't do it, so she had to.

Somehow. She'd had the wheels put on at the store two years earlier when she'd bought Ethan the bike for Christmas. They must have used a frickin' machine.

"Can't you do it, Mom?" Ethan asked, squatting down beside her and pushing his glasses up on his nose, as though staring at her incompetence would somehow get the baby wheels off his bike.

"Of course I can," she told him. "I just need some oil." Or some of whatever it was that helped loosen bolts. She'd read about it…

"Maybe you could call Tad," he said. "Or I can if you gimme the phone."

She wished it was the first—or even the fifth—time she'd heard the detective's name since he'd left the day before. But no…all afternoon, all night long, even that morning, Ethan had been talking about him.

Warning bells had been sounding so loudly in her head, it was a wonder she'd even heard her son's request—let alone finished the grocery and necessary-item shopping and then managed a trip to the movie theater with her son, followed by the fried chicken that he loved.

Trying to get his mind off Tad Newberry.

Didn't help that even when Ethan wasn't mentioning the guy, Miranda's mind was jabbering on about him.

Bike on its side, with the back wheel lodged between her feet, Miranda sat in the driveway and pulled on the wrench with all her might. It slipped off the bolt and slammed her in the knee.

She didn't swear out loud. Nor did she give up. She couldn't afford to do that. She stood. "Let's go." She got her keys and headed over to her car. Driver's license and credit card were already in the back pocket of her jeans.

She never stepped outside without the means to run, to take Ethan and disappear, if she had to.

"We going to take the bike back?" Ethan asked as she wheeled the bike out of their way.

"Nope, we're going to the store to find something to help us with the bolts." She'd look up on her phone what she needed when they got to the hardware store.

"Or we could just call Tad," Ethan said, under his breath and with a touch of belligerence.

She let that go, choosing her battles. "Tad's only going to be in town for a while, Ethan. I told you that already. We can be friends with him, but we can't ask for his help with stuff."

How did you explain life's hideous complications to a six-year-old?

"You could date him and then maybe he'd stay around."

"No, he wouldn't." *Make no mistake about that, little man.* Because she couldn't let him stay.

"He has an important job to go back to as soon as he's healed enough. Remember?"

Looking out the window he could barely see over, Ethan crossed his arms and harrumphed. "He doesn't act like he's hurt."

"Well, he is."

"How do you know?" She could feel those blue eyes turned on her.

"I'm a doctor's assistant. I'm trained to know." She almost mentioned having seen Tad's scars, but thought better of it. Remembering Danny's reaction, she couldn't take a chance that Ethan would share the seven-year-old's seeming fascination and ask to see for himself.

"But we can be friends," he said.

"Yep." Somewhere over the past six weeks, maybe even during the past twenty-four hours, she'd made that choice.

More like, it had been made for her.

"But we just can't need him, like, to fix my bike, right?"

"Right."

"Okay. Cool."

TAD HAD BEEN burning with anger after he watched Miranda and Ethan drive away from their house. Livid with a man who'd father a child and then beat that boy's mother to the point that she'd feared for her life and run away from everyone she'd ever known or loved just to keep the two of them safe.

Anyone she'd have called to help when she couldn't get the training wheels off her son's bike had been left behind in North Carolina.

He hoped to God that Miranda's husband really was dead, as the chief had testified. For Miranda and Ethan's safety, first and foremost. And, he had to admit, so he wasn't tempted to go for the man's throat himself.

Out of his car, he was halfway between it and the bike leaning up against Miranda's little house, intending to get those training wheels off and be out of sight before she got back, when he stopped.

He was still a newcomer to the world of domestic violence, but after six weeks as an honorary member of the High Risk Team, in addition to all the reading he'd been doing since agreeing to work for Brian O'Connor, he knew he shouldn't fix that bike. A woman in Miranda's position, a woman who'd lived with daily fear, would be more likely to panic at the idea that someone had been on her property, messing with her stuff. The fact that this person knew she'd been struggling to get training wheels off her son's bike would tell her he'd been spying on her. Chances were she wouldn't see her benefactor as a Good Samaritan, but rather, someone who'd found her and intended to control her again. Someone who was letting her know he was stronger than she was. That she needed him.

If the panic was too intense, that act, something as simple as fixing a bike, could even prompt her to run again.

He was being paid to keep Miranda and Ethan in sight. To keep them safe. Not to fix bikes.

Back in his older-model SUV, he drove away before he had any other stupid ideas.

MIRANDA SAW DANNY again on Monday. She'd removed his stitches on Friday and Marie was worried about a puffy redness on one end of the incision that had been made during the surgery, which was done to repair the muscle tear he'd sustained during his fall.

"I'm fine," Danny said, when Miranda asked him how he was doing.

As soon as she had a look at the incision site she knew what the problem was.

Fear. Marie's fear.

Not infection. Or further physical damage. The scar area was pink, not red. A healthy pink.

Asking a nurse to come and stay with Danny in the exam room, and giving the boy a handheld learning-game device with the permission of his mother, Miranda led Marie down the hall to her office, closing the door behind them.

"What's wrong? Is it infected or is the injury worse than we thought? Does he need more surgery? Should Dr. Bennet take a look at him?"

Max Bennet, the pediatrician who'd hired Miranda as his PA even before she'd completed her training, would be a good person for Marie to talk to. But not about her son's leg.

"Danny's incision is fine, Marie."

"But shouldn't Dr. Bennet take a look, just in case?"

Picking up her phone, Miranda sent a quick text to Max, who responded immediately.

"He's going in now, if you'd like to meet him down there," she said to the worried mom.

Her furrowed brow smoothing out, Marie shook her head. "He'll let you know if there's a problem, right?"

"He'll text either way."

"You called me in here to talk to you—separate from Danny—and since there's nothing wrong with his incision..." The other woman's words trailed off.

Miranda nodded, words tripping over themselves as they fought for release, while, for the most part, she was forced to remain silent.

For the most part.

"Danny's leg hurting…we know it's going to." She started slowly. "Surgery let us put the fibers back together, but there'll still be scars. We talked about how the nervous system sends messages when muscles have been compromised, inflaming the area to protect weak fibers, shortening the fibers…"

Marie gave a quick nod. "Rehabilitation is all scheduled, and we'll be there on time, every time," she said.

"Good."

"I just… I'm so scared, you know? Danny—he's all I have. I should've gotten him out sooner and now he's hurt, and Devon might try to take him from me and… I'm sorry. I shouldn't have wasted your time today."

Marie was in daily counseling through The Lemonade Stand. She didn't need Miranda to work through all the issues with her. Nor was Miranda professionally qualified to do that.

"I know," she said now, making a silent choice that she prayed she wouldn't regret. But what was the value of her life if she couldn't use her experiences to help others? She'd needed to speak to Marie since she'd first heard her story. "And that's why I called you in here. Fear is insidious. The thoughts it drives can consume you to the point of interrupting your ability to cope with daily life. The stronger those thoughts get, the more real they seem…"

Danny was only a year older than Ethan.

If Miranda hadn't left when she did, her son could so easily have been that little boy sitting down the hall. Or worse.

Her father had been after Ethan, just as Devon was after Danny.

"I know I'm being paranoid, and I'm sorry…"

"No, no, don't apologize," Miranda said, leaning forward with both hands on her small desk, in her small office, as she looked at the woman in the folding chair across from her. "What I wanted to tell you, still want to tell you, is that I understand. And that…anytime you have a concern, even if you pretty much know that it's just fear, you're welcome to call me. At home."

Taking a card from the holder on the front of her desk, she wrote her cell number on it. "Anytime," she said, handing Marie the card. "Sometimes you have to hear a professional opinion to stop the fear," she added. "You couldn't trust your own mind because you knew that someone else had manipulated it, that it played with you.

"I don't want you to put off calling the doctor, or to have to wait for the office to open, nor do I want you to run up medical expenses with urgent care and emergency room visits. Of course, if it's an emergency, go! But if you're not sure, even if it's the middle of the night—call me."

Staring at the card, looking like she was fighting tears, Marie didn't reach for it. "I can't do that," she said instead. "I can't bother you like that."

"I want you to." To communicate how intensely she meant those words, she laid her hand on Marie's, then turned both hands over and placed the card in Marie's exposed palm, closing her fingers around it.

"I have to do this on my own…" Marie's words were a trembling whisper.

"Some of it, yes." Miranda knew she might be overstepping a line between professional and personal, but she wasn't sure that mattered.

Not in this case.

"But you also have to know when to accept help," she said, realizing that she was speaking to herself, as well.

"Why?" Marie's eyes were moist as she looked at her. "Why would you do this? You've got your own life. You don't need patients, or mothers of patients, waking you up in the middle of the night because they're afraid..."

Miranda told herself to come up with some platitude. Quickly.

She couldn't break the promise she'd made to herself never to screw up again.

Couldn't speak of the past she'd left, ever. Doing so could expose her to someone talking to someone else who happened to be talking to someone who'd once known a woman named Dana and was looking for her...

"Just please...if your mind starts to play tricks with you, if you start getting paranoid that something's wrong with you or Danny, if he sneezes and you worry that he could be getting pneumonia, don't get scared. Don't let fear take over your senses. Call me instead."

"I don't..."

"Think of me as your weapon in that particular battle," Miranda said, finding strength out of nowhere. "Fear seems all-powerful, but the truth is, it buckles and evaporates when you stand up to it. Calling me is the way you look that particular fear right in the eye."

Marie needed an arsenal. She'd collect it one weapon at a time, to face down one fear at a time.

Just as Miranda had.

And she'd need to carry it with her for the rest of her life, too. Because although fear slithered away, it always waited, out of sight, to strike again.

Chapter Six

The Santa Raquel High Risk Team was meeting every Tuesday in a conference room at the police station—for those who could make it or had news to share. Eventually the meetings would taper back down to once a month, but while the team was building, they were keeping in close contact.

In jeans and a striped shirt, with the sleeves rolled to his elbows, Tad sat and listened. He wasn't an official member of the team, although he had his moment to report that during his dozen drive-bys of Danny Williams, he'd noticed nothing untoward. Everyone, including Danny's mother, Marie, was following established protocol.

Sara Havens Edwin, a licensed professional clinical counselor, head counselor at The Lemonade Stand, looked relieved, and Tad nodded in her direction. In a private conversation, Sara had informed him that one of the biggest concerns in a situation like the Williamses', one of the greatest threats to life was Marie herself. She not only loved her husband, but she'd been manipulated by him since high school. She was driven from within to keep him happy.

Miranda had her turn, too, telling everyone about Marie's visit to her office the morning before, leaving out specific medical information that wasn't pertinent to the case, but letting them know that while Marie had been concerned about her son's wound, the boy's healing was completely on track. There'd been no sign of any other injury. Sara took notes on that, too.

A few minutes of administrative discussion took place then. A new email loop was being set up; contact information was dispersed. Funding was mentioned, finances appropriated. He listened, but found himself paying more attention to the little park benches with primary-colored rainbows over them that dotted the scrub top Miranda was wearing.

They dipped and fell with the shape of her breasts and he knew he shouldn't be noticing that. Tried not to. And looked again.

Her breasts weren't the only ones in the room. And he wasn't the type of guy who generally went around noticing them in any case. A shapely, curved butt was his more usual distraction. But those rainbow-covered breasts across from him... They were so captivating. Like the woman.

Miranda's ability to nurture flowed from her with every breath. And he kept wondering how it would feel to lay his head on her breasts.

Wrong. Wrong, Newberry. Wrong. Wrong. Wrong.

They'd be soft, with hard nipples. Womanly softness with a core of strength.

And they'd smell like flowers.

Because she did. Something in her soap, probably. Or whatever lotion she used.

When he started envisioning himself rubbing lotion onto her back, into her shoulders and the sensitive parts of her neck, he sat forward. Brought his thoughts to a screeching halt—to catch her watching him stare at her breasts.

Their charged gazes held for a second.

How could something so not good feel so great?

TAD WASN'T FEELING too great half an hour later as he sat with Miranda over coffee in a shop they'd visited several times before. Others had been there with them, the last of them just leaving.

"Let's move to a smaller table," he suggested when she didn't get up with the others. He was pleased she'd stayed, but the look on her face didn't bode well. Something was bothering her.

And since she'd been fine until the others left, he was pretty certain that something had to do with him.

Or rather, his wandering eyes. He'd screwed up. Badly. Bringing sexual awareness into the workplace. He of all people. Back home, at the station, he'd developed a reputation for being the one guy who hadn't fallen under the spell of a young female cop who'd apparently joined the force to find herself a husband in uniform, not to serve and protect.

He'd also refused friendly advances from a forensic specialist he'd actually liked a lot because he knew better than to bring sex into work.

Letting Miranda pick the table, he followed her to a two-seater in the far corner, and his mood dropped another notch. He was supposed to be gaining her trust, not losing it. For her own safety. And because he'd given his word to a man he trusted.

It wasn't about the money. It had never been about the money for him—not one day of his working life.

He had to fix this.

"I'm sorry," he said the second they were seated

across from each other at a table so small he had to turn so his knees weren't touching hers.

Absolutely *no* touching. He had fences to mend, not further destroy.

"I was completely out of line, but I swear to you, I've never, ever had a problem keeping personal and work separated."

Miranda's frown made her look smart rather than confused. Assessing rather than seeking. "I'm sorry, did I miss something? What are you talking about?" She sipped from her half-full cup of latte, which had to be getting cold.

His straight-up black had been gone a quarter of an hour after they'd arrived. An espresso sounded good. He wasn't used to all the sitting in his car staring out at life that he'd been doing these past six weeks. If nothing else, the time off was letting him know that much as he loved detective work, he wasn't cut out to be a private investigator.

He was more of an action type of cop. Following leads. Hunting down the bad guys.

Not being one of them. "You and I... I appreciate the chance to learn about the High Risk Team, to help out while I'm here. I might have crossed a line and—" He stopped. "Uh, I want to tell you that—"

He broke off as she shook her head, and then looked him straight in the eye. "If anyone crossed a line, it was me, Tad. Letting my son talk you into playing video games with him..."

"I thoroughly enjoyed myself. I was kind of hoping for a rematch," he said. She thought *she* was the one being inappropriate?

"He is, too," she said. But she wasn't smiling. So he wasn't getting his hopes up. Or his worries, either.

He had to talk to her father. His current boss. To let him know he could be developing feelings for his daughter, so the chief had a chance to get him off the case before anything happened between them.

And then he'd lose his reputation for good. Lose any chance of resuming his career in North Carolina, and possibly anywhere else depending on how the internal investigation into his last case went down.

"I told Ethan I'd talk to you about it," she said, surprising him further. "But…this is all so awkward, you know? You haven't even asked me out, or hinted that you wanted to, and it feels like we're having 'the talk' or something."

"I'd say apologizing for possibly crossing a line could be construed as a hint." What the hell was he doing?

"So maybe it's a little complicated, huh?"

"Maybe." He should be walking away. Instead he was leaning in. Smiling at her. "I'm attracted to you."

He wasn't going to lie to this woman any more than he had to. She'd had enough hell in her life. Had already had a man betray her trust in the worst possible way.

"Yeah." She glanced away, licked her lips in a completely natural manner that turned him on, although it clearly wasn't meant as a come-on, and looked back at him. "I told you I haven't been on a date since Ethan's father died. What I didn't tell you was that…"

He waited, not even breathing. Was she going to tell him that the man had beaten her so badly, terrorized her so horrifically, she'd had to change her identity to get away from him?

Would she tell him the man's real name so he could verify his death and know for himself that she was safe?

He couldn't tell her who he really was without her father's say-so, not at that point, but if he could at least be certain that the fiend who'd hurt this woman was definitely gone, he'd be a whole lot happier.

"Well, the truth is, I haven't even been attracted to anyone..."

Becaauuusse...

"Which is probably why I'm behaving like such an imbecile right now," she finished, running the rim of her finger around the edge of her coffee cup.

Had she just told him she was attracted to him? Replaying the last minute or so without his own inner dialogue, he was pretty sure she had.

And while he was disappointed that she wasn't confiding in him, he was relieved, too. Anytime she spoke to anyone about her past, she opened herself up to the possibility of being found.

He was glad to know that Miranda was taking good care of herself and Ethan.

"We're attracted to each other," he said, adding a lightness to his tone he didn't feel. "We should drink to that. Can I get you another coffee?" He stood, needing that espresso in the worst way.

"Another latte?" she asked, gazing up at him, as though she'd just asked for a whole lot more and was confident he'd deliver.

He wanted to.

But was equally sure he couldn't. Not yet.

One thing was for certain. His weekly call with the man paying his rent couldn't come fast enough. Maybe he'd break protocol and move the conversation up by a few days.

Maybe.

Standing at the coffee bar, Tad was mostly just eager to get back to the beautiful woman waiting for him at the table in the corner.

MIRANDA'S STOMACH WAS in knots. Her hands shook. It didn't seem to matter that she'd made up her mind two days ago to have this talk with Tad Newberry, or that she'd rehearsed how it would go.

He'd looked her in the eye and told her he was attracted to her. Okay, not a major occurrence in the larger scheme of things, but in her world, it was a huge first. A guy she had the hots for thought *she* was hot.

In her old life, that had never happened. After all the counseling she'd had, she understood that the feminine part of her, the part that controlled things like budding sexual attraction, had been shut down by her father's abusive treatment. Her defenses against men, against trusting men, had been acute ever since.

And now?

Now she had to have the conversation she'd set out to have. Regardless of how her belly flip-flopped and her crotch got warm as she watched Tad walk back to her.

She thanked him for the coffee. Took a sip to distract herself while he sat down. No need for her to glom on to his fly while it hung there at eye level.

This situation was not going to get out of control. She couldn't let it.

Wouldn't let it.

"I'm not looking for a relationship," she said as soon as the sting of hot coffee subsided from her tongue. "No matter how I feel about someone, I'm not going to hook up, period. At least not until Ethan is older."

There. She'd done her deed. And if it meant he walked out of here and avoided her the rest of the months he was in town, so be it.

All the better, really. Meant she didn't have to be on her guard around him. Constantly fighting the insane need she had to feel his lips on hers.

To know how his tongue felt against hers.

When she and Jeff had conceived Ethan, they'd tried to kiss first, but had ended up laughing, instead.

Tad was still sitting there. Studying her. "Good to know," he said, leaving her with a strong desire to be privy to every single one of his thoughts.

"You're only here for, what, another nine months, at most?"

No. That hadn't come out right. As though, if he was willing to hang around, she might change her mind.

There could be no hint of possibility here. No cracks in any doors or windows through which he might slip.

"At most," he told her. He'd leaned back in his chair, was sitting partially sideways so that one arm was on the table, the other hanging off the corner of his chair. As though he didn't have a care in the world.

But the way he watched her…assessing…made her nervous. Like he was seeing more than she could ever allow.

This was a bad idea. Worse even than she'd feared.

What if she let something slip? Some little nugget of a fact that made him curious…

No.

She stopped that thought, too. She was *not* going to let paranoia take over again. She'd won that battle. Wasn't going to let fear and suspicion get close enough to have to fight them again.

At least not if she could see it coming.

Since returning to the table, Tad had contributed nothing to their conversation. If she wasn't still humming inside from his admission that he was attracted to her, preceded by an apology for "crossing a line," and followed by his backhanded admission that he wanted to ask her out, she might be able to convince herself that they had nothing to talk about.

That she'd been worried for nothing.

"I told Ethan we can be friends, the three of us, you and me, you and him, but that we can't *need* each other for things. Or rely on each other," she said in a rush.

Half hoping he'd miss the "you and me" part of that. And yet fearing he would.

"I'd like to be friends." He rested both arms on the table again, and she could hardly comprehend how relieved she felt. Almost giddy with it. Like she had to laugh out loud. And maybe cry a little, too.

"All three of us, me and Ethan and you and me," he added.

And she started to tremble.

Chapter Seven

In the spirit of friendship, with a phone call to North Carolina lurking in his very near future, Tad asked Miranda how her weekend had gone.

He knew she'd gotten the training wheels off Ethan's bike. The boy had been riding like a pro when Tad had checked on them later that afternoon. He'd found a place around the corner from them where he could park and still see their house between the other houses. And when he drove down the street behind them, he could keep tabs, too.

At first, watching them had felt good. Righteous. He was keeping them safe. But the more he got to know them, the less great he felt. The cause was important.

Still, did the end always justify the means?

The sixty-four-million-dollar question of his life these days.

The question Internal Affairs was pondering on his behalf.

"Ethan kept asking me to call you on Sunday." She'd been talking about a movie she and her son had seen and that Ethan had wanted him to see, too. With them.

"You should have."

"I'm sure you have things to do."

The things he was being paid to do were much easier when he was spending time with her.

"I do a lot of sitting around," he told her. "In meetings, in my car... I'm finding I'm not all that good at it."

"You want to be out saving the world," she said. He noticed a difference in her tone. Not necessarily negative, but...different. *Aware.*

And he figured he understood why. "You know someone like that?" he asked.

Her father.

The man, a true hero, must have been an incredible parent. Growing up with someone who was willing to take risks over and over again, to fight the hard fights selflessly, must have been remarkable. Such an inspiration. With Tad's father's defection from their family when Tad was just a baby, Tad had been the man in his family his whole life. He'd been all his mom and older sister had for protection.

And he'd failed them.

Just as Miranda's husband had failed her.

"Not personally, I don't," Miranda said, with no hint of subterfuge. "But since you were hurt on the job, I'm guessing you didn't make your living sitting at a desk. I imagine that for someone like you, who usually works in dangerous situations, it would be difficult to have, as the highlight of your day, driving around checking up on a little boy."

Her blue eyes were filled with warmth, and they directed her nurturing to him; he sucked it in like a man dying of thirst.

"But you must realize that what you're doing is far more than being ready in case Danny's in trouble," she continued. "You being out there, watching, gives Marie extra strength, too. And it reminds her that she can't give in and contact Devon because everyone would know and he'd be the one in trouble if he came around. She might not be able to protect herself, but she's been programmed to protect him."

The insight struck him hard. He'd been doing a lot of reading on domestic violence over the past three months. And gained more understanding in five minutes of conversation with Miranda. Her experience spoke to him.

Probably more than she knew.

Or maybe because *he* knew.

"She's at possibly the most critical point in her life," Miranda was saying, her voice low as she leaned closer to him. Tad could feel her intensity.

"If she makes it through this total break, if she can stay out from under Devon's mental control long enough to free her own thoughts from him again, to counteract his voice in her head, then she'll be able to work on recovery and building a new and happy life."

He felt like he'd just slipped a bit deeper into Miranda's own psyche. Wanted to be there. But only with her permission.

"I'll do whatever I can to help," he told her. And added, "If there's more I can do, please let me know."

He'd do whatever it took to help Marie stay out of harm's way. To help her win this victory over evil. And if he got any insights into how he could help Miranda as well, all the better.

"I will," she said. "I know that when you came to see Danny at the office, that really helped."

Dropping his pants, she meant. He'd relived that one a dozen or more times in the days since, mostly with mortification.

But he wasn't sure he'd do anything differently...

Ends and means and all that stuff.

"If I tell you something, do you think you can keep it to yourself?" she asked.

"Of course." What else could he say? The more of her secrets he knew, the better he'd be prepared to protect her.

Not that she was in any danger. He'd just feel relieved knowing firsthand that her husband was really gone.

"When Marie was in the office the other day I gave her my personal cell number," she told him. She sipped from the coffee he'd pretty much forgotten was there. But she met his gaze—standing up for the choice she'd made. Standing by it.

"Paranoia can be a lasting result of being a victim of domestic violence. When your trust is betrayed on such an intimate level—"

She broke off, and he needed to take her hands in his, or preferably, take her in his arms, let her know he'd die before he allowed anyone to hurt her again.

"I'll keep an eye on her, too, if you'd like." There was only so much he could do for Miranda at the moment. But he could help Marie get through the things he hadn't been there to help Miranda with. The first steps of the difficult journey to freedom.

Surprisingly, Miranda shook her head. "If she found out, it could do more harm than good," she said. "The point is for her to learn to trust herself. To be able to rely on herself, on her own strengths. To discern the difference between being dependent and asking for help. No one's good at everything. She needs to do all she can, and to know when she needs help and then ask for it."

He got that. More than he ever had before.

And thinking of her son's training wheels two days before, he wondered where Miranda was in the process.

"That's why I gave her my number," she told him. "It's not illegal or wrong or anything for me to do that, but it does go outside normal medical protocol. I just saw a chance to give her a tool to help her fight her demons and knew I had to do it."

And she was telling him this because…

She didn't trust herself all the time? Would she ever?

Even when you won the battle and became a survivor instead of a victim, did you ever fully lose the sense of having been there once? Did anyone?

Life shaped people. Changed them.

"I think it's great that you did that," he told Miranda now, meaning the words. She'd been dealt a horrendous hand, and she'd saved herself.

So much for needing the protection he kept trying to assure himself he was giving her. Truth was, maybe he needed to give it to her more than she needed to get it from him.

"I just hope she uses it," Miranda said, and then smiled at him. "This is nice," she added. "Being friends."

"You want to have a friendly dinner sometime this week? Maybe give me another shot at becoming a zoo-keeper your son can't easily obliterate?"

She hesitated, and he fell a little flat. "Or not."

"No." Miranda sat up straighter, took a visible deep breath. "I mean, yes, let's talk about that. I… I'm pretty odd about my house," she said. "I…don't invite people over. I know, it's weird, but being a single mom , you never know who you can trust, and I've always kept our home a safe place. You know, where it's just the two of us."

He remembered the way she'd rushed him through to the backyard on Saturday.

"I could invite you to my apartment," he told her. "It's not much, but there's a kitchen and a TV where we could hook up the game."

"No. I'm just being…"

Paranoid?

"Maybe it's time to open up Ethan's world a bit more. To expose us both to a society that's been good to us. Let me check my schedule and get back to you with a night. Would that work?"

Let me think about it, he translated.

"Sure," he said with a shrug. "I'm available."

"Do you like baked spaghetti?"

"Who doesn't?"

"It's one of Ethan's favorites. I'm off early on Thursday because I work Saturday this week. We could do it Thursday night."

"Does this mean you've already checked your schedule?" He grinned at her.

She grinned back. "Smart-ass."

Miranda had to go back to work, and he wanted to get in a workout at the gym before heading over to Danny's school for his afternoon watch. He walked Miranda to her car, moved on down to his own, but didn't unlock it until he'd watched her drive out of the parking lot and out of sight.

He'd never admired a woman, wanted a woman, as much as he did her. For the first time since his sister was murdered, something mattered to Tad more than getting the bad guys off the streets.

Suddenly, seeing a woman—and her young son—happy was what mattered more.

Marie and Danny's safety mattered most, certainly. Absolutely.

They had an entire team of people helping them. He was proud to be among them.

But his mission was much more personal, too.

It was time for Miranda Blake to be free to become Dana O'Connor again. To return to the father who adored her. The life she'd been forced to leave behind.

To be free from the past that clearly still haunted her.

She'd won her battle; now it was time to come home from the war.

Chapter Eight

Miranda waited until Wednesday night to tell Ethan that Tad would be coming for dinner on Thursday. Purely for self-preservation. She needed to have her own thoughts securely in place before dealing with her son's barrage.

Was she doing the right thing? Could she have someone in their home without somehow revealing any piece of their past that might help someone find them?

Would someone approach Tad in town, someone he thought she knew, and ask him some innocuous question? He might well answer, unknowingly, with something that could expose her. Her father's superhuman ways opened any possibility.

She'd been told to live a normal life. Had saved nothing from her past. Nothing. No pictures. Not even the fourteen-karat gold heart charm Jeff had given her the day she'd told him she was pregnant. A symbol of the love he felt for her, and the love she'd given him. The love they'd created in their baby, through their baby. He'd told her that whenever she doubted her worth or questioned herself, to hold on to that charm and talk to him—promising that he'd hear her from wherever he was and find a way to answer her.

The night she'd run, she'd taken a side trip back to college and buried the charm alongside Jeff's grave, thinking that maybe, someday, when Ethan was grown, she could take him there, tell him the truth about the wonderful man who'd fathered him and give him the charm.

Was it wrong to steal a moment of happiness for herself by inviting Tad over again? Was she risking Ethan's life?

Or was she hurting it by keeping them cloistered? Would her son grow up being afraid of the world?

He'd gone to bed ecstatic Wednesday night. And had jabbered about dinner the next evening, wanting to know what she was going to make, suggesting that she bake brownies, too, and asking if he could have a night off from homework.

She'd made the brownies as soon as she got home on Thursday. Crossed her fingers that there'd be no homework, and if there was that they could get it done quickly. She was smiling as she waited in her usual spot outside Ethan's school that afternoon. As she'd cooked and cleaned her way through the early afternoon, she'd had a long talk with herself. And maybe with Jeff, too. Listening to his voice in her mind, telling her how smart and capable she was.

Of all the friends he could've had in college, he'd chosen her—a normal-looking, quiet, shy loner—to hang out with. Jeff had always seen something in her she'd never seen herself.

"I don't like Tad and I don't want him to come over for dinner." Ethan's words were spewing out before he'd even climbed into the front seat beside her. His glasses made his eyes look bigger as he turned them on her. "You have to call him and tell him he can't come," the boy said, and then shoved his backpack on the floor at his feet and sat there, arms crossed, with his lower lip jutting out like it did when he was trying not to cry.

Heart thumping, Miranda went immediately into calm mode. "Why? What did he do?"

"I thought he was *my* friend. Our friend. But he's friends with any old boy."

"I don't understand," Miranda said, her tone filled with the love the little guy drew from the depths of her. She ignored the other cars and kids milling around outside her vehicle.

"I saw him," Ethan said. "He was here, on the other side, where they play baseball. At recess. I thought he came to see me, but when I started to run over to him, some other kid went over and Tad didn't even see me. Or wave. He just talked to that other kid for our whole recess and then… I don't know what. Maybe took him for ice cream or something."

"What other kid?" Miranda's senses were on alert for an entirely different reason now. She'd known Ethan and Danny Williams went to the same school; it was a big school and the boys were in different grades.

"I dunno." Her son's chin was down by his chest, and she had to fight the need to pull him close and rock him against her as she had when he was smaller.

"I'm sure, since the other boy was at recess, too, he couldn't just leave school. Do you really think Tad took him for ice cream?" she asked, seeing so many complications and not knowing what to tackle first, or at all.

"No."

"So you think Tad shouldn't have any friends but you?"

"I dunno."

"But you know, people care about more than one

person. Jimmy likes more kids than just you and you like more than just him."

"He's only a little kid like me."

"You liked Tad, and that didn't mean you didn't still like me, right?" As she tried to assuage her son's hurt feelings, it occurred to her that she'd failed him in a way she hadn't seen coming, focusing only on her work and on him, giving him unrealistic expectations of the adults in his life. Few as there were...

"I dunno," he said again. "I thought he was *my* friend."

Kids' feelings got hurt. It was all part of growing up.

Maybe some of them were better acclimated by the time they were six. More exposed to human interaction. Probably most of them had to share the caregivers in their lives. And they'd likely had more than one.

In an effort to keep Ethan safe, she'd sheltered him, figuring he'd have his own interaction with others when he started school. When he was old enough to protect himself. Or at least tell someone if he was hurt or afraid.

She'd had it all planned out. Had him prepared and...

You'd think, given that, he'd be jealous of sharing *her*, not jealous of Tad being friends with another boy.

The way he'd taken to Tad—the first person she'd shown real warmth to in front of him, other than the professionals with whom they came in contact...

Could be this wasn't so much a relationship thing as it was a "daddy" issue. Having a man around.

She had no idea what to do about that at the moment. How to explain...any of it.

"You said you wanted me to go on a date, right?"

"Yes, but not with him. Not anymore."

"It's a little late for that," she told him. "I already invited him over. And he's planning to be a successful zookeeper tonight." Dealing with children was her forte. Not only because of her training, but because it somehow came naturally to her.

Still, she felt completely, uncharacteristically, lost.

"Can you do me a favor and be nice to him? Just for tonight?" Give her time to figure out how to handle the newest bump in their road. She'd known bigger bumps were coming. Had been as prepared as one could be when facing the unknown.

"I dunno."

"He wants to see you, Ethan. He really likes you."

When Ethan looked at her, she could see tears in his eyes. "Then why didn't he notice me?"

"Did you ever think about asking him? You say you want to be his friend, but what kind of friend just gets mad and cuts you off without at least asking you about what hurt him?"

She had to text Tad. Give him a heads-up. Maybe sort this one out between the two of them before he arrived for dinner.

Telling Ethan the truth—that Danny was a victim of domestic violence, that his own father had threatened to kill Danny's mother and had tried to force Danny to leave with him, that Tad was on the team that was protecting him—was out.

Shouldn't be such a hard thing, lying to her son, with her whole life built on lies. And it still made her sick.

Tad wasn't afraid of storming into an office to face a man with a loaded gun. Didn't think twice about knocking down a door behind which men were waiting with weapons. He'd faced off against an assailant who had a bomb.

And he put off calling Miranda's father until Thursday afternoon. A lot could happen between Tuesday and Thursday. No point in borrowing trouble.

A couple of hours before he was supposed to show up for dinner, he was looking forward to the evening so much he knew trouble had arrived.

Pacing between the sock drawer in his bedroom and the living area of his small quarters, he gazed out at the ocean in the distance, listening to the ring on the other end of the line. Two and then three rings, although the chief always picked up on the first.

On Fridays, he expected Tad's call.

Figuring he was going to voice mail, knowing he couldn't leave a message, Tad shoved a hand into the pocket of his jeans—the black ones again—and repeatedly flexed his injured thigh muscle. Focusing on the exercise. Counting the squeezes.

"Is there a problem?"

To date the man had always answered his phone "Chief O'Connor." Every time.

"No."

"I was in a meeting."

"I'm sorry, sir." He didn't like feeling chastised and considered hanging up.

Let the chief wait until the next day to hear from him at their usual time.

"No. No, I'm the one who's sorry. I apologize. When I saw the number come up I got a bit tense. It's difficult not being able to handle this myself. To be there if there's an emergency. Please, forgive me."

Defenses immediately lowered, replaced by the respect the chief had earned from Tad, he walked out to his balcony, feeling a chill in the April air. The sun would be warm. It wasn't shining on his side of the building. He got the morning sun.

"I apologize for the unplanned contact," he said now. "I have a situation I need to run by you. Probably should've done that before now. I have a…meeting tonight and if you'd rather I didn't go, I need you to tell me."

"I told you before—you have free rein there. Whatever it takes to keep them in sight. To keep me apprised of their activities. To keep them safe."

"Your daughter and her son are befriending me."

"Good! Better than good. That's great. I couldn't have hoped for better." At his superior's enthusiasm, Tad squirmed. "The more inside you can get with them, the better you'll be able to protect them on the off chance that some of her ex's family is a danger to us. Or if she gets spooked and runs again."

"About that, sir. Have you actually found his family? Do we know if they pose a danger?"

"Some of them have been located. Others haven't. At least one, a brother, could pose a potential danger. We need to keep things status quo for now."

"If you give me the man's name, I can do some checking from here. It's what I do best. Investigate. Find clues. Put pieces together. Track down what others can't find. I've got the time."

"I appreciate your willingness, Newberry. I've got someone else, equally capable, working on this."

Yeah, the chief's eggs-in-different-baskets philosophy was frustrating the hell out of him.

And would be, even if he wasn't dangerously close to getting personally involved in this one.

"The thing is, sir, Miranda… Dana…has given some indication that there could be interest in a liaison between the two of us. I need you to know that I'm… I care about her. She's everything you'd want her to be and more."

A lot like the chief in terms of selflessly offering help to others. The way, for instance, she'd given Marie her phone number, telling the struggling woman to call day or night…

"Fine. That's fine, Detective. Your honesty serves you well. I've been following your IA review, and your integrity has come through loud and clear. Whether you resume your position with your current department or not, the state of North Carolina will definitely have a place for you at the end of your sabbatical."

But this wasn't about him. About his future. Though, maybe for some, it would be.

"They've invited me to have dinner in their home tonight." *In their home.* Just the three of them.

"I couldn't be more pleased. I knew you were the right man for the job. Just…treat her well, okay? If you feel something for her, then that's good, go with it. If not, don't let it go so far she gets hurt. I'll be looking forward to a more complete report on my grandson during our call tomorrow."

Had the chief just given him the go-ahead to sleep with his daughter? As long as he cared about her? It sure sounded that way to Tad. He'd been about to clarify when the chief was interrupted and ended the call.

Tad wasn't going to have sex with Miranda. Didn't think it was a good plan. But getting closer to her, maybe even close enough to hold her…

Shaking his head, he returned the burner phone to the sock in the drawer, grabbed the button-down shirt he usually wore with the black jeans, lined up the hanger with the others and shut his closet door.

He'd never done undercover work, but had a pretty

good idea of what it felt like. And figured he'd been right to steer clear of that option in his career. *Complicated* was all in a day's work for him. Mixing life with the job, though…not his thing.

He could quit. He'd found the chief's daughter. Could tell him to hire another man to watch over her.

That possibility had merit. He hated it, but it had merit.

The cell phone in his back pocket sounded an incoming text from the woman who was never far from his thoughts these days. So much so that he'd given Miranda her own ringtones—separate ones for text and calls.

Everything okay with Danny and Marie?

Had Marie called her? His adrenaline sped up. Devon Williams had been spotted near Marie's house that afternoon by a police patrol. Not close enough to disobey the restraining order, but enough that a notice had been sent out.

Had he violated his order, after all? Approached Marie?

As far as I know, they're fine. Why?

Get the facts, then act.

Ethan saw you with Danny at school today.

He quickly explained that he'd been asked to make visual contact with Danny just as a precaution and had waved at the boy, who'd actually come over to ask him a question about running with a hurt leg.

Guess you were right, the visit to your office went well, he finished. It felt good, sharing a victory with her, small as it might be.

A heads-up. Ethan's feelings were hurt. Thinks you chose Danny over him.

So much for feeling good.

What did you say to him? he texted back.

He paced back to the living area, to the balcony, as he awaited her response. The job wasn't supposed to be this emotional roller coaster he'd been on for the past couple of weeks. It was supposed to be his head fully engaged, not his heart.

After his sister's death, Tad had made it that way. He was going to be a positive influence on the world. A help, not a hindrance.

And he was never, ever going to love anyone again as much as he'd loved Steffie.

Told him to ask you. Sorry. I passed the buck, came the eventual response. And then, I drew a blank. Can't tell him who Danny is or why you know him.

He read her response twice.

Why not?

Seemed to him that telling her son about Danny might be smart. If the boy knew that sometimes kids were in danger from family members, it would give him an awareness he might need if any of his father's family came looking for him.

Chief O'Connor had mentioned one family member of Ethan's father who could pose a risk, and that had been on the edge of his consciousness since the second he'd heard it. Made him anxious to get to dinner and have a closer look at Miranda's house. To make sure she had dead bolts, the windows were all securely latched. That...

He'd look at it all. He'd add more watch time, too. He'd been loitering around enough to be familiar with the neighborhood, to recognize her neighbors as they came and went.

He's only six. He doesn't need to know about the seedier side of life yet.

He disagreed. Completely. Given her circumstances—about which he supposedly knew nothing.

But he got her message. He wasn't supposed to say anything about Danny's situation to Ethan.

Telling himself he'd find a discreet way to approach the topic with her, Tad settled for, Got it. And thanks for the heads-up.

Her response was almost immediate. Thanks. Complete with a smile emoji.

Chapter Nine

She had to do this. Not only for herself and Ethan, but for all those who came after her. For Marie and the Maries yet to come.

She had to be proof that life existed after domestic violence—even when the threat was so severe you had to run for your life. Others might not know her circumstances, but by living a happy, fulfilled life, she could teach others to do the same. She could teach with confidence.

Sometimes confidence was as much a factor in helping someone as facts were.

And someday, with life following a natural progression, her father and the threat he posed would be gone. Then she could use her story as an example to others.

Thoughts firmly stationed, she watched the clock, her stomach filled with butterflies as Tad's arrival drew close.

She'd originally planned for them to spend the majority of the early-evening get-together out on the patio, but the wind had kicked up, chilling the air, so she'd had to give up on that option.

Inside the cottage it was. She'd set the table in the smallish eating area off the kitchen. Ethan and Tad could play *Zoo Attack* from the game box controller attached to the living room TV. She'd cleaned the bathroom in the hall. And shut both bedroom doors. For privacy, not because they weren't equally spotless.

In skinny jeans, a dark blue tank and a white, mostly see-through top with three-quarter-length sleeves, she examined her appearance one more time as she did a last check on the bathroom. She'd left her hair down, happy with the natural waves for once, and the rest... She'd never been a heavy makeup kind of girl. Basic foundation, a hint of eyeliner and that was it.

A thrill of anticipation swept through her as she caught her eye in the mirror. She was hoping that Tad really was attracted to her.

As much as that scared her, considering her secrets, it also felt good. Damned good. Her escape from hell wasn't a success unless she and Ethan lived a normal life. Anything less made her remain a victim trapped by the fear of further abuse.

Back out in the living room, she noticed that her son hadn't budged from his cross-legged position in front of the TV, where he was cleaning up his zoo, when the doorbell sounded.

"Remember, if you want to have a friend, you have to be a friend," she told him quietly as she passed, bending down to kiss the top of his head, hoping he'd lighten up and let the whole Danny thing go.

Either way, she knew that Tad wasn't going to tell her son about Danny's abuse. She hadn't run three thousand miles, given up everything she'd had, everything she'd known, to have her young son exposed to domestic violence. In time, when he was older and his psyche had been formed with loving family values... then she'd tell him.

Ethan didn't lighten up. On the contrary, he was

pretty much a brat. A child Miranda didn't recognize as he insinuated himself between Tad and her, interrupting any time the two of them started a conversation, and refusing to answer Tad when he spoke to him directly.

Tad had been in their home less than ten minutes, and the evening was a disaster.

"Maybe I should go," he said to her, standing up from the couch several yards behind where Ethan sat on the floor. Setting the glass of red wine she'd brought him on the table, Tad pulled out his keys.

"I don't think a six-year-old has the right to determine our evening," Miranda said, surprising herself with the firmness of her tone. She didn't get demanding with her son, ever. He was a good kid. Rarely needed discipline, just guidance.

And she was not going to be like her father. Her son would never have reason to fear her. She'd promised herself, and him, too, when he'd been a baby on the run with her.

She stood, hands on her hips. "Ethan, turn around please."

At first, the boy didn't move, then, very slowly, he turned, looking up at her through his Clark Kent glasses. Her heart melted, as it always did, when he showed her the emotions he wasn't old enough to hide.

"Do you really want Tad to leave?" she asked him, praying he'd be honest with her. And with himself.

"I dunno."

"That's not good enough, Ethan. We have a guest in our home and you're being rude."

Not that she could totally fault him on his manners. If she'd ever had visitors, he might have been better equipped to be a proper host.

"I'm sorry." He sounded more petulant than contrite.

"The other day you asked me to come over," Tad said, dropping down to sit on the floor beside him.

The boy, his game controller in hand, stared at the television.

"You worried I'm going to win our next battle?" he asked, glancing at the screen.

Ethan shrugged.

While she didn't love video games, Miranda played them with her son. He'd never been a sore loser. Nervous, but also kind of fascinated, she got her glass of wine, had a seat on the couch and sipped.

"So…let me play, too," Tad suggested, picking up the unused game controller. He couldn't do much unless Ethan changed to a two-player version. She waited.

And let out a long breath when her son did just that.

Fifteen minutes into a silent but competitive game, she slipped out to the kitchen to put the finishing touches on dinner, telling herself not to make too much of Tad's advent into their lives.

Warning herself.

He was only with them for a short time. She could enjoy herself, *needed* to enjoy herself for her own and Ethan's health. Needed to introduce him to others.

And would continue to do so after Tad was gone.

He was just the first step on this next stage of her survivor journey. She'd start to open her home, their lives, more. Thanks to Tad.

The feelings he'd raised in her, maybe simply because she was ready and he was there, had forced her to confront her fear of inviting others in.

Ethan had forced it a bit, too, latching onto Tad as immediately as he had. Hearing their voices from the other room, she left the dressed salad in the glass bowl on the counter and went in to tell them dinner was ready.

"Why's it rude for me to ignore you when you ignored me?" she heard.

Oh, Lordy. Her son was not giving up. She wondered which one had broken the silence between them, and suspected it had been Ethan. Tad, with his honed self-control or discipline or whatever it was, probably could have waited it out for days.

"I didn't ignore you," Tad said calmly, his avatar racing around a checkerboard-looking thing, just ahead of the blockages that kept appearing on the path. "I didn't know you were there. But you know I'm here. That's the difference." Ethan, a full lane ahead of Tad in his own version of the same puzzle, was also two squares ahead of the blockages. And he had a hefty collection of blockage obliterators in the spare feeding trough in his zoo barn, meaning her son was winning soundly. "You knew Danny was there. Why didn't you look for me, too?"

"I was there to see Danny."

Wiping her hands on the towel she'd brought in, Miranda stopped. Stared at the back of Tad's head.

Should she put an end to the conversation? Call them in for dinner? Pull Tad aside to warn him, remind him, whatever?

"Who's Danny?" she asked, sensing she was overreacting even before the words were out of her mouth.

Tad's quick glance in her direction readily confirmed her suspicion.

Ethan, still looking at Tad, didn't seem to hear her. "Why were you there to see *him*? You know his mom, too?" The question wasn't as friendly-sounding as it might have been. More accusation than curiosity.

Clearly she had work to do where her son was concerned. He wasn't just her little boy anymore. It wasn't just the two of them against the world. She'd known the time would come. Had to give herself a second to swallow the sadness.

And endure the instant shard of fear that followed.

"I do know his mom," Tad said. "So does your mom."

No! She stepped closer to them, but before she could get words out, Tad gave her another look. Not condemning. Not a warning.

More like a promise of some kind.

"She can't tell you about him because he's a patient and it's against the law for medical personnel to talk about their patients, but he's not my patient and while his stuff isn't my business, I can tell you that he knows I got hurt. Your mom knew I got hurt and brought me in to meet Danny."

Ethan's gaze had been locked with Tad's through the entire explanation. Miranda was close to tears.

"But why?"

"He just had a question to ask me about my injury."

Which didn't explain, at all, why Tad had been at the elementary school. She waited for Ethan to ask.

"I got a scar on my leg, and got burned on my back, too, see?" Turning, Tad pulled up his shirt, exposing the scars on the lower part of his back. She'd seen them higher up, too, that day in her examining room with Danny.

"Wow. Did it hurt?" Ethan asked, eyes wide behind his glasses as he talked to Tad.

"Yep. A lot. More than anything else. Ever. Except maybe...you thinking I'm not your friend."

"How'd it happen? Did you get shot?" Ethan knew Tad was a police detective.

"Nope. It was an explosion."

"With some bad guys?"

"One bad guy."

"Did anybody die?"

"Just the bad guy."

"Cool."

She didn't think it was cool.

"So…are we friends again?" Tad moved right in.

"I guess." Ethan turned back to the TV and started to laugh. "Hey! I won even when we weren't playing!"

Their time had run out and he'd been ahead when they stopped, but Miranda had a feeling her son had also won for real, having a man like Tad to look up to for a little while.

She had a feeling she'd won, too.

Chapter Ten

He didn't get a look at all the window latches Thursday night. When he'd excused himself to visit the bathroom, he'd planned to check the bedrooms, but he'd found both doors firmly shut and couldn't risk getting caught inside the rooms.

He'd tried to get her to talk about the windows, noticing that the French door leading out the patio was sparkling, which only led to a conversation about cleaning windows and how she was good at dealing with the inside, but never got around to the outside. They'd only get dirty again next time it rained. He'd moved on to asking if she ever opened her windows to let the breeze in, and she'd said there was no need, since the place was small and she could open the front door, with the metal security screen locked, and get all the cool they needed.

So Friday, when he knew Miranda was at work and Ethan at school, he made a stop by the cottage to do a thorough check on the windows from the outside. To find out how hard it would be to break in. He brought along a squeegee, a spray bottle and a roll of paper towels as his cover, and washed the outsides of all her windows while he was at it. Which meant he'd have to tell her he'd done it, because she was bound to notice and get freaked out.

When he'd thought that Miranda's ex was her only threat, and had been confident—if not 100 percent certain—that the man was deceased, he'd contented himself with watching out for her as her father had asked.

Now that he knew there was a family member who could pose a threat, he was buckling down on his procedures. He was not going to lose a woman or child in his care. He wasn't going to let Ethan or Miranda get hurt, period.

And when he called her father for their regularly scheduled weekly chat later that afternoon, he was determined to get more information out of him.

"How'd it go last night?" Chief O'Connor asked as soon as he picked up.

"It went really well." Tad stood out on his balcony, needing the ocean view to keep things in perspective. To get away from his own interests and out into the world where he could help save lives.

"Tell me about Jeffrey. Is he a good eater? I'm sure he's smart, like his mama." The man's eagerness pulled at Tad, making him a bit sad for all of them. Jeffrey, whose name had been changed to Ethan, and who had no idea he'd ever been anyone else. Or that he had a wonderful grandfather. Miranda who'd lost the support of her family and friends. Chief O'Connor, with his unending well of unconditional love for his family which left him with such horrendous loneliness, and himself, too, because he'd never experience the depths of that kind of love again.

And then, with the next breath he took, reminded himself that he was alone by choice.

"She made his favorite dinner, so I don't know if the way he cleaned his plate is typical of his usual habits or not. And yes, he's a smart little guy. You'd be proud of him, Chief." He could have said so much more. Was probably being paid to say more…

And reporting details of his time with Miranda and Ethan, taking things he learned about them during the time he spent with them, seemed duplicitous. Or worse.

"What's his favorite dinner?"

See, that was one of those intimacies, those privileged pieces of information you got when you were invited into someone's inner circle.

"Spaghetti." Sort of.

"Baked spaghetti? In one of those long metal pans? Sauce and noodles mixed together with cheese?"

Tad half smiled as he leaned against the ceiling-high cement wall he shared with the vacant balcony next door. "Yeah," he said. "Clearly you've had it before."

"It was her favorite, too," O'Connor said, his voice growing soft. He paused, as though restraining emotion, and added, "It was one of her mother's specialties. She taught Dana how to make it, and other things, too, when we found out she was sick."

Tad might not want family of his own, but he knew, in that moment, that he had to get this one back together. Somehow, someway, he had to help them.

"How old was she then?" He had a feeling the older man never talked about his own pain. He was always too busy tending to others.

"Ten."

"And when her mother died?"

"Eleven."

He'd been fourteen when his sister was murdered.

Chin tight, he straightened, hating that Miranda, who gave so much, who truly cared about others, had suffered so much. And had to handle it all alone.

He had to right this wrong.

"I'm concerned about this family member of Jeffrey's father that you mentioned yesterday," he said. "I'm uncomfortable not knowing more. I can't do my job that way. I could have exposed her just by being here. She and Ethan could be sitting ducks…"

Surely the chief knew that.

"You think I'd risk the safety of my only child, my only grandchild?" The chilling tone came at him.

And he took the point. "Of course not."

"I appreciate your concern and I count on it, Tad." The chief softened his next words again. "And I respect that I've put you in a difficult position. You can understand, I'm sure, that I don't trust easily at this stage. Which is why I only give out information on a need-to-know basis."

Another point taken.

"I'm trusting you with their lives. You're the only one who knows I've hired you to find her. The only one who knows you've done so. If you're also poking around in things here in town, someone might be able to trace you to her. I need to make certain there's no danger to them."

Tad was on forced medical and professional leave. With no family. It hadn't been hard for people to believe he'd gone off by himself to heal.

And Chief O'Connor was on the money on every point—even to the point of not paying him directly, but rather funneling the money through a special police fund used for undercover work. As Tad would have expected.

"I'll watch them closely," he said, still uncomfortable with what he didn't know.

"How'd it go with Dana? She can be a little defensive, understandably. I'd like to think she has you for a friend."

His discomfort intensified—on a whole different front.

"Fine. She's accepted me as a colleague and a friend." He had to tread carefully, balancing on a fine line between allegiances.

But their goal—Miranda, Dana, safe and free, with familial support and love—was the same.

"Well, if it goes beyond that, I want you to know you have my blessing. Assuming it's what she wants, what makes her happy. I couldn't pick anyone better to see with my daughter…"

"I said good-night to her and Ethan—Jeffrey—together, as soon as the dishes were done," he inserted, not willing to have that conversation with his boss. He'd come clean with the chief about "caring" for his daughter for ethical reasons. And it stopped there.

He'd heard of mothers being matchmakers. The chief was both mother and father to his daughter. Still…the whole thing left him feeling like he needed a shower.

He was friends with Miranda and Ethan. He wasn't going to let it go "beyond that," no matter how tempted he might be.

For so many reasons.

One was that he had no intention of getting into a committed emotional involvement and Miranda deserved no less.

"I realize you feel I've left you somewhat vulnerable out there, but I can tell you that the family member of whom I spoke yesterday is no longer a concern," Chief O'Connor said, getting Tad's full attention.

He turned back to his apartment, went inside and shut the door.

"This same one who, yesterday, posed a threat?" he asked.

"Yes. The older brother. He's got a record, drugs and assault among other things, but he's been incarcerated for attempted murder for the past year."

"How long's he in for?"

"Twenty, with possible parole at seven."

Dropping onto his sofa, he wiped a hand down his face.

God, relief felt good.

MIRANDA HAD JUST tucked Ethan into bed and kissed him good-night when her phone rang Friday night.

"Danny's leg is itching and he's lying in bed crying, saying it hurts," Marie said, after apologizing for making the call. "I gave him the acetaminophen you said I could, but it doesn't seem to be helping. Are we absolutely sure there's nothing wrong there? Some infection we can't see?"

"What did Dr. Bennet tell you on Monday?"

"That everything was fine, but that was four days ago."

"Is he running a fever?"

"No."

She went down the list of other possible symptoms that would indicate a problem, all with no signs of any concern. When they got to the end of the list, she suggested that Marie have Danny soak in a warm bath for a while and eat a healthy snack before going back to bed.

"Devon's been watching us," Marie said then. "The police caught him just far enough away so they couldn't arrest him yesterday."

As a member of Danny's medical team, she wouldn't

have received the alert, just an update at their High Risk Team meeting on Tuesday, but Tad would have known.

Which was why he'd been out in the open, making it easy for Danny to find him during recess the day before.

"Have you seen or heard from him?"

"No."

"And your sister and brother-in-law are there with you?"

"Yes."

"So…our plan is working then," Miranda said, wishing she could climb into the other woman's psyche and help her with her battle, knowing that only Marie could do this part. "The police, they saw him, warned him, and he's staying away."

"I guess."

Marie was scared. She had reason to be. And she had to fight that fear, or it would consume her and the rest of her life, too.

"If the bath doesn't do the trick, it's okay to give him a little more acetaminophen," she said, in her most medical-professional-nurturing-a-patient voice. And then, speaking as a woman, she added, "If you get worried, call me back. I mean it, Marie. You're in the middle of the toughest part of this and I agreed to be a member of the team helping you because it's what I want to do. Your job is not to give in to feeling guilty, or apologetic. Just pick up the phone and call me. Or someone else who can help. You're not alone. I can't stress that enough."

Marie thanked her. A couple of times. Sounding more in control than she had at the beginning of their conversation. Miranda hung up, not sure she'd been able to do enough.

Five minutes later, when the phone rang again, she expected it to be Marie calling back. It was Tad.

Curling up on her couch next to the book she'd been intending to read, a feel-good paperback novel about two female best friends and how the friendship survived the different paths their lives took, she told him about Marie's call.

And received his assurance that there'd been no further notice of Devon's activity since the day before.

"I was wondering how you'd feel about me taking Ethan to the gym tomorrow?" he asked. "I offered to take Danny last week when I was in your office, and while Marie hasn't set anything up yet, she might. It would be good for me to do a test run with Ethan. And…good for Ethan to go there, too. The boys attend the same school. Ethan knows who Danny is now. They might talk at some point."

She didn't think so. More likely, Ethan would steer clear of the other boy.

That wasn't the reason for her hesitation.

"I take him to basketball camp when I work on Saturday mornings." Since January. Prior to that, she'd had him at the office with her, during the first year she'd been Dr. Bennet's PA. And before that, at a day care in the building where Dr. Bennet had his practice.

Ethan had declared, when he'd started first grade, that he was too old for the after-school day care, although it accepted kids up to the age of eight. She let him make the decision, because it was one she could allow.

"I can go anytime," Tad said.

Basketball camp hadn't been the cause of her hesitation, either.

"I'm worried about him spending too much time with

you." She finally just came out with it. "I've told him you're only here for a while, that you have your life in Michigan, a police force that needs you. He says he gets it, but after the way he was when he saw you with Danny, like he's taking ownership of you—I don't want him to get hurt…"

"My life in Michigan?"

Embarrassed that she'd remembered so many details about him, she admitted, "You told us, on your first day with the team, that you were from Michigan."

"Are you saying that you don't want me around him?" he asked next. She wasn't sure whether she was relieved or not, that they were getting back to the point. "You said on Tuesday that you were open to friendship."

"I know." She understood his confusion. "I do want that. I just don't want him getting the wrong idea."

"People are going to come and go from your lives."

He was right, of course.

"And maybe when I'm ready to go back to work, I'll look for something here."

Her heart rate escalated abruptly. Grabbing her attention.

"I…told you, I'm not interested in a long-term…anything. At least until he's older," she got out, wondering how much of her breathlessness he picked up on.

Figuring all of it.

Hoping none.

"Friendship," he said. "Just friends."

But she wanted so much more than that from him. The night before, after he'd left, she'd ended up taking a long soak in the tub, thinking about him.

About how he'd dealt with Ethan's jealousy over Danny. About the way he engaged in her son's video game as if it mattered as much to him as it did to Ethan.

His views on the state of the world, which they'd discussed over coffee after the past six team meetings. His awareness and compassion. His willingness to risk his life to help others.

His patience.

And his body. Oh, that body. What it did to hers. How could she have lived twenty-eight years inside her own skin and never known that she could feel like this?

"I know you've been through a lot, Miranda. Losing Ethan's dad. Having to raise him on your own with no family to help you…"

She'd told him she'd grown up in foster care—back during their first personal conversation. He'd apparently remembered things, too.

"All I'm suggesting here is that I hang out with you and Ethan for a bit."

He was new to town. Not there for long—if you discounted his what-if, and she was going to—and knew very few people. He was unselfishly and willingly volunteering a lot of time to help Danny and Marie.

"But if you'd rather I didn't, I understand…"

"No!" She couldn't just let him go. "I'd rather you did," she said quickly, trying to gather her thoughts.

Maybe she should stop now. End the friendship before any of them got hurt.

Go back to being who she was seven weeks ago, before she met him…

Even as she had that thought, she knew she was asking the impossible. Tad was changing her, *had* changed her. He'd awakened something—an awareness of herself, her needs—that she hadn't had before.

He'd brought Ethan's needs more acutely to her attention, as well.

She had so many silent battles to fight. Had been an

army of one for so long. She wasn't sure she had it in her to fight her own yearnings for some good feelings in her life. Even if they only lasted for a while.

"Surely in the six years you've had Ethan, another man has shown interest in you. Asked you out, or hinted at a desire to," Tad said, causing another surge of desire.

What was wrong with her?

"Yeah, there've been a few." Most recently, one of the volunteer coaches at the city-based basketball camp she'd enrolled Ethan in. "And I wasn't the least bit tempted."

Let him make of that what he would.

"You think Ethan's dad would want it this way?"

If he knew why, probably. But… "No."

"Ethan's dad. I feel kind of ridiculous saying that every time. I assume the guy has a name?"

Yep, and there was why she didn't do *intimate* with anyone. Or get close enough for *intimate* to be a risk.

She hated to lie.

And the more lies she told, the more chance she'd make a critical mistake. Counseling had pounded that one into her.

"Ethan's named after him," she said. It was the truth. His birth name just wasn't Ethan.

"Ethan what?"

Why? Why did he need to know a last name?

If she came across like a crazy woman, she'd raise more suspicion than if she answered.

"Grossman," she said, blurting the name of one of her mother's doctors. Colleen had contracted hepatitis C while on vacation with Miranda and her father down in Punta Cana. They'd thought for a while that she was doing better. That she'd be okay.

She wasn't.

"I'm not going to hurt you or Ethan." Tad's soft voice came over the line. She couldn't remember wanting to believe a man so badly in her life.

But she couldn't.

Chapter Eleven

Tad didn't take Ethan to the gym Saturday. He'd decided not to broach the subject again during his Friday-night conversation with Miranda. He'd almost made a critical mistake, pushing too hard, with his request in the first place. Had teetered on the edge of losing her friendship altogether.

And he'd learned a valuable lesson about survivors. They were as vulnerable as they were strong.

Or maybe the lesson had been about Miranda in particular. As strong as she was, she was vulnerable, too.

He thought about her all day Saturday. Wanting to call her. To see her and Ethan. And settled for a couple of drive-bys. Now that he knew the possible threat against her was in jail, he wasn't as worried about her immediate safety.

He'd looked up Ethan Grossman the second they'd been off the phone Friday night. He'd found no one of that name in North Carolina who'd been in college six years before. Or anyone close to college-age. Even using databases he still had access to, he'd only been able to find one listing. A man closer to her father's age than her own.

She'd lied to him about her husband's name. Not surprising. Smart.

Disappointing, too, on a strictly personal level. Which was at the bottom of his priority list.

Lying in bed Saturday night, thinking about her, he suddenly sat upright in the dark.

Ethan's named after him. She hadn't said the man's name was Ethan; she'd only confirmed the conclusion he'd drawn.

Ethan's named after him.

Ethan's birth name was Jeffrey.

He spent the next hour on his laptop, searching for Jeffrey Grossman in or around North Carolina.

And came up empty.

Frustrated, he pulled out his burner phone and texted the chief. I know the father's name. She told me.

It wasn't technically true. But he had to have answers. If leading the chief to believe he already had, by other means, the information that he wanted the chief to discuss with him, and the chief would then open up more to him, give him more complete information, then the end justified the means.

MIRANDA PASSED TAD on the road Sunday, on her way home from the grocery store. She waved. He waved. Ethan turned around, as much as the belt would let him, and kept waving.

She couldn't even pretend not to be thinking about him after that, and when her son was in his room, doing his weekly cleaning chores, she texted Tad, asking him if he felt like grilling a steak. The man was alone. Healing. Helping Marie.

It wasn't until after he'd said a steak sounded good that she told him it would have to be at the play park on the beach. She didn't own a grill.

Didn't have steak, either, but a grilled steak did

sound wonderful. And it was something she never had because Ethan hated steak. On her trip back to the grocery store for a couple of thick T-bones, she bought her son the hot dogs he wanted as his dinner on the grill. She'd planned to meet Tad at the park, which was really just playground equipment, some grills and picnic tables cordoned off in the sand of one of Santa Raquel's tourist beaches. But when he'd offered to pick her and Ethan up, she wasn't quick enough to invent a reason to refuse and said yes.

She told herself she wasn't going to make a big deal of her appearance. The meal wasn't a date. She and Tad weren't dating.

She wore leggings because they'd be comfortable to sit in on the beach. And the thigh-length off-white figure-hugging short-sleeved sweater was the only thing warm enough to wear with leggings on the beach in April. Running a brush through her hair was just polite, and she reapplied her minimal makeup because she'd rushed through it that morning.

The ride over could have been intimate, sitting next to him in the front seat of his SUV, but Ethan, strapped in the back in his shorts, long-sleeved shirt and tennis shoes, took over the space and didn't let go during the five-minute drive to the park. As soon as Tad answered his first question—had Tad ever been to the beach park?—in the negative, the six-year-old regaled him with all the things he could do there. How the slide was higher than the one at school, there were a lot more swings for big people, and if you got high up and wanted to jump out, it was cool because you landed on the sand.

The barrage went on. She was happy to listen. Her son sounded normal. Happy. Eager to face what was ahead of him.

She'd done some good as his only parent.

Ethan wanted to go down to the water first thing, so they left the cooler in the car and, after taking off their shoes, walked across the sand, down to the shore. The beach wasn't crowded, but it wasn't deserted, either, that Sunday afternoon. Seventy degrees and breezy was too cold to swim, but a couple of kids were wading, bending over, picking things up off the ocean floor. Another kid was building a sandcastle in sand wet from the surf. Three teenage girls walked past them, chattering and laughing. A few couples were scattered about.

Ethan liked to look for anything living on the shoreline.

"You're giving him a great childhood," Tad said, standing beside her just out of reach of the waves lapping at the shore.

"I do my best." The breeze was harsher down by the water, but she welcomed the coolness on her heated skin. Being around Tad, who needed central heat? Or warmth from the sun?

"I went to the beach once, as a little kid. In a town called South Haven on the shores of Lake Michigan across from Chicago. Mom rented a cottage there for the long weekend over the Fourth of July."

It was the first mention he'd ever made of his personal life. Avid for more, for a real picture of the man who compelled her to want to be around him, she asked, "Was your dad there, too?"

"Nope. He took off when I was a baby. Met someone else, divorced my mom and moved to North Dakota. It was always only Mom, my older sister, Steffie, and me."

"Did you ever see him?" Fathers were a tough subject. No matter what they did to you, you loved them. Felt like you needed them.

Until you had a child of your own to protect.

"Not that I remember. He left that woman, too, luckily for her before they had kids. Last I heard, he was in Florida, working as a casino dealer. As far as I know he never remarried or had other kids."

"Have you tried to get in touch with him?"

"Not in a long time."

The way he said the words had her looking up at him, and she was shocked to see the bitter sadness in his expression. Ethan was talking to the kids who'd been in the water, picking up things from the ocean shore, seemed to be comparing finds. He was a friendly kid. Outgoing. She'd been worrying too much that week about the way she'd secluded him.

"How about your sister? Is she in touch?" She wanted desperately to know. But didn't want to push.

She didn't want to be pushed, either.

"Steffie's dead."

Her heart dropped, and the breath caught in her throat. "What happened?" She turned to him and when he met her gaze…it was like his soul and hers…knew each other. Connected as friends, not strangers.

"She and I were home alone one night. I was a freshman in high school. She was a freshman in college, going to a local university. Mom was at work. She was a nurse at the children's hospital in Detroit."

"Your mom was in the medical field?" He'd never said. And at a children's hospital… Her entire being tensed with the need to help him—because she was a nurse, too? Or had been. Before she'd left herself behind, invented a new life and become a pediatric PA.

She liked being a PA. As much as she'd liked being a nurse. Maybe even a little more. She so badly wanted to share that with Tad.

"Yeah. My father was an X-ray technician when they met. From what I can tell, he's had a lot of different jobs since then."

"Where's your mother now?"

She wanted to know about his sister. Had to get back to that. But it felt like they needed a moment. Or at least he did.

"She's gone, too. After Steffie died, she fell into a deep depression that she never really came out of. She died of an accidental overdose of prescription medications when I was in college."

Miranda knew how horrible that felt—losing your mother. Couldn't tell him that, either.

"Oh my God," she said, watching as the children moved a few feet farther down the sand. Ethan wasn't allowed in the water without her. So far, he was remembering that. A breeze blew against them, lifting tufts of Tad's short brown hair. The ocean sounds could have taken his words, their conversation, away.

Instead, they seemed to be enclosed by it all.

"I'm so sorry."

He shrugged. "It was a long time ago."

And yet…right there with them. Life had a way of doing that to you. No matter how many years passed, some things remained. Hurting you still.

"Tell me about the night your sister died." He'd brought it up. As though he wanted her to know.

"She was watching a movie the last time I saw her. Eating popcorn. I went to my room, had my headphones on, listening to music. When I went out to tell her good-night, she was gone."

"Gone?"

"From what they pieced together based on foren-sic evidence at the scene, and later a confession from the guy, the perp knocked at the door. A guy she knew from college. He'd had a crush on her, thought she returned his feelings. He said his car broke down and his cell was dead. Asked to use our phone. She went back to the couch. When he got off the phone, she offered him some popcorn. Apparently he made a move, she rejected him. Popcorn flew all over. Then he dragged her out of the house. Turned out his car was just fine, and parked at the curb. He'd just been looking for an excuse to spend time with her. But after her rejection, he lost it. He shoved her inside his car, drove her to a field, raped her, beat her to death and left her lying there. The neighbors heard her scream, called 911. I'd already discovered she was gone and had called, too, but by the time they found her it was too late."

Oh. Just oh, God. He'd been in his room with headphones on. A fourteen-year-old man of the house. Coming out to see popcorn all over the living room.

There were no words. No way to fix this.

Sliding her hand into his, Miranda held on to him, hoping he'd know she was sharing his pain.

Hoping it helped.

"Look, I got three at once!" Ethan came running up from the wet sand, his hand outstretched, extricating Tad from an excruciating moment—and ripping him from a warmth he'd never experienced.

Miranda quickly pulled her hand from his and he tried to ignore the sense of loss as he bent to see the three sand crabs her son had in his hand.

"You want 'em?" Ethan asked him. "They don't hurt people, do they, Mom?"

"Nope." She shook her head, acting as though she'd

just woken up from a nap. A little out of it, not completely with them.

Tad could relate. What in the hell had possessed him to tell her about Steffie? People knew, of course. And that his mother had died during the first year of his criminal justice degree studies. He'd moved from Michigan to complete his studies in North Carolina—choosing the state because he'd never been there and was offered an academic scholarship with work-study opportunity. Background checks told the facts.

They didn't reveal the details he'd given Miranda.

He'd known he was getting in deep. That things were complicated. Nothing had prepared him for the jolt he'd felt when she slid her hand into his.

It was that feeling that prompted him to make another unscheduled call Sunday night after the picnic on the beach.

He and Miranda hadn't had any more time alone after Ethan shared his sand crabs. The little guy had announced that he was hungry. They'd traipsed up the beach, cooked, played some three-way kickball in the sand, then headed home early because it was a school night and Ethan had to have a bath before bed.

Miranda had invited him in. He'd read more invitation than just the glass of tea or cup of coffee she'd offered, and despite all the desire flowing through him, he'd politely declined.

And then called her an hour later to apologize. He needed to stay on her good side. Wanted to believe it was for her father's sake and for her own ultimate good, which she'd see when she learned the truth. But he had to admit that the phone call was mostly for himself.

Being vulnerable with someone was new to him. He didn't like it. Didn't know how to get out of it.

And was mesmerized by it, too.

"I felt a little awkward, unloading on you like I did," he said by way of apology for his abrupt departure earlier. "I should have handled it better."

"You were fine," she assured him, a little more distant than she'd been when she'd called earlier in the day to invite him to dinner.

He was glad he wasn't the only one who recognized that they had to maintain established boundaries, but he was disappointed, too. Perversely filled with a need to get them right back where they'd been on the beach before Ethan had interrupted them.

It was as though unfinished business lay between them. Something that hadn't been there before.

Maybe it was time to get back to work. To occupy his mind before it flew off permanently.

"I unburdened myself. Now it's your turn," he said, pushed from within to move on from the standstill he felt trapped in. Maybe if she talked to him about her father, indicated that she missed him, he could convince the chief that she was ready for the truth. That would get him out of this mess.

"Excuse me?"

"I told you about my family and I know nothing about yours."

If silence could be heard, he heard it then.

"I don't have a lot to say," she told him after a lengthy pause. "You already know I grew up in foster care."

"Like Ethan Sr.?"

Maybe he was egging her on. Maybe he needed her to trust him.

A selfish need at best. Miranda believed her safety lay in her silence. And her lies.

"Yes," she said. "Except that I stayed in one place, and he was shifted around among different families."

"And your foster parents, were they good to you?"

"Yes."

"Are you still in touch with them?" Frustration motivated him. He was aware of it.

"No. They took in a lot of kids. I, um, didn't actually go into the system until I was eleven."

The year her mother died.

"So you were with your parents until then?"

"My mom. I never knew my dad." Something in her tone touched him.

More than mere sadness. Much more. What was he doing? Forcing a woman to talk about her father, the person she'd loved and adored, a man who'd been a true hero, who'd not only kept her safe but been all the family she had. Of course, she'd have to wall herself off from any admission that he even existed.

Tad's excess energy started to seep slowly away, bringing back the calm with which he did his best thinking.

He wasn't happy to be on the phone with Miranda in the middle of their current conversation.

He needed to be able to tell her that her husband really was dead. That the story she'd made up about Ethan's father's death was now reality. That she could see her father again. That the chief knew where she was and was watching out for her.

But it wasn't his truth to tell.

And how could he know, really, the nuances between a daughter on the run and a father left behind? He'd never been either.

"See you for coffee after the meeting on Tuesday?" he asked her.

"Of course."

Tad hung up, completely dissatisfied, and yet relieved, too. They'd taken a step back.

And they were still friends.

Chapter Twelve

On Monday, Miranda took her lunch hour to visit The Lemonade Stand. She'd called first, found out that Sara Havens Edwin, lead counselor and the woman who'd counseled her when she'd first landed in Santa Raquel, had half an hour between appointments, and Miranda offered to bring lunch.

With her complete security clearance, she could park in the employee lot and did so, still wary enough not to want anyone to see her entering the Stand and assuming she was a victim. No one could know she'd been one, except the few who'd worked with her, those who'd initially helped her.

New identities had to be just that—brand-new. Zero ties to the old.

And yet her very existence was a tie to herself, to her own history, that would never be broken.

Placing two veggie pitas on the table between them in the little conference room Sara had booked, she sat, sipping from one of the two glasses of tea Sara had come in carrying.

"We haven't had a meeting like this in well over a year," the counselor said, her blue eyes piercing. "What's up?"

"I've met someone."

"Ahh." The woman smiled, and her dark blond hair seemed to halo her expression.

"No…it's not like that," she said. "It's not…we're just friends. It's Tad Newberry. He's visiting, as you know, but we've been spending some time together."

"I'm glad."

Yeah, well, she didn't need a go-ahead on that score, although she could understand why Sara thought she'd come for encouragement. Sara knew she hadn't had a close personal relationship since Jeff.

"I keep having to bite my tongue not to tell him about my past," she said in a rush, feeling like a criminal for even having the thought. "I mean, you know him. You know we can trust him. Yesterday we took Ethan to the beach and got to talking, and he told me some things about his past and I just… His mother was a nurse like I was. He lost his sister—and then lost his mom young like I did. I understood and I needed so badly to tell him that. And I couldn't." The words came pouring out of her. "I felt like I was shortchanging him. And me, too."

Putting down the pita she'd unwrapped, but not yet bitten into, Sara placed her hands on the table. The counselor was familiar with trauma. She'd lived through some devastating stuff of her own. Which was part of what made her so supremely good at her job. She was also a natural calming influence.

Miranda didn't feel at all calm. A little more so when Sara met her gaze, her tone dead serious as she started to speak.

"I want to be able to tell you what you need to hear," she said. "But I can't, Miranda." Miranda, not Dana. Always. Sara knew her birth name. She'd never used it. Not once.

"For your own safety, and Ethan's, there can be no

ties. None. Particularly with law enforcement. When you left, your father had the entire state of North Carolina convinced he was to be revered, giving him a greater ability to find you than most abusers ever have. We've got no idea how far he's risen now and no one here is going to risk looking him up, either, in case a search shows up somewhere and an IP address is traced..."

"Tad's from Michigan."

"It doesn't matter. And I think you know that. You just needed *me* to know that you're tempted, didn't you?"

With tears in her eyes, Miranda nodded. She was fighting her battle.

And Sara was her arsenal.

TAD'S BIGGEST TAKEAWAY from coffee on Tuesday was relief that he and Miranda were okay. Her eyes had met his a couple of times over the conference table during the High Risk meeting. She'd smiled at him once, as though they were sharing a private joke. And afterward, at the coffee shop, she stayed for an extra half hour after everyone else left—as had become their tradition.

On Wednesday all hell broke loose. As it had been told to Tad, Marie had called Miranda to ask about swelling and pain in Danny's leg, asking for a doctor's excuse to keep him out of school. Danny had missed so many days over the past year that they'd reached the limit legally allowed before authorities got involved.

She'd needed to see Danny before she could write such a letter, and told Marie to head straight to the office, and either she or Dr. Bennet would see Danny as quickly as possible. When an hour passed and she hadn't shown up, Max Bennet called the police, who'd already been contacted by Ruby, Marie's sister.

Tad was pulled into the loop when Detective Chantel Fairbanks called to find out if he'd seen Danny that morning. He'd already been by the school twice, but hadn't seen the boy—not all that unusual, since Danny would've been in class. He also hadn't seen anyone lurking nearby, which was what he was there to watch for.

Miranda called him a few minutes later, while he was still driving around the area, filling him in on the situation as she currently knew it. Apparently a friend of Devon's had seen Marie at a gas station where she'd been gassing up her car before taking Danny to school and then going on to work. The friend begged her to call to keep Danny out of school, so no red flags would be raised. And then to go home and call him. The friend just wanted to FaceTime with Danny, and would be at a restaurant, where Devon could look on from another booth and see his son.

Danny, overhearing the request, begged Marie to agree. She couldn't tell whether that was because he loved his dad and missed him, in spite of his rages, or because he was afraid of what his father would do if his mother didn't comply. Maybe they were both intimidated by Devon's friend, which was Tad's personal opinion, and he further suspected that Devon had intended them to be.

Regardless of the reason, Marie had agreed to wait half an hour and then do as the friend asked. She called her sister, who was already at work, to tell her she was taking Danny home to make the call. And then she'd called Miranda to get a doctor clearance to keep Danny out of school. Neither of them had been seen since, and Marie wasn't answering her phone. They were running a location trace, but so far had nothing. She could have turned her cell off.

Ruby had gone home immediately, hoping to talk her sister out of going along with wishes that had clearly come from Devon, and found the house empty. She'd called the police immediately.

No one had been able to locate Devon, either, but he wasn't due at work until later that afternoon, so it wasn't as if they could be certain he was involved in foul play.

"I'm finished with my morning patients," Miranda told Tad, "and I'm just sitting here, worried sick about her. I wish there was something I could do." He could hear the fear in her voice.

"Have you tried calling her? Maybe if she saw your number, she'd take your call."

"Twice," Miranda said. "It went straight to voice mail." She was sounding less and less like herself. Like the Miranda he knew.

And more like a woman who feared forces that were stronger than she was. Could be she was putting herself in Marie's shoes. Could be she was firmly planted in her own and living with the demons her ex had left her with.

He had to help her.

And to pretend he didn't know how much she'd suffered…and why.

"You want to go to lunch? We can wait together."

Expecting a refusal, he was surprised when she agreed immediately, asking him if he'd like to meet someplace or pick her up at the office. She mentioned a diner not far from the clinic and he headed that way, telling her he'd pick her up.

The fact that she'd even asked was a "tell" to him.

She was waiting for him at the door of the clinic and came out when he pulled into the lot. "I've got an hour," she told him, settling her purse on the floor. In her cartoon character scrubs, with tennis shoes and her hair tied back, she looked as she did every Tuesday when she came from work to attend meetings, but there was something different about her, too.

A tightness in her face, lines near her mouth. She was definitely tense. Her hand was shaking as she buckled her seat belt. Or was he looking too hard? He didn't think so.

He wanted to reach over to take her hand in his, much as she'd done for him a few days before on the beach. She gave and gave and gave.

He wanted to give back.

Wanted her to know how great it felt to receive.

He asked her directions to the restaurant; she gave them and then said, "I just feel we should be doing something. At least be out there searching for her..."

As a detective, he'd been out searching more times than he could count. "Do you have any idea where she might go? Where Danny likes to go? Anyplace she might hide?"

He didn't think Marie was hiding. She'd have called for help.

Unless she'd been prevented from doing so.

"Danny likes to climb that little mountain on the south side. Out by the new housing development. Seer's Point? He told me that's when he'd know his leg was better. When he could get to the top again. Apparently Devon had been taking him there before he was old enough to walk. It seemed like a good memory for him."

And something for them to do that felt more useful than sitting in a booth at a diner. "How about we go to a drive-through for some take-out food and head over that way?"

Gratitude filled her eyes, and she nodded.

Tad put the car in gear.

SHE COULD FEEL herself slipping. Knew that panic was close. She'd called the school to confirm that Ethan was in class and okay before she'd called Tad, recognizing the ludicrousness of her actions even as she did it.

Devon Williams didn't know Ethan, and wouldn't have reason to hurt him if he did. Unless he found out that she'd given Marie her number in case she needed help. He could be after anyone who was trying to take his wife away from him.

She knew how the abusive mind worked.

Maybe he'd somehow come across her number on Marie's phone, or learned that she'd been involved in bringing Danny's case to the High Risk Team. Maybe he knew Tad was involved, too, and had seen the three of them together.

"What sounds good for lunch?" Tad's voice felt so close, while she felt so far away.

Eating in general sounded unappealing at the moment. But it was time to eat. She'd been hungry an hour ago. Acting normal was the way to beat the panic.

She felt anything but normal.

"Salad," she said, naming a new organic drive-through salad place on the way out of the downtown area, trying to think about what she'd order.

Ethan was fine. He'd been at lunch the first time she'd called. At recess the second. If she called a third time she was going to look like a lunatic.

She knew he was okay. But she was scared to death for Marie, afraid her sister in victimhood hadn't been as lucky as she herself had.

And Danny… At least Ethan had been spared violence in his young life.

She'd done the right thing. And she'd done it well. Her son was safe. Jeff would be proud of her.

Thinking of her best friend, of how incredible she'd felt the first time she made a comment about her father and, instead of doubting her, he'd asked some very serious questions and then sat and cried with her as she found a way to answer them.

She'd been lucky. So lucky.

Devon Williams had been a victim of domestic violence, too. By his father. It happened that way so often, the abused growing up to abuse.

But not with her. She'd never even come close to experiencing the white-hot rage she'd seen seething from her father.

Jeff hadn't turned into an abuser, either. He'd been gentle. Kind. Funny and emotionally strong.

"Ethan's dad was abused as a kid," she told Tad. She couldn't give him the facts of her life, but there were some things she *could* say. Things her father had never known. Things he'd never associate with her so things he'd never mention as an identifier if he was looking for her. "In his first foster home," she added, when her gut clenched anyway.

It had actually been his birth home. And his birth mother. She'd been a single mom. An addict. She'd already been at her wit's end with his older brother, and then Jeff had come along…the son of her pimp, he'd always believed.

Ethan would be back in class by now. She couldn't call to verify. Had no legitimate reason to call.

They'd phone her if there was a problem. Reaching

into the pocket of her scrub top, she checked her cell. Just to be sure she hadn't missed a call.

And tried Marie again, closing her eyes as she waited for a ring, willing the woman to pick up.

"Voice mail," she said, dropping her phone back in her pocket.

"You mentioned Ethan's dad being like Devon—"

"No!" she interrupted him, horrified at where his thoughts were taking him. Where her stilted conversation had led him. "He was nothing like Devon," she said now, scrambling for safe words. "He was my best friend. The one you went to when the rest of the world was crashing in on you. He always made things seem a little less intense. I could tell him stuff I never told anyone else."

All true. All untraceable.

And talking about Jeff, with Tad, calmed her in a whole new way.

"How'd he die?" She should've expected Tad's question, especially after he'd told her how his mother and sister died. It still caught her off guard.

"He was in a car accident," she improvised quickly. In reality, he'd been playing intramural football with a group of fraternity brothers. Had taken a slam to his left kidney. When they got him to the hospital, they found he only had one working kidney. And it had been ruptured.

He'd recovered. Was on dialysis, and waiting for a kidney to become available, but there was one complication after another. Six months later, they'd told him he wouldn't survive a transplant, although he'd seemed fine at first, other than being tired a lot...

He'd already talked to her about his last wish. And

they'd conceived Ethan while there was still hope that he'd live to hold his child in his arms.

"What would you like?" Tad had pulled into the salad place. She had to think a minute. Asked for the turmeric with rice and cranberry because she saw it on the menu board. She wasn't fond of cranberries. But as she and Tad sat in his SUV at the foot of the mountain ten minutes later, she ate as much of the salad as she could.

"I'm worried sick about what he might be doing to her," she finally admitted when the silence was rotting her mind again.

"I know."

She put the lid on her bowl, noticing that he'd only eaten half of his roasted vegetable salad. "I can't eat any more."

"You want to walk?"

They'd already perused the small dirt parking lot at the foot of the trail. Not only was Marie's car nowhere in sight, there were no other vehicles, either.

"Can you?" she asked him, looking down at the thigh she'd seen in an examining room without jeans covering it. She'd never seen him limp, but he'd told Danny that he still hurt sometimes, when he pushed things.

"I can climb the mountain," he told her, looking up at the top of the peak. "I'll probably have to limp down."

Miranda couldn't go far, had to get back to work and was in her scrubs, but she got out of the car. She figured they could walk until the trail started upward.

And when he reached out, offering her his hand, she took it.

Chapter Thirteen

It took more emotional strength than he'd ever have guessed for Tad to do nothing other than hold Miranda's hand that Wednesday afternoon. They walked the trail for about ten minutes, then sat on a cement bench. It was in the sun and Miranda had said she wanted to soak up some of the warmth.

What she'd done was look over at him, sitting shoulder to shoulder with her out in a deserted patch of nature, with trees and brush and the mountain ahead of them obscuring them from view. She met his gaze and then stared at his lips.

He could tell she'd wanted a kiss. Maybe as a distraction. Maybe to assure herself that she wasn't Marie. That she was well and healthy and perfectly safe.

Or maybe because sexual tension had been buzzing between them since the day they met.

He wasn't a guy who was good at figuring out all those nuances. He didn't usually get himself in situations where he'd need to be good at it.

But he was a guy who knew that, even tempted as he was, hard as he was growing sitting there beside her, he couldn't act on the desire pulsing inside him.

Not with the secrets standing between them.

She hadn't pushed it. Hadn't actually leaned over

and kissed him. But she'd reached for his hand as they walked back to the car a few minutes later.

As though they were…a couple. Not just friends.

AN ALERT WAS sent out to the High Risk Team late Wednesday afternoon that Marie Williams was safe and at home. Whether or not she'd let Danny make the phone call, seen her husband or just skipped town for the day, Tad didn't know, but assumed he'd hear the details at the next High Risk meeting, if not before. He was asked to resume watch duty at Danny's school, and sent a text to Marie reminding her that he was happy to help out in any other situations, as well, if she needed him.

He got a "thank you" in return, and nothing else.

Miranda also texted—to thank him for lunch. He called, wanting to see how she was doing, but she didn't pick up.

Friday's phone call couldn't arrive soon enough as far as Tad was concerned. He wasn't going to break protocol again and phone the chief unexpectedly. He respected the man's position, the difficulty of his circumstances. And pissing him off or making him uncomfortable would be counterproductive to the goal he had in mind.

It was time to get Miranda and her father back together. To end a very long and difficult chapter in both their lives.

Where that would leave him remained to be seen. He'd be lying to himself if he didn't admit he was entertaining thoughts about some kind of future in which he knew Miranda. Dana. Whether it would be back home in North Carolina or here in California, he didn't know. He was open to various possibilities.

Once he had the older man on the line Friday afternoon, he got right to the point. "We were involved in an incident with another victim this week," Tad told the chief. "Nothing notable with that case, except that for a while there, it looked like the woman and possibly her young son were in immediate danger. I was with Miranda. She was beyond frightened, Chief. It was difficult to watch. More so because she doesn't have to live this way. I'm recommending that we tell her the truth. She deserves to know that she doesn't have to live in fear. That her ordeal is done."

"Was she afraid for herself on Wednesday?"

"No."

"Then her knowing the truth wouldn't have changed anything. I imagine she's suffering from some form of PTSD. Or at least memory-related stress. Wednesday's incident was a trigger, and there's no guarantee that will ever end for her."

Tad let the anger surging inside him burn silently for a few seconds. And saw the reason in what the chief was saying.

But did he have to be so…cold, so scientific about the whole thing? This was his daughter they were talking about. If he'd seen Miranda, seen his own daughter teetering in a hell of her own and yet managing to stay afloat, to tend to others…it would break his heart.

Which was why the chief had to approach the situation from a cerebral place. Understanding dawned on Tad as he stood there in his bedroom, looking at the open sock drawer from which he'd pulled the burner phone.

Brian O'Connor might be a hero, might seem larger than life, but he was just a man, too. One who'd lost his wife to illness and then his only child to a fiend who'd beaten her to the point of fearing for her life. Running for her life.

Like his daughter, the chief might grieve, but no matter how intense his personal pain, he managed to stay afloat. To tend to others.

"You two need each other," he told his superior.

"I'm not at all sure she'd agree with you on that." O'Connor's tone was less robust than Tad had ever heard. "I haven't been completely forthright with you, Detective."

Heading out to his balcony, Tad counted the black bars across the front of the space by rote. There were twenty-four of them, mounted on top of a four-foot-high stucco wall. Spaced four inches apart.

Do not tell me her husband's still alive. Not trusting himself to speak, knowing he had to learn the facts before he acted, Tad waited.

"The truth is, finding out that I know where she is could trigger Dana to disappear again," he said. "I don't *think* it would. If she's as far along in her healing as you've reported, then she almost certainly wouldn't. Trouble is, I'm not ready to take even that minute chance of losing her again."

Tad was trying to keep pace with him. And to understand what was being said behind and inside the words, too.

"You think that anyone from her past life finding her could trigger the fight-or-flight reaction?" he guessed. Miranda in no way seemed to him to be so vulnerable that she'd run without first seeking assistance. Her whole world was filled with professionals trained to help those in her situation.

That was no mistake, he realized. Even the doctor she worked for was dedicated to the fight against domestic violence; not only that, he was a donor to The Lemonade Stand.

And the man she'd befriended, with the clear indication that she'd be open to more, the first man she'd, by her own admission, been interested in since her ex's death, was a detective on leave volunteering on the High Risk Team.

As far as he knew, none of them had any idea about her past—except him, and she didn't realize that—but she'd planted herself in the middle of a fortress.

A surge of emotion flooded him—like nothing he'd felt in many, many years. Deeply warm. And fiercely protective. The woman impressed the hell out of him over and over again.

"I think my daughter could still be hugely angry with me."

Not at all the words he'd been expecting. Or any version thereof.

"Excuse me?"

"We didn't part on good terms," the chief said, giving Tad a feeling he didn't like at all. Like when an investigation took a bad turn. A really bad turn.

"Mind explaining that one?" He didn't consider himself subordinate at the moment. Or the receiver of a paycheck. This was news to him and he didn't like being misled.

"I was trying to get her to leave the bastard," O'Connor said. "She said I didn't understand, that she loved him and he loved her..."

Lips pressed firmly together, Tad waited.

"The truth is, he turned her against me, Tad. I couldn't believe it was happening at first. *Didn't* believe it. I thought she was just having a hard day or was taking it all out on me. She said she could handle him.

That I was making things much worse. Said she wanted her space, so I did my best to give it to her. And she'd go longer and longer between phone calls. Too late I realized he was isolating her from me, the one person who could protect her. She had few friends, had been a quiet child ever since her mother died. Didn't date in high school or go out much. She was ripe for him and no matter what I tried to do to help her, it was always the wrong thing."

Tad slumped into one of the two chairs on the balcony, elbows on his knees as he stared at the artificial-grass-covered floor. Having spent close to four months studying the insidious hell of domestic violence from all sides, he could hear the truth in every single unbelievable word O'Connor was saying.

His heart went out to the guy.

"I'm sorry, sir."

"No. No. Don't you be sorry," he said in return. "You being there, what you're doing, you'll never know how much it means. I just need you to be patient, Detective. Give me insights into her current situation. Give me a little time to get to know her again, through you. To figure out a way to approach this. But if she finds out I've got you looking out for her, it could ruin everything. Unless she understands that in the past, I wasn't butting in or trying to control her, but to save her life. And that now, I just want to give her life back to her. To see her again. To love her and Jeffrey and do everything I can to help them be happy. Keep doing what you're doing. When the time is right, I'll know."

"Okay."

The last thing he wanted was to screw up Miranda's life further. He'd read a ton, witnessed a small fraction firsthand, but he had no real experience with how either Miranda or her father would be feeling.

He was superimposing his own feelings onto theirs, colored by his own experiences.

He didn't like feeling he was spying on her. But there was no way he was leaving her, either. Whether he worked for her father or not. He had to know for certain that her ex was dead. That all the danger from her past was gone. That she had a chance to know real freedom, and to have her father in her life again.

He could quit working for the chief. But then O'Connor would find someone else. Someone who might not care about Ethan and Miranda as much as Tad did. Be as respectful of them. Someone who might tip her off and send her running again as her father feared.

He hadn't learned enough yet. So he was trapped.

"She told me Jeffrey's father was killed in a car accident," he said aloud. "Do you have any idea if that's true? Do you know how the guy really died?"

She'd also told him she'd never been married.

"He died of an overdose," O'Connor said. "And I'm not sure anymore that they were ever legally married. She told me they were. That they'd flown to Vegas, did it at one of those wedding chapels."

He could never, in a million years, see Miranda doing that.

But he'd never known Dana.

"Problem is, I haven't been able to find any record of the marriage."

Even in Vegas you had to apply for a marriage license.

Clearly there was more investigating to do. And he wasn't in a position to do it. O'Connor had been right on that score. If by chance a search was noted, if it was somehow traced back to Santa Raquel, someone could come looking. He'd done a lot more reading on identity change over the past week—including the risks.

And if Miranda and Ethan's father really *hadn't* been married, did it mean other things weren't the way they seemed, either? Like the man's death?

"Another concern has been brought to my attention," O'Connor said. "There could be others, besides the brother in prison, who know that Dana's the mother of this guy's son, and who aren't the most upstanding citizens, if you get my drift. Maybe this guy owed someone drug money. Anyone could be out there, knowing that she's my daughter, knowing the position I've reached, that I've amassed a substantial amount of money, and try to get to that money through her or Jeffrey. We just don't know enough yet."

O'Connor clearly had someone good on the case. Looking at every angle. Out to protect Miranda and Ethan, Dana and Jeffrey. And the money—Chief O'Connor had been left a huge inheritance by a man whose family O'Connor had once saved. It had been all over the news. Anyone who knew Miranda was his daughter would know he'd be able to pay a tidy sum for her return...

The chief might not have told Tad the full details of his and Dana's personal situation, but he hadn't lied to Tad, either. Tad had understood all along that he got information on a need-to-know basis. Chief O'Connor was absolutely certain his daughter's ex was dead. Tad had to go with that. Deal with feeling uneasy.

O'Connor didn't get where he was without having to prove himself, again and again. He'd climbed the ranks based on his deeds, not on who he happened to know. He was a fireman, a lifesaver. He wasn't going to risk his own daughter's life or that of his grandson. On the contrary, he'd do everything possible to protect them.

"I've got your back, sir."

He made the promise before ringing off.

"And your daughter's, too," he added after he disconnected the call.

Chapter Fourteen

Ethan had a surprising request for Miranda when he came out of school on Friday. She'd spent the past two days, since hearing that Marie and Danny were home and fine, alternating between wanting to hold her son, never letting go—and needing to push both of them out into the world to live. Fear and paranoia versus strength and mental health.

"Can I spend the night at Jimmy's tomorrow?" her son asked as he climbed into the car, shoving his backpack on the floor at his feet.

Spend the night away from her?

It was as if the universe was testing her. Ethan with Jimmy.

And her with Tad.

Could she be a normal mom? Give her kid a normal life?

And a normal woman? Surrender to the intense attraction she had for Tad Newberry?

"It's his birthday and his mom said he could invite one friend and that's me," Ethan continued, taking an envelope out of the front pocket of his pack and handing it to her.

Wanting to put the car in gear and drive away, she took the envelope and pulled onto the street.

She'd met Jimmy Randolph's parents a few times. The boys had participated in T-ball together the previous summer and James Randolph, Jimmy's father, had helped coach the team.

The boys had never played together outside of school and sports, though. Ethan had never even been to Jimmy's house.

"You've never spent the night away from home," she said, still holding the sealed envelope with, she assumed, a birthday invitation inside, as she drove them toward home.

What did she do with this? Stay safe? Or take a chance?

"So?" Ethan's defensive tone told her clearly what her son wanted her to do. She could coddle him, but only so much. He was growing into his own person. Would fight for the chance to live his life.

He was six and had no idea of the reality of their lives.

What should she do? She signaled a turn and made it around the corner.

"You'd have to follow Jimmy's parents' rules. Go to bed when they say. Get up when they say, even if it's different from how we do it at home."

"I *know*, Mom, I'm not dense." The blue eyes peering over at her from behind those dark frames just took her breath away. God, how she loved him.

What should she do? There was a car slowing in front of her. She slowed, too.

"And if it sucks, I can call you and you can come get me," he added. Practical. What she should have been.

"Don't say *sucks*. You know I don't like it."

What should she do? What should she do?

Stop it, she told herself.

"I want to go, Mom."

She knew what she had to do. What the rational part of her wanted to be able to do. "I'll call Jimmy's mom and work out the details," she told her son. But she wasn't thinking about Barbara Randolph as she turned into the driveway at home a few minutes later. She was thinking about Tad Newberry.

And wondering if, maybe, he'd be free to go on a date the next night.

She'd need some pretty stupendous distraction if she was going to survive this one—her first night ever without her son.

TAD STEPPED OUT of the shower Friday evening, having just come home from an extra workout at the gym—his third visit that day—to hear his phone ding an incoming text. Still dripping, he dried his hands, threw his towel around his neck and grabbed the phone. Very few people texted him anymore.

Recently, only one.

Miranda's icon showed on his screen.

You free tomorrow night?

Funny how in an instant you could go from sore and irritable to...

Sure, he texted back. He wondered what she had in mind. Maybe invite him to the movies with her and Ethan? He would've been glad to go with them the previous weekend.

Or another picnic on the beach.

Maybe Ethan was bugging her about another round of *Zoo Attack*.

Hell, he'd be willing to sit in a puddle with them on the back porch. His, hers or someone else's.

Feel like going out to dinner?

Sounds good. Uncle Bob's again, probably. Or somewhere he hadn't been that was equally pleasing to kids. Some pizza place where he and Ethan could play Skee-Ball or shoot hoops. Rubbing his hair while the rest of him drip-dried, Tad waited for more details.

And maybe a club or something? Adult time.

He read the screen while the phone lay on the bathroom counter, then pulled the towel from his head and wrapped it around his growing midsection.

At the word *adult*?

He stared at his phone, as though touching it would make it explode.

Unless you don't want to.

The sudden hesitation struck him. He knew what it would have taken for Miranda to issue that invitation.

Picking up his phone, he typed, Of course I want to. Sorry, just getting out of the shower, went to the gym for supper tonight.

They were going out for "adult" time. Just the two of them. He felt like a randy teenager. And a fool. He was on a job.

With permission for fringe benefits.

But Miranda didn't know that. Any of it.

Still, his feelings for her were as genuine as he could get...

If he pulled back now, she'd be hurt.

Ethan's spending the night with a friend, she texted.

When should I pick you up?

I drop him off at five. How about six? Let's dress nicely. My first time out in six years.

Images of Miranda in a form-fitting dress that showed some cleavage and shoulder immediately over-whelmed him.

Got it.

Got that they'd have all night, too. That she could very well be expecting the kiss he'd managed to avoid on the trail on Wednesday. And more.

Fully erect now, he noticed the bulge of his towel in the mirror's reflection and knew he was in serious trouble.

MIRANDA'S SATURDAY OFF meant cleaning day, and she hit it like a maniac. Ethan went along with her plans to clean out his closet until he realized that meant getting rid of things he hadn't worn or played with in at least a year.

He agreed to dust the living room and bedrooms. And to empty all the trash cans. He started to grumble when she suggested he sort through his video games and choose some of them to donate—the ones he hadn't played in quite a while.

She'd been spraying down the back patio, cleaning the table and chairs, and came back in to find him playing video games. Every one he hadn't touched in what he figured was the past year.

Errands were next, and leaving a completely spotless house that now smelled like cleaning solution mixed with lavender, she got them through six stores, including the toy store where Ethan dawdled as they chose Jimmy's present—an educational race car building kit. They were still back home with a couple of hours to spare before she had to drop him off.

She'd meant to shop for something to wear that night. Had glanced at some outfits as she breezed through the mall, but nothing had grabbed her.

Worried about shoes—mostly that she wasn't sure she had any that wouldn't make her look like a frumpy old mom—she tackled her own closet, rearranging, organizing, filling another bag of things to donate to The Lemonade Stand. What the women there couldn't use, they could sell in their thrift shop.

And why the hell had she said that about dressing nicely?

Or—she cringed—used the word *adult*?

Why was she going at all?

With the beginnings of a panic attack tightening her chest, she walked out to find Ethan and conjured up another job for him. He could rearrange the cupboard so all the cereal labels faced out, and the boxed dinners were all stacked together.

But her son was sound asleep on the floor in front of the couch, his glasses skewed and pressed against the bridge of his nose.

She'd worn him out.

Too bad her energy crisis was stemming from nerves and wouldn't give in to fatigue.

Back in her bedroom, she got practical. She had a

dress, one she'd purchased to wear to a fund-raiser for The Lemonade Stand—a fancy wine tasting and auction put on by Hunter Rafferty's company, A Time of Your Life. Hunter's wife, Julie, was the sister of Colin Fairbanks, millionaire husband to Detective Chantel Harris of the High Risk Team. The event had been held the previous Christmas at the Fairbanks mansion, hosted by Julie and Chantel together, with wine from Tanner Malone's local winery. Tanner's then-fifteen-year-old sister Tatum had been a resident at The Lemonade Stand for a while.

Tatum, now twenty and going to college to study public relations with a plan to work for her brother's growing winery, had organized a play night for the children of attendees in a different wing of the mansion, with popcorn and other treats, and a host of games for them all to play with prizes for everyone.

And the dress…

It was black, tight down to midthigh and then split on the sides to just above her knees. She'd still been on an extremely tight student's budget when she'd purchased it, and it had been the only thing at the overrun store that had been classy enough for the event, in her size, and with a price tag that wouldn't deprive her and Ethan of lunches for a week.

The top part of the low-cut dress consisted of satin shoulder straps. Had she been smaller-busted, there would've been no cleavage showing. That evening she'd worn a short red satin jacket she'd found on the clearance rack at the overrun store. It was Christmastime, so it looked as if she'd picked the perfect outfit for the occasion.

Tonight, mid-April, on a date…no way was she wearing the red jacket.

But she had a black sweater, short and a blend of

Lycra and wool. She'd bought it to go with the crop top she'd worn for working out in college, but who had to know that?

Which brought her back to shoes. She'd never be able to dance in the high heels she'd settled for...

She tried them on, studying herself in shorts and a T-shirt in the full-length mirror attached to the back of her bedroom door. Too sexy. Definitely.

Walking back and forth in front of the mirror, forward and backward, turning to see herself from behind, she bit her lip.

Her calves looked...attractive.

But when she walked in those shoes, her hips swayed back and forth.

Tad might notice. In fact, he might like the whole ensemble. Might want to partake of...

She shook her head. Kicked off the shoes. She'd had an erotic dream with him as the star two nights before. Probably because although they'd talked about their attraction, about being together, he'd still never even kissed her.

And she wanted him to. Badly.

It was a matter of wanting what you didn't have, she told herself.

Great way to get a woman to want you—lead her on and then do nothing.

Tad wasn't the type of guy who'd lead a woman on, though. Or do nothing about it if he did.

Other than Wednesday out on the trail, when would he have had a chance to kiss her? Ethan was always with them.

What if he kissed her and she messed up kissing him back? It wasn't like she'd ever had hot sex in her life. Or been all that good at kissing. Always too closed in on herself. Feeling like a loser because she'd let her father's issues do that to her.

She'd never been a raving beauty. And when you felt ugly, it was hard to imagine someone else finding you desirable.

With that thought, she lifted up her shirt, turning to see herself from different angles. Slender at the waist. Smooth skin, if a little too white in a state where tanned blondes were the norm. Her breasts looked good. She'd always thought they were her best feature.

Her thighs did, too, she decided, dropping her shirt as she put the shoes back on and paraded again.

Until she caught her gaze in the mirror. What was she *doing*?

She was a twenty-eight-year-old medical professional. A mother.

If he liked her enough to kiss her, then fine.

If she liked his kisses, she'd kiss him back. If he didn't like her kisses, they'd take it from there.

She needed to get Jimmy's present wrapped. And talk her son into taking a shower because he was sleeping in someone else's sheets that night. She checked the battery on the watch she'd bought him for Christmas. A kid version of a smartwatch, designed to keep kids safe when they were apart from their parents. They could make and receive calls with up to four people.

Hers was the only number programmed in it.

Might not be a bad idea to have Tad's there, too. Just in case. With something practical to do, she warded off the panic for another few minutes.

Chapter Fifteen

Tad was going to keep his hands off her. Or die trying. From the second she opened her door to him that evening, he'd been salivating. Wanting her like he'd never wanted a woman in his life.

Even more than the first time he'd had sex. He'd been eighteen, the summer before he'd started college. She'd been five years older than him—working at the same restaurant he had. He'd had women since, a fair share, but only those who were happy to keep things casual.

He'd done some research that afternoon, and took Miranda to a five-star restaurant with a renowned chef, but not because of the stars or the chef. The place was situated on a cliff overlooking the Pacific and had a wall of windows on the ocean side. He'd been lucky enough to get a reservation for a window table for two, and was glad he had when they were seated and he looked across the candlelit space to see the glow in her eyes.

"This is wonderful," she said, her voice caressing him like a warm massage. "I've never been to a place like this in my life."

Her hair, down as usual, was shining and curled around her shoulders. She leaned forward and, not expecting the move, he found that his gaze was trapped by her cleavage. Something he'd purposely been avoiding. He could see the swell of her breasts, right there, naked, in front of him, and got instantly hard.

Then her words registered. "Never?" he asked. Although the chief hadn't always been a millionaire, he'd done well for himself, making six figures by the time Dana would have been old enough to be taken out to fancy places.

"Nope," she said, still glancing around. And then, sobering, looked at him. "I…grew up in foster care, remember?"

Right. He knew better. And yet…when she'd first made the statement, he could have sworn she was telling the truth. Not just Miranda's truth, but Dana's, too. The whole truth.

Surely, even if it was only for her high school graduation, the chief would have treated her to an elegant dinner. Tad had been out with him twice, and that had just been for informal job interview conversations.

Brian O'Connor liked fine food.

So did Miranda, as it turned out. She enjoyed a good glass of wine, too, although they limited themselves to one apiece since he was driving.

"I have a bottle at home," she said as they were waiting for their check after dinner. They'd talked about innocuous things, like books they'd read, movies they'd seen, which ones they'd liked. They'd found several in common, and a couple not so much. She went for the more emotionally intense. He liked action. "The wine at my place won't be as good as this was, but it's in the fridge chilling…"

She was inviting him in.

He wanted to go in.

MIRANDA CALLED BARB Randolph as she waited for Tad to get the valet to bring the car around. She didn't feel like herself, was tingling with awareness and anticipation, but she was still a woman who knew she was solely responsible for the little boy she'd taken on the run with her.

To save their lives from a madman who should've been the one person in the world who'd protect her.

The man was famous for saving lives. Revered for it.

The irony wasn't lost on her.

And she wasn't going to let it taint this night, either. As soon as she heard that Ethan was doing well, had eaten three pieces of pizza and was with Jimmy and his dad in their workshop—where James was making both of the boys little cars out of wood—she was just a woman with the most gorgeous man on earth.

At least, that was how Tad seemed to her as he came strolling toward her, his long legs and firm body filling out that fitted black suit with the red satin tie. She could have worn her jacket, after all.

She could pretend he wasn't as hot as he seemed, except that she'd seen those legs. Knew how muscular and firm they were. Had seen the boxers, too…

Were they blue tonight?

Shivering with the need to know, she took the hand he held out to her and walked with him to his SUV, not caring that the slit in her dress rode up to the silken line of her black panties as she climbed inside.

She caught him looking. And smiled. Noticing how he pulled the corner of his jacket closed.

Being with a man, being in want, being wanted, was delicious. If this was healthy living, she was all for it.

After he started the engine, it was quiet inside, dark

and intimate. He reached for the radio controls, finding a streaming station that played soft music with no commercials.

"Dinner was delicious, thank you," she said as a love song that had come out a couple of years before filled the car.

She'd heard the song a hundred times. Knew the words. It had never meant a darn thing to her.

Suddenly every word was etching itself on her body.

And she got nervous.

She wasn't in love. Couldn't be in love.

But she was in a whole lot of like. Infatuation, even. Respect and a ton of lust...

And didn't know squat about casual sex. Not personally.

"You want to stop at the beach? We could take off our shoes and walk in the sand," he suggested as they drew closer to her part of town.

A reprieve. And romantic, too.

"We could stop at my place, pour some wine into plastic cups and walk over." She'd have to change shoes. Or go barefoot.

"You want more wine?"

Not as badly as she wanted him.

She nodded.

He stopped at her house. And poured the wine while she changed into flip-flops. He got a pair of his own out of the back of his SUV as they passed it on their way down the driveway.

"From my gym bag," he told her. "I don't go barefoot in the sauna."

Neither did she...when she'd gone to the sauna back in college. Her roommate at the time, a girl she'd only lived with for one semester, had teased her about it. That was the first time she'd gone to college. She silently took his hand as they started down the street.

TAD WAS ABOUT ready to explode. He'd clearly been without sex for too long, and he was having a hard time thinking about anything else. Found his thoughts thinning as though the synapses in his brain had gone numb. His penis had not. Darkness hid the evidence, for which he was thankful.

But he had to keep his wits about him or risk making a huge mistake. He couldn't afford another one of those. Which was why he was carrying a cup of wine but not drinking from it.

He didn't want to lose his closeness with her. And not because of her father. But because she'd come to mean more to him in eight short weeks than he could fathom. His life, a life that had been like a spinning top, had finally settled in a little beach town in California, thanks to the woman walking beside him in the dark, holding his hand.

And yet staying in Santa Raquel wasn't a reality he could seriously consider. More and more he knew that he needed to get back to work. That quitting what he did—putting himself on the line to save lives—would destroy part of who he was. He needed his work.

And he needed her happy, too. Such an odd concept, to care so much about a person that his or her happiness made you feel…satisfied.

The air was cool and although she was wearing a sweater, she shivered. Removing his jacket, he put it around her shoulders and then took her hand again.

"You'll need this," she said, turning as though to shrug out of it and give it back to him.

He knew he wouldn't need it. Not for the warmth. He was burning up.

And darkness was his cover.

She hesitated, but let the jacket stay where it was. Let herself accept the gift. And he could feel her struggle. Like she had to fight, constantly, to accept anything from anyone.

"I washed your windows." The asinine comment blew out of him.

"What?"

"The day after you were talking about not getting to the outside windows. I came over and washed them for you."

What the hell was he doing? Trying to piss her off?

Or ingratiate himself? No, not that. Definitely not that.

"Oh." She didn't miss a step. Didn't drop his hand. But she was quiet for a minute or two and he couldn't gauge her mood or come up with any guess as to what she was thinking.

"I didn't notice," she finally said. "I'm sorry. And thank you."

All appropriate responses. But he wanted the truths she held inside.

"I shouldn't have been on your property without letting you know. Shouldn't have touched your house without letting you know." One more block to the beach. They couldn't get there soon enough. Maybe he'd take a headlong dive into the ocean.

"So why did you?"

"Because I wanted to help you and had a pretty strong suspicion that if I offered, you'd refuse."

She chuckled. "You're probably right." Then, shaking her head, "I know you're right."

He didn't want her agreeing with him. He wanted her writhing beneath him.

"I took away your choice about making that decision," he said, feeling as cantankerous as he ever got. Playing to the victim in her, even though he was taking advantage of his private knowledge about her. His secret knowledge.

It was all to remind himself that their playing field wasn't level. To make her less into him because he wasn't sure he could trust himself to say no to anything she offered.

But one less secret felt pretty damned good, as it turned out.

"Being a friend means having someone's back enough to know when that person needs help," she said.

Oh. God, what was he going to do with this woman? The minute he felt he had it all under control, she surprised him again.

In ways that captivated him.

They'd reached the sand. Kicked off their flip-flops, leaving them on the edge of the sidewalk. No one else was out, but the beach, reserved for homeowners in the neighborhood, which included Miranda's cottage, seemed to beckon them.

Not only were the waves rushing in to shore, but lights shone out on the ocean from some kind of vessel, and the shoreline in the distance was dotted with lights from houses and establishments. The sand was cold between his toes, in direct contrast to the heat of her hand in his.

"You need your coat back," she said as a breeze lifted the hair on his head.

"I need the fresh air," he told her. And then said, "You ever listen to older rock bands? You know, the classics?"

"Like the Eagles?"

"Yeah, or Kansas. They have this song, 'Dust in the Wind.' You ever hear it?"

"Dah, dah, dah…" she hummed the tuned. And then recited a couple of stanzas about dust and wind and how small each person really was.

"Sometimes I think about that, how we're all little more than a grain of sand," he said, talking in a way he never talked aloud. Sharing thoughts that embarrassed him somewhat. "And I take comfort in that." He glanced over at her. Her hair was blowing back from her face, the moon shining on her cheeks. He moved in, not thinking, just moving, taking his lips to hers and then, in the last second, pulled back.

"It's good to know I don't always have to carry the weight of the world on my shoulders," he told her, hoping she'd see that she could feel the same way. That he could somehow find a way to truly lighten her load. Other than by washing a few windows. "Sometimes, I can just be one grain of sand blowing in the breeze, and the world won't even know I'm not doing anything."

"I heard a wise woman speaking once." Her voice was louder. They had to speak up to hear each other over the waves. "I can't remember the occasion or what exactly she was talking about. But at one point she said, 'All shall be well,' and the words stuck with me. Sometimes, late at night, if I wake up and the world seems too heavy for me to carry, I tell myself, all shall be well. In the long run, no matter what I do or don't do, no matter what does or doesn't happen, all shall be well. Usually, remembering that, I can let go long enough to fall back asleep."

Just like a grain of sand, able to lie on the beach and

not matter, for a minute or two. A moment to lay down your burden and rest.

She got it. And he was glad.

Chapter Sixteen

It was way too chilly to sit on the beach. Or even think about getting naked there. When Tad suggested heading back, she readily agreed, although she'd only had about three sips of her wine. She dropped the cup into the trash can as they passed it, and he did, too.

There was more at home, chilled. Mostly she just wanted to get there. To be alone with him.

The whole day had been building to this point and the walk on the beach had made it completely clear to her. She wanted this.

And all would be well.

The universe had sent her a man when she was ready to meet him, and yet, if he'd offered to wash her windows, she'd have turned him down.

For no good or rational reason.

She wasn't going to turn him down that night. She was ready to start living again. Being a woman, a person, not just a mom and a PA.

While she loved being both of those things, she needed more.

It was time.

And she'd met a man, developed feelings for him, and was ready to take this first step. To get on with her life.

It helped that he was only in town temporarily. She didn't have to worry about long-term consequences. About the secrets she couldn't ever share.

There'd be no need. He was going to be a lover—she hoped—not a life partner. Or even a lifelong friend.

And if, in the throes of passion, she let something slip from her old self—like she'd admitted that night that she'd never eaten out in such a nice place—then she had to trust herself to find a way out of it. To explain. To cover.

Just as she'd been doing since she'd signed Dana O'Connor out of existence. She knew how to do it.

Had become quite adept.

She could be a grain of sand. A speck of dust in the wind. For a little while. Her son was safe. For the first time since she'd run with him, she had an entire night ahead of her, a night without having to listen for him, to know that it was up to her to keep him safe if anyone broke in...

Tad walked her to the door and hesitated behind her, almost as though he wasn't going to follow her in.

"You want a fresh glass of wine?" she asked him. "You want to come in?" would probably have been better. She wasn't going to drink much more. An occasional glass of wine was it for her.

Her father had never raised a hand to her until he started drinking after her mother died.

Not on the job, though. No, he only drank at home. On his days off. When Miranda was trapped there with him, taking the brunt of his anger. All the bitterness at the death of his wife...and for years Miranda had been the recipient of that rage.

Tad nodded and followed her inside. She didn't ask

about the wine again. She just poured some for both of them. But didn't drink.

She watched him take a sip, knowing, somehow, that he didn't really want the alcohol any more than she did.

They could sit on the couch. Or go to her room. She had nightstands. They could set their wine down...

She wasn't all that up on seduction technique.

"It's nice here," Tad said, walking barefoot in his suit to the living room, taking a seat on the couch. "You've made it comfortable. Peaceful."

Smiling, she hesitated a second before sitting next to him, curling her feet up on the couch as she turned to him. If she acted all virginal, she might give him the wrong impression.

"My goal is for Ethan to grow up in a healthy happy space. Apart from the rest of the world. Which is why I have so few visitors."

As soon as the words were out, she knew they were wrong. Gave away too much. Freezing, she started to slide backward in her thinking. To...

"You've only been here for what, a year? Since you finished school?"

She'd told him during one of their coffee shop visits that she'd been a PA for a year. That she and Ethan had lived in an apartment building close to his school during the time she'd been in PA school, moving into their current home in Santa Raquel last year. All her hands-on clinical work had been done at the new children's hospital in Santa Raquel. The story that she'd had help creating for herself, and that she'd given to Tad early on, was that she'd gone to high school in Portland, Oregon—a place she'd visited, so she could speak of it believably—and that she'd dropped out of school to have Ethan. After that, she'd told him, she'd moved to Santa

Raquel because of the study program that allowed her to do much of her work online, since the Santa Raquel children's hospital worked in coordination with an online PA degree program.

The truth was, she'd chosen to become a PA because she'd been in Santa Raquel due to The Lemonade Stand, though she'd never been a resident at the shelter. Then she'd heard of the PA program. With a nursing degree she couldn't use, needing a new career, the situation had been ideal for her.

That was another time the universe had provided for her after she'd done all she could.

"Yeah we moved in last year during spring break, and most of the stuff is secondhand," she admitted. "I'm slowly buying new as I can afford it."

She made good money now. More than she'd ever have made as a nurse. But she put a lot of it away. Some in a bank. Some not.

If she ever had to run again, she wouldn't be doing it destitute. She'd make it an adventure for Ethan. Taking him someplace decent. Telling him they were on vacation.

Maybe it wouldn't ever happen. She hoped... Maybe she worried for nothing. But with her father, a man who never gave up, she had to be on alert.

"It doesn't look secondhand..." He was holding his glass, watching her, not studying her belongings.

His gaze, so warm and intimate, fired her blood, made her wet with wanting, and...he didn't move. Didn't lean in as he had at the beach. They weren't even touching.

He took a sip of wine, breaking eye contact. She sipped, too, a little taste, and when she saw how much her hand was shaking, put her glass down.

"Is there something wrong with me?" she asked. It was late. They were alone with wine. Wearing sexy clothes.

"What?" His wide-eyed glance might have been comical if she hadn't been starting to panic. In a way that was wholly new to her. "Something wrong with you? No! Of course not." And then, in that soft voice of his that made her feel...wanted all over again, he murmured, "Why do you ask?"

"You said you wanted to ask me out. Or you were hinting that you did. We're...you're...you and I, you and Ethan. You said you wanted all three of us."

"I do." He set his glass down, too. And somehow managed to move a little farther away as he turned toward her and took her hand. "I really do."

"So? Why is nothing...happening?"

He didn't say anything. Just studied her. Like he was reading a book or something.

"Ethan's usually around." His answer, when it came, was a huge disappointment. And a relief, too.

Only because he was confirming an excuse she'd already come up with. A reality she'd already created.

"But he isn't here tonight."

Her father had not taught her to be a woman who threw herself at men. On the contrary, he'd beaten her bloody the first time a boy had kissed her on her front step after a summer dance hosted by their high school—and the great chief had witnessed the unremarkable occurrence.

Buzzkill. Maybe this evening wasn't a good idea, after all.

"I'm afraid that if I touch you, I won't stop."

Tad's words brought her head up. She saw the truth

in the light in his eyes. In the way his jaw clenched. And when she dared to glance lower.

"Who says you have to stop?" she whispered, aware only of him again. Sand. Dust. All would be well.

"Sex complicates things. I don't want to lose you."

I don't want to lose you. She'd dreamed those words. Back when she used to fantasize about meeting a good man, having a husband who'd cherish her as much as she did him.

I don't want to lose you, she'd cried in Jeff's arms when she'd finally accepted what he'd known—that he wouldn't live long enough to see the birth of their son.

"You aren't going to be around forever," she reminded Tad.

"Like I said, it's complicated."

But not impossible.

He wanted her. And she needed him. To help her get to that normal life she was supposed to live.

She was a woman who didn't trust, but she trusted Tad. Enough to have him in her home. To give him time with Ethan. To want to share her body with him.

She was horny as hell and maybe she wasn't thinking straight, but it felt so…good. So right.

"I've never felt anything like this before. Been turned on like this." She couldn't keep it to herself anymore. "It's making me crazy. I think about you all the time, about how you looked that day in the examining room with your pants down around your ankles…"

Just saying the words made her heat up. She reached for her wine, took another sip. So yeah, usually one glass was her limit, but there was nothing usual about this night.

"Surely you must've been attracted to Ethan Sr.," Tad

said. He had a look in his eye, a wanting, that reached right inside her.

She didn't want the wine anymore. She wanted Tad. For real. Needing him to know her in ways no one else had.

"I...wasn't attracted to him," she said slowly. "Not sexually, at any rate." She was attracted to his heart. To his friendship.

And could tell this part of the story. There'd be no way to trace what had happened between her and Jeff.

They'd never dated. No one had suspected.

"You had a child with a man you weren't sexually attracted to?" His frown showed concern, but the edge in his voice sounded suspicious, and he seemed more like a detective sensing something criminal. "Did he rape you?"

She might have seen that coming if she'd been herself.

"No!" Oh, God, no. While the lie might be a good cover, she couldn't let it stand. "I'd just...never..." She faltered. "He was a friend. A close friend. I wasn't into partying and drinking, and sometimes he'd stay back and hang out with me. Mostly we talked. Trusted each other with things we never told anyone else. We'd both grown up in foster homes and it bonded us." Her father's abuse, his birth mother and then foster father's abuse, that was what had bonded them.

"The car accident I told you about, that killed him..." The football game. She'd been there, standing on the sidelines, cheering for his fraternity. "He didn't die immediately." He'd had long enough to find his long-lost brother, contact him. The guy had offered insincere commiseration, asked for money and then moved on.

"But he knew he was going to die," she went on.

"The one thing he wanted was to have a child, a legacy, part of himself to continue on in the world. He wanted that with me. And he wanted his child to be connected to me. Someone who would give me unconditional love. When he first talked to me about it, I didn't think he was serious. But he wouldn't let go of the idea. And the more he talked about it, the more I saw that if I did as he asked, he'd be able to die peacefully. I had to give that to him. I knew I wanted children someday, and if that day came sooner…"

Her biggest concern had been her father. He'd gone nuts when she'd just kissed a guy. The second she'd come in the house and shut the door. As far as she knew, he'd only taken it out on her, not the boy she'd gone out with. The date had been during the summer between her junior and senior years of high school, and she'd stayed home until she healed. But the guy had never called her again—not that their date, or the kiss, had been that great. And not one guy had asked her out in her senior year, either.

If that kind of reaction had happened after just a kiss, no telling what he'd do to her, or Jeff, if she turned up pregnant without a husband or full-time job. She'd been going home less and less since leaving for college and hadn't gone at all during the months her pregnancy was showing. She'd been petrified of what he'd do.

And had known that eventually she'd have to tell him. He was her father. He still insisted on birthdays and holidays together.

"You're saying Ethan was conceived on purpose with someone with whom you'd had no sexual relationship?"

She nodded. "And it wasn't all that terrific for either of us," she admitted. "The sex, I mean." Jeff had struggled to even make it happen. They were so close emotionally, and physically it had been so awkward...

"Was he your first?"

She'd hoped he wouldn't ask that. But nodded.

"And since Ethan...there's been no one?"

More to the point, "I haven't felt even a hint of wanting someone." She'd never been fully turned on in her life, until him.

Having endured beatings that escalated over time from a man she'd loved and trusted sometimes did that to a girl. Squelched her ability to feel attractive to men. To be turned on by them. Or so she'd been told in counseling. She'd only been eleven the first time he'd hit her. He'd apologized almost immediately and then gently explained how it had been her fault for clinging to him and crying, for reaching for him over and over, after her mother's funeral. With it being her fault, she'd been loath to mention her bad, clingy, needy behavior to anyone else.

He'd been smart, too. Always hitting her where it wouldn't show.

"And you weren't molested?" His gaze was intent.

"No." From what she'd learned since she'd reinvented herself, she was lucky on that score. She looked him straight in the eye as she answered him.

After a long moment of studying her, he asked, "So, why me?"

His question was fair.

"I have absolutely no idea." It was the truth. "I just know that if you don't kiss me, I'm going to cry myself to sleep tonight." Being honest was one thing; too much information was another. It felt as if once she'd opened her well of secrets, anything that could slip out by chance did so.

"Well, we can't have that…" His voice had dropped to almost a whisper, a guttural one, as he moved slowly forward, sliding his arm behind her, and pulled her closer to him. She ended up with her breasts against his chest. The contact sent immediate electric shards of warmth down to her crotch.

His lips touched hers and all thought fled. There was only sensation. Incredible, delicious, delightful sensation. She opened her mouth at his probing, eager for whatever he had to give her. To show her.

Eager to learn. To do.

To know what being with him would be like.

He moved lower, kissing her jaw, her neck. He smelled like some kind of musky man something and as his day's growth of stubble rubbed against her sensitive skin, she shivered with a need for more.

Her hands moved over him, exploring the muscles in his chest, his arms. Exploring his back. Noticing the differences between his body and hers. Getting turned on by those differences.

And from knowing those were Tad's hands on her. That it was *him* she was touching.

"Are you okay?" he asked, drawing her attention to the fact that she'd stopped moving.

"Better than okay," she told him. She could stare into his brown eyes all night. She ran her fingers through his hair. "I just like having the privilege of touching you."

Maybe she was odd. And no good at love talk. But she had to be herself. Her deep-down true self. The one without a name who lived both lives within her.

"I hereby grant you that privilege anytime you want it," he said, groaning as he drew her even closer, lying down on the couch with her mostly on top of him.

"We could go to my bedroom," she offered, playing

with a button on his shirt, wanting to unfasten it. To feel his skin against her fingers.

His hands were still touching her back but not holding on.

"I know," she added, "it's complicated. No strings attached, Tad. Just come to bed with me. Please?"

She'd probably die remembering these moments in the morning, but she was a woman who'd awakened from a hellacious nightmare and had this opportunity. He'd be gone soon, back to his own life.

She would come to her senses; she already knew she couldn't be part of a long-term, committed relationship because she couldn't lie to her partner, even by omission.

"Things aren't always what they seem," he told her.

She might have laughed at the irony of that statement, but was too far gone, desperate to get naked next to him while she could. Moving her pelvis against his rigid penis, she said, "It seems like you want this as much as I do."

It didn't take a lot of experience to know some things.

He kissed her. Long and deep. Then looked her in the eye again. "I've never wanted a woman more than I want you right now."

That was all she needed to know. Standing, she held out a hand to him. He took it. Stood up and then, when she would've walked down the hall with him, he scooped her up and carried her.

Chapter Seventeen

Tad was pretty sure he wasn't thinking straight—or thinking with his brain at all—as he fell down onto Miranda's double bed with her still in his arms. He just knew there was no way he was sending this woman off to cry herself to sleep. To believe she wasn't enough. Or desired.

This whole situation was beyond rationalizing, in a sphere where right and wrong didn't exist. The need was devastating. And mutual. It had to happen.

So he quit fighting the inevitable.

"Tell me what you want," he said as he pulled his lips from hers and saw her looking up at him, those big blue eyes wide. Her blinds were closed, but she had some kind of night-light in the adjoining bathroom and it spread soft, subtle light over portions of the bed.

"I want to unbutton your shirt."

Slipping off his jacket and tie, he tossed them toward the end of the bed, then lay back against the pillows. She had them stacked two deep and he sank into them with pleasure. "Have at it," he said, smiling at her.

Slowly, she tended to his shirt. With each button, he could feel the soft brush of her fingers against his skin, first his chest and then lower. He could feel the passion fueling his body's need for release growing more and more intense, too. Her movements were mind-blowingly hot and excruciating, but he didn't stop her. When she finally reached the bottom of his shirt, he waited— partially to give himself time to recover enough so he could continue without ending things prematurely, and partially out of curiosity.

What would she do next, this glorious feminine mixture of knowing and innocence? Of strength and vulnerability. The cleavage that had been teasing him all night was above him, a temptation he was savoring. But he willed himself enough control to be able to uncover her gifts slowly, to touch and taste and know them thoroughly.

Pulling wide the edges of his shirt, she put both hands on his lower belly, and his hips thrust upward with the force of his reaction. Seeming not to notice, she slowly moved both palms upward, fingers splayed, covering every inch of skin on his abdomen, his ribs, then his chest. She rubbed her face in the hair and flicked her tongue against his nipples before taking them between her fingers, touching softly.

She might be personally innocent, but she knew erogenous places, knew how to tantalize them, and it dawned on him—she was a medical professional. Had to have studied all the major nuances of the human body. She'd probably had a course in human sexuality.

He wanted to know every little thing she'd learned on that subject. Wanted her to show him. To do things to him.

He wasn't sure he had the time. Not on this first go-round. He groaned and she straddled him, settling her weight against his bulging fly. Not moving, just weighing him down.

"You're going to get more than you bargained for down there, missy," he told her, and she smiled.

"How do you know what I'm bargaining for?"

"How do *you* know so much about tantalizing a man?"

Her grin didn't change as she continued to tease his nipples. "I'm actually playing out my own fantasy here, but I'm glad it's good for you, too."

Not sure whether she was messing with him or not, Tad rolled to his side, and then, with another quarter turn had her underneath him. One tug and he had her dress up over her hips and his hand down her panties. She was as wet as he was going to be in a couple of seconds.

He yanked at those panties and got them down low enough. By the time he'd tossed them, her legs were spread and she had his belt undone and was working on the clasp of his pants. He helped with the zipper, pulled himself free of his boxers, then took a condom out of his back pocket and opened it with his teeth and slid it on with one hand.

"I'm sorry," he told her. "I wanted to take all night."

"We've got all night," she squealed as she thrust herself upward and over him. He moved as slowly as he could, wanting to remember every single sensation along the way, the tightness of her. The welcoming.

She wasn't as gentle as he was trying to be as she answered his thrusts, and within a few seconds it was all over.

Remarkably, for both of them.

BLISSFULLY SORE, MIRANDA still wasn't ready for sleep an hour later. She and Tad had made love twice more, taking more time, exploring.

"If I'd had any idea it could be like this…" Her sentence trailed off because she couldn't finish it. Even if she'd had an idea, there hadn't been a man in her life who could arouse these feelings in her.

Physical satisfaction came from more than just body parts. At least for her.

"I hope that means you'll consider repeat opportunities as soon and as often as we can arrange?" Tad half growled as he curved into her, his arm around her waist, his face snuggled between her breasts.

"I was hoping you'd be amenable to the possibility," she told him, grinning. Her hands, running lightly along his back, moved over the raised skin of his scars as they had several times during the past hour. This time they stopped there, tracing the lines. She sat up and climbed over him and then, lying behind him, began to kiss those scars. Lightly, one by one. Needing to know…

He turned, maybe uncomfortable that she was delving so completely into a different aspect of his life, but she couldn't let him disappear—back into their world of secrets. She sat up. "How'd it happen?" she asked. "For real," she added, letting him know she wasn't going to be satisfied with the generic answer he'd given Danny and Marie at the clinic.

Sighing, Tad rolled onto his back, put his arm over his eyes, and she wondered if he'd fallen asleep. Then he pulled himself up against the pillows and met her gaze.

"It started with a report of stolen property. A series of home invasions in an upscale neighborhood. A single perp. He didn't take electronics. Just jewelry, silver, some collections, an artifact. He'd hit eight homes that I knew of, in at least three neighborhoods, and at the last one, an old man was home and got hurt. There was no obvious point of entry, but the thief didn't seem familiar with the homes. You could tell he spent time in each place, looking for things. He always hit when the owners were on vacation. In the last case, a grandfather was cat-sitting for the family while they were out of town. He ended up in the hospital with—fortunately—minor injuries. Could've been a lot worse. There were never any prints at these sites. No sign as to how the guy was getting into gated communities, which told me he had to have access to them.

"I checked all the maintenance people they used, down to cleaning crews and pool companies. Nothing. Until I was questioning the old guy in the hospital and he said something about getting up to have a snack and all he could find were the pastry puff things the caterer had left after the party his son had the night before they left town. Turned out that the caterer had been to many homes in each of the neighborhoods, though not all the homes he hit were his clients'. He knew how to get in the neighborhood gates, though, without alerting anyone."

Listening to him was like watching an episode of a cop show on television. Miranda almost forgot why he was telling the story. Almost.

"The caterer denied everything, of course, but his wife said she'd seen some receipts from an antiques dealer that she'd questioned him about. They didn't have any antiques. She was able to find one of the receipts, which she gave to me. I showed up at the address on the receipt—an upscale antique store—early one morning, on a tip from a neighboring business that the owner usually came in an hour or so before he opened. As I get there, a woman's walking out and I held the door for her and went on in. I had a black-and-white backing me up, two officers, on the street. I was thinking I'd just question the guy, but the second he saw my badge it all went south. Fast. There was this little girl behind the counter and the man grabbed her, put a gun to her head and started backing toward this door, telling me that if I came any closer he'd shoot the kid."

He looked so…sorry. Like it was his fault. Miranda's heart pumped heavily. She knew this story wasn't going to end well. She'd seen his scars.

And remembered that he'd told Danny that only the bad guy had died. Of course, what else would you tell a seven-year-old who'd just narrowly escaped a beating from his father and ended up with a serious leg wound?

"I radioed outside, and then called for hostage negotiators. I was told to stand down, to wait for backup, but I could hear the little girl crying in there. Something crashed and the girl screamed. Like she'd been hurt. I tried to get the guy to talk to me, thinking that he couldn't hurt her if I kept him engaged in conversation. It worked for a minute or two. He told me he wasn't going to jail. No way was he letting his wife give his daughter another father. I figured I was getting him to trust me and I motioned for the two officers to come in and back me up. Others were arriving, coming in through the rear entrance, but the negotiators weren't there yet. I was standing right outside the door by then. I could hear a toilet flush. The guy said something about taking the girl with him, and then she screamed, 'No, Daddy, no!' and I burst through the door. I couldn't just stand there and let that little girl die.

"Turns out he'd rigged a bomb to go off when the door was opened. What he told me was that if anyone came in, he and his daughter would die. I saw the wires as I was pushing through. It was too late to stop the explosion, but I dived for the girl, pushing her out of the way and landing on top of her. The guy had been going through a divorce and didn't want his ex and her new man to have full custody of his daughter. He knew that if he was charged with a criminal offense, he'd lose her for sure. Apparently, he was dealing drugs out of the shop, too. Probably thought that's why I was there. Up until a few months before he'd been a law-abiding citizen. Ostensibly he was doing it all to have the money to pay alimony, child support and legal bills, according to a source who worked for him."

"Did the bomb really kill him?" He'd told Danny it had.

"It just knocked him unconscious. He killed himself in the hospital."

Miranda smiled, a sad smile, but still... "So you saved the little girl's life and all was well—other than your own need to heal, of course."

Tad shook his head. "I'm not just on leave," he told her. "I'm under an IA investigation. I tried to quit outright, but the department didn't accept my resignation. They want me back. They just have to work out how to get my fellow officers to believe I've got their backs."

"I don't understand."

"The bomb didn't completely detonate when I pushed through the door. It was still active and there I was, in there with a little girl who was going to die in my arms if someone didn't figure out a way to get us out of there. The shop owner was unconscious, dead for all anyone knew, but that girl was very much alive and aware.

"If I'd waited for the hostage team, chances are they either would've known there was a bomb and taken proper precautions or, best-case scenario, they'd have been able to talk the owner down. Get him to release the girl, at least."

"Sounds like he wouldn't have done that. Not if

he knew he'd be releasing her to her mom and this other man."

"Hostage negotiators are trained to find out what they're facing. If they'd had no luck, they could have rigged a small camera under the door, seen the bomb. People specially trained in volatile situations would have been on hand. As it was, there were two other officers and me, and a ticking bomb."

Mouth dry, she tried not to imagine the scene in the detail he was giving.

"So what happened?"

"Help arrived. Someone who recognized the type of bomb, the particular chemicals used, and knew how to disarm it in a way that curtailed the blast."

And all that time he'd been lying there, in excruciating pain based on his scars, with the little girl. Probably telling her that everything was going to be fine.

She'd seen his patience with Ethan.

"It was clear after further investigation that the shop owner was uncomfortable with his illegal activity and had been getting more and more paranoid. He'd been planning his way out for weeks. The theory was that he intended to blow up the office to hide his illegal activity. They think the flush I heard was him getting rid of cocaine. I don't know if he'd meant all along to take his daughter with him, though. I do know she wasn't even supposed to have been there that day. Her mother had been called into work on her day off. She's the woman who'd been leaving as I'd come in."

"And the girl? Is she okay? With her mother?"

"As far as I know. She was treated and released the same day."

Reaching underneath him, Miranda placed her hand on the scars. "You saved her life," she said. "If her father was as unhinged as he sounds, chances are he wasn't going to wait for the hostage negotiating team. He knew there was no way out for him and had already decided he'd rather die than be caught."

"Maybe. That was my take."

"I'd wear these scars as a badge of honor," she told him. "Life is complicated," she echoed his earlier words. "It's a messy situation and definitely doesn't follow the rules."

His raised eyebrow made her want to start kissing him again. Life got so unexpectedly ugly sometimes, you needed to lose yourself in exquisite sensation just to survive.

"Think about it," she continued. "Look at Danny and Devon." Look at an eleven-year-old girl whose mother had just died and whose father got drunk the day of the funeral and backhanded her for coming to him crying— begging him for solace.

He hadn't been able to handle his own grief, let alone hers. She'd understood. Which was why it had been so much easier for him to get her to believe that *she* was the problem. That *she* made him lose his temper. He'd never once hit her mother. Or her either, until that day.

"Rules and protocol are great for most situations," she said, overtired suddenly. "But when they don't work, you have to go with your gut. That's why we're given instincts as well as intellect."

It was a lesson she was still learning. To trust her instincts.

"Come here." Tad held out his arms to her. Miranda hesitated, afraid now to seek her own comfort.

She should be allowed to be happy. She had that right.

Just as she should've been able to seek comfort from

her father the day her mother was buried. Just as Tad should've been celebrated for saving a life, not put under investigation because he hadn't followed protocol. She should never have had to take her child and run, leaving her father to grow old all alone.

Tad's arms slid under hers and he lifted her up against him, sliding the covers they'd pulled down earlier over both of them.

Life wasn't fair. It was filled with tough choices.

And sometimes…miraculous moments, too.

Chapter Eighteen

The sun was shining all that next week. Tad had to make a conscious effort not to get lulled into a sense of laid-back, carefree California life. Marie and Danny were living their lives, going about their normal routines for the most part. Danny was in rehab, working hard and showing progress already.

They found out at Tuesday's High Risk Team meeting that Marie had taken Danny to make the phone call to her ex, but at the last minute, she'd felt herself being sucked in again and refused to go through with it. Danny had been upset with her and she'd just started driving. Afraid to go home. Not wanting to call the police for fear of getting Devon in trouble and having Danny hate her more. In the end, they'd driven up the coast, had lunch and talked, just mom and son. They were both undergoing counseling, but Danny was only seven; he'd witnessed a lot in his young life and the mom-and-son time had been good for both of them. When they returned home, he was no longer mad at his mom, and Marie was readier than ever to divorce Devon and get on with her life.

They'd also heard at Tuesday's meeting that Devon had gone to a couple of job interviews. And he'd been sober for them.

Tad had difficulty keeping his hands to himself when Miranda stayed for coffee with him after the others who'd joined them had left. The two of them had been texting back and forth since they'd shared breakfast in bed Sunday morning before saying goodbye.

He'd been hoping for a dinner invitation, but hadn't received one.

"I need to kiss you," he told her as they sat, looking into each other's eyes like a couple of lovesick kids.

"I know."

"I could come over tonight." He'd sworn he wasn't going to push himself on her. That he'd wait for her to set whatever pace she felt comfortable with.

Disappointment hit when she shook her head, but he quickly deflected it. He'd known, going in, that they weren't building to something more. They couldn't, not with the secrets that stood between them.

He shouldn't have slept with her at all. He'd known that, too. Had been determined not to. And then she'd bared her sexual self to him, told him she'd cry herself to sleep...

From anyone else that might have been a come-on, a tease. He'd been completely certain Miranda had been giving him the truth.

"I don't want Ethan to get the wrong impression." The intimate way she was looking at him wasn't at all disappointing. In fact, the opposite was true.

He had to be careful. And he cared so much, he couldn't snub her advances. "You don't want him to know we're anything but friends," he surmised.

"Right. You can't touch me or be anywhere near my bedroom when he's around. The way he's suddenly looking for more relationship contact in his life... I've told him you're only here for a while longer, but he's only six. Knowing that isn't going to stop him from making more of it than there is."

He understood completely. Knew she was right. "So, coffee and wanting to kiss you is it," he said.

He smiled. Remembered what it felt like to touch his lips to hers.

And remembered a whole lot more when she smiled back.

IT WAS ONE thing to know what was best. And another entirely not to want what wasn't. When she'd had sex with Tad, she'd been in that one moment. With a need so intense it had to be assuaged.

She would never have believed that when it was done, she'd need him even more. That wasn't generally how life worked. You built up to an event like that, had all these expectations, and even if it lived up to your expectations, when it was over, some of that anticipation was gone.

Nothing was as good as the first time, right?

That was what she told herself for days after spending all night in Tad's arms. She couldn't get into bed without smelling the clean, sexy scent of his body—although she'd washed her sheets Sunday after he'd gone.

It was what she was telling herself Thursday when she left the clinic at noon. It was her half day because she had to work Saturday morning, and she had errands to run. Things she liked to do while her son was still in school and she didn't have to make him tag along.

Like checking out clothes. Buying new underwear. Stopping at a jewelry counter just to look. Girlie stuff that bored Ethan to tears.

Sometimes she did the grocery shopping so he wasn't

constantly bugging her to buy junk food that wasn't good for him.

The current bottle of disinfectant was almost empty, which meant she'd be opening the spare that weekend. She didn't like to be without a spare.

She thought about getting her hair trimmed. Her usual place took walk-ins. Or maybe she'd see if she could get in for a massage. Or a pedicure.

With her current salary she could afford either. Or both.

They weren't things she normally considered. She didn't need them. And the more money she could stash away, the more secure she and Ethan would be. No matter what happened...

She hadn't even reached her car yet when she had her phone to her ear.

"You feel like lunch?" she asked as soon as the call was answered. Before she could talk herself out of it.

"Of course. When? Where?" His deep voice made her feel like liquid gold.

"My house."

"I'm on my way."

"I CAN'T BELIEVE it was even better than last time." Miranda let the words fall out as she lay, replete, in Tad's arms an hour and a half later. They'd been very careful about condom use, and then, when things had started up again, she'd used her hands to please him.

Her face on his chest moved with his chuckle. She ran her fingers through the hair close to her cheek.

So this was what got people to do crazy things to be together.

But she couldn't be like them.

Couldn't be crazy. Not completely.

"It's only for a little while," she told him, loving his leg between her thighs. She'd straddled him, was holding him down—sort of. He could move anytime he wanted to. He didn't.

"I know." He was playing with a strand of her hair.

"No touching around Ethan," she reiterated. "We aren't a family and can't give him the idea we might be. It's not fair to him."

"I know." He didn't sound any happier about that than she did. But he wasn't arguing, either. Had she wished he would?

She'd have had to say no if he'd offered any chance at anything more permanent. She had secrets she could never share. But he didn't realize that.

He had a job to get back to.

And a house.

He had a life to get back to, she reminded herself, back in Michigan. He wasn't married, didn't have family, but he had colleagues he'd known and worked with for years. He had people going to bat for him. Friends.

"So when can we do this again?" she asked.

His finger was drawing circles on her shoulder. "Tad going to Jimmy's again anytime soon?"

"No."

"Then give me a little time to recoup, say half an hour from now?"

She laughed, as she supposed he meant her to do.

And the subject was dropped.

TAD COULDN'T GET anything about that afternoon out of his mind. From the sight of her heart-covered scrubs on the floor, the bottoms, half inside out, trailing from the bedpost, to the ray of sun that had shone through the closed blinds. From the way she'd sounded when she'd come, like a fierce feminine warrior who'd found bliss, to the hint of emotion in her voice when she'd kissed him goodbye at the door twenty minutes before she had to go pick up her son.

He seemed to be smelling the lavender that pervaded her home in every room of his own place now. Even after he showered her scent from his skin.

He'd had lovers. Enjoyed his time with them. He'd never known anything like this…thing…he had going on with his client's daughter.

What was wrong with him?

Or had he found something very, very right? He made his trips to the gym on Friday, with drive-bys to the elementary school, Marie's house and Miranda's, with one scenario playing over and over in his mind.

He's with Miranda, alone, but they're dressed. On a balcony. His. He tells her who he is. Why he was initially in town. Tells her that her abusive ex really is dead—not from some imagined car accident, but from a drug overdose. That his criminal brother is behind bars. He tells her that her father loves her so much he sent Tad to find her, just to make sure she's safe.

She'd be shocked. It would take her a few minutes to assimilate it all. To come to terms with his duplicity. But she was so mature and wise, she'd see his heart. Her father's. Ethan's. And her own. She'd know that the way they'd become involved was meant to be. She'd be grateful to him.

It could happen.

When he stood on his balcony with his burner phone on Friday, calling Brian, he was determined to get things moving forward.

"Tad? You're a minute late."

Taken aback by the greeting, he apologized and didn't feel he should've had to. Really? A minute?

"Something wrong, sir?" he asked. The chief was a fair man. Reasonable.

"Damn straight there's something wrong! My grandson's across the country from me, that's what's wrong."

O'Connor's tone, the way he said his words, didn't seem quite right. He was slurring. Didn't sound tired, but...

"So let's bring him home." Tad jumped on the opening. "I'm ready anytime you are." *Now. I'm ready now.*

"Not time yet," the chief said, sounding almost petulant for a second. And it occurred to Tad—the irritation, impatience, petulance...

"Have you been drinking, sir?" He'd never heard of the man having so much as a beer at a dinner function, but it wasn't a crime. As long as he wasn't driving. Or working.

"Yes. I apologize." He sighed. "Today is the anniversary of my wife's death and I came home with a six-pack of beer. I'm afraid I nearly polished the thing off. I don't normally touch the stuff," he said.

"It's okay, sir," Tad quickly assured him. He'd had his own share of six-packs over the years. Usually after a tough case.

"No. No, it's not okay. I know better and should hold myself to higher standards."

Shouldn't they all?

"So...tell me about your week. Their week. How's Jeffrey?"

He told the older man about his grandson's first sleepover. About the friend's father building a wooden car in his workshop.

"I'd like to have been there," O'Connor said, not

quite sounding maudlin, again, but not himself, either. "There's so much I could be teaching him."

Tad didn't doubt that. He could barely imagine how hard it must have been, missing the first six years of his only grandchild's life.

Missing his only child.

"She told me that Jeffrey's father—Jeff, right?"

"Yes, Jeff, that's right."

"She told me they were friends, not a couple. That he didn't die immediately in the car accident. That he'd been injured and the injury led to his death months later. And it was only after he'd known he was going to die that they'd conceived Jeff."

He felt like scum, sharing Miranda's secrets behind her back, but this was her father. They were two men whose goal was to help her, protect her, give her back her life. He was doing what Miranda would do herself, if she could, telling her father whatever he needed to know to help her.

"Lies. All lies." Brian O'Connor sounded sad as he said the words. "That Jeff guy got hold of Dana good. Got her to lie about all kinds of things." His tone held definite tones of irritation now and a hint of bitterness, even as he said his daughter's name.

Tad's own anger rose with that one. This wasn't her fault. None of it was her fault.

The chief clearly wasn't used to drinking. He didn't seem to hold his alcohol well.

"I need more, sir," he said. He wasn't just the chief's employee now. He was Miranda's lover. That came with responsibilities.

"I can't keep doing this job for you without knowing certain things. I need proof that her ex is dead. That

I'm not somehow putting her in further danger, having found her, having ties to you and to her former life."

He'd tried his damnedest to get beyond an almost irrational need to overcome his inability to trust anyone or anything on a gut level. He'd come to terms with the fact that perhaps he'd thrown protocol to the wind on that last case because he hadn't trusted the system or his peers. He'd somehow seen himself as the only one capable of saving that little girl.

But he'd made love to Miranda. Trust in the chief aside, job aside, he had to know. Her father could fire him, but Tad wasn't going to leave Miranda now. He was going to finish what he'd started.

"I need to know for sure, or I'm done."

"You're falling for her."

"I need proof that her ex is really dead. That she's out of danger."

"Proof coming your way," Chief O'Connor said, and there was a beep on the line signifying an incoming text.

He wasn't ready to climb off his high horse yet. Which had probably led to the wrong decision in that antiques shop, too.

"I need one more thing," he said. "A list of car accidents in and around Asheville—" the North Carolina town where Dana had gone to college "—for the eighteen months before Jeff was born."

"Since my beer binge has trapped me at home with nothing to do, I'll get to work on it and have it to you before day's end."

Tad slid back down to reality. To being just a guy on a private payroll because he'd screwed up his job.

"Thank you for understanding, sir."

"Back at you, Detective. Not one of my best days."

Tad hung up feeling he'd gotten to know the man he'd long admired more in five minutes than in all the years he'd been hearing about him. Sitting there all alone, mourning his wife.

And his daughter and grandson, too. Having risked his life so many times to save others, only to have everything he cared most about stripped from him. It had to be emasculating to someone like the chief to sit back and let others tend to his family. To know there was nothing immediate he could do to help them.

Kind of like Tad's need to do more for Miranda, to end this. The chief's need, by comparison, would be that much greater.

You couldn't blame a guy for drinking on that one. Or for irritability and rudeness.

Chapter Nineteen

Tad had been expecting a death certificate. Really, really needed one. The text that he opened as soon as he ended his call was not a death certificate.

It was a coroner's report. A confirmation of the deceased's identity and the manner and cause of death. Not a matter of public record.

More than a death certificate.

Jeffrey Muldoon Patrick. Aged 23. Death by opiate ingestion.

It didn't get much more official than that.

Or more convincing, either. He'd had Dana's birth certificate from the beginning, but got Ethan's now, too. He knew that Ethan's real name, his birth name, was Jeffrey Patrick O'Connor.

Named after his father, just as Miranda had said.

Thank God. She was in no danger. Miranda and Ethan really were safe. The giddy feeling of relief carried him to dinner at a place not far from his apartment. And to the grocery store to restock some essentials afterward.

If only he could tell her, be honest with her. This was good news. She should be the one buoyed by it.

But he couldn't break the chief's faith in him, break his word to a man of honor.

No matter how much he wanted Miranda to be happy.

This mission belonged to Chief O'Connor. He had a right to determine how he reintroduced himself to his daughter. He knew Dana. Tad only knew Miranda.

But if Tad could somehow get Miranda to tell him the truth about her husband—take the huge risk of exposing her past to him... No, he still couldn't break his word to the chief. If he acted too soon, if Miranda was angry with her father, as the chief believed, and he didn't give O'Connor a chance to mend fences, she could very well cut him off again.

He couldn't be responsible for a hero losing his family for the second time. Or for Miranda and Ethan—Dana and Jeffrey—losing their chance to be reunited with the man who adored them both, even though he and Jeffrey, aka Ethan, had never met.

In other words, it was none of his business. Shit.

When the list of car accidents came over his burner phone later that evening, Tad perused it carefully, but wasn't surprised to find there'd been no fatal or near-fatal crash involving anyone named Jeff, or any other man in his early twenties, in or near Asheville around the time of Ethan's conception.

As he'd suspected, Miranda's story had been a lie.

LIVING A LIE had never been harder for Miranda than after she'd started sleeping with Tad. So many times she'd wanted to call him and tell him the truth about herself. She could trust him with the truth.

She knew she could.

And yet something held her back.

Sara Edwin's advice, for one. And the fact that Tad exhibited signs of a tendency she knew all too well from her father—one of the things she'd admired about him, actually. An inability to let injustice just lie there. Tad was a detective. A damned good one based on what he'd told her. He'd been willing to risk his life without hesitation to save a little girl.

There was no way he'd sit idly by, letting her and Ethan live in constant danger of having her father find them. He'd take on the man the state of North Carolina revered. He'd want her to prosecute her father.

He'd probably believe she could win.

What she knew was that there wasn't enough evidence. She'd never told anyone about the years of beatings. At first, because she'd felt responsible. And because she'd loved him. Because he was her only security and support. Her only family. If she didn't have her father, who did she have? There were no grandparents in her life. No aunts and uncles. Her mom's parents were both gone. Her father's dad had beaten him for much of his life. She'd never met her paternal grandmother, either.

Her father had an older brother whom she'd never met.

If she'd lost her father, she'd have been a ward of the state, and the one or two times she'd told him she'd rather be that than live with him, he'd not only punished her for the words, but had brought home reports of some of the things that happened to wards of the state. Of course, now she knew that most children in foster care were lovingly and well cared for. But back then...

Didn't matter. There was no way she'd be able to prosecute her father without evidence. No charges to file against him. Just like the courts couldn't file anything against Devon on Marie's behalf. Not yet, anyway.

You had to wait for the abuser to abuse in a big way

in order to get away from him, and then you'd have a chance.

So many times, in situations like hers, the victim died first. She wasn't going to let that happen. To her or her son.

Ethan was an unknowing victim.

The train of thought led her right back to where she'd started. She absolutely could not tell Tad about her past.

And so she tried not to think about the things she couldn't change, things she could do nothing about. She had a really easy way to do that, too, and found herself sinking into a world where she worked, took care of her son and then let her thoughts be consumed by Tad—and her body governed by sexual adrenaline.

The weekend following her Thursday tryst with him, if she wasn't working or watching out for her son, she was thinking about ways to be alone with Tad. Finding times in her schedule where there might be a possibility.

Barring anything else, they could squeeze in an hour on Tuesday morning, if they didn't go for coffee with the group after the High Risk Team meeting. And if she skipped lunch.

On Monday, she proposed as much in a text to him. And got his immediate affirmative response. Hell, yes.

Then she walked around hot for him the rest of that day, dreaming about him that night, as she anticipated being with him.

She shaved her legs with extra care on Tuesday morning and left the conditioner in her hair a little longer than usual. Chose her newest scrubs—a lavender pair with rainbows and bears—and used a touch of rose-scented essential oil on her wrists.

Buzzing with need, she walked into the police station for the meeting Tuesday morning, trying to look nothing but professional as she approached the conference room. Smiled and said hello to everyone before she let her gaze home in specifically on the chair Tad always occupied.

Trying not to falter when she saw it was empty. He always got to the meetings early because he was also in domestic violence training sessions at the station and in meetings with other detectives, listening in on discussions about other domestic violence–related crimes.

He didn't show up at all that day. Neither did Chantel Fairbanks, their High Risk Team detective.

Five minutes into the meeting, she knew why.

Tad had seen Devon Williams lurking outside a business near the elementary school that morning. He'd been wearing a janitorial jumpsuit and a hat. He'd turned to a dumpster, reaching inside as though looking for something when Tad first drove past. A dumpster-diving janitor had alerted Tad enough that he'd parked and taken a walk around the building. Devon hadn't seen him, but Tad made a positive ID and called Chantel, who'd asked him to keep Devon in sight until they could get to him.

Miranda was back at the clinic, seeing patients, before she got word that he'd been apprehended—and then let go. It turned out that Devon had been just far enough away from school property to be within his allowed limits.

All team members had been put on high alert. Devon was biding his time. Chantel—and everyone else involved—was sure of it.

Suddenly sex was the last thing on Miranda's mind. Leaving work as soon as she'd charted her last patient, she drove straight to Ethan's school. Didn't matter to her that she was half an hour early. She'd rather sit in her car and wait than have him come out a second early and her not be there.

She wanted him close.

Needed him close.

He was her life.

This was her life.

She was thankful for that reminder.

TAD HATED FEELING UNEASY. He went to the gym Tuesday night after texting with Miranda. On Wednesday he was at the police station for a while. There'd been another domestic call while he was there, regarding a first-time abuser, and he'd been asked to ride along. He stayed by the car, watching, and still got an eyeful and an earful. The man came out of the house brandishing a gun, clearly out of his mind with rage.

From what he'd heard on the way over, the guy was a high school teacher and coach. A good guy who'd come home from school sick to find his wife in bed with another man.

The officer who'd gone to the door knew the man. Talked him down. Got him to come to the station with them.

In the end, no charges were filed. He hadn't hurt anyone, only threatened. His wife wouldn't testify against him.

The next day, he'd filed for divorce.

And Tad was still uneasy.

Why, if Chief O'Connor missed his family so much—and it was clear he did—and if he knew for sure that Miranda's ex was dead—which he did—did he insist they wait longer before telling her?

Why postpone the reunion that would be so good for everyone?

Another thing was bugging him, too. The chief was

known to have nerves of steel. A man who could think clearly under the most severe pressure.

And now for the second time he'd gone off on Tad. The day he'd called a day early, and then, much worse, when he was drinking. Yeah, they were dealing with an emotionally intense situation, but wasn't that what he excelled at?

Granted, it was different when it was your own family. He of all people knew that.

But something felt off.

Could it be that Jeff Patrick was still alive? Maybe under an assumed identity? That idea was far-fetched. But Miranda wasn't Miranda, either.

So what if this Patrick guy had somehow gotten to the chief? What if O'Connor was being blackmailed, forced to find his daughter? That could explain why he'd put Tad onto her without anyone's knowing—and forcing him to remain silent now that he'd found her. Could also be why the chief was so adamant that Tad not do any checking that could lead anyone to California.

Had his original search already set things in motion? Did Jeff Patrick have a way of monitoring searches? Had he allowed the search with the understanding that when Tad found something O'Connor would turn it over?

Was O'Connor putting the guy off? Saying Tad hadn't found anything?

Yeah, right. The state fire chief of North Carolina was going to sit back and let a criminal abuser blackmail him.

But the chief had to be protecting his daughter and grandson from *something*.

Maybe, just as he said, he was waiting for the right time, the right piece of information from Tad that would give him a way in with Miranda. That would soften her heart toward him.

Didn't make sense to Tad. She might once have been under the control of a man who'd turned her against her father, but no one was brainwashing her now.

He couldn't do any checking into Miranda or her past life, couldn't risk leading anyone to her, but he could call a former colleague of his, using his burner phone, without saying where he was, and have her do a covert check on the chief for him. It would come from North Carolina. And had nothing to do with Miranda.

The idea had niggled at him all day Wednesday, and by Thursday, with no further invitation from Miranda, he made the call.

Gail Winton, a woman who'd been a partner of his on their force, knew him better than just about anyone. They'd had a brief, very brief, sexual encounter early on in their relationship. She was now married to an army veteran–turned–refuse company owner she adored. They had two young kids.

And had Tad over for dinner most holidays, too.

After getting up in his grill for not calling sooner, not letting her know he was okay, and after he'd assured her he was indeed following doctor's orders, eating right, resting and doing all his workouts, he got to the point. She agreed to help him, no questions asked, warning that it might take a few days since he didn't want anyone to know they were looking. She didn't ask why he wanted the information, either. Didn't know what information he might suspect she'd find. That was how they'd always worked. Let the facts speak for themselves, then come up with theories to further investigate.

"And, hey," she said when he was about to ring off.

"What?"

"I'm glad you're working on something. A year off, no way that could be good for you."

She knew him too well.

Chapter Twenty

Someone was watching her. In line at the grocery store Thursday afternoon, Miranda had the distinct sensation of prickles on the back of her neck.

"Are you mad at me?" Ethan, at her side, looked up, his eyes wide behind those Clark Kent glasses.

"No, but I do want you to remember to tell me when you need something special for school." Someone was definitely back there. In another line. Or down an aisle. Watching her. She'd seen the same gray baseball cap three times in two days, most recently over in the produce section.

"I thought we already had potatoes."

"Usually we do." And she was glad he'd volunteered to bring them. They were doing a group science project, putting potatoes in water to see the roots grow, and he was being an active participant.

"Jimmy hasta bring jars." He looked around. "Maybe he and his mom are here, too. He didn't tell her, either."

"Turn around." Her tone of voice, her whole demeanor, was off. She knew it. And couldn't relax.

Not saying another word, probably thinking he really was in trouble over a stupid potato, Ethan stood silently beside her.

WHEN HIS TEXT dinged on Thursday night, Tad's first thought was that it was Gail, with information on the chief. Until he realized the sound had come from his regular cell phone—an entirely different notification tone. He had the burner phone out, though, on the table beside his regular phone, while he sat and tried to watch a wildlife documentary.

You want to have dinner tomorrow night?

His body leaped to immediate attention. Had Ethan been invited for another sleepover?

Of course.

He was typing in another text, telling her to name the time and place, eagerly anticipating the response of *my place*, when she texted back.

Ethan wants to know if you'll play Zoo Attack.

Of course. His response was just as quick. The rest of his bodily reaction took a bit longer to be agreeable to the plan.

SHE WAS BEING RIDICULOUS. Miranda knew it. And yet, after Ethan was in bed Thursday night, she paced their small house, making certain multiple times that all the doors were dead-bolted. That the windows were latched. She kept her phone with her constantly. Placed her keys by the garage door.

In her closet, she checked inside the toe of a particular shoe, pulled out a roll of bills. Stuffed it in her bra. She was wearing it to bed that night.

And from under the bed, she dragged out a back-pack, making sure she had underwear and jeans that were Ethan's current size. Added some extra granola bars to the nonperishable food stash in the front pocket.

The poor kid had a mother who was a paranoid mess. She saw it. And couldn't stop.

The only way not to be afraid was to act. So she was acting like a woman who could keep them safe. Preparing herself to calmly get them out of there if she had to. Grabbing her extra set of car keys, she carried them to bed with her. And then decided to sleep on the couch.

Routine was bad when someone was after you. It made you an easier target.

What she wanted to do was sleep in her son's room, on the floor between his bed and window. She went in there for a while.

And realized that if he woke up, there'd be no good way to explain what she was doing. Or why.

She had to get a grip. Live normally. After all, lots of people had baseball caps. Gray was a common color.

Thinking back over the past couple of days, she couldn't even be sure that whoever was wearing the cap—or caps—had been the same person all three times.

She hadn't gotten a good enough look on any of those occasions.

She'd turned away whenever she noticed him, so as not to draw his attention.

She couldn't describe his clothes. They'd been different, but baggy all three times.

That similarity sent a spark of fear shooting through her again. This was what being afraid did to you. What domestic violence in particular did to you. It made you feel unsafe in your own home.

Out in the living room, she picked up her phone. It was almost eleven. Too late to call anyone. She wasn't Marie, assigned to a High Risk Team with people on alert on her behalf.

She didn't want to call "anyone." She wanted to call Tad.

Or at least, text him.

Instead, she lay down with her phone in her hand and thought about being in his arms. Pictured her head on his chest, listening to his heart beat.

Her nerves started to settle. The constriction in her chest loosened. And eventually, she fell asleep.

TAD HADN'T HEARD from Gail by the time he had to call the chief on Friday. After his week of high alert, frustration, theories and readiness, he was prepared for anything.

The call was as unalarming as it could be.

"I apologize for last week," the chief said on answering. "I knew you'd be calling and I was way out of line, allowing myself to get in that state."

"It's okay, sir. I know what it is to mourn a loved one." The chief, and everyone else looking into his suitability to resume his job, knew about Steffie. They figured he'd acted without thinking because he was responding to the possibility of another girl being hurt on his watch. That was partially why the chief had hired him to search for Dana.

Because he understood how it ripped a man up inside, losing one of his own, when he should've been able to protect her. Standing on his balcony in the jeans and T-shirt he'd be wearing to dinner, he felt for the guy.

"So what news do you have for me?"

He told the chief about dinner that night, without

mentioning that he hadn't seen Miranda or her son all week—not counting the day before, when he'd been driving by to make sure Danny got into his aunt's car, instead of his mother's, after school. He'd been alerted to the change. Marie had a meeting at work that she really needed to attend. As a precaution, everyone wanted to confirm that the meeting wasn't a fabrication Devon had somehow forced so he could get to his son.

While Tad had been watching for Danny, he'd seen Ethan run out to Miranda's car in a line of parents waiting to pick up their kids.

"I've been thinking about what you said, about moving things along," the chief said, gaining Tad's full attention. "Maybe this week, when you talk to her, ask her something about her father. I know she's lying about her past, I understand she has to be the person she's created, lies and all, but maybe some truth will come out, too. A nuance. A word. A missing detail that would normally be there. You're trained to notice such things."

He was. Interrogating people, getting to various truths, was one of his fortes. Which was why it was going so much against the grain to live with the secrets between him and Miranda. They were consuming him. Every minute of every day.

Glad to hear that the chief was at least considering an end to this, Tad readily agreed to his request.

MIRANDA DIDN'T SEE Gray Cap at all on Friday. And she looked. Everywhere. She had to get a good visual, just in case. Given how many people wore gray baseball caps, wasn't it odd that now there wasn't a single one anywhere in her vicinity?

Or maybe she'd been dreaming the whole thing up.

Making something out of nothing. Or her head was playing tricks on her.

For instance, when she came out of work a few minutes later than usual, she was sure that the person in the black sedan in the corner of the parking lot was watching her.

Why wouldn't he be? If he was waiting for someone to come out of an appointment, he'd be watching everyone who came through the door. She was going to get this under control. It was because of Marie and Devon; she knew that.

Everyone on the High Risk Team was aware that Marie wasn't safe. They were doing everything they could to protect her.

Sometimes everything wasn't enough.

She couldn't get over the feeling that someday, someway, her father was going to use all the tools at his disposal—the police forces, the power, the access to confidential information, the reputation that let him go anywhere, do anything he wanted without question—to find her.

And when he did…that would be the end. There was no doubt in her mind about that. He didn't want or need her. She was nothing more than a reminder of her mother to him. When she'd been little, maybe not so much, but after puberty, when she'd matured, everyone had said she looked just like her mom.

It had taken Miranda a long time to realize that where her father was concerned, that was a bad thing.

What Brian O'Connor wanted wasn't his daughter. He wanted his wife—and his grandson. The son he'd never had.

She'd die before she'd let him spend five minutes alone with her boy.

And she wasn't going to think about any of it that night. Tad was coming over. It had been more than a week since she'd seen him. The longest it had been since they met. She wouldn't be able to touch him, to feel his lips on hers, but safe in her home with her son, she was going to soak up Tad's presence. Let him know, somehow, that he mattered, and let herself believe that all would be well.

She was going to be a grain of sand. Mere dust in the wind. Just for a few hours.

TAD PLAYED *ZOO ATTACK*. He ate two helpings of chicken-and-rice casserole. Helped with dishes. Kept his hands to himself where Miranda was concerned. But not his gaze. From the second he'd seen her, in skinny jeans and a sleeveless, gauzy, flowing tie-dyed tank thing, opening the door to him, he'd been obsessed with the sight of her.

She was like the sun and moon in one. A natural Madonna with the power to take him over completely.

They ate out on the back patio. After finishing his chocolate chip bar with ice cream, a treat for when the dishes were done, Ethan asked if he could go in and watch a movie, naming a popular kid's flick that had just come on the streaming service. Miranda let him go.

Tad had never been so glad to have a boy want to watch television.

He couldn't touch Miranda. Couldn't kiss her. But…

"Do you have any idea how badly I want to hold you right now?" he asked.

"Maybe about as badly as I want you to?" She smiled, but her lips were trembling.

He got it. He was dying, too.

And had a job to do so he could get them out of this

misery and into the next part of wherever, whatever they'd be.

"You're incredible, you know?" he said, just because he wanted to talk about her, them, nothing else.

"I'm just me. Don't see more than what's there." She'd brought ice water to go with their dessert and took a sip of hers, then set her glass down next to Ethan's empty milk cup.

"I'm seeing what's there. You're both mother and father to your son, doing a remarkable job of raising a well-adjusted kid."

Her shrug seemed to be one of discomfort more than anything else, and he was acutely reminded that she was a woman forced to keep secrets. Trying to make her feel cherished, he was, instead, doing the opposite.

He asked her about her mom, about life before she was eleven. And spent the next half hour hearing wonderful things about a woman who'd clearly had spunk. Loved adventure. And her daughter.

"She never said anything to you about your father?"

"No. But I was only eleven when she died." She glanced toward the house, toward Ethan, for the first time in a while. He could see the boy. They could hear the television. But for some reason, mention of her father had her turning around.

The chief was right; Tad knew how to read nuances. He just wasn't sure what this particular one meant.

That she missed her father? That she hated seeing Ethan miss out on knowing him? And vice versa?

Probably blaming herself, he surmised, based on all of the literature he'd been reading.

"Have you ever tried to find out who he was?" he asked.

"No. Why would I? Clearly he wanted nothing to do with me."

Her lack of emotion struck him as odd. She didn't sound bitter, and she might have, given the circumstances as he knew them. If she was angry with her real father, some hint of that should come out in her talking about her fake father.

Unless she wasn't angry?

"Having no father isn't an issue for me." Again, her response seemed odd. As if she truly didn't care.

But she had to, didn't she? A young woman who'd lost her mother, been raised by a doting, heroic father—one who was beside himself with missing her? Who'd do anything to protect her and see her happy, even deny himself her presence? Growing old all alone.

Was she that good at hiding her feelings? Studying her, Tad felt off the mark for the first time since he'd met her. Unable to tune in. As though she was a complete stranger. Closed to him.

"What about for Ethan's sake?" He pushed where he would otherwise have dropped that line of questioning. He'd given the chief his word.

Her shrug, the expression on her face, held some regret. He paid eager attention. And then she said, "I hate that my son doesn't know his own father because he was such a great guy. Other than that, no. Our society gives us the idea that you need two parents to grow up happy and well-rounded, but I truly think that what it takes is unconditional love, continuity and security. That's why I won't let you stay here when Ethan's home. I won't let him grow up with a confusing message caused by different men staying in his home and then leaving. With different authority figures."

If they hadn't already established that he was only there for a period of time, he'd have been hit hard by that one. As though he was just one of a number. She'd ut it right out there without her usual compassion. It wasn't like her to be harsh.

And then he understood. She was being practical, with her emotions shut off, because she had to be. How else could she have faced leaving her father? She'd had to ignore the demands of her heart when she left that life. It was the only thing that made sense.

It wasn't much to give the chief, but he was done fulfilling that request.

Chapter Twenty-One

It was getting too messy. Miranda saw everything closing in on her and knew that her time with Tad had to end. She'd known it all along.

Just as she'd known she couldn't have a long-term committed relationship—with anyone. The closer she and Tad got, the more he tried to know her, to discover exactly who she was. And there was only so much "her" to know. His questions weren't wrong. His curiosity was perfectly normal. By the same token, she wanted to find out everything there was to learn about him.

Still, she didn't ask much. She couldn't take what she couldn't give.

But she wasn't ready to lose him. Not yet. He had at least half a dozen more months in town. Maybe she wouldn't be able to handle the lies for that long. For now, for this day, and maybe the next week or two, maybe even a month, she had to try.

Just thinking about him had pulled her out of the dark realms of paranoia and panic, to a place where she'd actually been able to sleep the night before. She'd woken around three in the morning on the couch and had managed to get to her room, crawl into bed and fall back asleep.

She hoped she was helping him, too. He didn't want

long-lasting relationship with her, either. He was far from home while he healed—not just physically, but emotionally. He had to be somewhat on edge, waiting to hear about the Internal Affairs investigation and his job. His entire career. She and Ethan did seem to be helping him get through it.

They might be ships passing in the night, but were meant to anchor together for this brief time. She had it all worked out.

She just had to quiet the clamoring of her mind and live in the moment. The day. The next week or two. A month…

She had to get through this stage of whatever step she'd reached on her life's journey. Ethan was branching out. She was branching out. They were getting through the changes.

And it was understandable that she'd be uneasy. That a bit of paranoia would present itself. It always would during moments of vulnerability. The trick was knowing how to deal with it. To beat it back rather than give in to it.

"Time for bed, little man," she said as she and Tad came in from the back porch just as Ethan's movie was ending. "Say good-night to Tad and then put your jammies on and brush your teeth."

Ethan got up from his place on the floor, his glasses bobbing on his face as he rubbed his eyes. "Night," he said to Tad, and headed down the hall.

A signal to her that it was Tad's time to go.

"He doesn't ever argue about going to bed," Tad marveled, after telling Ethan to "sleep well."

"Never has," she said, loving her boy so much. "When he's tired, he wants his bed." She didn't invite him to sit. To hang around. She stood there, listening while Ethan brushed his teeth.

"Mind if I use the restroom before I go?" Tad asked. "I thought I'd drive by Marie's place before I go home."

Of course she didn't mind. She told him to use her bathroom, since Ethan was in his. And then stood there wishing she could join him in his car, in the dark, driving slowly through town. Wished she could help him more than she did.

Perhaps they could go to the beach again on Sunday. The three of them.

Ethan crossed the hall to his room and she went to tuck him in, reveling in the small arms that wrapped sleepily around her neck. "Night, Mommy, love you," he said, and her heart lurched. He was already half-asleep as he turned on his side and curled his hands under his pillow.

Mommy. He hadn't called her that in a while, other than when he was particularly sleepy.

"Love you, too, sweetie. Sleep tight," she whispered.

This was why she lived as she did. Why she'd gone through everything she had to get Ethan out of North Carolina. And continued to sacrifice to keep him safe. She and Jeff had created a life—their son's— purposefully. Jeff had trusted her, even knowing about her father's power over her. And she was going to do everything in *her* power to give Ethan the life she and Jeff hadn't had. A life free of violence, with a caring parent who was capable of unconditional love.

She heard her bathroom door open and instead of returning to the living room to show her guest to the door, she pulled Ethan's door partly closed and continued into her own room.

She just needed a minute. Something to sustain her

as she spent the rest of the evening alone. The ghost in the black sedan that morning was starting to loom in her mind again, gray baseball cap and all. But she had it under control. Knew it for what it was. Now those memories were simply reminders that she'd never have a man in her life full-time—at least until Ethan was grown. She'd never know what it felt like to say good-night to her child and crawl into bed with his father.

Meeting Tad halfway between her bathroom and her bedroom door, she wrapped her arms around his waist, shivering as his arms came around her.

"I wish you could stay," she whispered.

His answer was to press his pelvis against hers, letting her feel how ready he was to crawl into her bed.

Conscious of the hallway, of her son's door just feet away, she pulled Tad into her bathroom, closing that door.

It was the one door Ethan was used to seeing closed. She'd decided when he was four, and getting curious about physical differences, to answer his questions as they came, and to shut that door so they didn't come too soon or too often.

She'd opened her mouth to tell Tad that she just needed a kiss before he left, but his mouth covered hers before she got the words out. She eagerly met his tongue with hers. He broke the kiss, breathing heavily, and trailed his lips across her jaw to her neck, sending tingles all through her.

Weak-kneed, she fell back against the counter, leaning there as her hands touched the bulging fly of his jeans. She rubbed it, wanting more access, but when he reached for the button on the fly, she stopped him.

"Not like this," she said. And not with Ethan in the next room. "But...how about Tuesday? After the meeting."

He laid his forehead against hers. "You're killing me, you know," he said, but he was grinning.

"So that's a yes?"

"That's a *hell, yes*! Of course."

With that he kissed her, hard, one more time, then let her go.

TAD HIT THE gym first thing Saturday morning, intending to be home, showered and ready to get to the baseball diamond where Danny Williams would be playing T-ball. Not running the bases yet, but practicing fielding and batting. Marie had texted the night before to say she was scared someone had told Devon she'd signed their son up for the intramural spring league, but she didn't want the police involved. She thought Devon was finally doing better, that they could part amicably, and she didn't want to raise his ire.

Tad had responded immediately, telling her he'd be happy to hang out and watch the practice.

Miranda, as she'd stood at the door the previous night, watching him walk to his car, had called out an invitation to go to the beach for another cookout on Sunday. He'd been happy to accept that invitation, as well. For entirely different reasons.

Everything felt like it was coming together. He didn't know how things would end up, but he was tentatively hopeful that his future would somehow include Dana O'Connor and her son. Probably at his job in North Carolina. More and more it felt like he needed to get back to what he was trained to do. What he did best. Didn't have to be in North Carolina, but if he had a job there...he really would like to pursue the idea of starting a High Risk Team in the area.

And figured, once she'd reconnected with her father, Miranda would want to head home, to be closer to him.

Tad didn't kid himself—there was a chance she was going to hate him, or at the very least feel unable to trust him, when she found out he'd been duplicitous with her from day one. Who wanted to hear that your lover was on your father's payroll to spy on you? But as bad as that sounded…when she heard the truth, when she knew why, surely she'd understand…

Just as he fully understood why she was still keeping her secrets from him. Hell, her whole life was a lie. But one that had to be told to save her life.

Because he was waiting to hear from Gail, he checked his burner phone before jumping in the shower. While he was eager to get out of his sweat-soaked T-shirt and gym shorts, they weren't the priority.

He had a text.

Not much yet. Looked at all finances that were filed as part of his campaign for office. Seem to be perfect. Tax records, the same. I've got a couple of people looking into how he spends any spare time. Will be following up with his public calendar. He's on vacation right now. Left a couple of days ago to go fishing.

That was it. Innocuous. Nothing at all, really, which was what he'd hoped he'd find. Not that any blackmailers, if they were any good at it, would likely show up in the first go-round. But if it was someone connected to her ex, chances were it wouldn't be a professional. Still, on the surface things were as they should be. Nothing obvious.

And yet… He stood there, reading the message again. *On vacation?*

He'd just talked to the chief the night before and he hadn't given any indication that he was vacationing. Out on a fishing boat, or at a lodge.

Not that the man owed him any explanations as to his whereabouts, but it seemed…odd. Under the circumstances.

They were talking about getting him and his daughter back together. About moving forward. If he were the chief, he'd have been waiting by the phone to see if Tad called with responses from the interrogation he'd agreed to do. A call Tad had planned for later that afternoon.

The news would be disappointing to the chief. But maybe not. If, as Tad was thinking, Miranda's lack of emotion, of any reaction at all, where her father was concerned was because she'd loved him so much, she'd had to block that love in order to leave him. To survive without him.

And he remembered the way she'd looked at Ethan at the first mention of her lack of a father, as though she regretted her son's not knowing him.

Just because the chief was on vacation didn't mean he wasn't waiting to hear from Tad. They hadn't specifically arranged a call outside their normal Friday ones, but the chief had said to keep him posted when they'd rung off the night before.

Deciding his shower was going to have to wait, Tad dialed the chief's private cell number.

He picked up on the first ring. Because he was on vacation? Or *had* he been waiting to hear from Tad? Hoping to hear from him?

He filled the older man in on his conversation with Miranda the night before, ending with, "It was my impression that she might be blaming herself for the fact that you aren't in their lives," he said. Could be his theories were based on what he thought, not on what actually was. He was getting too close to Miranda to be just a detective.

"You think she could be ready..." the chief began.

"I do, sir." With the man on vacation, the timing might be right. "If you want to fly out here, I can meet you if you'd like. Tell me how you want this to play out." The man was on vacation. Now was the time to tell Tad, to let him know that he could fly out there that day. Tension filled him as he realized that he might not have any role in the reunion at all.

Or any chance to tell Miranda he hadn't just been seeing her at her father's behest. To tell her how his heart was open to her in a way it hadn't been open in a very long time.

He hadn't thought this part through well enough.

"I'm kind of involved at the moment," the chief said. "Business I can't leave unattended. And, frankly, I want to plan the reunion. So much is resting on it. I'll go through some of her mother's things. Take them to her. That way, even if she rejects me, she'll have them. I don't know when exactly I'll go out there, but it'll be soon. Very soon. For now, if you could continue as you are..."

There was nothing for him to say but, "Of course."

In the shower, Tad was feeling rather glad the chief wasn't rushing right out. Now that he'd realized he might not have a chance to explain himself to Miranda, he needed time to think about his own plan. To figure out if there was anything he could do, prior to her learning the truth. To let her know that his feelings for her were completely personal. And not likely to end.

Yes, he was glad, but a little uneasy, too.

The chief had said he was involved in business that couldn't be left unattended. A fishing trip?

Surely his daughter and grandson meant more to him than catching fish.

Unless the "business that I can't leave unattended" had to do with blackmail—someone trying to force him to provide large sums of money for Dana and Jeffrey's safety.

In which case, he couldn't afford to expose their whereabouts. Any traceable contact between the chief and Tad could do just that.

If that was the case, O'Connor should've told him. Eggs in different baskets or not. Tad understood the man was in an impossible position, but Tad couldn't do his own job if he didn't know what he was up against.

Not to disrespect the chief, but he wasn't liking the guy all that much at the moment.

He couldn't rest easy unless he knew for certain that Miranda and Ethan were safe.

Chapter Twenty-Two

Miranda was cleaning bathrooms Saturday afternoon, with her son using the toilet brush to scrub his toilet and splashing water all over the rim and onto the floor, when the tone she'd set for High Risk Team notifications sounded.

Grabbing her phone out of the back pocket of her shorts, she clicked on the text.

Marie Williams and son Danny did not return home after T-ball practice and lunch as expected. Not answering cell. Devon not answering either. CF

CF. Chantel Fairbanks.

The notice went out to the full team, putting everyone on alert. And anyone who was available could join a search party to try to find them.

"Who's that?" Ethan asked, peering up at her from behind his glasses. The unusually solemn expression on his face alerted her to the fact that she must look concerned.

She didn't want him to know who it was. Didn't want domestic violence to be a part of his life.

She had to help. As many vehicles on the road as they

could get, as many eyes looking, would increase Marie's chances that someone would spot something and be able to alert authorities in time to save her.

If indeed she was with Devon. They didn't know for sure.

Which was why there wouldn't be an Amber Alert.

It was up to them, the team and anyone the team could contact, to be the equivalent of Danny's Amber Alert.

"You remember Danny, the boy you saw with Tad that day?"

"Yeeahh…" Ethan drew the word out as though hesitant about wanting to know more.

"His mom's car is lost and she's hoping some of us can drive around and help her try to find it. She can't get to work without it." The words came to her as though inspired.

Her son scrunched up his nose. "Huh?" he asked, the toilet brush dripping on the floor as he held it suspended above the bowl. "How does a car get lost?"

Okay, not inspired. "I don't know. Maybe it was stolen," she said, taking the brush from him and wiping the floor with the towel in her hand. "But I think we can help, don't you? Just drive around for a while and see if we see it. I'd need you to do most of the looking, since I'll have to pay attention to the driving."

"Okay." Ethan shrugged. "Can I have a hamburger and french fries for lunch, then?"

"Of course." Maybe he was playing her. Bribing her. Maybe she should teach him that doing good deeds for others meant you didn't get paid for it. Teach him a lesson in selflessness. At the moment, though, she'd be willing to buy him ice cream for dessert, too. She just had to get out on the road.

TAD KNEW FOR certain that Danny and Marie made it safely away from T-ball practice. There'd been no sign of Devon all morning, and no cars following Marie as she left the diamond. He'd been watching.

He hadn't followed them to lunch afterward. She'd texted, letting him know that Danny had asked for pizza and she was taking him to buy some at a place not far from home. That was the last he'd heard until he got a call from Chantel an hour later.

He was the last person to have seen the mother and son. He told Chantel that Marie had been wearing black capris and a ribbed white T-shirt, and Danny had still been in the jeans and T-shirt he'd worn to practice. He told her where they'd been headed.

She already knew both things and was just verifying what Marie's sister, Ruby, had told her. Marie had texted her after she'd texted Tad, to ask if Ruby and her husband wanted her to bring home any pizza.

She'd never made it to the pizza place. And she wasn't answering her phone.

He got the High Risk Team alert almost immediately after his call with Chantel. Was back out to his car and on the road immediately. She'd asked him to start from where he'd last seen Marie, to check around the ballpark, see if anyone remembered anything. And then to drive all the streets between the park and the pizza place.

Officers were going to be talking to neighbors along the route. And expanding the search farther out.

He reminded himself that they'd thought she'd gone missing once before, that she'd failed to answer her phone then, too, and that she'd eventually returned home, safe and sound.

He told Miranda the same thing when she called a

few minutes later to let him know that she and Ethan were out looking for Marie's car and would call the police if they thought they saw any sign of it.

"Don't approach, no matter what," he told her, instantly alert. They needed eyes on the road. He just didn't want Miranda or Ethan out there.

But he couldn't stop her. And probably shouldn't. As long as she kept her distance, she was in no real danger. Devon would have no idea that a woman out driving with her son would be any threat to him. It wasn't like he'd be shooting at every car he passed as he drove wherever he might be taking them. That would be the quickest way to get himself arrested.

If he even had them.

Marie had been told, after the last incident, to let someone know if she was going to change her schedule, told to call before she took off again. She'd apologized for the time everyone had spent looking for, and worrying about, her.

"Maybe Danny changed his mind about which pizza place," he said now, conscious of the fact that Ethan was in the car with Miranda, making it difficult for her to speak freely.

He'd caught the "looking for Marie's car" remark. Took it to mean that Ethan didn't know Danny and Marie had been in it or were in any danger.

And maybe she was right to keep the news from her son. Earlier, Tad had figured Ethan would be better prepared in the event of danger in his own life if he knew. He'd since changed his mind about that. She was raising a happy, healthy, well-adjusted child.

"Could be they went to Charlie's." A pizza place with gaming rooms. He'd driven by it but never been inside.

"She might not have heard her phone ring, or isn't getting cell service in there," he finished.

He was at the ball field. Had to get going. Talk to some people. He didn't tell Miranda that, though. He just asked her to please keep in touch, assuring her he'd do the same.

"And be careful," he told her. "No risks."

"You, too," she said, and he wondered if she was thinking about the time he'd gone rogue. If she was worried he'd get hurt. He had a gun on him, not that she knew that. He never took it into her home, leaving it locked in the glove box of his SUV. But he was licensed to carry and always did.

Telling himself that Ethan was his assurance that Miranda wouldn't take risks, he exited his vehicle and headed into the park.

"THERE'S A RED CAR."

"But see how it only has two doors? We need a car that's bigger, like ours," Miranda told Ethan as they drove slowly through the streets of Santa Raquel. She'd tried Marie's phone, just in case the woman would pick up a call from her, but it went straight to voice mail.

As she drove, trying to see every single car within sight, she prayed that Marie and Danny were okay.

And that Tad would be, too. Knowing that he was out there, also looking, was a comfort to her. Strange how in her most frightening situations, thoughts of Tad were what brought her back to a sense of being okay.

The sexual attraction she got. The other, the comfort part, not so much. Maybe she just didn't *want* to get it. Knew that she couldn't take it any further, so she didn't want to think about it.

"There's one!" Ethan said, pointing at a car that was

the same size and basic shape as Marie's, but a different make and model. She'd shown her son a picture of the vehicle before they'd left their driveway, having checked it out on the internet on her phone.

"That's almost it, but remember that symbol on the back of the car I showed you? That's what we're looking for."

They'd been at it for half an hour, up one street and down another, just driving and watching, when Ethan saw a car that looked exactly like Marie's parked in a driveway. Devon was staying with a friend in the area, which was why she'd chosen to search there, but she didn't know which house.

Picking up her phone, she dialed Chantel, gave her the address and prayed again.

It took too much precious time for Tad to make it all the way around that park. Parents and kids were filling all three diamond areas as different T-ball and Little League teams held practices and scrimmage games. He talked to at least fifty people, showing them Devon Williams's picture, but no one had seen him.

Anxious to get back on the road, to get to the part where he was out there doing all he could to find the guy, he nonetheless stayed his course. Chantel had asked him to cover the park. He was going to do that.

Others were out on the roads, cops and volunteers like Miranda. He didn't always have to be on the front line.

His call with the chief still plagued him a little as he walked from the second to the third diamond area, completely on the other side of the park from where Danny had practiced. Why had O'Connor led him to believe he was tending to an important business matter if he was on vacation?

Could Gail's source have made a mistake?

The possibility was highly unlikely. Gail checked and double-checked everything, just like Tad did. Needing to know firsthand. It was one of the shared traits that had made them such good working partners.

Approaching a woman who was sitting alone on a bleacher, watching a group of little boys gathered around a man on the field, Tad said, "Excuse me. I'm looking for my brother. You didn't happen to see him around here, did you?" He showed the picture of Devon.

"He's not from around here, recently had surgery, and needs his medication..." He'd invented so many stories over the years, he always had one handy.

Expecting to hear the same "no, sorry," that he'd been hearing for the past half hour, he was surprised when the woman took a second glance.

"Yeah, actually, I did," she said, looking up at him. Her eyes were squinting against the sun, but she appeared to be about Miranda's age, late twenties. She was dressed like almost everyone else, in jeans and a T-shirt, had short brown hair, and wasn't wearing a wedding ring.

Something about her expression had Tad paying close attention.

"It was kind of sad," she said, "the way he missed his son's practice."

"You spoke to him." *Careful now, he's your missing brother needing medication at the moment. Not a potential suspect who might be hurting his wife and son.* He softened his features.

"No." She shook her head. "I just heard him talking to the coach, right before practice started. He seemed to think his little boy would be practicing at noon. He acted somewhat…off, though."

"He needs his medication."

"He was really mad, like he thought the coach was hiding his son from him."

An angry Devon. Things didn't look good for Marie.

"Did you see which way he went?"

"Yeah." She tilted her head to her left. "He got in a blue full-size pickup right over there. I'm sorry…he obviously shouldn't be driving, but no one knew."

"It's not your fault," Tad said, hurrying away. She'd understand his urgency and even if she didn't, he couldn't worry about it. Pulling out his cell phone as he ran, he got Chantel on the line.

THE CAR ETHAN had pointed out didn't belong to Marie. He and Miranda didn't find her car. The police did. Abandoned on the side of the coastal road leading out of town. There'd been signs of a struggle. Of another car coming off the road right behind her, possibly backending her to get her to stop.

An all-points bulletin was put out for Devon's truck, and a text went out to let volunteers know they were no longer needed. Finding Devon was up to the police now.

"Why are we stopping, Mom? Did they find the car?" Ethan asked as she pulled into the drive-through lane of his favorite fast-food place.

"Yes, they did," she told him, trying her best to sound upbeat about that. "Isn't that lucky?"

"I guess." He didn't sound all that glad. "I was hoping it would be me who'd see it first and then I could tell Tad."

She hadn't told Ethan that Tad was involved in the search, but he might have assumed it.

"Can we go in? Please?" Even though he was too big, Ethan still liked to play in the jungle gym set up for kids inside the restaurant.

She wasn't getting out of her car until it was safely parked in her garage. "Nope. We've got cleaning to finish," she told him, which, of course, brought another groan.

She bought him a chocolate shake to go with his lunch to compensate for being a mom.

TAD WASN'T ON the scene when they found the Williams family. Chantel was, though, and called him personally to ask him to join them.

Devon was holding Marie hostage inside an abandoned shack. Whether it was one he'd known was there or one he'd just seen driving by was yet to be determined. He'd sent Danny out, unharmed, when the police arrived and now Danny was asking for Tad.

He made it to the scene, fifteen minutes outside town, in ten. It had taken another hour for negotiators to get Devon to let his wife go. But he didn't do it without first punishing Marie for making him miss his son's first T-ball practice. He'd roughed her up so badly her face was barely recognizable. And from the way she was holding her arm, Tad figured it was broken.

Tad wished he could wipe the vision from his mind. He was glad Marie was safe. Thankful that her husband was in custody. But all he kept seeing was Miranda in a similar state. Imagining her face behind Marie's bloody swollen bruises.

He called her as soon as he left the scene. Needing to say so much, to promise her she'd never suffer like that again, but unable to let any of it out.

"You're sure she's okay?" Miranda asked softly. "You saw her for yourself?"

"She was talking when they put her in the ambulance," he said. "Asking about Danny."

He'd let her know from the outset that the boy wasn't hurt. Physically. That he was with his aunt and uncle.

"Danny told me he was the one who called his father about the practice," Tad said. "He was afraid if he told the police he'd done that, they'd take him to jail, too."

"You assured him he's not in trouble, right?"

"Of course. He said he was scared to play without telling his dad because when he found out later he'd be in trouble. So he got hold of Marie's cell phone and called him. Somehow he messed up the time, or Devon would've been there this morning, I'd have seen him, and all of this could have been avoided."

"Poor little guy. No way he should be going through this."

She sounded angry.

And kind of frightened, too. He figured she was probably experiencing some of Marie's pain, her fear, vicariously. How could she not be? He remembered how frightened she'd been the last time Marie had gone missing.

She'd never ask for help, but…

"You mind if I stop by? A little *Zoo Attack* with Ethan sounds pretty good right now."

"Of course," she told him. "I'll thaw some hamburgers and we can have sloppy joes for dinner."

A community had come together and saved a life that day. And, for the moment, he had a place in Miranda's and Ethan's lives.

He started to feel a bit better.

Chapter Twenty-Three

Someone was following her. There was no doubt in Miranda's mind as she drove from the big-box store to Jimmy's house on Sunday afternoon. She'd told Ethan he could invite his friend to the beach with them, thinking it would be good for Ethan not to have Tad all to himself. It would be a chance to repay Jimmy's family's hospitality, as well, without having the boy running around their home.

She wasn't ready for that yet. There was nothing for him to find there that would alert anyone to the fact that she wasn't who they thought she was. But the idea of him going home to tell his parents about her house, or their private lives, or anything he found different from his… Nope, she just wasn't ready.

Turning two blocks before Jimmy's street, she noticed the black sedan doing the same. She couldn't be positive it was the same car she'd seen in the clinic's parking lot on Friday. Couldn't tell, from surreptitious glances in the rearview mirror, if the driver was male or female.

Didn't see a gray baseball cap.

But she was definitely being followed.

Watched.

It wasn't her first time. Or even her tenth. She had

no way of knowing when it had started. But she'd first been aware of it when she was only sixteen, and out after dark for the first time. Scared, but unwilling to admit that to her father, she'd been paying extreme attention to everything around her and had noticed the car turning whenever she turned.

Not knowing what to do, she'd hurried home, found her father there waiting for her. Sober for once, and in a good mood. She'd never told him that someone had been watching her.

She'd been afraid it was him. That he'd hired someone. And hadn't dared bring down his wrath by saying anything.

And now, heart pounding, she went over her car in her mind. Told herself to stay calm. Hyperventilating could get them killed. The roll of bills under the spare tire would last for at least a week. If she was careful. A duffel bag holding clothes and food rations was in the back, beneath the duffel that held her jumper cables and medical kit. She had an extra phone charger in her purse, and in the console, too, not that she'd use her phone if she ran. Too easy to trace.

"You know what? I'm not feeling very well," she told Ethan, turning again. And again, ending up on a main thoroughfare. A couple of seconds later, she saw the black sedan turn, too, far enough away that she couldn't make out a license plate. "I think I'm going to have to cancel today, sweetie. I'm sorry," she told Ethan.

"You sure?" His brow was creased. "Maybe you just have to go poop and then you'll feel better."

Because in his world, life was usually that simple. Thank God.

"Maybe, but we can't take that chance, not with other people involved." She glanced in the mirror again, not seeing the car. "Will you get my phone out of my purse and dial Jimmy for me?" she asked him. The car's Bluetooth system picked up when he'd done as she asked, and she spoke to Jimmy's mom, asking if they could do the beach trip another day.

The car was there, several vehicles back, when she got off the phone.

HEADING SLOWLY BACK to his place from the gym on Sunday, Tad tried to relax, still coming down from the weekend's events. But he couldn't lose the sense of unease that had been slowly building where Miranda and her dad were concerned.

He was falling in love with her. He saw that now. Didn't like it. But knew there was no way he could stop it, either.

And chances were good that when she heard he'd been on her father's payroll all along, she'd want nothing to do with him.

He'd still have it that way, though, if it meant she was happy and able to live free from fear.

He'd just pulled into his complex when his phone rang. Putting the SUV in Park, he grabbed it by the second ring.

"Would it be okay with you if we just stayed home tonight? I can cook the steaks under the broiler..."

"Of course." His standard answer with her these days. "Or you two could come here. We've got community grills at every building..."

She hesitated, and he thought she might accept the invitation, but in the end, she said, "It's probably better if we do it here," she said, sounding disappointed enough that he smiled. She'd wanted to come to his place. That was satisfactory for now. "Ethan's got all his things here, and that gives us time for adult conversation."

Even knowing that with her son at home, she just meant conversation, Tad was still wearing a full-on smile as he climbed the steps to his place. He was obviously growing on her as much as she was growing on him.

And that boded well for the possibility of a future.

Even after he dumped the big secret…

HER SECRETS WERE going to show. Miranda had debated canceling dinner with Tad altogether, but she'd needed the peace of mind being with him brought her, needed it too much to deny herself.

If she was being followed, she'd have to leave. To start over. Again. Lose not only her home, her life, but her career, too. She had enough saved to get her through school a third time. Maybe. But she wasn't sure she could do it. Just the thought of not having a solid way to support her and Ethan, the thought of losing her solid income, panicked her.

She needed to calm down. To think practically. Tad's presence helped her do that. And yet, when she jumped, hearing his car door in her driveway, she knew she was taking a huge chance seeing him when she was like this. The man was a good detective. Astute. He was going to notice if she was jittery.

He'd come at the time they'd originally designated for the beach, which meant they had an hour, at least, before dinner.

"You want to play *Zoo Attack* again?" Ethan asked before Tad was even fully in the door.

Wearing jeans and a black polo shirt, he looked so good to her. Way too good. She wanted to sleep with him, to lose herself in good feelings and then lie in his arms and rest, and didn't care—in that second—that she shouldn't.

"You got to play with him all last night," she said to her son. "Tonight's my turn." True to his word, Tad had come over the night before, played *Zoo Attack* for a while and then left. She hadn't invited him to eat with them. He hadn't suggested it, either.

"Can I watch a movie, then?" Her son was jumping up and down with the grin that told her he was being cute on purpose because he knew she usually gave him what he wanted when he did that.

"You may watch two episodes of *PAW Patrol* before dinner," she told him. He'd been watching the popular cartoon since he was a toddler, but he still liked it, so she allowed it when she could.

"You just didn't feel like the beach today?" Tad asked as he followed her through the living area toward the backyard.

"She didn't feel good, but she pooped and now she's better," Ethan blurted, and Miranda wanted to sink her chin to her chest and cry in embarrassment.

"You know, some girls don't like to talk about bathroom stuff like a lot of boys do," Tad said. "To us it's gross and funny and kinda cool sometimes, but to girls it's often embarrassing."

His words were offered so easily, naturally, that they stopped her in her tracks. Everything about Tad Newberry arrested her attention.

"Oh. Sorry, Mom," Ethan said.

The truth hit her then, in her dining room, talking about poop.

She was in love with Tad.

As the realization hit, she did start to cry.

TAD SAW THE TEARS. Miranda turned away, and there was no sign of them by the time they got to the patio, but he couldn't get past the sight of them.

He'd only known her a couple of months, but from what he'd seen Miranda wasn't a crier.

Already worried about her because of the rough weekend, he was growing ever more frustrated by his inability to bring everything out in the open between them and deal with the facts together.

Including the fact that he could very well be falling permanently, completely, in love with her.

"How'd you sleep last night?" he asked, taking the bottle of water she handed him as she sat down with her own. He'd hated leaving right after his gaming session with Ethan. Had wanted a chance to have a conversation with Miranda after the day's events, to make sure she was okay.

She hadn't invited the intimacy and he'd felt that pushing her would be wrong. At least he'd been able to stop by. To be with her so she'd have some sense that she wasn't alone in the world.

"I slept okay," she told him. "I was thinking about Marie a lot, of course. How could I not? I called the hospital today and spoke with Ruby. Marie's expected to recover, though I expect she's going to need some facial reconstruction. Ruby will be bringing Danny to his next appointment with me. He's in counseling, too, of course."

"I talked to Chantel this morning, and then had a brief conversation with Ruby, as well. I told her to call me if she needed any help."

With Devon being held without bail, at least until a hearing to determine the extent of further danger if he were released, the physical danger was over. For the time being, anyway.

Maybe he'd get some help. There were programs for abusers. Some benefited.

The whole incident must have brought back memories for Miranda. Ones she couldn't share. But there was a key difference in her case.

Her abuser was dead. The danger was over forever. She just didn't know that.

A sound came from inside the house. "What was that?" She jumped up, going through the sliding screen door.

The bang, faint as was, had been obvious to Tad, but he stood behind her as Ethan came down the hall back to the living room.

"I put the toilet seat up and it fell," he said, his attention already back on the television recording he hadn't paused.

"Did you flush?" she asked, her tone kind.

"Yes, Mo-o-om."

Tad was seated again when Miranda turned and rejoined him.

"You're not quite yourself today," he said, studying her. Frustrated and unable to sit and calmly chat. He had her answers, the information she needed, right there in his mouth and they were about to choke him.

With a glance at the living room, she said, "I'm being followed."

Thinking he'd misheard her, Tad frowned. "What?"

"I'm being followed," she repeated, glancing toward the house again, as though making certain that Ethan couldn't hear them.

"What do you mean? Being followed." No need to

fake relaxing chat now. Sitting up, he leaned forward. "Who's following you?"

"I don't know," she told him.

He didn't know, either. Her abuser was dead.

Although...could this be a manifestation of the paranoia she'd spoken about regarding Marie? The reason she'd given the woman her private number? So she could help Marie fight off the insidious effects of domestic violence–based fear?

"When were you followed? Where?" he asked, thinking that if he could talk her through it, she might see things differently.

"I first noticed a gray baseball cap. Earlier in the week. I saw it three times, three different places, the last one at the grocery store. But I'm not even sure it was the same person, or the same hat."

Okay, good. She was talking herself down.

"But then Friday, when I left work, I noticed this person sitting in a black sedan in the corner of the parking lot. I couldn't tell if it was a male or a female, but...he seemed male to me, based on shoulder width. There was no gray cap. The head was in shadows, and I couldn't make out hair length, but I think it was dark. And he could've just been watching the door, waiting for someone inside having a procedure or appointment."

He nodded, almost smiling as he listened. Miranda was impressive. He'd known her such a short time, but was so damned proud of her. Her strength. Her determination to be accountable for her life and make the best of it.

She didn't need him to help her beat any residual paranoia. She was doing fine on her own.

"Yesterday, I didn't see anyone, but since we were out looking for Marie, I wasn't paying as much attention, either."

"You were watching every single car on the road. I'm guessing you'd have at least noticed if a similar black sedan was anywhere nearby."

Meeting his gaze, she nodded, sitting upright in her chair—as though she were on the witness stand in court.

"Then today…he was back. Never close enough for me to make out facial features, but again, very clearly a male physique, based on shoulder and chest width. He was wearing dark, loose clothing, I think, so it was hard to tell anything for sure. He was clean-shaven. His hair's dark. And kind of long. Not like mine. It didn't cover his neck, but it wasn't short like yours."

All his emotions went on hold as Tad listened. She hadn't just superimposed the fact that someone was following her on a random person in her area. She was attributing it to one person. As though readying herself for a police report.

"Where were you when you saw him? Another parking lot?"

"Driving," she said. "I was on my way to Jimmy's. He was there for a couple of miles and two turns, so, instead of going straight to the Randolphs' house, I took some nonsensical turns, you know, going in a circle, and he was still there."

Yeah, and now he wasn't smiling. At all.

"That's why I canceled the beach. And Ethan's visit with Jimmy, too. No way would I involve an innocent little boy in anything that could potentially be dangerous."

She was serious.

And she hadn't called him. Or anyone.

Because…she wasn't going to. It was like the chief had said, Miranda's fight-or-flight mechanism went naturally to flight mode. She'd run if the danger warranted it.

Something had made her not trust anyone to help her. As though she didn't believe anyone *could* help her. That the danger would always be there. It was stronger than anyone's ability to stop it. He was reading her easily. On that, at least.

"Who do you think it was?" he asked, all detective now as he worked his way through the situation.

He waited. Was she going to tell him about her ex? Clearly that was who she thought was behind this.

She shook her head. "I don't know." She looked him right in the eye as she said the words.

She wasn't going to tell him.

So why was she still there? Why hadn't she run? Or called Chantel?

"It was weird. He followed me, and then he didn't. I got to Ocean Street and he was there, and then he turned off. I saw him go."

Ocean Street ran from one end of town to the other.

"How far were you from home?"

"Five miles. I wasn't going to bring him here!"

In about five seconds he'd head out to the street. To check her house, and every one within a two-or three-mile radius. Just in case.

"Have you seen any black sedans around here? Any that you don't recognize as belonging to a neighbor?"

"No. Again, I wouldn't be sitting here if I had."

He nodded. Whether she'd be at the police station, or on her way to becoming someone else, he didn't know.

But he understood one thing. She was still sitting there only because the threat hadn't become real enough.

So he had to make sure it never did. Even if it was imaginary, if she truly believed Ethan was in real and immediate danger, Miranda and Ethan Blake would cease to exist. Just like Dana and Jeffrey O'Connor had.

Chapter Twenty-Four

Miranda considered not going into work and keeping Ethan home from school on Monday. Briefly. A few times. But she recognized that if she did, she'd be reacting to the negative stimulus, not acting in a rational manner.

She'd very knowingly put Tad on their detail, now that he no longer had any reason to watch Danny. Her belief that she had someone following her gave away no clues to her former identity, or even that she had one. So she'd chosen to tell him about the black sedan.

If not for him, for knowing that Ethan would be protected by a top-rate detective, they'd have gone already. Maybe they should be. Maybe they would be soon. And it would kill something vital in her to leave Tad without saying goodbye.

Before she gave in to instincts that could be tainted by the week's events with the Williamses, before she gave up a great career, a home in a town where both she and Ethan were happy, before she pulled her son away from school and the beginnings of friendships that could prove lifelong, she was going to be very sure there was legitimate cause.

Tad texted her three times on Monday while she was at work, to let her know that Ethan was at school, that there'd been no dark sedans hanging around—either near the elementary school or her clinic. She hadn't asked him to check or to keep her informed. But she'd known he would.

And thanked him profusely when he did.

Still, she looked around carefully before exiting work that afternoon, and then watched her rearview mirror as carefully as she watched the road in front of her when she drove to Ethan's school. If they were truly in imminent danger, keeping to her normal routine wasn't wise, which made her a nervous wreck by the time she arrived safely at the school with no sedan sightings. There'd been some black ones, but none that looked the same, with only a dark-haired male driver. None that had turned every time she had, or missed a turn and shown up behind her again.

She could be experiencing a particularly severe bout of paranoia. Because of Marie. The timing made the possibility rather obvious.

And still, she was certain she was being watched. A gray cap. A black car. Maybe it would be a bicycle in her neighborhood next.

If it was, Tad would see it.

Unless her father didn't want him to. There was nothing out of the realm of possibility where Brian O'Connor was concerned. She'd spent the first twenty years of her life watching him in action. Everyone she knew in her old life—other than a few people from college in Asheville—knew and loved her father. He'd lived an exemplary life, every place but in their home.

"How does going on vacation sound?" she asked Ethan as they drove home after school. Her scrubs, the bears with hearts, had a stain on the front from a can of orange drink she'd dropped while eating lunch in her office. It was bugging the crap out of her.

"Where to?"

"I don't know. We haven't been to Disneyland yet." A person could get lost there for a day or two. Mostly she needed him to be prepared for the fact that they might go on a trip soon. She'd work out the rest as it came.

"What about school?"

"Maybe it would just be for a weekend. Maybe we could go to Yellowstone National Park. You said you wanted to do that after you learned about it at the beginning of the year."

"Is Tad coming?"

"I haven't decided if we're going yet or not," she told him, trying to sound vague, a "talk about the weather" type of conversation. "But if we do, no, I was thinking just you and me. We've never gone on vacation."

"If we go, can I swim in a hotel pool?" Jimmy had talked to him about his family trip to a resort in Mexico over Christmas. According to him, the best part had been the pool.

"Yes."

"Cool!"

She'd stopped at a light. She turned to look at him. "If you had to pick your five favorite things, what would they be?"

"Why?" He looked at her, eyes wide behind his glasses. "You aren't going to make me give away more stuff, are you?"

"I have no plans to pack up your stuff," she said truthfully. "It's a game." For now. "I think I know what they are and I want to see if I'm right. Then you think of five of mine and see if you're right."

"That's a dumb kinda game."

Probably. But it was the best she could come up with at the moment.

"Tell me anyway," she said. Depending on what they were, she'd know to grab them if she had a chance in the event that they had to leave.

Not that he could keep them long-term. If they had to start new lives, everything would go. Or be buried somewhere, like her gold heart charm from Jeff.

But having them with him in the short run would help. She knew. Been there, done that.

"My blue teddy bear, but don't tell Jimmy. Or anyone," Ethan said, his small face serious. He was watching out the front of the car as if getting them home safely was his responsibility.

"This is our game, sweetie. I don't tell anyone our private stuff."

"Not even Tad?"

"Nope, not even Tad." Though that was getting increasingly more difficult. It was breaking her heart. "Okay, what else besides the teddy?"

"*Zoo Attack*, that award I got at Charlie's for winning Skee-Ball, my model car and the M&M's from Easter that are still in the 'frigerator."

Smiling, she said, "Ready for mine?"

"Wait." He frowned. A minute or so passed, and he said, "Okay, now I'm ready."

"The charm bracelet you gave me last Christmas, the picture you drew of us in preschool that's in my bedroom, the clay bowl you made last year, pictures of you when you were a baby…"

"You said only five things. Pictures are more than five in one thing."

Smart boy. "Okay, the one with you in the little blue suit." Because baby pictures could never be replaced.

She'd cried so hard, leaving his newborn photos behind. And one of the first things she'd done as Miranda Blake was get new photos done. He'd been three months then. "And for my last thiinngg…" The memory of making love with Tad Newberry. "My PA certificate."

"Oh, dang!" Ethan exclaimed, causing her heart to jump.

"What?"

"I got one wrong." Oh.

He was so damned cute she couldn't help adoring him.

"Which one?"

"The certificate," he muttered, clearly disgusted with himself. "You hung it and everything."

She hadn't expected him to guess it. But she was curious. "What was your fifth guess?"

"Me. I thought you'd choose me."

She had, of course. A long time ago. Which was why they were playing the game in the first place.

HE'D SEEN NO black sedan. Though he'd left Miranda's right after dinner on Sunday night, after having already made a run around her neighborhood while she was preparing dinner, he'd stayed in the area half the night. And had spent all day Monday and a good part of Monday night cruising between Ethan's school and her office and then their neighborhood after he'd seen them get home safely.

If he'd somehow put her in danger by finding her, he was damn well going to keep her alive.

And if she was imagining that she was being followed… Well, it didn't hurt to keep the vigil. He missed going to the gym and his leg was a little stiff Tuesday morning as he rolled out of bed after only a few hours' sleep, but he felt better than he had in a long while.

It was preferable to be doing something, rather than just waiting. Miranda had unknowingly freed him to watch her closely without freaking her out.

The burner phone, which he was keeping out of the sock drawer and close to him whenever he was in his apartment, dinged a text from the nightstand beside his bed.

Nude except for his boxers, he practically dived for the thing. Brian or Gail. Either way, the message could be critical.

It was from Gail. And not at all what he'd expected.

Totally off the record… Brian O'Connor was diagnosed with terminal lung disease four months ago. Mesothelioma, is what I was unofficially told. Maybe the "vacation" is to get treatment?

Shit. The news hit him hard. Just…damn. Gail's point about the vacation made sense. O'Connor clearly didn't want Tad to know he was dying. Treatment would explain why he hadn't told him he was on vacation. And why he'd said he couldn't come immediately because he had "business that I can't leave unattended." It could also explain the apparently drunken state the man had been in. Chemo and other treatments, with heavy pain meds, could've had the same effect. Or he could have been drinking as he'd said. The medications could also explain the unusual irritation. The mood changes.

Dropping his phone on the bed, he walked to the living room, looked outside, entered the kitchen, then left again. Miranda and Ethan were going to get back with her father only to watch him die? She'd lost the last years with him?

Back at the sliding glass door leading out to the small balcony, he stared at the ocean in the distance. And...

God, no.

Had Brian contracted his services to find her, in spite of the danger to all of them, because he couldn't die without seeing them?

Had he fudged that coroner's report? Was that why he'd been so adamant about refusing to let Tad know any more about Miranda's ex, Jeff? Because the man really wasn't dead?

The string of words that came out of his mouth as he headed back to his bedroom weren't ones he normally used. They were profanities and referred to improbable sexual acts. And eased his anger not at all.

Forgoing a shower, he shoved his legs into jeans. Pulled a shirt off the hanger and let the clothes holder lie untouched on the floor where it landed after flying off the rod. He grabbed socks, leaving the drawer open, and, yanking on tennis shoes, left them untied as he collected his keys, wallet and both phones and hightailed it out of the apartment.

Miranda was pretty certain she was being followed. If Brian O'Connor had lied to him—and he had by omitting his illness as it would be at least part of the motive for Tad's employment—then there was every possibility that Jeff Patrick was still alive.

And, because of Tad, right there in Santa Raquel. Lying in wait.

ETHAN'S LITTLE TUSHY looked too darned cute as, in jeans and a T-shirt, he ran toward the school building wearing his backpack Tuesday morning. Watching from the car, as she always did, she saw him turn at the door and wave at her. She waved back, and he was gone. For another day.

And this afternoon she'd have some alone time with Tad. Right after the High Risk meeting they were going to her place. Pulling out into traffic after checking for black sedans, heading down the street toward work, she couldn't help the little thrill of anticipation that shot through her. In fact, she reveled in it. She could use a huge dose of naturally induced euphoria.

Her phone rang, and thinking it was work with some schedule adjustment—a patient cancellation or the addition of one who'd woken up too sick to go to school—she pushed the button on her steering wheel to answer.

"Hi, it's me," Tad said. "I'm a couple of cars behind you."

She glanced at the rearview mirror. Didn't immediately see Tad's SUV. And then she did.

Another thrill shot through her. He really had her back.

The only other time she'd felt like that since her mother died had been with Jeff.

"I've seen no black sedans, gray baseball caps or any other indication that anyone is watching or following you, but I need to talk to you, if I can. Is there any way you could skip going into work this morning? I realize it's a horrible thing to ask, but I hope you trust me enough to know I wouldn't ask if it wasn't important."

She could call Annabelle, the PA who was off on Tuesdays. There were three of them who worked for Dr. Bennet and they were permitted to exchange hours however they saw fit. She'd just never asked before.

But she'd exchanged shifts with Annabelle a couple of times when the other woman had requested it.

"I'll have to make a call… I'll see what I can do. I can't leave patients at the clinic unattended."

"I understand. Call me back as soon as you know."

Looking in the rearview mirror again, she saw that he was still only two cars behind her and nodded. "You're scaring me."

"I'm sorry. I don't mean to. I just have something to tell you that I think you'd want to know."

"Are you leaving Santa Raquel?"

"Make the call, Miranda. Please?"

Less than a minute later, she had him back on the phone. "All set. You want to go to my place?"

"No. And not mine, either. You know that car dealership out by the freeway?" He named a cash-for-your-car type of lot. One that didn't ask many questions if you had enough money, which made her even more uneasy.

"Yeah."

What was he doing? What could he possibly have to say?

Unless he'd found out who was watching her…

"Head over there," he told her. "I'll be right behind you."

"You're sure I'm safe?"

"Yes."

"You're really scaring me now, Tad."

"Call Chantel," he said. "She'll assure you that my request is valid."

"You've talked to her today?"

"I had to tell her I wouldn't be at the High Risk meeting."

Oh. So he *was* leaving. Which didn't explain why she was on her way to a car lot.

And suddenly she didn't want to know. Life without Tad was inevitable. But did it have to happen right now? When the rest of her world could be caving in?

Chapter Twenty-Five

Tad didn't want to scare Miranda, but his first priority was to keep her and Ethan safe. His first call as soon as he got on the road to Miranda's place that morning had been to Chantel Fairbanks. In short, distinct sentences, he'd told her everything he knew.

She'd been on board immediately. It had been her decision to have Miranda take Ethan to school as usual. She'd assigned an officer who'd be positioned with Ethan in sight until further notice. Until Tad could talk to Miranda, and maybe after that, they were going to act as though Jeff Patrick was in town, looking for his chance to snatch his family back.

While he'd been sitting around the corner from Miranda's house, waiting for her and Tad to leave for school, keeping his eyes on the place at all times, he'd emailed Chantel the documents he had on Miranda. He'd slid the SIM card into his phone only long enough to do that and then returned it to an inside pocket of his wallet. Chantel had already begun a full investigation of Miranda's past.

He followed Miranda into the car lot, parking directly behind her, and, with a hand at her back, walked her inside.

"How much would it cost me to rent a car for a few

hours?" he asked the older guy behind the counter drinking coffee and eating a doughnut. "I'll leave you the keys to both of ours, sitting out there..." He nodded toward the lot. Put his keys on the counter and asked Miranda to do the same.

She clicked to unlock her car first, saying, "I need to get my bag..."

Tad flashed his detective badge, a North Carolina detective badge, while Miranda had her head turned toward her car. The badge wasn't technically valid in California, but he didn't figure the guy was going to know that.

"Cost you nothing," the older man said, handing him a set of keys. "As long as you return it in a coupla hours, not wrecked and full of gas. We'll call it a test drive."

Yeah. He could've just asked to take a car on a test drive. Might have if he hadn't been surging with adrenaline.

Not the good kind.

It was a warning to get himself in check. He had to be a cop first.

Their ride was a newer-model lowest-end Cadillac. Blue.

"I need my bag," Miranda said again, going for the hatchback on her car rather than the front seat where he'd assumed she would've left her purse.

Watching the area for anyone who might be watching them, Tad hoped that whoever was following Miranda, if anyone really was, assumed she was on her normal routine. That this person wouldn't know she wasn't until he cruised by the clinic and saw her car missing.

He noticed that she was fooling with the spare tire on her car.

"You need help?"

"No! No," she said, shoving her hand into the front pocket of her scrubs, as though she'd hurt it and didn't want him to see. "I accidentally pulled the tire up when I went for the bag." The duffel had been hidden in the wheel well. He pretended not to notice that he'd noticed. With a quick side trip to the front seat, she got her purse, and put both in the front passenger seat of the Cadillac.

The guy with his doughnut had been watching them the whole time. Let him think he was taking Miranda to a quickie at a motel. Tad didn't care.

On the road again as quickly as possible, away from cars that might be known to them, he drove back into town and straight to the police station.

Frowning, Miranda looked at him. "We're going to the High Risk Team meeting?"

He shook his head, leaning over to kiss her on the lips. He was sure the move was completely inappropriate and equally sure he had to do it.

Her lips lingered on his, kissing him back, and when he pulled away, he said, "Trust me for a few minutes longer and then you'll be fully in the know."

She nodded.

And he hoped to God he hadn't just had her trust for the last time.

Or kissed her for the last time, either.

MIRANDA KNEW HER way around the police station. She'd been there many times in her scrubs, as she was that Tuesday morning. She'd planned to be there later that morning, for the team meeting. And it felt weird as hell, being shown, with Tad, into a different area. One she'd never seen before. Various desks dotted the room, and as Tad approached one in particular, Chantel stood up.

She greeted Miranda with a smile, and then said,

"You can use this room right over here. It used to be a storeroom, but it's become a place where we can go for quiet conversation among ourselves."

Ushering them into a room with a couple of worn tweed couches in black and beige stripes with scarred wooden legs, and a single equally scarred coffee table, Chantel closed the door behind them.

She was no longer in fear for her life, but Miranda still felt uneasy.

Standing by the first couch, she faced Tad—aware of Chantel's presence just outside the door. "What's going on?" Maybe she and Ethan weren't on the verge of running or dying, but this wasn't good, whatever it was.

Taking her hand, he sat down. "Sit, please."

It was Tad. He was touching her. So she sat.

"I know who you are."

Heart thudding, she felt as though the cereal she'd had for breakfast was coming up. Clogging her airway. Swallowed a couple of times.

"I'm Miranda Blake."

Chantel's smile a second ago had been…compassionate. Was it Sara? She'd told them?

She'd told Miranda not to say anything!

Which could only mean…

"He's here." Shaking, she stood. She had to go. Get out. Now.

Tad pulled her back down. "There's no evidence that anyone's following you," he said. "And no evidence that you're in any immediate danger."

Immediate.

Ethan! She had to get to Ethan. Jumping up, she reached in her pocket for her keys. Didn't have them.

Tad had ditched their cars—the cars someone might recognize as theirs.

"I have to get Ethan."

"Chantel has an officer assigned to him until further notice. It's probably not necessary. But we're taking no chances."

"You don't know my—"

Tad took her hand again. "Dana, it's okay."

Trembling like she'd never trembled before, she couldn't answer him. And wasn't sure she could even stand.

She had to get Ethan. Go.

"Please, just listen to me for a minute?"

She nodded. Mostly because she needed a minute to get herself under control. To figure a way out. She had her bag in the car. Had stashed the money in it.

She didn't have a car, didn't have access to her own.

"There may not be any danger at all," Tad told her. Not at all what she'd expected to hear. Chantel was involved. Ethan was under guard.

She wasn't an idiot.

"You don't know him like I do…"

"We think he's dead, Dana."

"Don't! Don't call me that. My name is Miranda. Miranda Blake."

"You don't have to be! That's what I'm trying to tell you. Chantel's just waiting on final confirmation, but it would appear he really is dead."

Elation flooded her system. And then immense grief. Relief. And…disbelief.

"How?" She could only get out a whisper.

"Overdose."

Fitting, and yet, other than alcohol, her father had never taken drugs of any kind. Not even aspirin. It had to be another one of his tricks. Playing with her head.

"Dana…"

Her gaze shot from her hands up to Tad's. "Do not call me that," she said through gritted teeth. And then, "I'm sorry. But please, don't ever call me that again. I'm Miranda now."

And then, slowly, her mind started to work. "How did you find out?"

When he looked away, she got scared again.

"What?" she asked.

He took both her hands. Kissed them. "I've known all along," he told her. "Your father, he knew that Jeff was dead, that you were free to come home. He hired me to find you. And then to watch over you until he thought it was time to get in touch with you himself."

Anger smoldered through her. White-hot. Burning her from the inside out. Pulling her hands from his, she jumped up. Ran for the door. Tried to open it, but couldn't get a grip on the handle. Her hands weren't functioning.

"Miranda." Tad was there, his arm around her.

"Don't *touch* me," she screamed, elbowing him away. And then, "Chantel! Detectives!" she cried out.

Chantel was at the door almost instantly, along with a couple of other detectives. She saw them and began to gasp for air. Could feel it slowly filling her lungs again.

"He's… Don't let him take me," she said, motioning to Tad. "He's…"

"Okay." Chantel's tone was understanding and commanding at the same time as she led Miranda away from that little room, down the hall and into a women's restroom. "We're alone here," the detective said, her blond ponytail moving as though to punctuate every word. Miranda focused on that hair. And then let herself look into the brown eyes an inch or so above hers.

"He's working for my abuser," she whispered. "I…

invited him into my home. I… I…*slept* with him. I let him near my son…"

Ethan was safe. Chantel had an officer with him.

Tears blinded her, and sobs took her air again as the horror overwhelmed her. Sinking down to the floor, she leaned against the wall, curled in on herself and let the emotion out. She had no power to do anything else.

At some point Chantel sat beside her. Maybe within seconds. The door opened. No one came in, and it closed again. And Miranda cried. She tried to think but was blinded by pain. Mentally and physically.

And then, slowly, the rage of emotion inside her stopped. Calm started to seep in. Maybe just exhaustion that felt like calm.

She had to take care of this. Of Ethan.

"I need a way out of here," she told the detective, looking her straight in the eye. Sara and everyone at The Lemonade Stand trusted Chantel. Dr. Bennet not only trusted her, he was the reason Chantel was in Santa Raquel. They'd been friends for longer than either of them had known their spouses. "I have a bag in the car. And money. I need Ethan, and a way to escape. We can figure out the rest from there."

Shaking her head, Chantel said, "You don't have to run, sweetie. It's over."

"No, it's not," she said, the words surprisingly strong and clear. "Tad's working for my father."

"I know. He told me this morning."

With horror, it dawned on her. They could all be under Brian O'Connor's thumb. He was insidious when he believed he was right about something. He got away with it because most of the time, he *was* right.

"Have you talked to Sara?" Miranda asked. If she had, then Miranda knew she couldn't trust any of them.

"Not yet. I put a call in to her, but she's with a resident who was admitted early this morning."

For a long moment she stared at Chantel. "You were Max's first wife's partner," she said, verifying what the doctor for whom she worked had told her himself.

"That's right."

"You saw her die."

"Yes."

"And your sister-in-law, Julie. She was a victim."

"Yes."

"One who wasn't believed for over a decade because her abuser had a lot of power…"

"Her brother always believed her. And it was her abuser's father who really had the power, but he believed his son."

Chantel was exhibiting patience, seemingly willing to take whatever route Miranda needed to get where they were going in this conversation.

"I can trust you."

"Absolutely."

She hadn't been asking a question. "Tad told you that Jeff was my abuser," she went on, guessing, but sure, too, based on what he'd said in the other room. *Your father, he knew that Jeff was dead.* As if that made her free. No shit he knew. She'd told him.

"Yes, he did." And then, pinning Miranda with a steely look, Chantel asked, "Isn't he?"

She shook her head, then collapsed, and this time it was Chantel who screamed for help.

Chapter Twenty-Six

"Sam!" Chantel's voice could be heard through most of the detective squad room. Tad, who'd been standing with Detective Sam Larson, locked eyes with the older man for a second before they both ran for the door of the women's restroom, bursting inside without hesitation.

They were all trained in basic CPR.

"Get Ethan," she said. "Bring him here." She was talking to Sam, but Tad was going, too. If something had happened to that boy...

"Tad, stay here." Chantel's command was just that. A command. Not a request. Or open to options.

With a glance at the departing back of the detective, Tad forced himself to stand down. He had to admit he was influenced by Sam's history; he'd just discovered the detective was married to a woman he'd promised to keep safe, only to have her first husband, a noted psychiatrist, find her and beat her almost to death.

"Jeff Patrick is not her abuser," Chantel said, biting the words out with such anger, Tad didn't question her.

"Who is?" The chief was wrong. The chief, who was never wrong.

"Her father." Chantel's words came in the same instant as recognition.

He went cold. Could feel the blood draining from his

skin. And nausea forming. He'd led Miranda's abuser to her doorstep.

His worst nightmare coming true.

He looked at her, huddled there, refusing to look back at him. He'd done this.

"I'll be right back," he said, throwing the door open. He pushed into the small bathroom next door, barely made it to the toilet and puked his guts out.

MIRANDA DIDN'T NEED Chantel's urging to get up off the floor. To wash her face, pull herself together. Knowing that Ethan was on his way was enough to propel her outside herself and into doing whatever had to be done.

Within minutes of Sam's leaving, Miranda was sitting in a kitchen with Chantel, drinking orange juice.

"I've asked Tad to come in and tell us what he knows," the detective said. "I need you to listen, to corroborate, or not, the things he says. He's our only lead to your father's thinking and we don't have time to waste."

"I can just go, get another identity, start over. It worked before, it can work again."

"Did it?" Chantel asked, staring her down.

For six years, it had.

"Trust us, Miranda. I realize it's a tall order, but you've been in Santa Raquel four years now. You know Lila and everyone at the Stand. You know me. You definitely know Max. And we know you. We don't know Brian O'Connor. He has no power here."

She wanted to believe that. So badly.

"Give us a chance to get him. To put him away. Give us a chance to give you your life back. A real life. One where you don't have to keep wads of money and emergency bags in your car. One where your son can make friends he can keep for a lifetime if he wants."

She wanted help. God, how she wanted help. She'd been alone for so long. Eleven years old was far too young to take the weight of the world on your shoulders.

But she was her mother's daughter. Had to make her proud. She wouldn't be a victim. Wouldn't let him win.

"Sometimes it takes the most strength to stay and fight." Chantel's words hit her at her core. She'd been fighting for so many years.

But she'd never stood up to her father. She'd only run. To college. And Jeff. To Miranda Blake.

She'd made the right choices then.

Maybe, now, the right choice was different.

"Fine," she said.

AT CHANTEL'S URGING Tad walked in, sat down. Miranda wouldn't look at him.

The three of them were at a round table with four chairs. Two vending machines lined the wall directly across from him, behind Miranda and Chantel. One held packaged junk food. Chips. Pretzels. Candy. The other, microwave meal choices. Soup. Pasta. The microwave was on the counter behind him. He'd seen it when he came in.

The refrigerator, next to the vending machines, had smudges on the handle. And the Formica floor beneath the table was cracked.

Apologies were choking him in their need to escape. But this wasn't his show. He waited for permission to speak.

"Miranda, tell me about the man you know your father to be."

Surprised that Chantel had turned to Miranda, Tad

looked at her, too. He'd been under the impression that he was only going to be allowed to speak about his part in what could turn out to be criminal charges against him.

If someone wanted to try to prove that he'd knowingly aided a man in his attempt to abduct his grandson. Or assault his daughter.

As far as Tad was aware, Brian O'Connor had never had charges filed against him. He'd never even been exposed as an abuser. But he knew that his daughter had fled his abuse. Tad knew none of the details, but he'd put that much together.

"He's insidious." The way Miranda said the word suggested she'd thought it many times before. Like it was just something she knew. "All the great stuff he did, the lives he saved, the volunteering, the caring for the community, it was all real. He didn't fake a bit of it. He can see a burning building falling down at his feet and instinctively know how to save one more person before it collapses completely. And he's got nerves of steel that let him act on what he knows."

Tad nodded. And then stopped himself. He didn't want to admire one damned thing about the man. Was still sick at his own culpability. Still trying to make sense of it all.

Miranda had been lying to protect herself. But the chief had been lying, too. Tad...well, he'd been nothing more than an effing pawn—all puffed up with his own ability to save and protect.

"Your greatest challenge is going to be not to underestimate him," Miranda said, looking straight at Chantel. "Don't think you're his equal. Assume he'll be outthinking you." Her sentences were clear. Each one a lecture in itself.

"If you need proof, look at what he just pulled off. He takes a strong, powerful detective like Tad Newberry who, it seems, isn't from Michigan, after all, and makes him into a patsy—apparently with very little effort."

He felt the dig clear to his soul. Took it like the man he wanted to believe he was.

"But don't stop there," she continued, still with little inflection. A professor, teaching a class. "He knows me, knows enough about Tad, knows human nature. You can't give him any information. He builds profiles of people from what he learns and intuits about them. He allowed Tad to get close to me in whatever way he could, even if that meant having sex with me."

"I did not, absolutely not, have any kind of personal relationship with you at your father's behest." He hadn't been asked to speak yet, but there was no keeping that one down.

With an eyebrow raised, Chantel glanced at him. The retribution he expected for his outburst didn't come, though. She looked back at Miranda without saying a word.

Miranda did, though. Glaring at him, she asked, "Did he let you know that it would be okay with him if you did?"

His answer was his silence. And with sickness spreading through him, he thought of all the information he'd fed the man over the months he'd been in town. All the little tidbits that would reveal his daughter's current state.

"My father knew I'd fall for Tad," she said, turning back to Chantel. "The plan would be to let me fall in love, to think I'd finally found happiness, only to let me know that it was all his idea, his plan. That he'd been the one to pick my man for me. To show me that he's in control of my life even now."

Tad wanted to blurt out a denial. To prove she was wrong.

He couldn't do that when his instincts were telling him she was right. He'd been played. Thoroughly and completely played.

"Girls usually go for men like their daddies. They don't mean to, don't necessarily even want to, but it's human nature. And human nature is his biggest tool. He knows when and how to cash in on it. Probably helps him save lives."

Because every side had its opposite. Good versus bad. And bad versus good, as well.

"He wants me to know I can't run. I can't hide. And if I'm ever going to be really happy, I need him to watch out for me. His end goal is that I'll feel I have to come home, so I'll bring my son to him. That's who he really wants. Ethan."

She shuddered, and Tad could only imagine what she was remembering. But he was fully confident that whatever it was had to do with the reason she'd run. Whatever final catalyst had prompted her to never let her father near Ethan.

"He truly believes in his own power over others and in his ability to control the world," she said. "In North Carolina, he pretty much is that powerful. He's revered, and it sticks because he's earned the reverence. Everything his admirers know him to be is true. But it's created a man who thinks he's invincible. And that's your biggest challenge. He'll do things you wouldn't expect anyone to try. And he'll succeed."

"Not this time," Tad said. He was going to see the man stopped if he had to give his own life up to do it.

If that meant shooting him in cold blood and spending the rest of his life in prison, so be it.

MIRANDA COULDN'T REMEMBER when she'd ever felt so tired. Bone-deep, just "lie down and go to sleep" exhausted. Being unconscious for an indeterminate amount of time sounded good.

But she knew she wasn't going to be sleeping anytime soon.

The minute they got Ethan to her, she'd look for her chance to get away. She'd find a "vacation" spot for them until she could figure out the next move. She just needed him to arrive safely.

Talking about her father had reminded her all over again that Chantel, the High Risk Team, Santa Raquel—they couldn't save her from him. Legally, he'd done nothing wrong. Finding her—there was nothing preventing him from doing so. No restraining order. No charges to file. There'd never been a single police report. The broken bones over the years had all been readily explained away as accidents. A lot of kids had bumps and bruises along the way. For the most part, the chief had made certain that hers didn't show.

Except the summer she'd kissed a boy on her father's front porch. Then, he'd just suggested she stay inside until she healed. And she had.

Even if he *was* in town now, had been watching her, which she was certain of now that she knew Tad had turned him on to her, they couldn't arrest him. He'd broken no laws.

He was simply letting her know that she belonged to him. That he could always get to her. That he wanted her back, out of possessiveness, control, vindictiveness. But mostly because he wanted Ethan. The son he'd never had. The son she should have been. The wonder was that it had taken six years…

Because he wanted her to think he'd changed? Had given her a cooling-off time? She might never know the reason, but she was certain he had one. And that it had to do with her doing what *he* wanted.

The whole thing made her sick to her stomach. Ethan should be there any minute. She'd rest better with her hands on his bony little shoulders.

"How certain are you that O'Connor's in town?" Chantel asked Tad.

"I'm not. I've had a colleague of mine, my partner, Gail Winton, checking up on him." Tad's words brought her gaze to him. He'd had doubts?

And how close was he to this Gail?

Were they lovers?

She wanted to ask, to distract herself, but knew she'd come across sounding like a crazy woman.

And it didn't matter, she told herself firmly. Tad Newberry wasn't who she'd thought he was. He'd used her…

Pain sliced through her and she had to stop letting it in.

"She said he's recently been diagnosed with terminal lung disease, asbestos-induced, probably due to fighting fires in older buildings…"

Her father was dying?

She stared at Tad. Was that true? Could it really be true? Dare she believe there'd be an end to this madness? Or was it him, up to something else to get her to come home? Playing on her sympathy?

"He's on vacation, according to his staff," Tad was saying, and fear pounded through Miranda.

"Gail suspects he's actually in for treatment."

He wasn't. He was in Santa Raquel. Following her. Biding his time. She could feel it.

She couldn't look at Tad. And couldn't help looking at him. He knew her father.

Chantel asked for Gail's contact information and Tad gave it to her. "Let me get this to Sam," the detective said, going to the door to call out to her coworker, who came over immediately.

She obviously wasn't leaving Miranda alone with Tad. Before Miranda could process how she felt about that, the thought of being uncomfortable alone with the man she'd trusted with her life, she heard her son's voice.

"Is this where they keep the bad guys?" He sounded curious, maybe a little excited, not at all worried, and her heart leaped. Tears sprang to her eyes, but she blinked them quickly away.

As she watched the doorway, needing him to appear, she could hear a male voice, couldn't make out the words, and then, closer, and louder, Ethan again. "Can I see where they keep the bad guys?"

Standing, she forced herself to remain calm, and when Ethan came into the room, didn't rush to him, didn't grab him into her arms.

"Hi, Mom. Hi, Tad. They said I get to tour the police station today, while you do your meeting that you do here every week. Kinda like school outta school."

They were making sure her son wasn't scared, turning his trip to the station into an adventure. She felt on the brink of tears again, but managed a smile. "That's right. And then you and I, we'll go out to lunch, okay?"

She had to give him normalcy.

"Can I have a hamburger and french fries?"

"I guess."

"Can Tad come, too?"

"I've got some work to do, buddy, but we'll meet up later, okay?" Tad preempted her response, as though he didn't trust her not to diss him to her son. She wouldn't. Not for his sake, but for Ethan's.

The detective who'd brought her son in, Sam, had a couple of quiet words with Chantel while Miranda was speaking with Ethan, and then he led the little boy away.

"There's a room with toys and a television down the next hall. After they show Ethan around a bit, they'll sit with him in there until we're done."

They were done there, as far as Miranda was concerned.

"We've put a call in to Lila Mantle," Chantel was saying, naming the managing director of The Lemonade Stand. "And to Sara Edwin, too. They'll be ready for you and Ethan…"

She wasn't going to The Lemonade Stand. "There's no point," she said. "We'd only be prolonging the inevitable. My father's done nothing actionable at this point. There's no proof of any abuse. It's my word against his—in a North Carolina court because that's where the crimes took place—and his reputation is golden. If I go to the Stand, we'd only be playing a waiting game with him."

It wasn't as though her abuser had recently abused her. They weren't getting her out of his home, and they weren't on a manhunt to arrest him.

"But you'd be safe, both of you," Tad spoke up. Miranda wanted to ask why he was still there. He'd given them the information he had.

This was no longer his business.

And she no longer trusted him.

"Excuse me, Chantel?" The door had opened and a

uniformed officer stood there. "There's someone here, asking to speak with the chief."

Frowning, Chantel shook her head. "I don't think he's in…"

"I think you'll want to see this visitor," the young female officer in the doorway said. "He says his name is Chief Brian O'Connor, from North Carolina. He showed his credentials and said he's here to talk to someone about his daughter."

Tad's hand covered Miranda's on top of the table. She pulled herself free.

Chapter Twenty-Seven

Chantel offered to speak to Miranda's father alone. Miranda shook her head. She couldn't afford to play the victim. She had a son to save. Facing her opponent was the first step in doing that. She had to know exactly what she was up against. He'd taught her that.

"Do you want Tad to join us?" Chantel asked.

She didn't. Wouldn't even look in his direction. But… "Yes," she said. Because she had to see for herself that the two men knew each other. Wanted to hear what they had to say to each other. Masochistic, in a way, and yet she needed the information to take with her into the future. She was going to have to make peace with all of this.

Including the fact that she'd given her trust, her body, even her closed-off heart, to a man in her father's employ.

Tad followed them down the hall, slightly behind Miranda. She felt his hand slide to the small of her back and sidestepped. She wouldn't fall for him again.

Wouldn't be wooed by the false sense of peace and future he'd brought to her world.

She couldn't afford to be weak.

Pausing outside a closed door to a room with no visible windows, Chantel turned to her. "You ready?"

Of course not. She was about to see her father—
a man she'd promised herself she'd never have to see
again.

A man she still loved. A man she feared even more.
She nodded.

"Dana! Baby! Oh my God, it's good to see you."

Chief Brian O'Connor didn't seem to age. His hair
was still as dark as hers, although he was approaching
his fifty-fifth birthday. His eyes as blue. Standing up
from his chair at a conference table, he reached out to
her with both arms, but didn't approach.

She followed Chantel to the other side of the table,
taking one of the four seats there, as far from the chair
her father occupied on the other side as she could. Tad
took a seat at the end. Closest to Miranda.

Playing both ends against the middle?

That was fitting.

Chantel landed right next to Miranda.

Maybe they were protecting her by sitting on either
side. Maybe she liked the feeling.

Maybe she didn't need it.

Brian moved closer, taking the seat across from her.
They were doing what they'd always done. Communi-
cating with every move, every look, as much as with
the words that weren't being said.

He was cat to her mouse.

She could choose her chair, he'd stand back and allow
it. And then he'd move in. If she'd been a good girl, a
smart girl to his way of thinking, she would've immediately made the right choice, the obvious choice—plant-
ing her butt in the seat across from him.

Or next to him, depending on how he wanted this
to play out.

Trouble was, she had no idea what he was up to.

Other than the ultimate win of getting Ethan to his home in North Carolina.

"You're so beautiful," he said, his hands reaching across the table as he leaned in, looking her in the eye.

She looked back. Said nothing. Her face remained flat, not because she willed it, but because she was on hold. Every system in her body. Holding.

With his eyes narrowing, probably imperceptible to everyone else, he met her gaze for another long, uncomfortable minute, and then turned to Tad.

"Thank you, Detective. I owe you a debt of gratitude. A lifetime of it. You've brought my daughter back to me."

Tad took a breath, Miranda felt it, although she wasn't touching him. She prepared to hear his response, but her father wasn't giving up control of the floor.

"I'd hoped we could have this conversation in private," he said, turning his full attention on Chantel.

"Tad and Miranda have chosen to be here," Chantel answered, pleasantly enough, but without a hint of being willing to give his request consideration.

"Tad, yes, that's fine. But Dana—Miranda—we might be better served if I could have a moment alone with Detective Fairbanks."

What game was he playing? Clearly he knew Chantel wasn't going to give him what he was asking.

So why ask?

"Your daughter has expressed a desire to be here," Chantel said. "Can you tell me why she shouldn't be?"

Brian looked at her again, and for a brief moment, she thought she saw regret in his eyes. Her heart pounded and her chest grew tight.

He'd loved her once. In her deepest heart, she knew he still did.

Just as she knew that the ugly parts of him, the pained and bitter pieces inside, ruled his relationship with her.

"I'm sorry, sweetie," he said. "I didn't want it to go this way. For your mother's sake, I'd hoped…"

He'd invoked her mom. It was going to be no-holds-barred. Miranda had no idea what was coming, but she grabbed the sides of her chair with both hands and held on, because she knew it wasn't going to be good.

TAD STARED AT the man he'd revered. In a dark suit and tie, the chief embodied authority with every move he made, every word he spoke. Tad wondered how he, and thousands of others, had so misjudged him?

Could it even be possible?

And yet…he knew Miranda. There was no doubting that her father was the abuser from whom she'd run.

With almost no money, she'd taken her newborn from the small apartment she'd moved into from her dorm shortly before she'd given birth, left behind everything familiar, everyone she knew, everything she held dear, and started a new life for herself and her son. She'd gone to school. Had a well-paying, respectable job she loved. A career, not just a job.

The former he'd found out from what her father had told him in the beginning—that she'd left her apartment in the dark of night. That O'Connor knew for a fact that she'd had little money.

Now he said, "My daughter needs help." Not at all the words Tad had expected to hear from the chief, who sat with a closed manila folder in front of him. "She's mentally…unstable. Has been since shortly after her mother died. She refused to go to school. Threw fits if

I tried to make her. Sobbed until she made herself sick. Eventually, I had to get her help."

He pulled a sheet out of his folder, placing it before Chantel. "That's a signed letter from her psychiatrist and it's in her school records, as well. It states that she could have recurring episodes later in life." He looked briefly at Tad and then back at Chantel.

"Her psychiatrist believes that her mother's passing just as Miranda was entering puberty was likely the catalyst that sent her over the edge. Her emotions became too much for her handle, and her psyche invented a way for her to check out. She'll do fine for a while, and then she'll relapse. Often in cycle with hormonal changes. Which is what happened shortly after my grandson was born. She got it in her head that I was going to try to take him from her and so she ran, taking him from me."

The man looked from Chantel, to Tad, and then back, his tone soft, compassionate. "I never intended to take him. A child needs his mother, and it was obvious that she adored him. And that she was taking good care of him. But knowing her…challenges, I felt it was my duty to keep them close by. A newborn baby—if something happened to him, and I knew about her issues and did nothing…"

His voice trailed off, leaving the obvious unsaid.

Maybe for Miranda's sake.

"The night Dana took Jeffrey out of his crib in the middle of the night and fled into the dark, I'd driven to Asheville, stopped by her apartment, asking her to move back home to Charlotte. She was living alone, said the father of her baby was dead, but I couldn't believe her at that point. When she has her episodes, she tells lies that even she believes are true."

Tad listened. Hearing sense. Logic. A tragic, tragic correlation of events.

Glancing at Miranda, he was struck by the lack of emotion on her face. It was as though she wasn't there with them.

And then he saw the whiteness of her knuckles against the seat of her chair.

"She accused me that night of abusing her," the man said. He had Tad's attention. "Said I'd been getting away with it for years, but that it was going to end right then. That her son wouldn't grow up as she had."

"Had you been abusing her, sir?" Chantel's question was nonjudgmental in tone. They were having a conversation. Tad's interrogation skills tended to go in another direction.

"Of course not."

He turned to Miranda. "Did I ever, ever raise a hand to your mother?"

"No."

"And did I ever, ever even look like I might raise a hand to you or speak to you in anger while she was alive?"

"No."

He looked back at Chantel. "I'm telling you, these delusions started after my wife died."

White knuckles against dark wood. They stayed in Tad's peripheral vision.

"When she first went missing and I was out of my mind with worry for her, I called her psychiatrist. Told him what she'd said. He suggested to me that since there'd been no abuse in our home, chances were good she'd suffered it elsewhere. Said it didn't sound like something she'd just made up. We came to the obvious conclusion that it was her ex she'd been afraid of. That she was, in her own confused way, trying to tell me something. That she'd said the guy was dead because she'd wished him to be."

One hundred percent focused, Tad was aware of every crack on the wall, the floor, the scars on the table. Every line on the chief's face.

And those knuckles. Still white.

"You told Tad when you hired him that you'd had recent word that her ex was dead," Chantel said as Tad was reaching a point of no longer being able to hold his silence.

His time would come. When he knew it all.

O'Connor bowed his head, then met Tad's gaze. "I lied to you about that," he said. "I didn't know. I wasn't even sure who he was. I suspected it was that kid she'd hung out with, talked about a time or two, but I never met him. Or knew his name. But I knew about you. Your reputation. And when events happened in such a way that you were out of work, I looked into your record more completely. I knew that if anyone could find my kids, you could."

"You were willing to put them at risk of an abuser possibly finding them through my search? Of me leading him to them?"

"I knew that wouldn't happen. You'd be there every minute, until I could ascertain enough about her mental state to come myself. You'd keep them safe. You always do. Keep those you're protecting safe. You'd give your life if you had to. Because of your sister. Because of Steffie."

He sucked in air at the mention of his sister's name. The man was right. He'd have given his life to protect Miranda and Ethan.

"At the same time, I was doing everything I could to

locate Jeffrey's father. You telling me that she'd named the boy after his father—that was my big break. Once I had a name, I could go to Asheville and learn about any Jeff who might have spent time with my daughter."

"That's how you got the coroner's report," Tad said.

Opening his folder, O'Connor pulled out the original. Along with a death certificate. Cause of death, overdose. Not car accident.

Tad glanced at Miranda. Like a recalcitrant child, she sat quietly, allowing the three of them to talk around her.

"You told me he died because of a car accident," he said, expecting her to ignore him.

Instead, with eyes that had little life in them, she addressed him. "It was an intramural football injury, actually. And an overdose. He'd been told he only had a couple of months to live. He knew it wasn't going to be long enough to see his baby born. So he mixed his pain medication with alcohol and some over-the-counter sleep aid, leaving a note so that I'd understand he wasn't running out on me, but was preventing me from having to care for him at the end. He'd said he was also providing for us financially, in that he wouldn't be eating up what money he had left on his medications and medical care. He left it for me, instead."

Tad wasn't sure what to believe anymore. Had no basis with which to make that decision. Just as Miranda no longer had reason to lie.

Chantel was allowing him the floor, so he turned back to O'Connor. "Why now?" Tad asked, wishing to God he could know what Miranda was thinking.

"Because I was diagnosed with mesothelioma. Time was up. I couldn't go without knowing they were okay. Without seeing them. Without letting her know they were set for life, financially. Without having a chance to teach my grandson some things about being a man.

"But as it turns out, it was a misdiagnosis. I had a biopsy soon after you came out here and what they'd found in the lining of my lungs was nonmalignant."

Miranda's chin tightened.

"So now, I've come to collect my family and take them home," the chief said, looking at Chantel, as though Miranda wasn't even there.

"Miranda is a grown woman with a successful career. You can't force her to go with you," Chantel said.

"I think I can," the man said. "Actually, I know I can." He opened his file again. "I've been in touch with her psychiatrist and I have here a signed commitment order—"

"It's okay." Miranda shook her head. "You don't need to do this. I'll go with you." She turned to him, tears in her eyes. "You win, okay?"

Brian O'Connor looked almost sad for a second before he reached across the table, holding out his hand.

Tad could hardly believe it when she let go of the seat she'd been clutching and put her hand in his.

Chapter Twenty-Eight

Miranda hadn't had any idea what her father was going to do, but she'd known he'd do something. He never left himself unprepared.

Or left stones unturned.

Briefly, sitting in the conference room with Chantel and Tad, she'd had moments of hope. When her father had confirmed his illness, she'd figured that even worst case, she'd only have to fight him off for another year or two, less depending on how quickly he grew weaker.

When he'd admitted that the illness had been misdiagnosed, she'd known where it was all going.

How it would end.

So she'd play it out.

She asked her father, in front of the others, if she could please have an hour or so back at her house with Tad, so they could clear out her stuff and Ethan's, because she knew that if she asked without the others there, he'd likely say no just to establish that he was the one in charge.

Sitting there, listening to him render her powerless, it was as though she'd become him. If she was going to save Ethan, she was going to have to play her father's game. Know him better than he knew himself.

Her son had his favorite things. She was going to get them for him.

Her lease and so on she'd deal with later.

Reminding her that she could have everything packed and shipped if she wanted to, he said, "I have us on a flight back to Charlotte that leaves in a little over four hours. I'm expected in my office Thursday morning. Will half an hour do?"

If he'd refused outright, he'd have looked bad in front of Chantel.

Five minutes would do. She knew what she was after. The money. And Ethan's things. And couldn't take more than she could easily carry. She'd be leaving it all soon enough, but if she could give Ethan his favorite things, just for the first few days...

She might have to get on the flight. Might even end up in her father's home, where he'd most likely have her under guard, a guard no one would ever see, including her. But when she saw her chance, she'd take Ethan and run.

If she had her way, she wouldn't be leaving Santa Raquel with her father. When Tad offered to bring Ethan in a few minutes, so she could have time to collect his things without having to answer the child's questions, she shook her head immediately.

Tad's tone was so respectful, conciliatory even, she wanted to puke. Or cry.

"I'm not leaving without my son," she said, reacting. Not thinking first.

Tad looked to her father, his brows raised, giving him the last word. He, of course, then said, "Thank you, Detective, thank you. I'd rather the boy meet me in his own home, rather than a police station."

"Okay, then, I'll bring Ethan. I can meet you and Miranda at her house in, say, twenty minutes?"

"You're a good man, Detective."

Instinctively, she wanted to argue, to see her son, but knew that to balk would do her no good. Tad wasn't going to run off with Ethan. Chantel was there. They were all doing their jobs. Pandering to her father was part of that.

While she was with her father, she'd see Ethan again. She just had to play along. To get along.

Until she could snatch her son and get away.

Tad hadn't looked at her since she'd said she was leaving. And why should he? What she'd thought they'd shared—it hadn't been.

He couldn't know, as she brushed past him in the hall, with Chantel as her escort, that the way his hand accidentally connected with the small of her back sent a shock of life into her.

And she hated herself for still reacting to him.

"You know I love you." Brian's words broke the silence in the car he'd rented—a black sedan, no surprise—as he drove Miranda to her home. She might have feared that he'd dump her off a cliff, but since everyone knew they'd left the station together, that he was the last person to see her alive, he'd be the prime suspect.

He'd never allow his reputation to be tarnished like that.

"I know you're angry with me, girl, but I only want what's best for you. You and Jeffrey. You can move in with me for the time being. Get a job. Maybe something at the hospital. And we'll see how it goes."

How *he* decided it should go, she translated.

He told her about the money he'd been awarded.

About his new position as North Carolina chief fire marshal. He told her how much he'd loved her mother. And that she'd be glad now, knowing they were all back together.

He talked about coaching Jeffrey's Little League team.

"He likes basketball," she said, and then, at his assessing glance in her direction, wished she'd kept her mouth shut.

She'd just given him something. She wasn't sure what. Some glance into her mind. A tidbit no one else would have noticed.

And she was going to pay for it.

ALL THE WAY to Miranda's house, Tad kept up a constant stream of chatter with Ethan, asking the boy about his tour of the police station. What he liked best. He wanted to prepare him, but realized he couldn't. He needed Ethan to act as though he knew nothing, and the only way to get a six-year-old to do that was to make certain he knew nothing.

Tad pulled into Miranda's drive in his own SUV, which had been returned to the station, along with Miranda's car, in exchange for their "rental." It took his full strength of mind to let the boy hop out. To run up to the front door, filled with stories to tell his mother.

He'd told Ethan she'd driven separately because they'd come in two cars, and the boy hadn't questioned why he'd been left to ride with Tad. Tad would've made up some story about her not feeling well if he'd had to.

As it was, he was on full alert. He had two goals. First and foremost, get Ethan and Miranda into his car and disappear with them. The second, do it without anyone getting hurt.

He'd take down the older man if he had to. His gun was loaded and in the back of his jeans.

He didn't want Ethan to witness any violence. Miranda had sacrificed her entire life so her son could grow up free of violence.

As he turned off the car in Park, he felt a second's hesitation. He was risking everything.

The chief *could* be telling the truth. His story had been convincing enough that Miranda had given up. Or maybe she'd given up *because* he'd been telling the truth.

He'd seen the psychiatrist's letter. And the rest of the paperwork her father had left behind in his file.

Miranda had had a psychotic break when she was eleven. And again at sixteen. She'd grieved beyond her ability to cope.

Maybe because her father had been beating her?

There'd been a report of a broken arm. She'd fallen off the monkey bars at school. At the age of twelve.

And the same arm had been broken a second time, in a different place, when she'd missed a step in the dark at sixteen. She'd been going outside to take out the trash and missed the last step. That kind of thing happened.

"Come on, Tad, let's go in! I wanna tell Mom about the cell I got to walk in."

He wasn't so sure Miranda would be pleased to hear her son's excitement at being in an actual jail cell. As a guy, he got it. The boy wasn't imagining himself ever being locked in one. It was just cool to see stuff that was on television. To see where they kept the bad guys after they caught them all.

With one last check to make sure his gun was in place, he followed Ethan into the house.

W‌HEN M‌IRANDA SAW Tad and Ethan get out of the car, she zipped up the bag she'd been filling—the backpack from under her bed, which now held more money and her and Ethan's favorite things, in addition to one change of clothes for each of them. The pajamas had to go. As did most of the food. She'd kept the jerky, some applesauce and a package of sandwich meat.

That should all make it through security. If it got that far.

Her father had allowed her privacy to pack, and was waiting for her in the living room.

"You want him to like you?" she asked him as Tad and her son came up the front walk.

"He will."

"You want him to like you, call him Ethan. And let him get to know you a bit before you tell him who you are."

She'd purposely waited to make that suggestion. He'd listen, or not. Without giving him time to assess, she had a better chance that he'd take her advice.

He wasn't a stupid man.

"Mom! Guess what?" Ethan came barreling in the front door with Tad right behind him. And then, seeing Brian O'Connor, stopped.

"Who are you?"

"He's someone I knew before you were born," Miranda said, coming forward to draw her son closer to the man she wanted him farthest away from.

Play the game, she reminded herself. It was the only way to free her son.

"This is Chief O'Connor. He's a fire chief. So now, today, you saw a police station and you get to meet a fireman."

"Cool!" Ethan looked his grandfather up and down. "You're kinda old to slide down poles."

Her father knelt down, reaching out to draw a light hand across Ethan's jaw. "I can teach you how to do it if you want," he said, grinning.

Because she couldn't bear to see the awe on her son's face, Miranda looked at Tad, expecting to see his beaming approval. If that was the case, she couldn't really blame him. He'd been under her father's influence long before he'd ever met her. And Chief O'Connor told a convincing story with credible "proof."

The truth would come out in the end. She had no doubt of that. If she didn't get away, he'd hit her again. Maybe even kill her.

But then it would be too late to protect Ethan from the residual effect of living with violence. She wanted her son to grow up with the ability to trust others. The cycle of violence stopped with her. She'd promised herself.

Tad wasn't looking at Ethan and her father. He was watching her. Intently.

"Well, if we're ready to go…" the chief began.

"Go?" Ethan asked, frowning at her.

"Remember that vacation I talked to you about?" She said the first thing that came to mind. "You wanted to go to Disneyland or Yellowstone, remember?"

"Yeeaahh."

"Well, how about we go to North Carolina instead?"

"Why?" Ethan frowned again. "And you said a weekend trip. What about school?"

It wasn't that the boy loved going to school. But his life was routine. He expected that.

"I'm going to head to the little boys' room, and then we'll go." Her father took that chance to bug out of the awkward conversation, leaving her to be the bad guy.

As he left the room, he sent a look to Tad, as if to say, *they're in your care.*

Telling Tad to watch them, she was sure.

Miranda had no doubt he'd had someone in California draw up appropriate paperwork to at least get her into some kind of mental health facility for a check. After all, he would've argued, what woman just up and ran, changing her identity, for no reason?

He'd used her earlier trauma, incident-induced and long gone, to lay doubt with others about her current mental state. It was cruel in the extreme.

And he'd already let her know, the night she'd run all those years ago, that in North Carolina, as in most states, grandparents could go to court to be granted visitation rights.

"Mom? What's happening?" For the first time Ethan looked scared.

As soon as the bathroom door shut, Tad grabbed the pack she'd dropped to the floor. "Run this out to my car, Ethan," he said with enough authority that Ethan did as he asked. "Let's go." He didn't touch her. But the look in his eye... He was giving her a choice.

He'd get her out of here if she wanted to go.

She didn't trust him. Didn't even feel she knew him anymore.

But for whatever reason, he'd offered her the chance she'd been waiting for.

Chapter Twenty-Nine

"Marry me."

They'd been driving north and mostly east for a couple of hours. Before they'd even left town, Tad had her take the SIM cards out of their phones. And in some obscure little burb half an hour into the country, he'd traded his SUV for a newer model, complete with a DVD system and drop-down screen for the back seat. He'd told Ethan they were going on an adventure.

"To Yellowstone?" Ethan had asked.

Tad had never confirmed or denied the question, he'd just talked about various natural forests, ones he'd been to, ones he'd liked.

And for the past ten minutes or so, her son, with headphones on and a movie they'd purchased for him at a gas station, had been asleep.

"Marry you," she said, keeping her voice low, but letting her incredulousness seep through.

What she kept to herself was the warm delight that shot through her at the very idea.

"We'll be in Vegas by eleven. We could be married before midnight."

And the world thought she'd lost *her* mind.

"Why would I marry you?" she asked him. "You used me. Set me up. Because of you, I'm having to leave everything I care about and expose my child to a life on the run."

"For one thing, if we're married, he can't force you to go with him for emotional or mental evaluation. Not even for your own good. I'm guessing those papers are signed by a doctor who trusts and believes him and signed based on things your father has reported not on meetings with you, which could put him in danger of losing his license, not to mention jail time, but it's not like you have time to prove all that. If we're married I'd be the only one who could request evaluation."

She hadn't thought of that. If she was married, some of her father's power over her would naturally disappear. Psychiatric papers or not.

She had to think. The future. Ethan.

"We could get married, and then head back to town," he told her. "Take a day to give Ethan his adventure and he could be back in school by the end of the week."

It sounded so easy.

And crazy.

Anything that seemed too good to be true usually was.

"He's not just going to go away, Tad. If it was that easy, I'd never have had to run in the first place."

"You were younger. A lot more vulnerable. Completely alone. You had no training yet, no counseling, to help you stand up to his manipulation. And Lord knows, in North Carolina, you'd had no way to compete with the power he wields. It would've been your word against his."

She stared at him. "You believe me."

"I thought that was established the second you left with me," he said. "The second I asked you to go. Either I was going to trust that you were telling the truth and not delusional, or I wasn't. And either you were going to trust me or you weren't. There weren't a lot of options, and no time to find any more."

She'd had similar thoughts rushing through her mind as they'd driven, but Ethan was right there. She hadn't been free to speak...

"I've never been so thankful to hear a man say he had to pee," Tad said, smiling over at her. "I'd have figured out a way to get you out of there, even if I had to hold the man at gunpoint, but this way Ethan is none the wiser..."

She nodded. Staring out the front windshield. "I left with you because I believed I'd have a better chance of escaping from you than from him."

He'd shared her most vulnerable confidences with her father. Brian O'Connor had made sure that arrow landed on her heart during their conversation at the police station that day. He'd let her know he'd had the power to get Tad to "tell" on her.

"You're free to go anytime," Tad said, totally serious as he looked over at her. "I swore to myself that I'd get you away from him. That I'd undo what I could of the damage I'd done, but you owe me nothing."

She had money. Her emergency pack.

"You want some jerky?" she asked him, reaching into the back seat to retrieve the pack on the floor behind her.

She removed the jerky. He took a piece. She chewed one.

"It could be that all that time you were working for my father, you genuinely thought you were saving me." She told him what she'd realized at some point during that very long day.

"Or that I did what it takes to do a good job. That I

was on the payroll and, being off work, needed the pay-check. That, after letting down my peers on that last case, I wasn't going to be disloyal to another man in uniform. Particularly not the state's fire chief."

"On the other hand, it could be that you care more about the end in mind than the means," she told him.

"Or it could be that I went to California to do a job and fell in love, instead."

Her heart jumped. Her stomach jumped. She wanted to be happy. She could feel happiness out there, right in front of her.

"He has the power to see that you won't work as a detective again. Especially now. Taking me away like this…"

"You haven't been declared incompetent. His paper-work only gave him permission to have you examined. You'd have passed with flying colors."

"I never intended to let it get that far."

"I know."

She turned to look at him. "You did? You do?" She needed the honest-to-God truth, whatever that might be.

"Your knuckles, they were white on the chair. You weren't giving in to him. You were pandering to him. Patronizing him."

"I was taking it," she said. "To do anything different at that point would have been stupid."

"You had to get home to get Ethan's things." He said, nodding toward the bag still on her lap.

She'd needed things for Ethan, either way.

"You told him he was going on the vacation you talked about. You'd prepared him. In your quiet, care-ful, intelligent and completely sane way, you were tak-ing care of your son."

Irritated by the tears that sprang to her eyes, she looked ahead and said, "It's what I do."

"It's what I'd like to do, too."

He reached for her hand. She hesitated.

And then she took it.

"DEARLY BELOVED, WE are gathered here today in the Crystal Heights Casino and Chapel to witness the union of this man and this woman in holy matrimony."

The Elvis impersonator even talked like the legend.

"And me, too," Ethan interrupted. "This man and this woman and don't forget me…"

Standing there in his jeans and T-shirt, with Miranda still in her scrubs and Tad in the jeans and shirt he'd pulled on that morning, the boy didn't seem the least bit fazed about the strange turns his life had taken that day.

Pushing his glasses up his nose, he glanced at his mother. "Are you sure Tad really knows what he's doing?"

Grinning, Tad looked at the boy. "I think it's the mom and dad who have to get married first, and then the kids," he said.

"Wait a minute." Ethan took a step back. "*Dad?* I'm going to have a dad?"

"Is that okay with you?" Miranda asked. She'd been handed a cheesy bouquet of flowers when they'd walked in the door. It was shaking in her hands.

"Yeah!" The upward lilt in Ethan's voice left no doubt that Tad had a place in this family if he wanted it.

What Tad wanted was to give her a proper wedding, as soon as their lives settled down. She deserved so much better than this.

What he wanted just as much was to take away Brian O'Connor's power over them.

"I don't mean to be rude, but can we get on with this?" Elvis whispered. "We got people waiting and time is money, if you know what I mean."

A minute later, with two quick *I do*s and no chance even to kiss the bride, they were pronounced husband and wife.

THOUGH ETHAN WAS all about seeing the lights, getting ice cream and visiting a hotel swimming pool, he was asleep five minutes after they were back in their newer SUV.

Pulling off to the side of the road, Tad grabbed a phone she didn't recognize out of the glove box. "It's the burner phone I've been using to communicate with your father so that no one could trace me to you," he said. "Now that the deed is done and we're married, we need to call Chantel. You want to do it or do you want me to?"

"She knew your plan to kidnap us?"

"She knew I planned to marry you if you'd have me."

Oh.

She took the phone. Looked at him in the darkness. "What are we doing now?"

Getting out of town safely, getting a car, getting Ethan something to eat when he woke up, getting married…one thing led to another.

And now, here they were, parked on the side of a desert road outside Vegas with no bed to sleep in.

"I say we find a place to stop for the night. And then head back to town in the morning."

"You were serious? We're just going back?"

"Either your father will see the wisdom in admitting defeat on this one, with the hope of one day seeing his grandson, or he's going to lose his temper, in which case, I'll be there when he breaks the law and we'll have something to charge him with."

She frowned, shaking her head.

"What?"

"I hate what he did. How scared I am of him. I really believe he'd have killed me and somehow justified it. But...he's done so much good, too. He really is a hero to the rest of the world. It's just such a shame that it all has to come tumbling down."

"It doesn't have to. He can go home. Leave you and Ethan alone to live your lives."

"I don't think he's capable of that."

She thought about that last night in Asheville, when he'd come to her apartment. His eyes had been glazed. He'd been like a madman. No one was going to keep him from his wife's grandson.

Not his grandson. His wife's.

"When I look back on the three of us as a family... I think my father always struggled with his shadow side. Whether it was the adrenaline rush from work, the need to be strong and forceful to do what he did, or events from his past... I don't know, but after my mom died, I was always afraid to be alone with him."

"You said he never hit you, or your mother, while she was alive."

"He never did. When my mom was around, he was different. I liked being with him then. It was like she tamed something in him, quieted whatever lion roars inside him. After she died, it all fell apart."

He touched her face and she turned to look at him in the moonlight. "As I went through puberty, matured, he drank more, lost his temper more, got meaner and meaner. He said it was because of my belligerence, my inability to do what was right. But I think it was because I resembled her so much. I'd cringe when people mentioned how much I looked like her in front of him. I was a constant reminder, a stab of pain every time he looked at me."

"Then as far as I'm concerned, he's lost the right to look at you," Tad said softly, leaning over to give her a kiss. It wasn't sensual. Or passionate.

But it made her cry.

IN THE END, Miranda opted for Tad to call Chantel. There'd likely be plans to make and she figured the two detectives were better suited to do that than she was.

That was the moment Tad knew she'd placed her trust in him.

Chantel suggested they hole up in a safe but off-the-grid hotel for the night. And call her back in the morning.

"She said they're watching your dad," Tad relayed to her as they looked for a place. "He drove around like a maniac for hours, she said, checking every place you've been in the past week."

"He was there all that time, watching me."

He thought so, too.

"And then he bought a bottle of whiskey and is holed up at your place. He has to realize you aren't going back to the cottage with him there."

"I've given up trying to figure out what he knows. My guess is he's planning. And has to have somewhere to sleep. He believes he owns us, so he owns my house, too. Believes he has a right to be there. Could be he's searching through all my things, looking for whatever he can use to get to me."

"He did that a lot, didn't he? Find out what hurt you,

what you cared about, what made you vulnerable, and then used it against you."

"He used it to get me to go along with him."

It would be best if the chief caught a plane to North Carolina and then hoped that Tad never had cause to return to the state.

"I'm going to put my house in Charlotte on the market," he told her. It was something he'd thought about doing. "Have everything packed up and shipped out here."

She stared at him in the half light. "This marriage. It was just to get me away from him. You don't have to go through with it."

He'd spotted a motel and pulled in. Turned to her. "I want to go through with it," he said. "If you do."

She touched his face, studied his eyes. "I do, Tad. But I'm scared. I'm just so scared."

He nodded. Started to tell her he was afraid, too, but went inside to get them a room instead.

THE SUN WAS shining when Miranda woke up the next morning. She didn't know where she was at first, and then felt a leg brush up against hers.

She was in her jeans. On top of a bed with a blanket over her. Tad was lying there next to her, watching her.

Turning her head, she saw Ethan, still in his clothes, asleep under the covers of the other bed.

"Guess we didn't have to worry about shocking him," Tad said, glancing over at the boy, who was so zonked his mouth hung open and drool trailed from his mouth down to his pillow.

She wanted to say that she was there, in that hotel room, married, for Ethan's sake. That she was doing it all for him.

"I want a life," she said softly, looking back at Tad. "I love him so much, I'd give my life for him, but I want a life, too. I want a partner, someone I can talk to when I'm scared or worried or so proud of Ethan I could burst. I want to make love on a regular basis. To not sleep alone. I want to be able to open my heart and love. Really love. Without fear."

He traced her lips with his finger. Ran his hand along her neck.

"I want all that, too," he told her. "But only if I can have it with you."

She could feel a tear drip from her eye down to the pillow. She was crying so much lately, as though all the emotion she'd bottled up for so long couldn't be contained anymore. There was no room for it.

She'd taken on as much as she could.

Clasping his hand, she brought it to her lips. "I love you."

"I love you," he said. "And Ethan, too, in case you hadn't figured that out yet."

His love for Ethan wasn't anything she'd worried about. Strange how she could accept it for her son, but was struggling so hard to allow it for herself.

"I suspect the fear's become a part of you," Tad said. "It's like you said, when you grow up with it…"

She nodded.

"But it's a part of you that makes you who you are," he told her. "You're more aware, more compassionate. You don't take things for granted."

She took a deep breath, and then took a huge leap. "You don't think it makes me crazy?"

He didn't gush. Or exclaim. Either would have been hard to take.

"Do you think I'm crazy for diving through that door and saving that little girl?" he asked.

"Of course not! You saved her life."

"I acted, at least in part, because of what had happened to my sister. In the process, I put others' lives at risk."

"That's understandable, Tad. Not crazy."

"Exactly."

"WE SHOULD PROBABLY wake him up and get going." As much as Tad wanted to lie in bed talking with Miranda, his wife, he couldn't do that easily until he knew they were settled. That Brian O'Connor was either on a plane or in jail. Miranda could request a restraining order against the man, that would probably be granted on a temporary basis, until she could get proof that her father had obtained papers to have her evaluated without her actually having been examined in the last ten years. At that point she'd probably be granted a full restraining order. For a period of time.

She couldn't prove prior abuse, but she could testify about it to a judge for a restraining order.

He'd talked to her about it the night before, and it was already on their agenda for that day.

They had breakfast at a diner up the road and then Ethan was settled in the back. He'd chosen the third seat this time, and he was watching another movie as they headed back across the desert.

"I was thinking... I'd like to go into private detective work," he told Miranda as they drove, and it occurred to him that if their marriage was real, he wasn't alone anymore. He should include her in life-changing decisions. "Not regular PI work, that's not me, but working domestic violence cases, you know, for the High Risk

Team. Maybe hire myself out to police departments. The Lemonade Stand. Individuals. As long as I'm licensed in the state, I could do any of it."

The plan was fluid. But he was liking it so far.

"I think it's a great idea," Miranda told him. And then asked, "Would you want to move? Into a different place, I mean?"

He'd been thinking about that, too.

"All those things you said last night," he began, "about what you wanted… You didn't mention babies. Do you want any more?"

He hadn't thought he did. Or ever would. But he'd been wrong about a lot of things.

"With you? I'd have one tomorrow if we could," she told him. "I did it all alone, with Ethan."

He took her hand. "Then yes, I'd want to move eventually. We'll need a third bedroom, at least. But I'd like to stay in Santa Raquel, if that's what you're asking."

She nodded.

And as he turned onto the highway that would lead them the rest of the way across the desert, he felt something he'd never expected to feel again.

Like he was going home.

THEY'D JUST STOPPED for lunch and were about an hour from home when Tad's burner phone rang. He'd asked Miranda to wait to put her SIM card back into her phone, and he hadn't put his in, either. Not until they knew more about her father's plans.

Their plan, as determined mostly by Chantel, was for Tad to take Miranda and Ethan to The Lemonade Stand, where an attorney would meet her to fill out paperwork for a restraining order, while Chantel tried to talk to Brian and get him to leave town willingly.

She listened while Tad talked, surmising from the conversation that it was Chantel. And then realized, when he mentioned North Carolina, that it wasn't. He was talking to a woman; she could hear enough of the voice to know that. And didn't like how proprietary she felt.

Or how threatened.

"That was Gail," he told her as he hung up. "Good news!"

She'd gathered that from his tone of voice. "Chief Fire Marshal Brian O'Connor is back in North Carolina," he said. "Apparently he chartered a plane, and just landed."

Right. Her father was a millionaire now. He could charter planes. She didn't care about his money.

"He left," she said, hardly believing it. "Gail's sure? Someone's physically seen him?"

"He's at his office right now."

"Chantel told him we were married," she guessed.

As she said that, his phone rang again. This time it was Chantel. She explained that she hadn't wanted to call until she knew the chief had landed on North Carolina soil, but now it was confirmed, Tad relayed when he got off the phone.

"Apparently he saw reason in Chantel's point that if he ever hoped to have a chance to talk you into seeing him again, and letting him see his grandson, he should go home and wait for you to contact him," Tad said.

She couldn't believe it.

She'd won?

"Maybe seeing me reminded him why it was best that he not spend a lot of time around me," she said. "He's happier without the constant reminder of my mom. Or maybe seeing his grandson really does matter more." Loving Ethan like she did, she got that.

"And maybe seeing you again reminded him how much he loves you, and with the health scare giving him a new perspective, he doesn't want to grow old alone."

"He could get away with beating me up, manipulating and controlling me back then. He could do it without risk to his reputation. He'd never get away with kidnapping Ethan. I guess his need to do good in the community really is the stronger part of him." She wanted to hope so.

"He wasn't always an abuser," Tad said, as though wanting to help her believe that her father could change.

Time would tell.

"If I ever see him again, or introduce him to Ethan as his grandfather, we aren't going to do it alone," she said. "You're there or it doesn't happen."

His expression was serious as he looked over at her. "You love me."

"Yes, I do. More than I ever thought I'd be able to love anyone but Ethan."

"I love you, too. With all of me."

They were words she trusted.

* * * * *

COMING SOON!

LET'S TALK
Romance

For exclusive extracts, competitions
and special offers, find us online:

f facebook.com/millsandboon

🐦 @MillsandBoon

📷 @MillsandBoonUK

Get in touch on 01413 063232

For all the latest titles coming soon, visit
millsandboon.co.uk/nextmonth

MILLS & BOON
Desire

Indulge in secrets and scandal, intense drama and plenty of sizzling hot action with powerful and passionate heroes who have it all: wealth, status, good looks… everything but the right woman.

MILLS & BOON
True Love
Romance from the Heart

Celebrate true love with tender stories of heartfelt romance, from the rush of falling in love to the joy a new baby can bring, and a focus on the emotional heart of a relationship.

JOIN US ON SOCIAL MEDIA!

Stay up to date with our latest releases, author news and gossip, special offers and discounts, and all the behind-the-scenes action from Mills & Boon...

 millsandboon

 millsandboonuk

 millsandboon

t might just be true love...